Under Her Wing

ALSO BY DANIELLE GRAINGER

THE DENTON HEIGHTS SERIES

Under Her Wing (Book One):
The Shasti and Madison Story

In Her Cage (Book Two):
The Jaleesa and Tina Story

Within Her Grasp (Book Three):
The Marta and Shanice Story

THE BERNADETTE SERIES

Wrecking Bernadette (Book One)

(S)mothering Bernadette (Book Two)

Becoming Bernadette (Book Three)

Desiring Bernadette (Book Four)

Loving Bernadette (Book Five)

UNDER HER *Wing*

DENTON HEIGHTS BOOK 1

DANIELLE GRAINGER

Bibi Books Publishing Company

Paperback ISBN   978-1-953734-13-6

First Edition 2022

9 8 7 6 5 4 3 2 1

Cover design by Sarah (Forcoverservice)

Bibi Books Publishing Company, LLC

UNDER HER
Wing

DENTON HEIGHTS BOOK 1

DANIELLE GRAINGER

Bibi Books Publishing Company

Paperback ISBN   978-1-953734-13-6

First Edition 2022

9 8 7 6 5 4 3 2 1

Cover design by Sarah (Forcoverservice)

Bibi Books Publishing Company, LLC

Dedication

This work is dedicated to those who are working through trauma, past and/or present. It can be a tough road, and I wish mindful and dedicated caregivers for you and the ability to tap into that inner strength everyone says you have – Yes, you do have it.

Acknowledgments

This book wouldn't have been conceived in this author's mind if it wasn't for the readers clamoring (quite politely) for a story about Madison, one of the beloved *littles* residing in Denton Heights, OH. I couldn't tell Madison's story without telling Madison's Mommy Domme Shasti's story as well. So, a big thank you goes out to the readers who've embraced the lifestylers in Denton Heights and those who told me they wanted more.

Thanks also go out, as always, to my wonderful beta readers and editors. Jiske and Olivia, you've always come through, and I thank you.

Table of Contents

Dedication..5

Acknowledgments...7

Chapter 1 1

Chapter 2 13

Chapter 3 24

Chapter 4 36

Chapter 5 55

Chapter 6 66

Chapter 7 76

Chapter 8 89

Chapter 9 102

Chapter 10 114

Chapter 11 129

Chapter 12 143

Chapter 13 156

Chapter 14 169

Chapter 15 185

Chapter 16 199

Chapter 17 212

Chapter 18 224

Chapter 19 239

Chapter 20 252

Chapter 21 265

Chapter 22 277

National Sexual Assault Hotline 291

Newsletter Signup...292

About the Author 293

Books by Danielle Grainger 294

National Sexual Assault Hotline 291

Newsletter Signup...292

About the Author 293

Books by Danielle Grainger 294

Chapter 1

Madison

Something irritating woke Madison Kim, who had been perfectly sleeping, thank you very much. She pulled the pillow over her head and rolled over. Who cared if she was late for school, anyway? School sucked.

"Girl!" the obnoxious noise made itself clear through the baby monitor. "Get in here," the noise said in Korean.

"Shoot. Mrs. Park." Madison bolted out of bed and raced to Mrs. Park's room. She wasn't in stupid high school anymore and hadn't been for four years. She rubbed the sleep from her eyes and tried to look awake as she surveyed the scene.

Mrs. Park lay on her back in the hospital bed. She had raised the top part and was trying to get the safety rail down.

"Hang on, Mrs. Park," Madison said. She carefully pinched both clips and lowered the bar. Even though Mrs. Park was infirm and in her early nineties, she swung her legs around without help and zipped up into a sitting position. Madison lowered the bed until Mrs. Park's feet were on the floor.

"Help me up," the wrinkled old woman barked.

Madison had been at Mrs. Park's condo for a little over six months, right after New Year's Day. That was the day her mother packed some clothes, gave her bus fare and a little money for food, and sent her away from home on a smelly bus. Yeah, Madison had been there long enough to know the morning drill. She helped Mrs. Park to the porta-potty right next to the bed. Before she sat, Madison pulled off the disposable adult diaper Mrs. Park had worn overnight, hoping to all things good and righteous that there was nothing in it. Nope. Couldn't get so lucky today. She tried not to gag as she rolled the diaper into a plastic grocery bag and knotted it tight. She'd toss it and any others in the dumpster on her way out that afternoon – once the home health aide got there. Ooh, and maybe she'd see Ms. Elena, the property manager. Sometimes she was in the mailroom office. She was so pretty and so nice to Madison.

"Clean me, girl!" Mrs. Park commanded in heavily accented English.

Madison jumped. She'd been daydreaming again. That had gotten her into trouble on more than one million occasions.

"Yes, Mrs. Park," Madison said the word 'yes' in Korean and got to work. Madison wasn't anything close to fluent in Korean despite growing up in a house where her grandparents spoke the language. She knew a few words, definitely some good curse words, but that was about it.

Madison's parents didn't speak much Korean either. Her mother more than her father. In fifth grade, Madison proclaimed to her family that she wasn't Korean. She was American, she'd declared at the dinner table one evening. In hindsight, she should have waited until *after* eating because that got her sent to her room by her grandmother instantly. That was okay, though. She'd take one for her cause. Some things needed to be blurted right away. Before her grandmother could send her to her room that evening, her mother gently reminded her that although she was indeed American, she was Korean-American. Madison refused it. Why did she have to be an *Other*-American? That had incensed her ten-year-old self then and still incensed her twenty-two-and-three-quarters-year-old self now.

Sure, she may look Korean with her Asian eyes, features, and boring thick black hair. She hadn't looked like anyone else in school except her younger brother in the grade below her, but she adamantly refused to be this thing called Korean. Both her parents had been born in the United States. Her father's mother, the one they lived with, had been born in Korea but was brought to the United States as a baby as a Korean War refugee. She wasn't sure about her grandfather. And her mother's parents had passed away a long time ago, so she didn't know much about them.

Being grounded for a week by her grandmother back then and not allowed to eat dinner was no picnic, but she had plenty of candy and snack cakes and chips stashed in her room to tide her over. She had dug in her heels – she was firmly American, and no one and nothing would change her mind.

Madison had thoughts like these daily as she absent-mindedly bathed Mrs. Park. Okay, sponge-bathing this ninety-something year old's body, including her private parts, wasn't exactly fun, but living with Mrs. Park had its perks. Oh, not the private-washing part. The rent-free part. The fact that she got paid directly into a brand-new bank account Mrs. Park made her set up. But the best part might be all the snacks, ice cream, tacos, and pizza Mrs. Park's credit card would buy. Madison even got four hours to herself every day when the home health aide came each afternoon, including weekends. Today she wanted to go to the Cincinnati Zoo, but she had to pick up Mrs. Park's prescriptions in town, so a Denton Heights field trip it would be. Maybe she'd hang out in that coffee shop. She'd gone in a couple of times but never stayed. There were always way too many people inside. Maybe today, she would be brave. She could use the e-reader on her phone to read the book she was in the middle of. It was a good one, too. Ooh, ooh. No! She'd pick up a new coloring book at the drug store. Did she have crayons? Yes. Or, or, or maybe…maybe she'd buy a set of colored pencils and a fancy sharpener. You know, the kind with a compartment to hold all the shavings?

"Girl!" Mrs. Park's voice pierced her reverie.

"Yes, Mrs. Park?"

"Get moving." More Korean. It was amazing how Madison understood what Mrs. Park wanted. Not the words as much as the tone and gestures.

Madison put her charge into a fresh adult diaper and clean nightgown and then helped her into the electric wheelchair.

Once Mrs. Park had mobility, Madison was free to dart into the bathroom and relieve her aching bladder, brush her teeth, and wash her face. Sometimes she forgot the teeth brushing part, but not today. She was going out! Toiletry done, she got dressed and headed to the kitchen.

"Coffee or tea, Mrs. Park?"

"Yes," came the affirmative answer.

Which one? Madison sighed. She hated making decisions. Okay, whatev. She'd make one of each and take whichever one Mrs. Park didn't want.

Madison snapped the tray table on the wheelchair and set the cup of tea on it. Ahh, Mrs. Park was in a reflective mood today. Instead of sitting in front of the television for the daily morning talk shows, she had positioned her wheelchair in front of the floor-to-ceiling windows overlooking Denton Heights and Cincinnati beyond.

"This is such a great view, Mrs. Park."

"Thank you, Madison."

Madison grunted in surprise. Mrs. Park was having a lucid moment. She'd remembered Madison's name.

"You are a beautiful child," Mrs. Park said, grinning at her. "Taking care of me in my old age. You should be out doing young people things."

"That's okay," Madison said. "I—"

"Like falling in love," Mrs. Park continued as if Madison hadn't spoken. "Making your career. Buying a house. Traveling."

"Yes, Ma'am," Madison said. She was in listening mode. Listening without interjecting something was hard, so hard, for her. A thousand thoughts ran across her brain, many onto her tongue, but she fought hard and swallowed those trying to escape.

"You're going out today, yes?"

"Yes." Madison wanted to elaborate but didn't want to interrupt her elder.

"Good. Go make some friends. They can come here to visit while you're strapped down to this old lady."

"Okay." Madison said the word, but she knew it would never happen. Not in a million years. Friends rarely were actual friends. They were people who made you think they liked you and then took what they wanted from you and made fun of you like everyone else. Nah, she didn't need friends. "Mrs. Park?"

"Hmm?"

"How do you know my mother? She was the one that sent me here to work for you. She said you were an 'old family friend.' What does that mean?"

"Yes," Mrs. Park agreed with a nod. "I am old!" She threw her head back and laughed with her mouth wide open.

Madison couldn't help but giggle.

"Tell me about your grandmother," Mrs. Park said, not answering Madison's initial question.

"You know her, too?"

"Mm hmm," Mrs. Park said. "Is she still a sourpuss? With that permanent disapproving scowl on her face?"

Madison merely chuckled softly. Mrs. Park was trespassing into dangerous territory. Madison secretly agreed with Mrs. Park's version of her grandmother but knew it was a trap. To be disrespectful like that to an elder? No, no, no. Even thinking thoughts like that was dishonorable. Respecting your elders was deeply engrained in Korean families. It was almost law. And, okay, fine. Madison didn't want to be thought of as Korean, despite her appearance screaming it everywhere she went, but there were some things like respect that transcended national origin.

Madison stared out the windows at the view as Mrs. Park told the story about how she was pregnant during the Six-Two-Five war and her husband was killed, but then an American soldier named Eddie brought her to Ohio as his wife after the war. He was one of her great loves, she'd said. Madison wondered if she'd ever have a great love like that. Someone who would take her to "new heights," as Mrs. Park slyly called the lovemaking she'd experienced with Eddie. Nah, probably not. And apparently, Mrs. Park had many great loves. Madison tuned her out as she launched into another of her rambling reminiscences.

No, Madison reaffirmed. *There is no one for me.* She was fine all by herself. Why even think about it? All Madison wanted was to be left alone.

~~~

Madison stood in the short line at the coffee shop, grateful there weren't too many people around. She got to the front counter and waited to be addressed by the uber-pretty redheaded woman taking the orders. She looked like a manager. She was definitely the one in charge, that was for sure.

"How is your day going?" the woman asked once Madison stepped up to the counter.

"Good," Madison said, her cheeks getting warm. She always felt wonky and weird whenever *pretties* talked to her.

"That's it? Just 'good?'" The woman's smile was kind. And gentle. "Are you coming from school?" She gestured to the backpack strapped to Madison's back.

Madison shook her head.

"Got all your treasures in there, do you?"

"Mm hmm." Why was this *pretty* talking to her so much? It was weird.

"Well, what can I get for you this afternoon?" the *pretty* asked. Oh, right. She wants my money.

It was June and already so boiling hot outside that Madison did the only sensible thing and ordered an iced coffee with whipped cream and sprinkles. She wished they had muffins or something to go with the coffee. Maybe one day she'd get brave and suggest it.

The woman took her cash and said she could wait at the far end of the counter for someone to call her name when the beverage was ready. "If you need anything else, Madison, just ask for me." She pointed to her nametag. "Rikki."

Madison's jaw dropped open. Rikki? That was the name of the coffee shop—Rikki's Coffee Shop. Holy guacamole! The owner was talking to her. The owner! Practically paralyzed at this realization, Madison simply nodded and slinked away.

Once she got her coffee, she made good on her promise to stay in the shop and not bolt immediately. Mrs. Park was fine in the condo with Phaneesa, the Friday afternoon home health nurse, so Madison didn't have to worry about that. She just had to be back by 4:00 pm. She found a seat in an empty part of the shop and sat on the couch with her back against the wall. She put down her backpack and began the arduous process of unpacking. Down on the low table went mints, tissues, paper clips—yep, she might need these things. She pulled out her brand new coloring book, pack of colored pencils, and sharpener. Oh, look, a power bar. How long had that been in there? No worries, it was still sealed and might make a tasty snack with the coffee. A rubber band, some stamps, a clean envelope—all of it went on the table next to her coffee.

The noise level in the shop had risen steadily while she unpacked. She looked up to see that a hefty line had formed. An old fat Black guy was looking right at her. He had no expression on his face, so she didn't know what to make of it. *Shut up,* she said to him with the power of her mind. Some white kid was looking at her, too. He was too far away for her to make out his face, but he wore bright red shorts and red suspenders and was beaming at her like she was his long-lost friend or something. His hair was sandy blond and short like Captain America's. He didn't have Captain America's muscles, though. Or the all-important shield. She couldn't really tell from this far away, but he had to be in his early twenties. He was holding the hand of a much older man. Madison mentally stuck her tongue out at him and, in a huff, stood up and moved to the couch on the other side of the low table, facing away from everyone. *What? You've never seen an Asian girl before? I'm American, you jerks.* Boys were stupid. Very very stupid.

Madison reached for her shiny new "Birds of North America" coloring book and turned to the first page. The cutest little mama bird held her wing out tight over her baby. The caption read, "A mama Canada Jay huddles her baby under her wing during an unexpected spring snowfall."

"Aww," Madison gushed. "That is so cute." She picked up her phone and searched for the bird to make sure she used the right colors. Ahh, boring. Mostly grays and whites, but that was okay. She could get creative with a colorful background. Yes, yes, and that way the birds' cuteness would stand out more. "Brilliant, Madison," she said out loud.

"Is that your name?" a voice asked right beside her. "Madison?"

Madison jumped and whipped her head to the side only to see the guy in the red shorts and suspenders coming around to sit near her. "Yes," she said quietly. She didn't like boys. They were…not nice.

"I was talking to you, but you didn't hear me," he said.

She shrugged. *Who cares?*

"Do you want to play a game with me?" he asked and sat down in her original seat against the wall.

"No."

"It'll be fun." He bounced up and down in his seat, making Madison wonder if he was retarded or something. She didn't think it in a mean way, just in a "what's his deal" kind of way.

"What's your name?" Madison asked.

"Billy," he said. "I'm twenty years old, and Seamus is my Papa." He pointed to the older man he'd been holding hands with on the long line. "I mean, he's not my biological father or anything. He's my Daddy Dom."

"Hmm?" Madison said, clearly confused.

"Oh, that means he's like my boyfriend, but we've agreed that he takes care of me and makes all the rules."

Madison looked from Billy to the man named Seamus and back again. She wasn't weirded out by the same gender thing or even the age difference, but the 'he makes all the rules' thing was kind of confusing. "You call him Papa?"

"Oh, yes," Billy said as he pushed Madison's stuff to one side and dealt out a hand of cards to himself and to Madison. "I call him 'Sir' sometimes, too, but that's usually only if I've done something wrong. Like not cleaning my room or not listening carefully. And sometimes I call him Sir when we…" he hesitated and added, "you know, when we have private Papa/Billy time."

Madison nodded as if she understood, but she kind of didn't. Was he talking about sex? She was okay with people having sex. She'd had lots of sex in Columbus. Lots. It was good sex, too. For a while. And then it wasn't. When her mother packed her up and sent her to Cincinnati to take care of Mrs. Park—it had been good because no one knew her in Cincinnati. She didn't have to think about *pretties* or *stupids* anymore.

"Match the color or the number on the open deck with a card from your hand. If you can't, you have to pick a card from the pond."

"Kind of like go-fish?" Madison rearranged the cards in her hand by color and then by number. Her coloring book lay open on the couch next to her abandoned.

"Sort of," Billy said, "but you can't ask me for a match. You have to match it from the pile. You keep going until you can't make a match, and then it's my turn."

They played a few hands of the easy game and giggled whenever one of them had a killer run of four or more matches. Madison pumped a fist in the air when she threw her last match down and declared herself the winner of all time, having beaten him three out of the five games.

Billy laughed at her antics and said, "C'mon, you have to give me a rematch."

"Okay." Madison lowered her victory arms and took a sip from her almost forgotten frosty beverage.

"Do you like boys or girls?" Billy asked as he shuffled the deck.

"You mean for a girlfriend and sex and stuff?"

"Mm hmm."

"Girls."

"I knew it," Billy said triumphantly. "Papa says I have good gaydar. But where's your Mommy Domme?"

"My dum?"

"Mommy Domme. D-O-M is for boys, and D-O-M-M-E is for girls," he spelled out.

"What do you mean by Domme?"

"The woman who takes care of you. You have a Mommy Domme, don't you?"

"No, should I?"

"How are things going, you two?" the man named Seamus asked and set a frosty cold beverage in front of Billy.

"She's beating me, Papa."

"Aww, poor kid. You'll live," Seamus said with a chuckle and then blew on his hot coffee. "Introduce me to your friend, Billy."

"Yes, Sir." Billy sat taller and said, "Papa, this is my new friend Madison. She doesn't have a Mommy Domme, and I feel bad for her because having someone take care of you is so special and amazing."

Madison's heart got warm and oogly as she watched Seamus pull Billy into a hug and whisper soothing words. He sat back but held Billy's hand.

Seamus turned to Madison. "It's nice to meet you, young lady. I hope Billy has been a gentleman?"

"Oh, yes, Sir," Madison said. "He has." She wondered why she'd called him Sir, probably because Billy had.

"Having fun over here?" The *pretty* named Rikki asked. She leaned forward with both hands on the back of Madison's couch. Her blouse opened a little, and Madison noticed her lovely cleavage. It also made her feel oogly but in a different way. It was like how Katia used to make her feel until she was done with Madison and gave her away.

"Yes, Miss Rikki," Billy gushed. "Madison is my new friend."

"Oh, that's great," Rikki said, her face beaming as she looked between Billy and Madison.

"She doesn't have a Mommy Domme, though." Billy's smile faded, and he looked down.

Not having a Mommy Domme must be the worst thing in the world, Madison thought. But how do you get one?

"Is she a *little*?" Rikki asked Billy.

Billy's expression was one of disbelief as he kept eye contact with Rikki and gestured to Madison's open coloring book, her pink backpack covered with Trolls stickers, and her unicorn t-shirt.

"Ahh," Rikki said. "Takes one to know one, I guess."

Billy nodded emphatically and then gasped. He raised his hand high in the air like they were in school and bounced on the couch.

"Yes, Billy?" Rikki said with a chuckle.

"Can Madison come to Miss Tilda's tea dance tomorrow? Please? Sometimes the other *littles* don't come, and it would be soooo much fun to finally have someone to play with." He said the last part so dramatically that Madison's laughter joined the grownups.

"Of course, she can come to the dance," the *pretty* named Rikki said. "It's up to her, though."

Billy's laser beam focus landed on Madison. "Say you'll come. Please, please, pleeeeeeease say you'll come."

"Umm, okay. When is it? And where? I can only be out from noon to four."

"Perfect," Seamus said. "It's from noon to six." He turned his attention to Rikki and said, "Will you give her the address?"

Rikki nodded. "Sounds like a plan. How old are you, Madison?"

"Twenty-two and three-quarters," Madison said. "How old are you?"

Rikki burst out laughing but answered the question. "Thirty-two and a half. And I am officially inviting you to my Aunt Tilda's party tomorrow."

"Thank you," Madison said, feeling her cheeks get warm.

"Miss Rikki," a faraway voice called. Madison couldn't make out the rest but knew someone needed Rikki's attention.

Rikki stood up, taking that wonderful cleavage with her. "Ahh, Lydia needs me." She turned to look at Madison and said, "Don't leave until I write down that address for you. Okay?"

"Yes, okay," Madison said. "Thank you for the invitation." What a grown-up thing to say. How unlike her.

Chapter 2

Shasti

Shasti Balakrishnan let out what was supposed to be a cleansing breath and sighed. Yoga usually calmed her, but not today. There was too much on her mind. The young patient whose illness was still a mystery for one. The new *little* in town that Tilda had called to tell her about for two. And this enormous house she could barely afford for three. Were there more? Probably.

Her young patient and family were counting on her to find the cause of the girl's unexplained illness and "fix it." Shasti would like nothing more, but this one was elusive. A fourteen-year-old girl should not have persistent drowsiness, dizziness, bouts of diarrhea, or nausea. No treatments had worked so far. Shasti needed a miracle to figure it out. She'd even take a small one.

She stood up and shook out her arms and legs. Rolling up her mat, she glanced at the clock in the spare bedroom she used for yoga. She had plenty of time. She took in the boring antique-white walls and wondered if someone would ever claim this room as their own. Would she ever have a *little* one day to care for and love? Someone who would be excited to pick out a new paint color? Pink? Yellow? Wacky purple with polka dot flowers? They would have so much fun painting it together, wouldn't they? She sighed, rolled up her mat, and stashed it in the empty closet. Maybe one day.

"That's why you bought this huge house," she murmured to no one as she headed for the shower in the master bedroom. "You want someone to take care of. Someone who will appreciate your guidance and helping hands. Unlike—" No. She would not think about Amber. That had been a mistake. Amber was submissive, yes, but she wasn't a *little* like she'd claimed. More of a selfish brat who took and took and took. The day she broke it off with Shasti was not only heart-breaking but was also a relief. That very evening Shasti contacted three headhunters for help finding a position far, far away from D.C. At that point, she still lived at home, even at age thirty-one, and her parents were asking too many questions about her lifestyle. That was something she never wanted to talk to them about. They knew she was a lesbian. They'd come to terms with their eldest daughter's sexual orientation, but the young and immature young women she brought home on occasion—all of legal age, of course—no, that wasn't flying anymore. Time to fly the coop and live on her own. Was she running away? Probably.

Why had she bought such a big house? It was stretching her budget big time. She'd had to ask her parents for help with the down payment, for goodness sake. And in a gated community? In Denton Heights, of all places? It was one of the most affluent bedroom communities of Cincinnati and was just the "right kind of place" for a young medical doctor joining her first practice as a full partner. That's what the realtor had told her, anyway. She liked the neighborhood well enough, and after only a few weeks of living there had her neighbors just about convinced that it was okay to have a dark-skinned woman of Indian descent living in their privileged white community. The fact that she was a doctor probably had much to do with their acceptance.

Enough! With a Herculean effort, she pushed the all-consuming thoughts aside and took her time grooming and dressing. Tilda had called late the night before to tell her that a twenty-two-year-old young lady who claimed to be a *little* was going to be at Saturday's party. Tilda would make introductions if that suited Shasti. It did, but Shasti was not going to get her hopes up. And this *little*? The one that was new in town? She was certainly not going to throw herself at Shasti, anyway. So, there was absolutely no sense getting excited about something that probably, most definitely, was *not* going to happen.

Showered, shaved, and dressed in a modest summer sundress with light makeup, Shasti pulled the trigger and actually got in the car. After a quick ten-minute drive, she pulled her decade-old BMW along the curb of Tilda's corner house. The car had been a gift from her parents the year she started medical school.

She tucked her purse under the front seat, probably not the brightest thing to do, and then grabbed the bag of rope she'd finally gotten in the mail. It had taken forever to arrive from the specialty BDSM shop, but the colors were vibrant, and the texture Tom had recommended she order. Tom promised to show her some rope techniques on his submissive Lydia that afternoon. And if Lydia agreed, Shasti was going to tie her as well. Rikki had offered up her submissive Eileen as a rope bottom, but there was something off-putting about Eileen. Shasti couldn't put her finger on it, and she would never tell Rikki about her unease around Eileen. Rope was proving to be a cathartic endeavor for her. It was relaxing. Almost Zen-like. And she didn't want Eileen to ruin it. Would the new *little* like rope play?

Stop. It's not going to happen. She checked her hair in the rearview mirror. She'd decided on a loose ponytail for her dark hair—one that didn't scream "extreme control freak over here" but also one that didn't scream "walk all over me." Funny how one ponytail could convey so much.

"Do you need help?" Rikki called from the side gate to the backyard, where the sounds of soft music and excited conversations promised a fun time. "Ooh, is that rope, or are you just happy to see me?" Rikki teased.

Shasti laughed and headed over the side lawn toward her friend. Good thing she'd worn knock-around sandals and not her expensive Italian leather flats. Shoot, she should have painted her toenails. Would the new *little* like girly things like painting nails? Or was she a tomboy who'd rather change the oil on her motorcycle? Both maybe?

Rikki leaned in close before letting Shasti in the yard. "She is positively adorable." The *she* obviously referred to the new *little*.

"Yeah?" Shasti said, her heart fluttering a little. "Don't get my hopes up, Rikki. There may be no chemistry."

"No worries. She doesn't know she's meeting you today. Aunt Tilda said it was better that she had no expectations. You know? That way, you can see the real her."

Shasti nodded as she took a huge breath.

"Nervous?"

Shasti nodded again and rolled her eyes.

"Just breathe." Rikki held open the gate and let Shasti into the oversized backyard.

They walked up the three steps to the large wooden deck, where Shasti greeted another local Domme. "How are things, Victoria?" Shasti asked.

"Going alright," Victoria said with a nod. As always, her short butch hair was styled perfectly and didn't move in the slight June breeze. Her light chinos, button-down shirt, and opened vest suited her style. Victoria never lacked companionship. The femmes fell all over each other to get to her. And she complied. Regularly.

Victoria's attention was laser-focused on a curvy brunette across the deck wearing provocative clothing. If you could even call it clothing. The see-through tube top left nothing to the imagination, and the thong barely covered anything. But that's how Victoria liked her women to dress—barely.

Shasti cleared her throat. "Your new sub, I take it?"

"Mm hmm," Victoria answered. Her voice was low. She was obviously enthralled with the brunette.

"Good luck," Shasti said, exchanging a glance with Rikki. "She's quite good-looking."

"I know," Victoria grunted.

Rikki leaned close and whispered, "She's inside," referring to the new *little*.

That brought Shasti's blood pressure down slightly. She had been nonchalantly scouring the many faces in the yard, trying to find the *little* named Madison. Now she could focus on breathing.

"I should greet your Aunt Tilda," Shasti said and looked for their host.

Tilda noticed her and motioned for her to stay right where she was. She leaned down and said something to Josef, her long-term submissive kneeling at her feet. He stood and hurried away to do her bidding. Tilda was the very definition of a matriarch. From the way she dressed to the way she stood tall with her head held high. That afternoon she wore a flattering caftan, and her completely white hair was tastefully done up in a beehive. Josef's work, no doubt.

Tilda was in command of any and every room she entered. The recent masquerade ball in May was proof of that. She was a celebrity. Everyone wanted to be near her. Shasti included. Magnetism. That's what Tilda had. Shasti hoped to be that well put together at Tilda's wonderful age of eighty years young. Tilda was Rikki's grandmother's sister and had introduced Rikki to the *life*.

"Ahh, my three girls," Tilda said to Victoria, Rikki, and Shasti. "My treasures. Tilda's treasures. I like the sound of that."

Shasti chuckled and was glad that Victoria had the absolute sense to give Tilda her full attention. Victoria understood protocol, as did Rikki, of course. The two of them continued to help Shasti understand the expectations of the Denton Heights power exchange community she'd found herself immersed in. She had been a quick study. There were Dommes, and then there were Domme's Dommes if that made any sense. Tilda was one of those. No one challenged her throne.

"Where is that sub of yours?" Tilda asked Rikki.

"She'll be down. She's finishing up a task for me."

"Picking up rice from the floor? One grain at a time?" Victoria asked, her expression hopeful. Ahh, it seemed that Victoria wasn't an Eileen fan either.

Rikki chuckled. "No, she's cleaning our bathroom."

"With a toothbrush, I hope," Tilda said. There was no mirth to her statement. Nope, she wasn't a fan either.

"I learned from the best, Aunt Tilda," Rikki said with a grin. "And there's also this." She held up her phone and showed them an app. "This is the on/off button." She pressed the on button. "And this one ramps up the vibrations."

"Ass or pussy?" Victoria asked. She was never one to sugar-coat anything.

"Ass," Rikki said. "Butt plug. She wanted the bigger one, but I wasn't in the mood to follow her orders."

Just then, an incredible racket tore through the relatively quiet party. Two human streaks bolted out the back door and onto the deck. They dodged people left and right and then flew down the stairs to the grass below, swords brandished. Ahh, plastic swords. With rounded tips, Shasti thought with relief.

Billy held his sword high, "I, William the Conqueror, will defend my kingdom against you, Madison the Marauder."

"Oh, is that her?" Shasti gushed to Rikki.

"Mm hmm. Isn't she adorable?"

Shasti nodded. On the backyard lawn below her stood the cutest Asian girl she'd ever seen. Her slim figure, cute button nose, expressive eyes, and untidy shoulder-length hair drew Shasti in. And the way she confidently held her sword, all of it caused something to shift inside Shasti. What that was, she wasn't sure yet.

"Get that squirt a hair tie," Victoria muttered, referring to Madison. She was serious.

"How old is she, Tilda?" Shasti asked. She knew but wanted confirmation because the girl looked so young.

"Twenty-two and three-quarters. She told me that when she got here," Tilda said. "She was emphatic about the three-quarters."

Seamus sidled up next to Shasti. "Billy is over the moon that he found a new friend."

Down on the lawn, the battle continued. "I will avenge the death of my father, you scourge of the earth," Madison replied and smacked Billy's sword with the tip of her own.

"As soon as one of them dies, I'll arrange for the two of you to meet," Tilda said to Shasti with a chuckle.

Shasti barely registered the glass of chardonnay that Josef handed her as she watched the riveting fight scene below her. Both parties claimed to have been wronged by the other and sought revenge. Their thrusts and parries looked almost choreographed.

Billy lunged forward, and for whatever reason, Madison let his blade slide between her arm and her side. She clutched her chest with both hands and groaned dramatically. "The final blow," she exclaimed. "You shall be cursed, William the Weenie Wuss."

Her death scene was spectacular, and the crowd burst into applause when she stopped moving.

Billy pulled his sword out of the dead Madison and held it high in the air, declaring himself the king of all the lands.

With his back turned to her, Madison leaped to her feet, grabbed her sword, and struck down the unsuspecting newly minted king. "In a surprise move," she announced, "Madison the Magnificent defeats the evil king!"

Billy's dying scene took over an entire minute as he gasped for air and circled around, grasping for something to hold onto. He reached a hand toward Seamus. "Goodbye, Papa. Fare thee well, kind Sir." And with that, he plopped to the ground and died.

Madison, to her credit, didn't take her eyes off him and, after a moment, gently nudged him with her foot. When he still didn't move, she whispered, "Billy, are you okay?"

"Yeah," he whispered, keeping his eyes shut. "I'm dead."

"Oh," Madison said. Without missing a beat, she asked him, "Where are the keys?"

"What keys?" Billy sat up, and she pounced on him like a professional wrestler.

"The keys to my new kingdom!" Her evil laugh made everyone laugh. Even Billy started giggling as he struggled to get out from under her.

Shasti laughed along with everyone else. She felt her cheeks get warm and knew it wasn't from the wine. Tilda cleared her throat and asked Seamus to call the *littles* over so she could speak with them.

Shasti rolled her eyes at the grass and dirt stains covering the two young people's clothes as they made their way back to the deck. It wasn't her place to reprimand them.

Billy bowed and said, "Hi, Miss Tilda, Daddy Vic, Miss Rikki, Miss Shasti, and Papa."

Each of them returned his greeting. An awkward silence followed until Billy whispered in Madison's ear, "Protocols, remember? Protocols? I told you about them."

She turned to him with a scowl on her face. "Robocalls? What are you saying?"

Billy facepalmed and then looked up at his Papa for help.

"It's okay, Billy," Tilda said. "She's new to our ways." She turned to Madison and said, "It's expected that submissives and *littles* greet the Dominants politely. As Billy just demonstrated."

"Oh, I'm sorry," Madison said, her face falling. "I didn't know."

"No worries," Rikki said. "Want to try?"

"Okay," Madison said, took a deep breath, and in a rush, repeated the exact words Billy had said in greeting. She even called Seamus *Papa*.

Tilda nodded at Seamus. It was her signal for him to correct her. "I appreciate the respect, Madison, but you either call me Mr. Seamus or just Sir. Papa is a very special term used only in an agreed-upon dynamic. Like the one I have with Billy."

"Ohhhh," Madison said, dragging out the word. "That's why he wants me to find a Mommy Domme. So I can call her Mommy or Mama or something like that, right?"

The Dominants on the deck chuckled at her naivete.

"Umm," Seamus said, clearly thrown by Madison's innocence, "yes, if that's what you want and if your Domme agrees to that."

"Interesting." Madison whipped her head toward Tilda. "Can we have cupcakes now, Miss Tilda?" Madison asked in all seriousness. "I saw Josef putting them in a plastic container when I first got here." The last part was sing-songed. No one, not even the matriarch herself, could resist that.

"Come give me a hug first, dear child," Tilda commanded. Her expression looked like she wanted to eat Madison up with a spoon. It was kind of how Shasti was feeling at the moment.

Madison complied immediately, her face beaming at the attention.

"Okay, how about this," Tilda said after releasing Madison. "Why don't you and Miss Shasti go in the kitchen and get the cupcakes out of the refrigerator? Bring the whole container out here and put it on the dessert table." She gestured to a small table to one side of the big table laden with summer salads and other summery foods.

Shasti looked over, too. Ahh, there were hotdogs for the *littles*. Shasti bet that's what Madison would have. And a cupcake, of course.

"Shall we?" Shasti asked. All on its own, her hand started reaching for Madison's. She pulled it back to her side and groaned inside. *There could be no chemistry. She's new to all of this. Slow down, Shasti.*

"Yep," Madison said and, without waiting, rushed into the house and headed toward the kitchen.

Shasti turned to the others and shrugged before following the vicenarian inside. Out of the corner of her eye, she saw Rikki and Seamus high-five each other.

Once inside the house, Shasti gently nudged Madison's discarded sliders to one side. She'd obviously flung them off her feet without caring where they ended up. Shasti found Madison in the kitchen yanking open the refrigerator door. She pulled out the cupcake container and plunked it on the granite-top island. She reached back with her foot and slammed the refrigerator door closed. The sheer force of it caused a magnet to fall and crash onto the porcelain floor tiles.

"Slow down, Madison," Shasti said gently. Wow, wow, wow. She hadn't wanted the first thing out of her mouth to be a reprimand. But there it was.

"Sorry," Madison said, seeming unperturbed. She stroked the edges of the container's lid lovingly.

Shasti reached down and picked up the fallen magnet. It was a tiny coffee cup, a promotional item from Rikki's grand opening over a year ago. Luckily it hadn't broken. The tile was also unmarred. She carefully placed it back on the refrigerator and then turned toward Madison.

She could not believe her eyes. The lid had been removed from the container, and it was obvious that one whole cupcake was gone. Oh, wait, there was frosting around the edges of Madison's mouth. Shasti couldn't believe what she did next. She hadn't planned it, it just happened. With a finger, she wiped a glob of frosting off Madison's mouth. Before she fully understood what she was doing, she popped the finger in her mouth and sucked off the sugary goodness.

"Mmm," Shasti said. "So good."

Shasti expected a giggle but didn't get one. Instead, Madison's serious gaze was riveted on Shasti's mouth. She looked from the mouth to Shasti's eyes and said quietly, "You're really pretty, Miss."

Shasti's face flamed hot at the compliment. Words. She should use words, but she couldn't find any. Instead, she reached for another glob of pink frosting on Madison's lips.

Just at that precise moment, heavy footsteps entered the kitchen. "Whoa, pedophilia in progress. Let me *not* be a witness."

Shasti jumped away from Madison and turned to see the judgmental glare of Rikki's submissive Eileen. "Good luck with that shit, Shasti." She gestured to both Shasti and Madison and then headed for the backdoor.

It hadn't gone unnoticed that Eileen did not use the honorific *Miss* to address Shasti. Ahh, but that was nothing new when it came to Eileen. Early on, Shasti pegged Eileen as one of those career submissives who bounced from Dominant to Dominant in search of their fix. Shasti hoped Rikki wasn't betting the farm on Eileen being "the one."

Shasti closed her eyes momentarily, cleared her throat, and said, "C'mon, Madison, let's bring those out to the table."

"Okay," Madison said and then added in a conspiratorial whisper, "I don't think I like her."

"I know what you mean. But maybe it's best to keep that opinion to ourselves, okay?"

"Like a secret?"

"Mm hmm," Shasti said.

"I like having a secret with you," Madison said shyly.

"Oh, yeah? Me, too." Shasti reached out, grabbed that glob of frosting still on Madison's face, stuck it in her mouth, and said, "After you, peanut. After you."

Chapter 3

Madison

After two more cupcakes and one bunless hotdog, Madison lay on her back, rubbing her full tummy. Billy's Sir had thrown a blanket on the ground for her and Billy to sit on while they ate. Kind of like a picnic. Oddly, he put the blanket right over the spot where she and Billy had died their most spectacular deaths in the epic battle of the universe earlier. Was no ground sacred in this kingdom? She tried not to giggle because it was Billy's turn to find a shape in the clouds. She barely listened as he pointed out his nine-hundredth poodle and instead snuck a peek at Miss Shasti sitting on the deck eating a salad. Why would you eat a salad when there were hot dogs and cupcakes? It made zero sense.

Madison hadn't lied when she told Miss Shasti that she was pretty. Her dark eyes were kind. Her skin was deep brown and looked so smooth that Madison wanted to run the tips of her fingers over her face, but that would be weird. Miss Shasti had her hair pulled back behind her head, exposing her lovely neck. Those earrings were so nice and dangly. Madison wished she knew how to dress the way Miss Shasti did. So elegant, even at a backyard party. And she had called Madison *peanut*. Was that a good thing? Or something else? She didn't know.

"Hey, Billy?" She smacked him on the stomach with the back of her hand.

"Oof! What?"

"Why is this called a tea dance? There's no tea, and no one is dancing."

Billy looked as confused as she felt. "I have no idea. I'll ask Papa later. Hey, what time is it? Don't you have to leave at like 3:30 or something?"

"It's only 2:00," Madison said, grateful she could observe Miss Shasti in the wild a little while longer.

"Yay. You can stay for the demonstrations in Miss Tilda's dungeon."

"There's a dungeon?" She sat bolt upright and looked at Billy in disbelief.

The grownups on the deck chuckled, and all eyes were on her. She looked down and frowned. She hated when people laughed at her.

Billy sat up and said, "C'mon. Papa's calling for us."

Madison looked up. She hadn't heard Mr. Seamus.

"It's time to go to the dun dun dun…" He paused for dramatic effect and then said, "dungeon." He leaped to his feet and ran toward his Papa's outstretched hand.

Madison got up and took two steps before realizing they'd left a mess on the blanket. She reached down, picked up all the trash, and looked around for a trash bin.

"Over here," a voice called from the deck. It was Miss Shasti. Her smile was so bright and kind. Madison turned to look behind her. Miss Shasti chuckled and said, "Madison, I'm talking to you. You can put your trash in this barrel right here."

"Okay." Madison felt her whole body flush. Having Miss Shasti's help made her feel one part good but one part embarrassed. Usually, people only talked to her when they wanted something. "Okay," she said again and made her way over.

"Ready to see the demonstrations?" Miss Shasti asked. She was so cheery. Was she always like this? It was nice but weird.

Madison still wasn't sure why Miss Shasti continued to interact with her. She obviously wanted something, but Madison couldn't figure out what. "Okay," was all Madison could think of to say. "I'm kind of scared of dungeons, though."

"You'll be safe there. Anything done in Miss Tilda's dungeon is consensual and usually worked out ahead of time."

"Okay," Madison said again. The urge to reach up and grab the kind woman's hand was overwhelming, but she didn't. It was stupid to think Miss Shasti wanted to be her friend. She was, like, so much older anyway. She was just being kind to the other Asian at the party. You know, the awkward one. That's all it was.

They made their way down the bright and well-lit stairs to a basement that spanned the entire length of the house. The walls were painted black and red, and there were a lot of contraptions and benches and stuff hanging on the walls. There were whips, paddles, and, holy macaroni, all kinds of scary-looking things!

"X marks the spot," she said when she saw a human-sized X attached to the far wall. Maybe that's where Miss Tilda tortured her prisoners with whips and chains. She wanted to ask Miss Shasti but decided against it. She didn't want to be laughed at again.

A woman that Madison recognized from Miss Rikki's coffee shop was sitting on a tall stool. She wore short shorts and a tight white short-sleeved t-shirt. Her arms were held away from her body, and her wrists tied with rope to this big metal U-shaped structure with hooks and bolts all over it. The woman was really pretty with her long blonde hair and curves in all the right places. She was a prisoner, wasn't she?

"Lydia's Dom bound her to those support posts," Miss Shasti said.

"Why?" Madison asked quietly.

"For the demonstration." Miss Shasti said. "Don't worry. Like I said, consent is paramount in any BDSM relationship."

"Lydia gave permission to be a prisoner?" This was a weird place, Madison decided firmly. She glanced toward the stairs and knew she could sprint up them, grab her shoes, and make her escape before any of these old people could catch her. She wasn't her high school softball team's leading base stealer for nothing, which was good because there was no way she would become one of their prisoners. She eyed Billy sitting in the well between Mr. Seamus's legs. Did Billy invite her so he could watch Madison be captured and then tortured? Is Miss Rikki in on it, too? All of these people seemed so nice. See? People suck.

"Madison?" a soft voice said near her ear. "Are you okay? Do you want to leave?"

It took a moment to quell her growing panic and realize that Miss Shasti was talking to her.

"Umm, what?"

"You don't have to stay if this is too much for you," Miss Shasti said. "You have a frightened expression on your face."

"Umm," was all Madison had to contribute to the conversation.

"Here, sit next to Billy. He can explain things as we go, okay?"

She looked over at her new friend. Or was he? Billy beckoned for her to sit on the floor next to him and his Papa. She glanced toward the stairs but said, "Okay."

Miss Shasti walked her over and then headed directly toward Lydia's Dom.

Billy whispered, "Mr. Tom is going to teach Miss Shasti how to tie a harness on Lydia. It will be like a vest or something. I'm not sure, but Shibari rope is really cool."

Madison wasn't sure what to make out of Billy's words, but she kind of knew a few things about BDSM. Kind of, but not really. Senior year, Katia had tried lots of stuff out on her, and Madison had kind of liked being on the receiving end, but when Katia insisted they switch roles so she could see what it felt like, neither of them liked it. At all.

So, there you go. Some people like to receive, and others like to give. Like Lydia – she was going to receive. And Miss Shasti and Mr. Tom were going to give.

"Ready, Shasti?" Mr. Tom asked and gestured toward his tied-up submissive.

Miss Shasti waggled her eyebrows at Madison and then picked up a red coil of rope.

"No," Madison blurted and leaped to her feet. She grabbed the teal-colored bundle and handed it to Miss Shasti. "This one will go better with her eyes."

The soft chuckle from the crowd made Madison jump. She wanted to bolt for the stairs, but the soft beaming smile on Miss Shasti's face halted her flight and almost melted her to the core. She turned to go back to her seat by Billy when she noticed Lydia's growing blush. "Hi, Lydia. You work in Rikki's coffee shop." It wasn't a question.

Amusement filled Lydia's eyes as she nodded back at Madison.

"Are you not allowed to talk because you're a prisoner?" Madison whispered.

Lydia looked at Miss Shasti as if asking for help.

Madison felt bad immediately. "Sorry, I didn't mean to get you in trouble."

"You didn't," Tom the Dom said, gesturing for Madison to return to her spot. "Lydia often falls into sub-space when we do rope, and she goes quiet. Being restrained like this sends her on her way." He pointed to her bound wrists, then turned to Miss Shasti and asked if she was ready.

She nodded and turned to Lydia. "Thank you for being my rope bottom today, Lydia." The pinking of Lydia's cheeks was obvious and made Madison wonder if Lydia was embarrassed or something. Shy, maybe? Scared? Happy? Wait. If it was possible to smile with your eyes, then Lydia was doing it. Miss Shasti cradled Lydia's chin and said softly, "You are a wonderful submissive. Your Dom should be very proud of you." Ahh, there it was. A real smile, albeit a small one, creeping up Lydia's face.

Madison watched in fascination as Miss Shasti followed Mr. Tom's instructions. Madison leaned forward and learned words like bight, anchor point, rigger, taut-not tight, and a bunch more. She also learned that the accepted term for Lydia was "rope bottom," not "rope bunny." The word bunny was offensive for some reason. It made sense, Madison supposed, because Lydia didn't look like a bunny. C'mon, where were the ears? Or the puff tail?

The relaxed look on Miss Lydia's face made Madison wonder what it felt like to be restrained and covered with rope by someone as calm and wonderful as Miss Shasti. She watched the sure and strong hands maneuver the rope around Lydia's body over and under the existing rope. The knots were done skillfully and sure. Madison couldn't help thinking that she wanted to be the one entangled in all that lovely rope. Miss Shasti also looked relaxed, as if doing this rope stuff was soothing for her, too.

Madison was about to tell Billy she wanted to go next but thought better of it as the rope tightened around Lydia's boobies from above and below, squishing them for all to see. No way was Madison doing that. Everyone would laugh at her A-cup mosquito bites.

"Yellow, Ma'am," Lydia said a bit breathlessly.

"Oh, oh." Miss Shasti stepped back. "Where?"

"Left wrist," Lydia said.

"Oh, goodness. I didn't even think to check there." Miss Shasti ran her hand down Lydia's arm to her wrist. "Warm here." She examined the wrist rope and said, "Ahh, A bit too tight. Your hand still has good color and good capillary refill when I press. But, Tom, let's go ahead and undo these wrist restraints." Without waiting for an answer, Miss

Shasti undid the wrist rope on the left side. Mr. Tom the Dom undid the right.

If the relief on Lydia's face wasn't enough to tell you how grateful she was, her long sigh was.

Miss Shasti pulled Lydia into a hug. "You are such a good girl, Lydia." She pulled back and placed the palm of her hand lovingly on Lydia's face. "Thank you for using your safe words." Lydia leaned into the kindness and nodded.

"What do you say?" Mr. Tom said, his voice kind of gruff.

Lydia cleared her throat and said, "Thank you, Ma'am. Thank you, Sir."

"Better," he said, his voice still stern.

Madison had so many different feelings fighting for dominance inside her, but the one that pushed to the surface was jealousy. She recognized it because she'd felt it before. This felt exactly like that time she saw Katia at the diner with some girl. That was right after Katia had passed her on to the *pretties*. That was four years ago and counting. She had no reason to be jealous of the attention Lydia was getting from Miss Shasti. But still. Madison wanted Miss Shasti's hand on her face, telling her she was a good girl.

"Madison," Billy hissed, "You're making weird noises. Lydia will be okay. Miss Shasti is a doctor."

"A doctor?" Madison said in full voice, and the room laughed at her again. Even Lydia and Miss Shasti were grinning at her.

Tears filled her eyes. Why did everyone make fun of her? Even these supposed new friends. She sprang to her feet and bolted up the stairs leaving all those *pretties* and *stupids* behind. Forever.

~~~

Madison sat on the floor of her room, coloring. At first, she used her new colored pencils, but she was pressing so hard that the tips kept breaking, so she finally decided to give in and switch to actual crayons. It was close to 4:00, and Phaneesa would be leaving soon. That was fine. Madison would focus on Mrs. Park instead of, you know, the other stuff. And now that Mrs. Park was on oxygen—that wonderful surprise she'd come home to earlier—she had even more things to think about. She wasn't exactly sure what was wrong with Mrs. Park, something about C.O.P.S. and Emphasim from years of smoking cigarillos or whatever. All she knew was that Mrs. Park now had to have tubes in her nose, giving her oxygen 24-7. She even had to wear the contraption when she slept at night. That sounded like it sucked.

"Hey, Madison," Phaneesa called from the other side of the closed bedroom door.

"Yeah?" Madison said, not even looking toward the door. She was busy.

"I'm heading out," Phaneesa said gently. "Are you sure you're okay, honey? You seemed kind of upset when you got home."

"I'm fine."

There was a long period of silence, and Madison thought the day nurse had left or something, but then Phaneesa said, "Are you all set with the tank and everything? You know how to read the gauges and attach the hoses?"

Madison sighed and put her artwork aside. She went to the door, opened it, and said to the short, stout middle-aged Black woman, "I'm fine with it all. Thanks for showing me."

"You're welcome. This is a lot of responsibility hoisted on you."

"I know, but Mommy sent me here to care for Mrs. Park, so that's what I'm doing."

"I'll be back tomorrow, but Eugenia will be here on Monday. We'll be starting six-hour shifts then. She'll show you a few more things you need to watch for, okay?"

"Okay."

It looked like Phaneesa wanted to say something else but didn't. She patted Madison's arm and picked up her nurse's bag. "I'll see you tomorrow, honey."

"Bye," Madison's retort was short and not very sweet. Whatevs. People were not her thing. Not now. Not ever again.

"Girl!" came Mrs. Park's shout from the living room.

Coloring abandoned, Madison made her way into the living room, where Mrs. Park was in her electric recliner. It went way back so that you could lay completely flat. And then it went the complete other way and spit you out into a standing position.

"Hi," Madison said.

"See what they did to me?" Mrs. Park gestured to the tubes snaking out of her nostrils and around her head.

"What's it feel like?"

"Weird," Mrs. Park said.

"Do you need anything?" Madison asked. She stood with her arms folded, wanting to get back to coloring her cardinals. At least they didn't make fun of her.

"Sit." Mrs. Park gestured to the gray couch that went with all the other gray and black and white furniture. There was, like, no color in the condo anywhere. Even the kitchen and bathroom towels were black, white, and gray. Madison sat.

"What do you want to do with your life, girl? You won't be taking care of me forever."

Madison shrugged.

"Find a life here," Mrs. Park said. Madison handed her the sippy cup with a straw that Mrs. Park had been reaching for. It looked like

Phaneesa had set her up with one of those disgusting protein drinks for sick old people. Madison tried a sip one day early on and almost gagged; it was so disgusting. But Mrs. Park drank them religiously in spite of the icky taste.

"Madison," Mrs. Park said quietly, "don't go back to that place. Columbus. Don't go back. They'll only continue to suck the life out of you up there."

Madison took the sippy cup back and placed it on the side table.

"But where am I going to go? What am I going to do?"

"Stay here in Denton Heights. This morning you were so excited to see Billy and meet some new friends at your party. Maybe Billy is a new boyfriend, ehh?" Mrs. Park laughed to the point of coughing. Madison leaped up and adjusted the chair into a sitting position. She made sure the oxygen hose was properly in place before sitting back down.

"My mother needs me," Madison said quietly. "I have to go back."

"Your mother is the one who sent you to me," Mrs. Park said. "She wanted you away from that environment."

"She told you that?"

Mrs. Park nodded. "Now, your mother is a different story. She needs professional help for her depression, but your grandmother rules that roost and won't let any form of weakness show in the Kim household. And you know that your grandmother has Golden Son Syndrome, don't you? Sons are highly valued in traditional Korean culture. Your brother and father can do no wrong in your grandmother's eyes. Well, except when your father married your mother. Hugest mistake he ever made according to her."

Madison's head dropped, and she stared at the socks on her feet. It was kind of warm in the condo, maybe she should go barefoot. It was summer. Who would care?

"I think your mother is a wonderful person," Mrs. Park continued. "But sensitive souls like hers can only take so much beating down, and her mother-in-law—your grandmother—is not a kind person."

"Grandma does think my brother Kwan is a Golden Son," Madison said, preferring to move the subject away from her mother. "He's twenty-one and still in community college." Memories came springing back unbidden. Kwan getting praise for doing mediocre things like breathing. On the other hand, she wore herself to the bone, trying to get acceptance and praise from her grandmother but getting none. Her mother would give her hugs and praise in private, but never in front of anyone else. Madison's father would only nod his head in approval now and then. Madison had even gotten perfect 5s on every AP exam she took in high school. She wasn't trying to show up her younger brother like her grandmother said. She wasn't. She just wanted to please. No, it was more than that. She wanted to be seen.

When the tears flooding her eyes spilled over, she fled to the floor-to-ceiling window, her back to Mrs. Park, and looked toward Denton Heights below. The coffee shop where she'd met Billy was right about there. Miss Tilda's house was over there. Where did Miss Shasti live? What kind of doctor was she? Madison felt her stiffness relax slightly.

"Your grandmother thinks in the old ways," Mrs. Park said. "Even though she was just a baby when she came to America, she clung fiercely to the Korean community instead of trying to assimilate into American culture. But then again, she grew up in the fifties and sixties when being anything other than white wasn't acceptable."

Madison wiped at the tears on her face before turning around. "How do you know my family again?"

"Bah," Mrs. Park said, obviously not interested in answering. She waved her off and said somberly, "You won't be taking care of me forever, Madison."

Madison tried to fight down the emotions bubbling up from Mrs. Park's unspoken words. She was in her nineties. She now needed oxygen to help her breathe. Home health aides were coming for six hours every day instead of four. Something was happening.

"So, tell me what you want to do," Mrs. Park pressed. "Do you want to be a zookeeper? Tame the lions?"

Madison cleared her throat and said, "I worked at PETology in Columbus. That's a pet store. They have them here, too."

"So maybe you'll get a job here for a while," Mrs. Park said. "But that's just a job. What about a career? You're still young. Don't just *work* in a pet store. *Own* the pet store. Don't feed the pets, be their doctor!"

"Like be a veterinarian or something?"

"Yes!" Mrs. Park poked her finger in the air. "Think like that. You have lots of life left." She leaned toward Madison, who had made her way back to the couch. "Madison, listen to an old lady. There is bliss in this world, even for you. You just have to find it. Sometimes it sneaks up on you when you're not looking. Angels—they nudge us toward things. You have been nudged toward your new boyfriend Billy, ehh?"

"He's not my boyfriend. I don't like boys that way," Madison interrupted. Her heart pounded as she admitted that natural part of herself. "That's part of the reason Mommy sent me here. To get away from my grandmother who kept calling me abnormal."

Mrs. Park groaned. "She is so repressed. Did you know that I had a female lover for a while?"

Madison's jaw dropped open. "You did?"

"Oh, yes," Mrs. Park said matter-of-factly. "Our husbands would go to the factory every morning, and we'd 'have tea' while the babies napped." She laughed big. "That might have been the best sex I've ever had. It was the most intimate, anyway."

Madison kept her eyes down but couldn't help the smile splitting her face. She didn't really want to talk about sex with Mrs. Park.

"I did meet someone, though," Madison said shyly. "At the party this morning. She's pretty. And nice. She called me 'peanut.'"

"Sounds like you like her. Does she like you?"

Madison shrugged. If she did, it was probably for all the same reasons most *pretties* and *stupids* liked her—for what she could do for them. And *to* them. No other reason.

"Madison, the angels seem to have nudged you toward her. Be open. Be curious. Be teachable. Learn and grow from all that information coming at you."

"I don't know how."

"Bah," Mrs. Park waved her hand as if discarding Madison's statement. "You're smart. Your mother told me you got top grades in school. She said you were a sports superstar, too." Madison shrugged. "You have to live, Madison. Listen to those nudges from the angels."

"Yes, ma'am," Madison said, still not looking up. She wasn't sure how one 'listened to angel nudges.'

"You cannot rely on other people for your own happiness. This was and still is your grandmother's and your mother's mistake. It's up to you to find your own happiness."

Madison looked up. That sounded good on paper, like communism, but… how did you do that?

Chapter 4

Shasti

Shasti checked her phone for the thousandth time since getting home from Tilda's. Apparently, no one had gotten a response from Madison yet. Billy had been reluctant to share Madison's phone number with her, but Seamus convinced him they were only looking out for her best interests. Billy had no idea where she lived. He only knew that she cared for a Mrs. Park, whoever that was. Did she live with this Mrs. Park?

"She was so upset," Shasti murmured to her teacup. She yanked the tea bag out and tossed it in the sink. Tea splashed all over the granite countertop, but she didn't care. She forced herself to sip the *Stomach Ease* concoction slowly. What set Madison off? Something had clearly panicked her. She seemed fine with Lydia being bound at the wrists, so what was it?

Shasti took a deep breath, held it, and let it out. Mind over matter, she reminded herself as she willed her stomach to stop churning. She headed to the formal sitting room, looking out the front window as if Madison would magically appear in her driveway. She sat in one of the two high wing-backed chairs she'd just had to have. She set her teacup down and closed her eyes for some meditative breathing. The loud ticking of the pendulum clock grated on her nerves, and then the neighborhood kids racing bikes up and down the streets of the gated community tipped her over the edge.

She urged her flippy stomach to settle down. "Mind over matter, Dr. Balakrishnan," she told herself again, this time out loud. "You can't help her if you're not calm yourself." She nodded at the wiseness of her words, fully intending to heed them if given the chance.

Both Rikki and Lydia promised to keep an eye out for her at the coffee shop that evening and over the next few days. Shasti thought it was a long shot, but it was something. And Billy—he had been so upset. Poor kid.

"He's so innocent and naïve, isn't he?" Shasti said to the rigid space no one except Rikki had seen in her two months living there. "Madison's an innocent, too. Such sweet wide-eyed innocence about both of them." Shasti let herself think about the cute Asian girl who was so full of questions. As Shasti tied Lydia that afternoon, she couldn't help thinking what it would be like tying Madison. Would she like it the way Lydia did? Go into sub-space? Would Shasti go into Domme-space the way she almost but not quite did when she tied? It would take the right partner for that. Would Madison be the right partner?

"Stop," Shasti said out loud. "You just met her." Another sip of tea went down her throat. "She's so young. Are ten years too much of a gap? At this stage of her life, you're an old lady to her, not a..." *Whatever.*

Maybe Eileen was right. Maybe this was bordering on pedophilia. Madison was just a girl, after all. Age-wise she wasn't. She was twenty-two and three-quarters—clearly an adult who could make her own decisions. Shasti smiled at the insisted upon three-quarters. Okay, so she was almost twenty-three, technically making it just over nine years between them. But the physical age wasn't the thing. It was Madison's emotional age. She didn't seem to be an adult emotionally or mentally. And *that's* what made the whole thing confusing.

Shasti checked her phone. There was no sense in sending Madison another text. She probably deleted them anyway since she didn't know the phone number they were coming from. Instead, Shasti called Tilda, who picked up on the first ring.

"I haven't heard anything," Tilda said. "Have you?"

"No," Shasti muttered. "I think our only hope is Billy. That and the coffee shop connection."

"You may be right. Rikki went to the shop to close up, and she said Mark hadn't seen any customers fitting Madison's description."

Shasti groaned. "I wish I knew what set her off."

"She needs a guiding hand, Shasti," Tilda said gently. "She's a lost soul. You saw that, didn't you?"

"Yes, definitely. I was going to ask her for a coffee date after I finished the rope harness on Lydia."

"So, you were taken by her, too, I gather." The smile in Tilda's voice was clearly evident between the cell towers.

"I was. I am. I'd love to see where this could go, but…"

"Give it time," Tilda said. "Let things unfold naturally."

"I know, but…" Shasti couldn't figure out how to voice all her reservations.

"But what?"

"There's a big age gap between us."

"I'm eighty-two, Shasti. Josef just turned sixty. You do the math."

Shasti took a sip of her quickly cooling tea, willing it to do its stuff. "But emotionally, she seems to be so much younger."

"Give it a trial period, dear," Tilda counseled. "If things don't work out, then they don't work out. That's life."

"A trial period?" Shasti liked the sound of that.

"Coffee date first. If that goes well, then a dinner date. At your house. You cook. Plan on those two events for now. Don't worry about happy ever after or disaster ever after. Just those two events."

"I can do that," Shasti said, hearing the conviction in her own voice. She even believed herself this time.

She said her goodbyes to Tilda and checked her text messages to Madison. Her stomach flipped when she saw the three dots dancing. Madison was reading her text. When no message came back, Shasti typed one of her own.

> SHASTI: This is Miss Shasti from the party. (As I said in my first two texts). I just wanted to make sure you're okay. You seemed pretty upset. You don't have to tell me why.

> SHASTI: I was wondering if you'd like to meet me for coffee tomorrow afternoon. We can work around your schedule. What do you say? 1:00 at Rikki's Coffee Shop? I'm buying.

> MADISON: Okay.

Shasti's pounding heart slowed. She's okay. Shasti tried to play it cool, even though she wanted to pummel the girl with questions about what had happened and then maybe, just maybe, reprimand her for bolting so rudely. But, no, that wasn't the right approach.

> SHASTI: Excellent! You left so fast this afternoon that I didn't get a chance to tell you how proud of you I was. You cleaned up your and Billy's trash from the blanket without being asked. That was a very grown-up thing to do.

She tapped the send button before she could change her mind, but as soon as she did, she cringed. Was it over the top? Would Madison consider the praise juvenile, inappropriate, or just plain idiotic? Shasti was working blind. She really didn't know this girl at all.

MADISON: Proud of me?!?!? Really?

SHASTI: Yes, of course. You seem like a very caring young lady.

MADISON: LOL. I'm not really a lady. You are. Not me.

SHASTI: Oh? Are you a boi, then? Or a boy? Or neither?

Shasti wasn't sure if Madison identified as non-binary. Shoot, maybe she had overstepped.

MADISON: No, I'm a girl, but I'm no lady. Ha ha ha ha ha. (laughing emoji).

MADISON: Is everyone mad at me? Am I in trouble for leaving without saying goodbye?

SHASTI: Not at all. Everyone is simply worried that we did something to hurt you.

MADISON: Well …

SHASTI: You can tell me.

Shasti's stomach had a new sensation. Butterflies. Madison was responding.

MADISON: Okay.

MADISON: Everyone was laughing at me.

SHASTI: Farthest thing from the truth, peanut. Everyone loved you. They think you are adorable and that you say the cutest and most innocent things.

MADISON: Because I'm stupid and worthless?

Shasti's heart was breaking for this poor kid. What would make her say those things?

SHASTI: Who makes you feel stupid? Because the girl I met today was intelligent and fun to be with and made me feel good. Like I made a new friend.

MADISON: Really?

SHASTI: Yes.

MADISON: Okay.

Hmm, Shasti thought. She doesn't quite believe me.

SHASTI: Might we talk more about this tomorrow? Over coffee? Because I think this is more of a face-to-face kind of conversation.

MADISON: Okay. And guess what?

SHASTI: What?

MADISON: I like your face.

Shasti chuckled in her not-so-lonely sitting room.

SHASTI: I like yours, too.

SHASTI: Do me two favors, okay? First, please put my name in your phone, so you'll know it's me.

MADISON: Okay. What's your last name?

SHASTI: Balakrishnan

MADISON: God bless you!

MADISON: (sneezing emoji) (winking emoji) (laughing emoji)

SHASTI: Ha ha! What a comedian!

MADISON: What's the second favor?

SHASTI: Text Billy to let him know you're okay. I'll text Tilda and Rikki, who'll text everyone else that you are fine and well.

SHASTI: You are "fine and well," aren't you?

MADISON: Yes.

SHASTI: Are you home?

MADISON: Yes, well, no. I'm at Mrs. Park's condo. I kind of live here, so yes, I guess I'm home.

SHASTI: Okay, good. And how is Mrs. Park?

MADISON: Good, except she's on oxygen now. I didn't know that was going to happen today or at all.

SHASTI: I'm glad she's okay. You can tell me more when I see you tomorrow. Okay?

MADISON: Yes.

Shasti didn't want to stop chatting. It felt like they had just gotten started. But then she remembered Tilda's words. "Give it time. Let it unfold naturally."

SHASTI: See you tomorrow then. 1:00. Rikki's Coffee Shop. I'm buying.

MADISON: Good night, Miss Shasti.

SHASTI: Good night.

MADISON: Don't let the bed bugs bite. What are bed bugs, anyway? Are they, like, real things?

SHASTI: Put your phone down (after you text Billy). I'll see you tomorrow.

MADISON: Okay. Bye.

Shasti stared at the text exchange waiting for Madison to engage her some more. When she didn't, Shasti let out the breath she didn't know she'd been holding and then scrolled back to re-read their exchange.
"Rikki was right. She is positively 'adorable.'"

~~~

Shasti sat in her car and took a moment to settle her thoughts. She had been so busy with Tilda's tea party and tying and worrying about the new little that she didn't check her emails until this morning. The labs had come back on the Henderson girl. They were practically perfect. There was no anemia or iron deficiency which was Shasti's leading thought on why the fourteen-year-old girl was experiencing dizziness, persistent drowsiness, and headaches. She'd had them check for abnormal blood sugars as well. They were fine, so she ruled out diabetes. In fact, all the blood counts, electrolytes, and thyroid numbers were well in the normal range for a fourteen-year-old girl. The Denton Heights Medical Clinic hadn't been the first stop on Mrs.

Henderson's quest to find out what was wrong with her daughter, but Shasti was determined to make it their last. She still had a few ideas.

With a sigh, she pushed the troubling case to the back of her mind and got out of the car. Once on the sidewalk, she smoothed her knee-length print skirt and checked her matching belt and sandals. Her form-fitting button-down blouse was modestly buttoned, but the dangling necklace hanging over the blouse was designed to move the eye toward her breasts. It was sneaky, but it was her way of testing the waters without being too overt. Would Madison's eye follow the necklace? Would her gaze linger on her chest?

She stopped just outside the door to Rikki's Coffee Shop and pretended to look for a non-existent item in her purse while she got control of her lustful thoughts. "There might be no chemistry," she muttered. "You're probably too old for her." She closed her eyes momentarily and put on her game face.

The hanging plants inside the large front window framed the gold lettering spelling out *Rikki's Coffee Shop* artfully. It was such an inviting space on the outside and so calming on the inside. From what Rikki told her, her shop had once been one of those chain electronics stores, which explained why the space was so big. She needed that space, too, because there were customers that camped out all day long even though Rikki didn't provide free Wi-Fi. She'd said it was in her plan, but since most new business ventures only lasted two years, she would wait until the shop's two-year anniversary to install it.

"Shasti," Rikki called from behind the counter as Shasti walked in. She tossed a rag aside and greeted Shasti at the door. "She's here." Rikki pointed to the black-haired girl facing away from them.

Shasti felt her face flush. With all her thoughts about the Henderson girl, she hadn't really made time to steel herself for her coffee date. The nerves she should have had all morning arrived in full force.

At Shasti's sharp breath, Rikki put a hand on her arm. "It'll be fine. She's the cutest."

"I know. I know," Shasti said. "Do you know what she drinks?"

"Lydia already made her an iced caramel latte with whipped cream and sprinkles."

"Sounds terrible," Shasti said and made a face.

Rikki chuckled. "What'll you have? She left a ten-dollar bill for your beverage of choice."

"Why did she do that? I told her twice that I was buying."

Rikki shrugged. "She wanted to be independent? Or she wanted to impress you?" She shrugged again. "Go with it, Shasti. You'll get her next time."

Shasti didn't know what to make of it. She wasn't used to dates treating her. Even in med school, when she could barely afford gas for her car and had to live at home, her dates took advantage of her generous and nurturing nature. "I'll take the usual, I guess."

"One large dark roast, three creamers, no sugar."

Shasti smiled. That was one of the reasons Rikki's shop was going to succeed. She made a point of making sure her customers felt seen—like remembering their drink orders. It was a trait she had immediately incorporated into her own medical practice. Not that she had been inattentive to her patients, but...yes, she needed to do that with the Henderson girl. Get to know the family better. Maybe something in her environment was causing the issue.

Stop. There would be time later to think about the Hendersons.

"Lydia working today?" Shasti asked Rikki as she waited for one of Rikki's baristas to make her coffee.

"She is, but I sent her to Kroger for brownie mix."

"Brownie mix?"

Rikki's smile was strange. "Madison suggested I sell brownies to go with the coffee. Well, she said 'brownies or muffins or rice Krispie treats or candy.'"

"What, no cookies?" Shasti laughed. "And so, you're indulging her by having Lydia make brownies?"

Rikki nodded. "I'm not letting Eileen make them." She pointed to the closed office door with a flick of her head. "She burns cold cereal."

Shasti laughed and held her tongue. At this point, Rikki had been Eileen's Domme for about six months. Shasti had only known Rikki a little over a year but had seen her with four submissives in that time. Eileen came on board about a week after Jessica broke up with Rikki at the last Christmas Masquerade Ball. Apparently, Jessica had a crush on Victoria and pursued her mercilessly at the ball to the point of breaking up with Rikki to show how serious she was. To Victoria's credit, she honored her friendship with Rikki and had none of it. Poor, poor Jessica went home alone that night. It had been excruciating to watch Rikki's heartbreak at the party. The fact that Rikki got with Eileen a week later made more than a few heads shake in disappointment. And that included Rikki's Aunt Tilda. Shasti wasn't sure who the true Domme was in that relationship, Rikki or Eileen. Shasti was sure that Eileen's picture was next to the phrase 'topping from the bottom' in the BDSM dictionary. Rikki must see something in her submissive that everyone else could not, Shasti reasoned. Either that or she had on the most expensive rose-colored glasses money could buy.

The barista brought Shasti her coffee, and Rikki promised to send Lydia over when she returned from the store. A good Domme, even a temporary one, always checked in with aftercare, and Shasti wanted to make sure Lydia was still okay after their tying session the day before.

Shasti walked up behind Madison and said, "Is that Madison the Magnificent I see?" Getting no response, she realized Madison must have been lost in her task. She was using colored pencils to fill in a beautiful picture of a bluebird. Her shading and pencil strokes were quite impressive.

Shasti moved to sit in the chair next to Madison's side of the couch.

"Oh, hi," Madison said, looking up. "Did you, oh, yes, you did." She pointed to Shasti's coffee.

"Thank you so much." Shasti put her purse down on the small table between them. "It was a very nice surprise."

"You're welcome," Madison said and closed her sketches. Oh, it was an actual coloring book. Interesting.

"How are you doing this fine afternoon?" Shasti asked and took a sip of her coffee. "Mmm, this is so good," Shasti added before letting Madison answer. It was a tactic her mother often used when she wanted credit for asking a question but didn't really want to know the answer. But Shasti actually *did* want to know. It was just her nerves. She was *not* becoming her mother. She refused.

"I know," Madison said. "Rikki's shop has the good stuff."

"Feeling better today?"

"Mm hmm," Madison said and then looked down. "I'm sorry I worried you guys."

"What happened?" Okay, nothing like going right for the elephant in the room.

Madison shrugged and worked her mouth as if embarrassed.

"Words, please," Shasti said in true Mommy Domme fashion.

Madison looked up and took a big breath. "I, uh, …" she paused and searched Shasti's face as if gauging whether she could trust her or not. Shasti softened her expression with a slight smile. "Everyone kept laughing at me. The whole time I was there. At Miss Tilda's. Like some things I don't know, but why do they have to laugh at me? You can't know everything all at once. A dungeon? Come on. Most people don't have a dungeon in their house. No one else thought that was weird? And I guess everyone knew you were a doctor except me. They laughed at me. All of them. And it was then that I realized that I didn't know anybody there. They were all strangers, and I wasn't sure what they wanted from me, and then…" She looked toward the front windows and said softly, "And then I left."

"Did you go right home?"

Madison nodded but then said, "Yes, to Mrs. Park's. I guess that's my home right now."

Shasti wanted to reach over and pat Madison's hand but decided against it. It was too intimate a gesture.

"No one at that party was laughing *at* you, peanut," Shasti said, risking the pet name. "In fact, everyone was enthralled with you. You gave them joy."

"Enthralled? What do you mean?"

"Enthralled means captivated or mesmerized. You are so full of life and fun and wonder, Madison. You've captured our hearts." She resisted referring to her as 'little one,' even though she really wanted to.

Madison furrowed her brow. "I don't understand."

"That's okay, sweetie," Shasti said, her heart melting. "Just know that no one was making fun of you. You were delightful."

"Are you 'enthralled'? You know, by me?" She looked directly into Shasti's soul.

Emotion clutched Shasti's throat closed, and she had to clear it twice before answering. "We're getting to know each other, you and I, aren't we? Coffee together? Conversation? Right?"

"I guess." There was a wariness to Madison's tone.

A change in tactic was needed. "So tell me about Mrs. Park and how you came to work for her."

Madison's wariness seemed to wane as she spoke about the woman she cared for and how she was a family friend even though Madison didn't remember her.

"And you said your mother sent you down here?"

"Yeah, when I lost my job at PETology because they didn't know how to take care of the animals, and I did it but forgot to pack out the stock, and then the stupid manager got mad at me for not doing my job, but that's because Joey doesn't know his ass from his elbow when it comes to taking care of the cats and dogs up for adoption. And the birds? He knows even less."

Ahh, wow. That was a lot to process and would absolutely be something for Shasti to pursue. But not yet. "What do you do for Mrs. Park? You said she was in her nineties?"

"Yes. And she can still get around kind of okay. I help her get into the wheelchair and stuff. And wash her and take care of her diapers and dress her. She has, umm, C.O.P.S. and Emphasim. That's why she can't breathe."

"C.O.P.D. and Emphysema?"

"Yes," Madison said, pointing a finger in the air as if in victory. "I can't ever remember what they're called. She's on oxygen now. The home nurse is there now, so I get a break. Phaneesa told me that I'm the morning and night shifts. She's one of the day nurses that comes."

Shasti nodded that she understood. Taking care of Mrs. Park sounded like a very big responsibility, and she said so. And then added, "I'm impressed that you've handled your new job so well. Have you ever thought about going into medicine?"

The confused expression on Madison's face was priceless.

"I mean, have you ever thought about becoming a doctor or nurse or something like that?"

Madison shook her head. "You have to go to college for that, and I'm not smart enough to go to college. And, besides, Kwan goes to

53

college, and you know that boys have to have the opportunity to go first and then, oh, well, there's no more money for you to go, so go get a job and do something with your life."

Shasti was flabbergasted at the obvious parroting of words Madison had endured. What kind of mother said that sort of thing to their child? She suddenly felt remorse for all the times she'd wished her own mother would back off in her life, even though there had been nothing but support—financially and emotionally—from her.

"I mean," Madison continued, "Mommy said she saved a little bit of money for me, but Grandma caught wind of it and wouldn't let her help me."

Ahh, it was the grandmother that was the issue.

"Where is your mother now?" Shasti asked.

"Home."

"Where's home?"

"Columbus," Madison said succinctly. Her short answers told Shasti that this was a touchy subject. She would tread lightly.

"Ohio?"

"Mm hmm," Madison said. "Mrs. Park wants me to stay in Denton Heights and not go back home. I guess she means like later when she, you know, passes?"

Shasti nodded. "And how do you feel about staying in Denton Heights?"

"I don't see how I could. I have no real job or place to stay. I'm driving Mrs. Park's million-year-old car, so I don't even have my own car. I used to borrow Kwan's car back home."

Shasti was fit to be tied; pardon the pun. Why did this young woman's family treat her like yesterday's garbage? She was a beautiful soul. She closed her eyes for a moment and took a cleansing breath.

"Do you get paid for helping Mrs. Park?" Shasti asked, fearing the worst.

"Oh, yes. It goes into a direct bank account Mrs. Park set up for me. I had to sign stuff when I first got there. Phaneesa looked at my earnings and said that Mrs. Park was very generous."

"Well, that's good," Shasti said and almost sighed out loud in relief. "Will you show me your sketches?" Shasti pointed to the coloring book. She had to change the subject somehow.

Madison showed her the book, and they chatted for some time, never falling into awkward silences. And Shasti was pleased when Madison asked questions about Shasti's life and family. She'd even hinted around about Shasti's past romantic partners, but Shasti didn't bite. The only thing Shasti confirmed was that, yes, she was a lesbian. An out and proud lesbian.

Shasti saw movement out of the corner of her eye and looked up. Rikki and Lydia were both sneaking up behind Madison. Lydia held two small plates, each with a hefty-sized brownie.

From behind, Lydia thrust the plate around Madison's side and in front of her. "Brownie?"

Madison jumped and then squealed with delight. She looked up at Lydia with adoration. "You're not a prisoner anymore?"

Lydia laughed and said, "I am not. And I never was a prisoner, little one."

"Oh, good." The look of relief on Madison's face was precious. "Is this for me?" She took the offered plate.

"Mm hmm," Lydia said. She handed the other plate to Shasti, who took it, but placed it on the table in front of her after nodding her thanks.

"How are you, my dear?" Shasti said to Lydia.

Lydia nodded and said, "I'm fine. Thank you for asking. I love rope." She turned to Madison. "You need to try it."

"Rope? Getting tied up?"

"Mm hmm."

"I don't want to be a prisoner."

"Don't knock it until you've tried it," Lydia said, barely able to hold in a laugh. She pulled her phone out of her back pocket and showed Madison a picture of the completed rope harness. "You didn't get to see the final result."

Madison leaned in closer. "That looks so cool."

"And Mr. Tom liked the color you picked out," Lydia said.

Madison bounced on the couch, obviously liking the praise.

Lydia tucked her phone back into her pocket. "I need to get back. Apparently, I have to wrap up the rest of those brownies to sell at the register since, for some reason, we are now selling brownie squares to our customers."

"Yay," Madison said, bouncing up and down like she'd won the lottery. "It'll help sales," she called after Lydia.

Rikki sat in the chair opposite Shasti. "That was a great idea, Madison. Thanks for suggesting it."

"Welcome."

"Soooo," Rikki said to Shasti, "how's it going over here?"

"We're having a great time getting to know each other. Aren't we, peanut?"

"Yes," Madison said, holding the plate with a brownie in her hands. "Are you going to eat?" She asked Shasti.

"No, no," Shasti said. "But, please, you go ahead."

The brownie bite was large. "Miss Rikki, did you know that Miss Shasti went to medical school at Georgetown?" Madison's mouth was full as she spoke, and it wasn't an attractive look.

"I did," Rikki said and raised her eyebrows. "Impressive, isn't it?"

Madison nodded. "Former president Bill Clinton went there also. Not at the same time, though. Miss Shasti isn't *that* old. And since she has no brothers, she got to go."

Rikki's perplexed expression was back, but Shasti simply put a hand up and signaled that she'd fill Rikki in another time.

"Okay, then," Rikki said and stood up. "I'll send Eileen over with refills."

"Just water for me," Shasti said.

Madison hesitated but then said, "Me, too. Just water. Thank you." She reached into the cutest pink backpack and pulled out an even cuter pink wallet.

"Oh, no, no," Rikki said. "The brownies and waters are on me."

"Thank you, Rikki," Shasti said, echoed by Madison a moment later.

Eileen not only delivered the bottles of water but also pointedly asked Madison if that was a coloring book in her possession. When the affirmative answer came, she said, "Hmm, imagine that," and looked at Shasti in such harsh judgment that it was all Shasti could do not to wither away in shame.

"She doesn't like me," Madison said without looking up.

"I think it's more that she doesn't like *me*," Shasti said.

"No way. Everyone likes you, Miss Shasti." Madison's hurt expression almost melted Shasti's heart.

"Even you?" *Oh, way to push that,* Shasti berated herself. What happened to taking it slow and letting it unfold naturally? Out the window, apparently.

Madison didn't respond. Well, she didn't respond verbally. Instead, her gaze locked onto Shasti's for a moment and then traveled lower to her lips. Shasti took that inopportune moment, or maybe it was opportune, to lick her lips under Madison's gaze. Madison momentarily looked into Shasti's eyes as if asking permission for something. Permission must have been granted because Madison's gaze followed the path of the dangling necklace around Shasti's neck and then lingered on Shasti's chest. Madison swallowed hard and then looked away as if embarrassed.

"Yes, even me," Madison said, her voice thick with emotion.

Shasti cleared her throat and said, "Would you like to have dinner with me later this week? Friday?"

"Yes," came the quick answer.

"Excellent. I'm pleased."

"I, I, I can only get out from noon to six. That's when Phaneesa or Eugenia are there. They stay for six hours now, not four. Friday will be Phaneesa. She's the weekend person, even though Friday isn't technically the weekend. She—"

"That's fine," Shasti interrupted. She was beginning to understand that Madison could ramble when excited or nervous. "A midday dinner then. A lunch slash dinner."

"Linner," Madison said, proud of the new word she'd made up on the spot. There was more bouncing on the couch. Her now-empty plate fell off her lap and onto the floor.

"Perfect word for it." Shasti picked up the plate. "Okay, we're agreed then. Linner at my house at, say, 1:00 or so?"

"Your house?" There was hesitation in her tone.

"Yes, is that okay?"

Madison's cheeks tinged the most adorable pink as she said, "Mm hmm."

"Great. It's a date." Shasti cringed invisibly. She hadn't meant to scare Madison with those words. Shasti covered her discomfort by asking what foods Madison liked and if she had any allergies.

Madison answered as if Shasti hadn't just blown it. Thank goodness she hadn't brought up protocols or mentioned a trial period. All of that was too soon. Follow Tilda's advice, she told herself. Let it unfold naturally—hardest words to ever follow.

Chapter 5

Madison

"Don't let them tell you what your place is, Mulan!" Madison grunted at the Disney movie playing on her phone. She grabbed her three-inch plastic Mulan figure dressed in armor, holding a sword. She'd gotten it from her mother when she was in third grade. It was one of the few things she'd brought with her to Mrs. Park's. "You tell them—no, you *show* them where your place is!"

Madison swung her Mulan figurine and smashed it into the lineup of green plastic soldiers she'd gotten at the pharmacy the other day. With her help, Mulan annihilated the ignorant opposing forces that thought they could dictate her life and tell her what to do and who to be.

She held the figurine high in the air in victory. "No one messes with Mulan," Madison growled to the universe. The conviction in her voice was almost believable.

"Girl!" came the bellowing voice through the baby monitor, even though Mrs. Park wasn't a baby.

Madison groaned. Every time she wanted to play alone in her room, Mrs. Park or one of the nurses interrupted. She pressed the button and said, "Yes?"

"Your mommy is on the phone. Come here. Now."

Madison tossed Mulan on the bed and bolted out of her room. Mrs. Park was in her recliner in the living room and held out the landline phone toward Madison.

She grabbed the phone and whispered, "Mommy?"

"Hi, Madi," came the soothing voice.

"Are you okay, Mommy?" Madison asked. "Are you in the bathroom again?"

"I am, so I have to make this quick. I'm fine. Mrs. Park says you're doing great there. Taking care of her like the good girl I know you are."

Madison melted under her mother's words. "I'm trying, Mommy. I made a friend. Well, a couple of friends."

"That is so good to hear." There was an odd lilt to her mother's voice. Relief maybe?

There was a rustling sound like her mother had dropped the phone, and Madison knew not to talk in case her grandmother was listening at the bathroom door again. After a moment, her mother's hurried whisper said, "Madi, know that I love you, sweet daughter. I have to go." And with that, there was silence on the other end. Her mother had hung up.

Madison put the cordless phone back in its cradle and plopped on the floor at Mrs. Park's feet.

"Bah," Mrs. Park said with a wave of her hand, mumbling something Madison couldn't quite make out. "Your mommy is a prisoner. She needs to go out on her own. Her husband—your father—is a good man but can't stand up to his mother. And your mother is…" Mrs. Park hesitated momentarily and then finished, "dying inside."

Madison's chest tightened as tears filled her eyes. It was true. Madison had tried to help her mother, but her mother would only say, "Go to your room now, daughter. Let Mommy rest."

And Madison would go.

"I'm going to a friend's house today," Madison said to Mrs. Park.

"A new girlfriend, perhaps?"

Madison laughed. "No, just a friend. She's making me food. I don't know why." But she had an inkling about why. And she didn't want to let that inkling grow. Better to go in not anticipating anything, right? Right. Sure.

~~~

Madison stepped into the house past Miss Shasti's outstretched arm holding the screen door open. She smelled so nice. Nothing overpowering. She just smelled like a fresh shower and maybe some light lotion on her skin.

"It smells really good in here," Madison said truthfully when the aroma of food hit her nose. "Almost smells like home."

Miss Shasti made a slight noise as she closed the door to the house, but Madison couldn't interpret it.

Madison wasn't sure what she had expected to see once inside the house, but she hadn't expected a formal grandma-like sitting room on the left—the kind that was only for show and that no one ever sat in. Two tall chairs that looked really uncomfortable sat facing the outside windows. The colored pattern on the chairs was entirely out of sorts with the color of the carpet. On the other side of the entryway was the dining room. The wooden table was this heavy-looking ugly thing that sat on the thick carpet, and it looked like you couldn't even move the monstrous chairs without a struggle. Madison hoped they weren't going to eat there. But in a flash, she understood. These were the rooms for company. Miss Shasti surely had a fun living room where she could let her hair down and, hopefully, a real kitchen table for real people.

Madison slid her sneakers off her feet and pushed them off to the side so they wouldn't be in the way.

"Oh, you didn't have to take your shoes off," Miss Shasti said with her pretty face, gentle smile, and straight white teeth.

"It's okay. My grandmother would kill me if I disrespected your home."

"I hope you don't mean that literally."

Madison scrunched her face and grinned. "Ah, well, any given day, I suppose."

Miss Shasti narrowed her eyes as if wondering if Madison was telling the truth. *Nah, she's wondering if I'm insane*, Madison thought. *Ha ha ha. Maybe so.*

"I got you these." Madison reached into a plastic Kroger bag and pulled out some flowers she'd picked outside the condo office where Mrs. Park lived. They had so many, and they wouldn't miss a few. And she'd been careful to brush all the dirt off, too. Very thoughtful, indeed.

Miss Shasti made an odd noise, and her face got all pink. "Thank you, Madison," she said softly. "I love impatiens. The pink ones match your shirt, don't they?"

"Oh, yeah," Madison said, rocking back and forth on the heels of her feet.

"Come into the kitchen. I'll put these in water."

Madison followed and watched Miss Shasti pull a vase out of a big closet and then put the flowers in the vase with water. Madison looked around, trying not to seem too nosy, which was far from the truth because she wanted to open every cabinet and door and go from room to room, trying to unlock the true Miss Shasti.

There was a definite struggle going on in the kitchen, Madison decided. On the one hand, it was trying to be formal and high-end with its fancy faucets and shelving, but on the other hand, it was functional and usable, as evidenced by the old coffee pot, well-used water boiler, and worn wooden tea caddy. Her bedroom probably showed the real her, too, Madison thought. Hopefully, there was a real living room where a TV and gaming systems would be. That's got to be where Miss Shasti lived. The real Miss Shasti, not the for-show one.

And the outside lawn and landscaping? Sure, her big house fit in with the other big houses with their manicured lawns, nary a dandelion in sight, but it was sterile and almost too perfect. There had been no love put into it. Not that it looked bad, except for the lawn that needed mowing. But…yes, that's it. Madison figured it out and looked up to find Miss Shasti looking right at her with an expectant expression. Madison had discovered what the issue was. Miss Shasti's house and yard were lonely. Madison smiled at her host. And that could only mean one thing. Miss Shasti was lonely, too.

"Are you okay?" Miss Shasti asked. "You look sad all of a sudden."

"Me? Nah. Just hungry." Madison bounced on her toes. She held off doing a pirouette, even though she really wanted to shake off some of her nervous energy. "What's for linner?"

"Help me set the table, and you'll see." Miss Shasti opened a high cabinet revealing plates and bowls.

Madison was grateful for something to do, and they made quick work setting the table. The relaxed table, not the monstrosity in the fake room by the front door.

Miss Shasti made her eat a small salad, much smaller than the one she had, to "make sure she got some leafy greens in her." Madison wasn't thrilled about it, but she was a guest, and in Korean culture, you ate whatever your host gave you, even if that meant swallowing it quickly. Yeah, like those slimy tomatoes in her salad. Thank goodness the onions had been put in a small bowl, "just in case Madison didn't care for onions." Ya think? Who in their right mind liked onions? Gross. But Madison was on her best behavior and simply said, "No, thank you," to the onions. Too bad the tomatoes hadn't been in a separate bowl, too.

After the salad, Madison sat at the kitchen table and looked out the sliding glass doors onto Miss Shasti's really big backyard. The sun was still high in the sky, it being only mid-afternoon, and the birds were chirping excitedly in the birdbath. There was a birdfeeder on a shepherd's hook, too.

"Ooh, look, Miss Shasti," Madison called to her. "A goldfinch. A male. Ooh, another one. A female. They're at your feeder."

"Look at that," she said with awe. And it wasn't condescending at all. Her tone didn't say she was humoring Madison and rolling her eyes. She was actually impressed.

Madison sat up taller and bounced in her chair. "You know, if you put out Nyjer seeds in a thistle feeder, you'll get even more. They're pretty much year-round in Cincinnati."

Miss Shasti set down a serving dish filled with traditional Indian chicken curry and then set down a smaller bowl of plain chicken cubes and white rice in case Madison didn't like the spicy meal or was a "picky eater."

"You know a lot about birds, don't you?" Miss Shasti asked as she sat down. She put her cloth napkin back in her lap, and Madison checked her own. Yep, by some miracle, it was still there.

"I learned about birds at the PETology store I worked at in Columbus. The birds weren't looking good, so I researched what they needed to thrive, and that's where I learned it. Except Joey, the jerk-off, found out I was taking thistle seeds from the store shelf and feeding the finches. I got that reprimand added to my growing list, and finally, my tower of reprimands toppled over, and Mr. Hannity had to fire me."

"I'm so sorry that happened, peanut," Miss Shasti said. It sounded like she meant it, too. Her brow was furrowed like she wanted to give Mr. Hannity or maybe even Joey the jerk-off a piece of her mind. "How about we watch the birds outside while we eat inside, okay?"

"Okay."

Miss Shasti put the tiniest spoonful of the orangey curry sauce on a small plate and suggested Madison try it for flavor and spice. If she didn't like it, she didn't have to eat it and was welcomed to eat the plain chicken and rice. "But I insist we get some protein in you and that you don't load up on just carbs, okay?"

"Okay," Madison said and was about to stick her index finger in the sauce when Miss Shasti made a clicking sound with her tongue.

"Use your fork or spoon, please."

"Okay." Using her spoon, which made so much more sense than a fork, she dipped it in the sauce and cautiously put it in her mouth. "Soooo good," Madison gushed and spooned the rest from the plate into her mouth. "Nice and spicy. May I have some more?"

"Of course," Miss Shasti said, filling Madison's plate with rice and the chicken curry mixture. "I'm pleased that you like it. I made it 'company spicy,' so if it's not hot enough for you, I can make it 'family spicy' next time."

"Next time?" Madison said before she could stop the words from exiting her mouth—a frequent problem she'd been told.

"Why not? We're enjoying each other's company. And, anyway, everyone has to eat, right?"

"Yep," Madison said and waited in what she hoped looked like her most excellent patience of all time.

"What are you waiting for? Dig in."

"Always wait for your elders to start eating before you do," Madison parroted the rule from her childhood.

"Ahh, I see. You're calling me elderly."

Madison's eyes flew open wide. "No, no. I didn't mean it like that. It's just—"

A soft hand on her forearm stopped the impending stream of words. "I'm completely teasing you, Madison." She placed a forkful of food into her mouth and gestured for Madison to start eating.

Madison felt so bad. Miss Shasti was older, sure, but she wasn't 'elderly.' Holy crickets, that was the stupidest choice of words. She felt her entire face flame hot. She focused on her food until a thought hit her.

"Are you married, Miss Shasti?"

Miss Shasti cleared her throat as if almost choking or something. "No, I'm not married. Never have been."

"Engaged? Current girlfriend?"

"No. There've been a few relationships over the years. Some I thought were serious, but I found out differently when they left me."

Madison thought that was the saddest thing she'd ever heard. "I'm sorry," she said quietly.

"How about you, Madison? Are you married?"

Madison burst out laughing. "No!"

"Why not? Ever engaged? Do you have a current girlfriend?" Miss Shasti's eyes were filled with amusement.

"You're teasing me again," Madison said. She scrunched her face at Miss Shasti, but the smile on her face hopefully conveyed that she didn't mind. Far from it. The hot South Asian woman sitting in the chair to her left had cooked her linner. Madison still wanted to run her fingertips along the curve of her cheeks and tuck that stray lock of hair behind her ear with the others. The buttons of her sleeveless top were almost straining Miss Shasti's curvy breasts.

Madison swallowed hard and realized she had stopped eating altogether and was out and out staring at her host's chest. She cleared her throat and said, "My parents—well, it was my grandmother, but she has been trying to marry me off to these stupid men since forever. Like since I turned sixteen. These random old guys would show up for dinner at the house, and then she'd make me sit in the sitting room where no one was supposed to go in, and I had to talk to them. I didn't catch on at first, but when the third man came—he had graying hair and was older than my mother. I still had no idea why I was supposed to talk to him. It was when I saw the worried look on my mother's face that I understood everything. Grandma was trying to get rid of me."

"I'm sorry your grandmother was doing that to you," Miss Shasti said. The warm hand was back on Madison's forearm. It was nice.

"I heard Mommy and Grandma fighting about it sometimes. My mother rarely stuck up for herself, but she always stuck up for me. She told me that if Princess Merida of Dunbroch could decide who she married for herself, then I could, too."

Judging by the confused look on Miss Shasti's pretty face, she had no idea who Princess Merida was. But that was okay. Maybe one day they could watch *Brave* together. It was one of Madison's favorites.

"I'm glad she stuck up for you," Miss Shasti said. "We all need someone to be in our corner, don't we?"

"Mm hmm," Madison said and went back to her food. "So, no. I am not married, engaged, or had a girlfriend. Not a real one, anyway."

It seemed like Miss Shasti wanted to say something else or ask a question, but she didn't, and they ate in silence for a while.

"Look at you," Miss Shasti beamed. "Clean plate club."

"Huh?" Madison looked down and realized she had eaten everything on her plate. "Wow. That never happens. You must be a good cook." She pushed her chair back on the hardwood floor and leaped to her feet. "Can I help clean up?"

Miss Shasti's mouth said, "yes," but her expression and body language said something else entirely. It wasn't hard to read. If energy lines and intent were seeable in the air, then Miss Shasti's were totally reaching toward Madison. Madison decided to play it cool as always. She'd let Miss Shasti lead.

Wordlessly they gathered the dishes and put them in the sink to soak. They gathered the food from the table and placed it on the countertop. Miss Shasti pulled out several glass containers from the closet in the kitchen—it was called a pantry, Madison found out, and Miss Shasti spooned the leftovers inside the bowls while Madison leaned back against the countertop.

The silence was getting kind of awkward, and Madison got a sinking feeling in her tummy. But maybe Miss Shasti was different. Maybe she wasn't just a *pretty*. Maybe she was…something else.

Miss Shasti cleared her throat and said, "I made cookies for you."

Madison's hopes were shattered.

"I put them in a bag for you to take home. Or we can have some later if you want." Miss Shasti pointed to a plastic bag ziplocked tight. "I hope chocolate chip is okay."

"Yes, of course. That's fine," Madison said. She had wondered what they were going to do after linner because Miss Shasti never said anything about that the whole time they'd been eating. Now she knew.

"Good. I'm glad." Miss Shasti stacked the now-filled bowls and headed toward the refrigerator. She successfully got the first three bowls inside without incident, but before Madison could dive in to help, the last bowl's lid opened up and spilled orange curry sauce all over Miss Shasti's clothes and on the floor. To Miss Shasti's credit, she didn't curse but looked like she wanted to.

Madison ran for the paper towels and wiped up the small amount that had hit the floor.

Miss Shasti handed the curry mess to Madison. "I have to go upstairs and change. Would you be a doll and clean this up and put it in the fridge?"

Madison nodded. She understood. Completely.

"Thank you for helping." She turned back at the bottom of the stairs and said, "I'll be upstairs." She turned away from Madison and then hurried up the stairs.

Madison nodded. Upstairs. Yep, everything was clear. Crystal.

She cleaned up the outside of the bowl and rinsed off the lid. And then, making sure the lid was tightly snapped on, put it in the fridge next to the others. She heard a noise upstairs and figured that was her cue.

She headed up the wooden staircase and turned left toward the sound. The bedroom door was ajar. Yep, that was an invitation if she'd ever seen one. She opened it quietly. Most *pretties* didn't like it when she talked, but this one was new, so she'd have to play it by ear.

"Oh, Madison," Miss Shasti said, covering her nakedness with the towel she'd been using to dry herself. "I'm fine. I don't need help." The towel did little to cover Miss Shasti's beautiful body.

Madison locked eyes with her and took no time erasing the space between them. "It's okay. I understand what's expected." She turned Miss Shasti around and walked her backward to the side of the bed. When the back of Miss Shasti's legs hit the mattress, she stumbled and sat down hard. Madison pulled the towel away, leaving Miss Shasti completely naked and vulnerable. "I'll take care of everything."

"What are you doing, Madison? We haven't—"

"Shh, shh, shh," Madison said, maneuvering Miss Shasti onto her back. "Let me take care of you. I know what you want." She crawled on top. "I'm very good at what I do." Keeping much of her own weight on her left leg, she let the other fall between Miss Shasti's, clearly hitting the mark.

"Madison..." came the lustful plea as Miss Shasti's pelvis rose and pressed against Madison's thigh.

Chapter 6

Shasti

Shasti heard herself moan. Oh, how she wanted this. It had been so long. But they hadn't talked about sex or anything. Madison's thigh had insinuated itself between Shasti's legs, and before she could bring up any sort of objection to the situation, soft lips were devouring her neck and cutting off her mental protests.

Madison, fully clothed, rocked against Shasti's naked body causing Shasti's aching need to simmer low in her belly. It was a need that had grown throughout the meal, but she hadn't intended to act on it. Madison's kisses turned to nips and bites as she made her way lower. But then teeth sunk into her shoulder, sending Shasti into a mass of pure moaning, quivering need. She hadn't planned this liaison, but she was powerless under Madison's witchcraft.

A hand caressed one of her breasts. The light touch over her peaking nipple sent a fresh wave of desire rolling through her body. Lips replaced the fingers causing Shasti's core to clench.

"Yes," Shasti said with a moan. Both hands found the back of Madison's head and pressed it hard against her aroused breast. "Fucking, yes." She had accepted her fate. She was letting this happen. Did she really have any choice?

The lips and tongue torturing her breast broke free and made a slow and sensual trail down Shasti's body. The lingering kiss on her mound almost sent Shasti into orbit. It had been so long. Her breathing was heavy as she petted the head with one hand and fisted the comforter with the other.

Tender lips pressed gently against her erect nub. But they disappeared too quickly, making Shasti moan at the teasing loss. The hardening tongue lapped a long stroke down through her center and back up again. Shasti's hips rose without her permission causing strong arms to wrap around her thighs to hold her open and steady. The tongue worked its way around her swollen arousal.

Shasti's head lolled back, deeply indenting her pillow. Her eyes, all on their own, rolled back inside her head. Excruciatingly light fingertips traced the wetness around her aching clit. It was a wispy touch, not enough to detonate but enough to quicken the fuse.

"Let go, Miss Shasti," Madison urged. "Let me give you this."

The tongue replaced the fingers, and the increasing pressure sent Shasti over the edge. She ground against Madison's tongue and lips and chin. "Fuck, Madison. Oh, fuck."

Shasti's body seized as she slammed her thighs tight on the head caught between them. Her body convulsed as wave after wave of ecstasy slammed through her entire body. Her frenzied muscles shook on their own accord as curse words flew out of her mouth, joining the rest of her body in an otherworldly release.

She struggled to breathe as the tongue, now inside her, continued to work. It was too much. She groaned but couldn't stop the torment. Nor could she open her eyes. She gave in to the groundswell of sleep that claimed her body.

Shasti's mind, desperate for consciousness, fought through her body's overpowering desire to stay prone and asleep. "Mmm," she groaned as she fought against the weight of unconsciousness. Best. Orgasm. Ever. Holy fuck.

With a struggle, she finally got one eye opened and then the other. A sheet had been pulled up over her nakedness. She reached both arms over her head and stretched. The tips of her fingers down to the tips of her toes and everything in between seemed to sigh and say thank you. "Mmm," she said again, this time in pleasant bliss.

"Madison?" Shasti called. "Sorry, I fell asleep. I do that sometimes." She got no answer and heard no movement in her room or anywhere. She sat up, adrenaline pumping softly. "Madison?" Still no answer. Maybe she was downstairs eating the cookies. Was she having milk with them, too? That would be adorable. Maybe Madison was lactose intolerant. She'd have to look into that. No, she hadn't mentioned it when they talked about food allergies before having linner together. Best to double-check, though.

She threw the sheet off and stood up, reaching for her robe. She put on her bedroom slippers, feeling silly because it was mid-afternoon. "How long was I out?" she called out her bedroom door, hoping to get an answer but getting none.

She hustled down the stairs calling Madison's name. She came to a screeching halt in the kitchen when she saw the note sitting under the vase of flowers Madison had brought her.

Hi, Miss Shasti. Thank you for the cookies. I told you I knew what I was doing. (smiley face) We didn't go over our story, so you can probably just say that I was here to help you with home projects (I fixed that loose cabinet door under the sink, by the way. See? Doesn't have to be a lie). Or you can say I was here to interview for cutting your lawn or something. Either way, let me know what you come up with, so our stories are the same. Thank you, Madison Kim

Shasti clutched her robe tightly around her. She reread the note as confused as ever. "Do you think I invited you here just for sex?" *What unknowing signal did I give her?* Madison had been so aggressive. No, that wasn't the right word. Assertive? Forceful? Dominant?

"I wanted it," Shasti murmured out loud and stroked the petals of one of the pink flowers in the vase. *I wasn't expecting or anticipating it, but I sure wanted it.* "And Madison thought I was expecting it." Realization hit Shasti hard. "Oh, no. She thought the whole reason I invited her here to my house was to have sex with her." Why did she leave? Was she embarrassed?

She rushed to the front window to confirm that Madison's car was no longer in the driveway and splayed her hand against the warm glass. "What happened today, peanut? Something is not right with this."

Shasti closed the blinds and wandered back into the kitchen. Yes, the bag of cookies was gone. Madison hadn't rushed out in a hurry. She'd taken the time to fix the cabinet door, write a note, and take the bag of cookies. Shasti found her phone by the coffee pot where she usually stashed it and texted Madison.

> SHASTI: Peanut – I am so sorry I passed out on you. We need to talk, little one. I think we may have a misunderstanding or something. Why did you leave so quickly?

Oh, no. What if she's upset? Or hurt? What if she's not okay?

> SHASTI: Are you okay? Send me a quick message letting me know that you're okay. Okay? (That's a lot of "okays" in one sentence, isn't it?)

73

She hoped that by keeping the text message light, Madison would feel comfortable responding. Expecting an immediate answer but not getting one, Shasti raced up the stairs to shower and get dressed. She checked her phone. No, there was no return text from Madison. She pulled up Rikki's number.

> SHASTI: 911. I need your advice. May I stop by the shop?

> RIKKI: You okay? Do I need to come there?

> SHASTI: No, I'll meet you at the shop. Be there in fifteen.

> RIKKI: Is Madison okay?

> SHASTI: I don't know.

> RIKKI: Make it ten minutes.

> SHASTI: Okay.

Shasti got there in twelve. She refused a caffeinated beverage and let herself be ushered into Rikki's soundproofed office just off the serving counter of the coffee shop. Rikki reached into a small refrigerator and handed her a bottle of water. Hydration. Yes. That would be good.

Shasti took a sip and paced the length of the small office and back again. Rikki took a seat on the couch.

"Shasti," Rikki said, breaking the growing silence, "what happened? Wasn't today the big linner date with Madison?"

"Yes, it was. And what happened? I don't know." Shasti paused for a moment gathering her thoughts, and then blurted out the events of the afternoon, from the flowers to the linner to the spilled curry to the sudden physical liaison upstairs. In her bedroom. Upstairs. Unplanned.

"Wait, what?" Rikki said. "You had sex with her?"

Shasti knew her face betrayed the stricken shame she felt. "It was more like she had sex with me. Something shifted when I told her about the cookies I'd baked for her to take home. I expected her to gush over them or, in the least, say, 'Thank you,' but she didn't do either of those things. She simply said something like, 'I understand.' It was confusing. It made no sense."

"It doesn't. What is there to understand about cookies?" Rikki's brow was furrowed. "And then she showed up in your bedroom without invitation?"

"Yes." Shasti plopped down in Rikki's executive desk chair. "I should have been stronger. I should have said no. But it happened so fast. I wasn't expecting her to act like that, and then she was on top of me and kissing me, and my body just reacted to her without my permission." She hid her eyes behind her hand. "Permission to speak freely and openly?"

"Yes, of course," Rikki said softly. "Always What's said here will stay here."

Shasti let herself feel relief. "Thank you." She chugged some water and said, "Rikki, she knew what she was doing. This wasn't her first rodeo. I mean, she read me like a book. She knew how to touch me and make my body respond." She leaned forward and said low, "Rikki, it took, like, less than a minute for her to make me cum."

"Whoa."

"I know. I passed out afterward. It was that powerful." Shasti sighed. "I mean, I know it's been a while, but wow. And you know what else? It almost felt rehearsed."

"Rehearsed?" Rikki tilted her head to the side, clearly confused.

"That might not be the right word. Don't get me wrong, it was amazing, but it almost felt mechanical," Shasti continued. "Like she'd done this type of thing before. Many many times before."

Shasti sat listening to her own anxious breathing as a realization was starting to dawn on her. "She's very experienced, Rikki."

"Maybe she's had a relationship? Back home in…where?"

"Columbus."

Rikki nodded. "She's almost twenty-three, Shasti."

"I know."

"She's a grown woman with youthful hormones. Maybe she had or still has a long-term girlfriend there."

"We had that conversation. She said she's never had a girlfriend."

Rikki's sigh said precisely what she had been feeling. Frustration. Confusion.

"I want intimacy, Rikki. I want to take care of someone. I mean, I don't know if it's her yet. Something happens whenever I think I'm taking a step forward with her. Maybe it's not in the cards for me this time."

"You don't know that," Rikki said softly. "What does Aunt Tilda always say? Something about not forcing a puzzle piece even though you're one-hundred percent positive it fits."

Shasti nodded.

"She's told me that many times about Eileen." Rikki gestured toward the shop.

"I've heard her. She's not a fan." Shasti shot her friend a sympathetic expression, refusing to voice her agreement with Rikki's aunt. She couldn't hurt her friend that way, even if she did agree. "I'm sorry."

Rikki just nodded and let out a sigh.

They sat in silence momentarily, each moment more miserable than the last as Shasti replayed every conversation she'd had with Madison that afternoon. "Wait, I just remembered something. She said she's never had a 'real' girlfriend. What do you think she meant by that?"

Rikki closed her mouth.

"And this note. Sorry, I forgot about it." Shasti reached into her skirt pocket for Madison's note and handed it to Rikki.

After reading it and handing it back, Rikki said, "That's very telling, I think. She thinks you need to find an excuse for her being at your house."

"Like I'm ashamed of her or something. That she couldn't possibly be coming over as a friend." Shasti searched Rikki's face for clues that she wasn't thinking the same thing. "Do you think it could be true?" Shasti asked quietly.

"I'm going to let you say the words," Rikki said.

Shasti nodded. That was fair. "Do you think she was a sex worker? Or still is?"

"That or some kind of sexual slave," Rikki said with a sigh so sad it almost made Shasti let loose the tears that had been balling up in her chest.

The silence that filled the office was almost crushing. "There's only one way to find out," Rikki said. "You have to go directly to the source."

Shasti nodded and chugged down the rest of the water.

A loud bang bang bang on the door made them both jump.

Rikki opened the heavy door, and a voice said, "Hey, babe, I wanted to ask you something about next weekend." Rikki's submissive

Eileen popped her head inside. Her severely short hair made her hard features even harder. She oh-so-obviously recoiled when she saw Rikki's company. She said, "Trouble in the nursery, Shasti?"

"What did you just say to her?" Rikki demanded. She stood up to her almost six feet in height. "Get in here." Eileen came into the office but didn't cower. Instead, she kept her head high.

"I'll talk to you later," Shasti said. "Text me if she shows up."

"Will do," Rikki said. "Keep me posted."

Instead of passing by Eileen near the door to the actual shop, Shasti snuck out the side door to the alley. Before the outside door to the office closed, Shasti heard Eileen say, "I got us a hotel room at that Cedar Point Amusement Park. Can we go?"

"No!" The door closed before Shasti could hear the rest.

She got in her car that was parked along busy Market Street. She loathed the idea of going home. Home was confusing right now. And even though she'd taken the afternoon off, her car picked its way toward the office. Yes. Paperwork was precisely the kind of thing she needed right now—something to get her mind off the troubling afternoon.

She rechecked her phone when she pulled into her reserved parking spot at the health clinic. No response from Madison. At this point, worry fought with another emotion. Anger.

"This disappearing act of yours, little girl?" Shasti said to her steering wheel. "That is going to get nipped right in the bud." Unsure how to do that exactly, Shasti shoved the thought to the side and made her way to her office via the side door to the clinic.

The hours slipped away while she tidied up her charts and paperwork. Her emails were handled as best they could be. She'd learned early on that having an empty desk or empty email inbox was just not possible and found ways to cope with this uncontrollable aspect of her career. She was still waiting for lab results for many of her patients and couldn't finish some of the charts. Medicine was fluid, wasn't it? Constantly changing. You think you have it all figured out, and then—bam—life socks something new on you. Jessie Henderson, for example. Her online calendar showed that Jessie had a follow-up appointment on Wednesday of next week.

She opened Jessie's electronic chart. The young girl's case wasn't ever far from her mind, and Shasti's brain continued to marinate on it in her subconscious. She typed in a few more suggested tests to try if the parents agreed to them. No, there was just the mother. Shasti vaguely remembered that there had been a recent divorce.

They still had yet to explore inner ear issues, vertigo, and a host of other things that could be causing the dizziness and nausea. Ménière's disease, maybe? The darn blood tests kept coming back normal, which truly was a good thing, but frustrating, nonetheless. It was an elimination game at this point.

"I'm not reading the signs correctly," Shasti mused. "Clearly, I'm missing something."

With a sigh, she checked her phone—no text from Madison. *I've missed something with Madison, too. Obviously.*

"How am I this far off-sync?" Shasti asked her office and stood up. Frustrated, she knew it was time to go home and face the feelings.

Chapter 7

Madison

"I'm going out," Madison announced to Mrs. Park and Phaneesa as she headed for her shoes by the front door. "To the zoo." No one bothers you, makes cookies, or expects anything from you at the zoo. Well, except the money to get in. And then there was that weird phenomenon about suddenly starving once you got inside the gates. "Tacos today," Madison said to herself as she shoved Mrs. Park's car keys into her pocket. "And then a pretzel for dessert. Or ice cream. Yes, with gummy bears for sure."

"Girl!" Mrs. Park bellowed.

"Yes, Mrs. Park?" Madison stepped into the living room, shoes in hand.

Phaneesa smiled at Madison, but it was a sad sort of smile.

"What's going on?" Madison hoped her zoo trip wasn't about to be called off.

"Sit," Phaneesa said and patted the open spot on the couch next to her. "Mrs. Park said she had a rough night last night."

"Yeah," Madison said. She pointed toward the oxygen machine behind them. "That alarm is loud when it's empty. I got the backup tank on in no time. I'm pretty handy, you know."

Phaneesa grinned. "You are. And the other things?"

"Oh, yeah," Madison said. "Mrs. Park never seemed to get comfortable in her fancy hospital bed, no matter how much I raised her head and then her feet and then lowered her head. Nothing seemed to work." And then there was the thing she really didn't want to talk about. "I got her cleaned up and got new sheets on the bed after she overflowed her," Madison leaned in closer and whispered behind her hand, "diaper."

"Mm hmm," Phaneesa said. "You did a great job. She's lucky to have you."

"It was really stinky," Madison said, hoping Mrs. Park couldn't hear her. Her eyes were closed, and she was probably dozing anyway. The sound of the oxygen machine was kind of like white noise and was pretty soothing, actually. Even Madison had fallen asleep on the couch to the rhythmic background noise after coming home from the *pretty's* house the day before.

"A decision is going to have to be made soon," Phaneesa said. "The hospice doctor is coming by one day next week." Phaneesa looked stricken, like she'd said something she wasn't supposed to.

"The *hospital* doctor?" Madison asked, confused by the word hospice.

Phaneesa cleared her throat. "Uh, yes. The *hospital* doctor. We're trying to schedule it while Eugenia or I are here, but that means it's during your usual going-out time. We need you here for the doctor's examination, okay?"

"Okay," Madison said. Phaneesa sounded so serious. Maybe it was serious. "I don't have any plans for next week, anyway. Except maybe going to the coffee shop in town."

"Rikki's? I love that place," Phaneesa said. "They're serving brownies and muffins now. Did you see that? I want to suggest they serve those little quiches during the breakfast rush. I'd buy one or two, for sure."

"Keeshes?"

"They're so good. You haven't lived until you've tried one. Once you do, you'll never be able to live without them."

"What are they?"

"A flaky pastry shell filled with an egg mixture, cheese, and whatever else you want. Some people like sausage or bacon. I like spinach in mine." Phaneesa laughed at Madison's stricken expression. "I'll bring you a box of plain cheese ones to try tomorrow. A reward for you since we're stealing your free time next week."

"Okay." Madison looked toward the door. "Can I go now?"

Phaneesa patted her on the knee. "You go. Have fun. Say hi to the kangaroos for me."

"Ooh, yeah." Madison leaped to her feet. "I'll go to Roo Valley first thing! And then the bird show, of course." She moved closer to Mrs. Park and put a hand on her shoulder. "I'll be back soon, Mrs. Park. Phaneesa's here if you need anything."

Mrs. Park's eyes remained closed, but her bony hand reached up and patted Madison's where it rested on her shoulder. It was right then that Madison truly understood that something was changing. Something was happening with Mrs. Park. She pressed the frail hand gently and then placed it back down on the armrest of the wheelchair. Choking up, Madison turned quickly and headed toward the door. She jammed her feet into her sneakers. She'd lace them up in the lobby downstairs.

"Bye," she called to both people in the living room and closed the door gently behind her.

She stopped at the mailboxes hoping to catch a glimpse of the hot Ms. Elena, but no such luck. Oh, well. She tossed the mail on the passenger seat and started Mrs. Park's old gold Cadillac. The car was a boat, that was for sure, but it beat taking the bus.

"Oh, my phone," Madison said, noticing it unceremoniously lying on the passenger-side floor where it had obviously fallen and spent the night. She picked it up. As suspected, it was dead. Oh, well. She tossed it in the glove compartment since there was no charger in the car.

She'd power it up when she got home. Maybe she'd watch Princess Merida defeat the bad bear and restore order to the kingdom once her phone was charged. Madison held her hands in a bow-and-arrow pose and then let the imaginary arrow go. Where it would go, she had no idea. Maybe it would go where all those other imaginary arrows went—back to Columbus and into those *stupids* who bothered her so much in high school. "*Stupids*," she muttered and backed the car out of the assigned spot.

~~~

Madison woke late Sunday morning, close to noon, close to the time Phaneesa would be there. She bolted off the floor where she'd slept in Mrs. Park's room all night. Ahh, good. Mrs. Park was still sleeping. The rhythmic oxygen machine was working fine, and the diaper change at two a.m. seemed to be holding. A quick sniff test told her that.

After returning from the zoo the day before, Madison had wanted to watch *Brave*, but her phone took forever to charge, and then by the time it did, she was knee-deep in helping Mrs. Park, who had choked on her evening medicines scaring Madison to death. Mrs. Park finally spit them all out and refused to try again. And then she ripped the oxygen tube out of her nose repeatedly and wouldn't leave it in no matter how many times Madison replaced it. Madison finally gave up.

The best sound ever was Phaneesa's knock on the front door.

"She's not up?" Phaneesa said, putting her bag down in the usual place.

Madison shook her head.

Phaneesa was wearing the pink scrubs with the kitty cats all over them. They were Madison's favorite. "Rough night?"

Madison nodded.

"You're quiet this afternoon," Phaneesa said softly. "You're never this quiet."

"I just woke up."

"Mm hmm," Phaneesa said. "Tell me how the evening went."

They went into Mrs. Park's bedroom, and as Phaneesa did her usual blood pressure and pulse checks, Madison told her about the pills, diapers, oxygen, and everything. She gestured to her pillow and blanket on the floor, showing where she'd slept.

"Thank you for the update, Madison," Phaneesa said, kind of business-like. "Oh, I brought that box of mini-quiches for you." She went back into the living room and showed the box to Madison.

"Those look kind of good."

"I'll pop a couple in the toaster oven for you and put the rest in the freezer," Phaneesa said. "Why don't you go shower and get dressed? They should be done by the time you finish."

"Okay," Madison said, heading for her bedroom. "And then can I go out to the coffee shop?"

"Of course, you can, dear," Phaneesa said. She turned her head, wiping at her eyes.

Yes, something was happening. Madison wondered if she should just stay home. She needed a shower, either way, so she grabbed fresh clothes and noticed her phone when it dinged an incoming text. She picked it up. Whoa! Twenty-three text messages. Almost her age in text messages. What the heck?

She plopped down on her bed. The first few were from Miss Shasti and then a couple from Billy. The one that just came in was from Miss Shasti. Crap, she sounded really worried.

MADISON: Hi, Miss Shasti. I'm okay. Sorry everyone was worried. I went to the zoo yesterday.

She wasn't sure what else to say. To be honest, she was kind of confused about why everyone was so worried about her all the time. She was fine. She was living her life and taking care of Mrs. Park.

> MADISON: I saw the bird show and had ice cream.
> No salad. They were out. Ha ha ha.

She shrugged, not knowing what else to add, and hit send. She tossed the phone on the bed and took her usual speed shower. You don't want to use too much hot water; someone else might need it, right?

She dressed in khaki cargo shorts and a yellow Star Wars t-shirt with Rey holding her light saber next to the speeder she built all by herself from scavenged parts. Madison's hair was towel-dried and still a little wet, but she didn't care. It would dry eventually. She checked the contents of her backpack, satisfied that she'd be ready if a coloring urge came on her at the coffee shop. Should she bring Mulan with her today?

Another ding came in on her phone. Oh, shoot, she'd missed four messages when she was in the shower. Holy Toledo on a stick. What is so important? She went back and read the first.

> SHASTI: I'm glad you're okay, peanut. Did you read
> my other text messages? The ones from yesterday?

> SHASTI: Hey, where'd you go just now? You were
> just here.

Uh oh. Miss Shasti was mad, and Madison understood why. "She thought we were having a text chat. Shoot." Madison read the next three messages.

SHASTI: Hmm...Okay, well, maybe you're avoiding me. But I would like to see you today. We need to chat.

Madison chuckled. Oh, is that what she wanted to call it? "Chat? " Madison chuckled. That was a new one. "I need you to 'chat' with me, dahling," Madison mimicked. "Up in my bedroom. With you between my legs." Mm hmm. They always wanted her back. Until they didn't.

SHASTI: Not at Rikki's shop. At my house. Downstairs in the living room. We have some things to discuss.

The living room? That could work. Probably in a chair this time. They loved when she got on her knees in front of them, didn't they? Hands in her hair, pulling her to their hot spots. Mm, hmm. Living room it would be.

SHASTI: You keep disappearing, and it makes me worry. Please text me back as soon as you read this. No matter what time.

MADISON: Here I am. I was in the shower. I wasn't avoiding you. Phaneesa's here. She's making me try a keesh from the toaster oven, and then I can leave. I can meet you at your house. I know the neighborhood gate code now. Ha ha.

SHASTI: Oh, good. And did you mean "quiche"? Eggs baked in a pie crust?

MADISON: Y

SHASTI: Full words, please.

MADISON: Okay. Sorry. Yes. Eggs in a pie crust.

SHASTI: You'll have to let me know if you like it. I
can make it for you if you do.

Miss Shasti didn't have to make quiche for her. The cookies were
good enough. That's what the *pretties* usually gave her anyway. The
ones Madison had gotten from Miss Shasti on Friday were pretty good.
She wouldn't mind a repeat of that. And besides, she probably
wouldn't like quiche anyway. And Miss Shasti would find a way to put
leafy greens, onions, or something equally disgusting inside. And that
would *not* be fun. At all.

After snarfing down both quiches, which were amazingly good,
and with assurances from Phaneesa that everything was under control
concerning Mrs. Park, Madison made it to Miss Shasti's house within
twenty minutes of their last text message exchange.

Miss Shasti opened the door and let Madison in. Madison ditched
her sneakers by the door and waited. Miss Shasti was gorgeous in her
flowing burgundy skirt. It had a pattern of subtle, softer off-white
tones that flattered her skin color. The blouse was neatly tucked into
the skirt and was tight across her breasts.

"Eyes up here, Madison," Miss Shasti said.

Shoot, she'd been caught.

"In the living room, please." Miss Shasti led the way, and
thankfully, they were going into the TV room and not that stuffy
formal room or sitting room or whatever hoity-toity people called it.

Miss Shasti pointed to one end of an excruciatingly comfy-looking couch. "Sit."

Madison sat. Her gaze darted around the room as her nerves escalated. This felt like those times when her grandmother yelled at her for…whatever. Anything and everything.

"Did I do something wrong, Miss Shasti?" Madison pulled her feet up under her hoping that wasn't against the rules. It just felt better to be small and tucked right now.

"I want to talk to you about Friday afternoon."

Ahh, Madison felt her shoulders relax a little. "Okay." She wanted to discuss terms.

"I don't know where to begin here," Miss Shasti said. She finally sat down on the other end of the couch. "Before we begin, do you want some water?"

Madison leaped to her feet. "I'll get it." She hurried into the kitchen and yanked open the fridge door. She grabbed two water bottles from the sea of water bottles on the bottom shelf that she'd seen last time she was there. Miss Shasti sure liked water.

She headed back but slowed her pace. She put the water bottles on a side table and stood behind Miss Shasti. She placed her hands on Miss Shasti's shoulders and began to massage them. "You seem tense, Miss Shasti."

"Madison," the tone was stern, "stop that this instant." Madison pulled her hands away. "I didn't give you permission to touch me."

"I'm sorry," Madison said. "I just thought…" She grabbed the discarded water bottles, handed one to Miss Shasti, and kept one for herself. She retreated to the far side of the couch and opened the water. Keeping her gaze down, she took a small sip.

"And that's what I wanted to talk about with you," Miss Shasti said. She paused as if searching for the right words. "In our community—"

"What community?"

"Please don't interrupt."

"Sorry."

"The community you witnessed at Miss Tilda's party last weekend. We have certain ideals that we all try to adhere to. To live by. One of those is consent. There are others like honesty and communication, too."

"Okay," Madison said, not quite understanding where this was going.

"I didn't give you consent to touch me on Friday."

Madison wanted to protest but held her words.

"You took me by surprise," Miss Shasti continued.

"You seemed to like what we were doing," Madison said meekly.

"Ultimately, yes, I did, but I wasn't prepared for it. I don't think you and I know each other well enough to do those intimate things together. Do you understand?"

Madison shook her head. No, she didn't understand.

Miss Shasti cleared her throat. "Have you, uh, have you done that sort of thing with other people?"

Madison nodded.

"Can you tell me more, so I'll understand?"

Madison looked away at the fireplace. It was a gas fireplace with fake logs. Why did you need a poker and log tongs if it was gas? That made no sense.

"Madison?"

"Hmm?"

"Communication is important," Miss Shasti said. Her tone was softer this time. "I like you, peanut. I want to get to know you better, but I need you to trust me. You can tell me things. I hope you want to get to know me better, too. Maybe?" She shrugged.

Madison glanced at Shasti's soft expression and then looked down at her own intertwined fingers. Her grandfather called them the people in the church fingers. She wiggled them. "People only want certain things. I know that."

"What types of things?"

"I mean, maybe not Billy. He's fun, but he might turn into a *stupid* at any time. And you had those cookies."

"Cookies? I was just trying to do a nice thing for you. Did someone else give you cookies?"

Madison shrugged. Why did Miss Shasti want to bring up that stuff? She was hoping to be past that. Of course, back in Columbus, she'd sometimes see somebody from high school, and they'd tease her all over again, especially if they came into PETology, where she worked. Joey, the jerk-off, heard about it and thought he could… that he could bother her in the back room. That's why she quit. She told everyone she got fired, but that wasn't entirely true, now was it, Joey? No, it wasn't.

She swiped at the tears in her eyes and hid her face underneath both hands as the tears flowed out like the tub faucet at Mrs. Park's.

The weight shifted on the couch, and she felt Miss Shasti sitting beside her.

"May I put my arm around you, Madison? Just for a hug."

Madison nodded and leaned toward the kind voice.

Miss Shasti pulled her in close. She rocked them both. Why was that so soothing? Soft lips kissed her on the forehead. "Oh, I'm sorry. You didn't give me consent for that."

"It's okay," Madison said, hearing the tears in her own voice. "I liked it."

"You did?"

"Mm hmm." Madison sighed when Miss Shasti kissed her again and then used her thumb to wipe the kiss away. "Don't wipe it away."

Miss Shasti chuckled. "I got lipstick on your forehead."

"You did?" Feeling better, she sat up and took a deep breath.

"Mm hmm," Miss Shasti said. "Do you feel safe here? In my arms?"

Madison nodded.

"Can you tell me more about the cookies?"

Madison nodded but couldn't look Miss Shasti in the eye. "Katia would sometimes make me cookies or whatever, but when Katia gave me to Brooke, Brooke only gave me store-bought cookies—the cheap kind. Alaina baked them herself—they were okay, except there were eggshells in them sometimes, so you had to be careful. Latisha baked them, too, and they were really, really good. She could open a bakery. I liked Latisha."

"But you didn't like the others?"

"I mean, I liked Katia, of course. Except when she gave me away. I didn't know she was going to do that."

"I'm sorry that she hurt you. Why did she give you away?" Miss Shasti reached for Madison's hand and held it. She stroked the back of it with her thumb. That was nice. Madison looked up at Miss Shasti and saw kind yet concerned eyes. Madison felt herself relax a little more.

"Umm, she said she had tried everything with me that she could think of and that she had met a girl from another school and wanted to date her, like, for real. Not like what she and I were doing. The whole time she kept telling me that we weren't girlfriends and that we weren't dating. I wasn't allowed to tell anyone why I kept going to her house after softball practice and on the weekends. She said if they asked, to tell them I was tutoring her in math. I even told my mother that."

"Katia was a classmate of yours in high school? She was, what, seventeen or eighteen?"

91

"Mm hmm. She was eighteen, and I was seventeen. She was the shortstop, and I was the catcher. We were both seniors. She cornered me in the locker room and asked why I always stared at her. I didn't want to tell her," Madison said and sighed.

"But she figured out you had a crush on her?" Miss Shasti finished.

Madison nodded.

"So, what did you and Katia do instead of math tutoring? Why did Katia want you to go to her house?"

"We went to her bedroom. She only had a mom, no dad, and her mom worked like two jobs or something and was never home. The first time I went over, I was so happy. Maybe she'd be my friend, but then she said she wanted to see my body and made me take off all my clothes while she examined and touched me. Everywhere. She touched me everywhere."

Miss Shasti made a noise of disapproval.

"I know," Madison said, "I shouldn't have let her do that."

"You are not to blame, Madison," Miss Shasti said. The anger in her words was scary. "This Katia predator is to blame. Did she ever ask for your consent to look at your body or touch you?"

Madison shrugged. "I kind of gave it to her when I did those things for her. Didn't I? She kept telling me that we both wanted this, so I believed her after a while. She always sent me home with cookies or money or something. As a gift, she always said, because I was good at pleasing her."

"Let me just pause here for a moment," Miss Shasti said. She swallowed big like she was really upset or something. "This is a lot for me to hear. I can only imagine what it must have been like to live it. So having said that, I want you to know that you can speak freely with me and if there's anything you do not want to tell me—" she poked the air on each of the last few words and then paused to clear her throat. "You don't have to. I don't want to force you into something too uncomfortable for you."

"Miss Shasti?" Madison said quietly.

"Yes, peanut?"

"Can I snuggle against you again? Oh, not like sex stuff, just like the hug before."

"Of course." Miss Shasti pulled her tight against her with both arms. Another lipstick kiss followed, and Madison let herself relax into the comfort.

"How long did this go on?" Miss Shasti continued, still holding her tight.

"The whole spring of my senior year. Right before school let out, the boys found out what I did, and they, uh…" Emotion closed her throat. No, she didn't want to talk about the *stupids*. Her chest tightened again, and more tears came.

"Shh, shh." Miss Shasti rocked her. Another kiss graced her forehead. "My poor poor peanut." Her voice hitched as if she was also crying. Why? "No one was looking out for you. I am so angry right now."

"I'm sorry," Madison said quietly and tried to pull away. Why did everyone get so mad at her?

Chapter 8

Shasti

Shasti wouldn't let Madison retreat and squeezed her tightly before relenting and holding her at arms' length. She looked Madison in the eye and said, "I am in no way angry at you, little one. I'm angry at those people who preyed on your innocent and submissive nature." She took a deep breath and added, "I think I want to table this talk for a little while. Would that be all right? I want to show you something."

"You're not mad at me?"

"No, of course not. You're not to blame for what happened to you. None of it. I would like to hear more about your experiences, for sure. If you want to tell me, that is, but for now, I think we both need a rest. Is that okay?"

Madison nodded. She took the tissue Shasti offered and wiped the tears off her face.

Leading Madison by the hand to the kitchen table, Shasti wondered if she was doing the right thing asking Madison to open up like that. Shasti was no psychologist, but she wanted to help. Maybe once she uncovered the major issues, she'd be able to find Madison the appropriate professional help she needed. Shasti certainly didn't want to do the young woman any harm.

"Have a seat." Shasti gestured to the same chair Madison sat in during their curry linner two days prior. She placed a tablet on a stand in front of Madison and said, "I want to show you something. A website that will help explain what our community is all about. Would that be okay?"

The most precious smile crept up Madison's face and lit up her eyes. "Is this you asking me for my consent?"

Shasti couldn't help the grin on her face. "I guess so. You're very bright, aren't you? Before I show you this, tell me about school and what classes you took."

Shasti willed her face to remain relatively impassive as Madison ticked off the half-dozen AP courses she'd taken, the accolades she'd gotten for academics and athletics, and the third-place GPA rank she'd earned in a high school with almost seven hundred seniors. Shasti had been right. This was one bright young woman sitting at her kitchen table. But this same bright woman told her early on that she wasn't "smart enough" to attend college. Two plus two was not equaling four in Madison's world. Two plus two was equaling something far more sinister. Shasti couldn't help wondering how far the abuse from the home life and her classmates went.

But before she would dig deeper into all of that, she needed Madison to understand a few things.

"So, this is the *Kinks.com* website." Shasti pointed to the webpage on her tablet. "It's a place for those of us who like a certain lifestyle. That lifestyle can mean so many different things to so many people, but I'm going to show you my page on *Kinks*. This way, you'll understand who I am a little more. Okay?"

"I give you my consent," Madison said, bouncing in the chair.

Shasti reached over and captured Madison's chin between her thumb and index finger. "You are adorable." She let the chin go.

Madison sat up taller and flicked her clean yet disheveled hair behind her shoulders. Victoria was right, Shasti thought with a smirk. *I need to get this girl a hair tie.*

Shasti took a deep breath, feeling like she was about to dive into the deep end of the pool without a lifeguard. No. *She* was the lifeguard. She had to remember that. In she went.

She swiped and tapped on the tablet until her *Kinks* homepage was up.

Madison took a big intake of breath. "Your picture is nice. I can tell it's you. That color looks good on you. What is that type of shirt called?"

"A corset. Pretty, isn't it?"

"Mm hmm," Madison said. "Why did you only post a picture of your chestal region? You're so pretty. Everyone should know what a pretty face you have. And why are you holding a hairbrush? It looks like someone's about to get a beating, aren't they?"

"I don't beat my submissives," Shasti said quietly.

"Submissives? You used that word before to describe me, but what is that?" Madison glanced at Shasti and then back to the screen. "Like Lydia, who was taken prisoner?"

"Being a prisoner implies you didn't consent. Lydia consented," Shasti instructed. "Being submissive basically means that you instinctively yield to others who are more dominant. Like your teammate Katia."

"Oh," Madison said. "But then I wanted to stop, and she wouldn't let me, and then she gave me to Brooke, who was always drunk when I got there like she couldn't stand the fact that I was there to go down on her and make her cum. After a couple of weeks, I was almost glad when she passed me along to Alaina."

Shasti's heart broke. This poor young thing. They took advantage of her. She clenched a fist but realized that Madison would pick up on her anger. She squelched it for now, but she would love to have a chance to confront those idiots—Katia in particular.

"Yes," Shasti said, "Katia's behavior and the rest are examples. Submissives tend to like when others take the leadership role. But I want you to understand that being submissive does not in any way mean that you are a doormat. It doesn't mean the person or people who have leadership over you can make you do whatever they want."

"No?"

"Absolutely not. Remember that part about consent?"

"O-oh," Madison said, dragging out the word. "I kind of gave Katia my consent when I didn't tell her to stop." It wasn't a question. Madison seemed to be making some connections on her own, which was a healthy thing.

"That's exactly right," Shasti said. "Here, read this part of my page. It's my introduction."

Madison turned her attention back to the screen and read to herself, occasionally breaking up the silence by reading parts of it aloud. "You're a Mommy Domme?"

"Mm hmm," Shasti said. "Read this next part. Out loud." She pointed to the second paragraph.

"Okay." Madison turned back to the screen and read, "'I am looking for a female *little*. A woman who needs nurturing and help with the more difficult aspects of life. Life is hard, sometimes. I know. I'd be honored to help you get through those tough times. You would be someone I would be friends with first, and then if it blossoms into more, that's something we can explore.'" Madison inhaled through her nose and said, "That rhymed, Miss Shasti."

"It did, didn't it?"

"And I like how you changed in the middle to talking right to the person—using the word 'you.'"

"A lot of profile pages do that. You'll see." Shasti pointed to the following line. "Go on."

"'I would, of course, be in charge, and there would be rules my *little* would need to follow. Should rules be broken or unheeded, then there would be consequences. And you would know and understand why. Consequences would fit the transgression, of course. I don't punish with violence and will never strike in anger. Fun-ishments may be employed if both of us enjoy that. Finding and respecting boundaries are also important, but it's okay to push up against boundaries sometimes in order to grow.'"

Madison sighed. It seemed like a content sigh, but Shasti wasn't sure.

"Are you okay, peanut?"

"Why do you call me that?"

Shasti wasn't quite ready to be so open, but she was the one that had opened that box with the *Kinks* website. "The truth is that the Mommy Domme in me recognized the *little* in you. I just want to scoop you up and protect you from the mean-spirited people of the world."

"You do? Why would you want to do that?"

Shasti's heart cried as she looked at the genuinely perplexed expression on Madison's face. It was as if this young woman never had someone care or watch out for her best interests. Those high school classmates certainly didn't. "Some people just like to take care of other people."

Madison's dark eyebrows scrunched together as she tried to make sense of things. "Is a *little* a submissive? I mean, like, a kind of submissive?"

"Yes. A *little* can be so many different things. But in general terms, a *little* is typically someone who needs guidance, maybe not all the time, but sometimes. In my opinion, I think some *littles* feel safest when doing childhood things. Not *childish* things, but activities like coloring or wearing a Star Wars t-shirt like the one you have on.

Things that make you feel safe and secure. Who knows? A *little* might just want mountains of cuddles some days."

"Like on the couch just now?"

"Mm, hmm. You asked why I want to be a Mommy Domme. I get to brush my *little's* hair and call her pet names like peanut or sweet pea. I get to protect her and guide her. That fulfills me. I don't have children, and I don't feel that I want children. It's something that took me a long time to figure out."

"And you want to help me?" Madison looked around the room as if trying to make sense of things. "Me?" she asked again, pointing to herself.

Shasti nodded. She wanted to rub her knuckle along that cute face less than a foot away, but this might be the make-or-break moment. She hoped she'd been explaining this well enough.

"Tell you what," Shasti said. "Why don't you click this link here. It's someone's journal post about *littles*. And this one here is an MD/lg journal post about Mommy Dommes and their little girls."

"Is Billy a *little*? And is Seamus his Mommy Domme?" Madison burst out laughing. She must have heard what she'd said and how wrong it was. "Billy's *Father* Domme?"

"Usually, it's called a 'Daddy' Domme, but yes, that's their relationship."

"I was jealous of it," Madison said. "When I saw how Mr. Seamus took care of Billy. He took care of me a little bit at the party the other day."

"Oh?"

"Yeah, he got us those swords to play with and put out the blanket, and he said I could have another cupcake with lunch." Madison looked up at Shasti shyly. "And you took care of me, too."

"How?"

"Lots of ways." Madison's cheeks turned bright pink, and she looked away.

Shasti pulled back and said, "Read those two journal posts. You can click wherever you want on this website but be aware that there are many thirsty people on here that only what one thing."

Madison nodded knowingly. "Like this guy that posted a picture of his *stupid* thing on your chat section down here."

Shasti rolled her eyes and put up a hand to block the erect penis. "Ugh, delete that, please."

Madison did as asked. "And is that why you didn't put your real name up there? *Cincy_MommyDomme* is your alias?"

"It is. I tried an online Mommy Domme relationship, but that isn't what I want. That's why I put Cincinnati as part of my name, so only *littles* in my area would contact me."

"So, you want a real live *little* submissive to Mommy dominate?" Madison asked, making Shasti chuckle. At least she was trying to make sense of it.

"Yep," Shasti said. "Go read."

Madison moved the cursor back to the *littles* journal post. Shasti excused herself so Madison could read in private. Preparing a snack was the only thing she could think of doing. As she cut cheese and apple slices in the kitchen to go with the whole wheat crackers, she couldn't help but smile when Madison excitedly blurted out words every now and then. The latest one was "stuffies." Before that, she'd said, "Disney movies. Oh, yeah!"

"Bedtimes?" Madison said in disgust. "Vegetables? Come on now." Oops. Things were taking a turn.

Yes, there was no mistaking that the young woman sitting at her kitchen table was a *little*. She just had to realize it for herself.

~~~

Late Monday afternoon Shasti hung her white coat on the hook by the door to her office. She could do this. She held her head high and made her way to the side door after making sure Reggie, the office manager, knew she was officially heading out of the building.

"It was your idea," Shasti said to herself as she opened the car door. "Mm hmm." Meeting Mrs. Park sounded like such a great idea yesterday when Madison was over. Now, though? Shasti was nervous. It was like meeting a girlfriend's parents or something. Mrs. Park was in her 90s and a survivor and refugee of the Korean War. She was a woman with quite a fighting spirit—not that Shasti knew that firsthand or even from Madison, but you would have to be strong to survive being pregnant and suddenly homeless. And her husband was killed in the war. Shasti couldn't even imagine that. Thank God for the American soldier who fell in love with her, pregnant and all, and brought her back home with him after his tour was over. But where was Mrs. Park's family now? According to Madison, Mrs. Park had a daughter, still living.

Shasti shrugged. Maybe she'd find out more this evening while visiting. She pulled out of the well-kept grounds of the medical center and onto the main road. The day before, Madison had read the two journal articles on *Kinks* and even found a few more until Shasti suggested they move back to the couch to talk about what she'd read. Madison was eager, especially when she saw the snacks heading into the living room.

During their chat, Madison asked a lot of questions. A lot. Shasti asked Madison a few of her own to make sure she understood what she'd read. Still, all in all, Shasti got the definite impression that Madison understood the concept of *littles* and the concept of Dominant caregivers. Bless Billy and Seamus for being such good role models. Their ears must have been burning since their names and examples of their behavior with each other were often brought up.

Oh, how Shasti wanted to ask Madison to be in a relationship with her—for a trial period, of course. So that they'd both know if a power exchange relationship was first and foremost something that Madison would want and would benefit from and also to find out if they genuinely had chemistry before making anything more official. There was chemistry already, Shasti mused. When Madison asked for more cuddles on the couch right before she had to leave, Shasti's heart had soared. It wasn't sexual. It was nurturing. And then, when Madison asked for another kiss on her forehead, she wouldn't let Shasti wipe off the lipstick. Madison wanted to keep it so she could look at it later and "remember." What she was going to remember wasn't clear to Shasti at the time, but when she recalled their closeness, she remembered how soothing it felt. And what was the best word? Ahh, how *right* it felt. Yes, there was chemistry.

"But I can't rush this," Shasti said out loud. "It's better to go slow. Madison has to have time to think about it, to marinate on things, to make sense of what I'll be proposing. She might just think you are a raving lunatic and want nothing more to do with you."

Of course, those thoughts ran counter to the fact that Shasti was now driving to Mrs. Park's apartment to meet the older woman that Madison worked for. Shasti asked to come over mainly so she could see how Madison was living. She was prepared to scoop the young woman up and bring her home with her if conditions at Mrs. Park's were not to her liking. Madison had such a trusting nature that it wouldn't surprise Shasti if the environment was deplorable.

She needn't have worried.

The three-story luxury condominium complex was built high on a hill overlooking Denton Heights below and Cincinnati beyond. The manicured lawns surrounding the entryway and the impeccable flower gardens were incredibly inviting. Ahh, impatiens. Now, Shasti understood where the dirt-filled flowers had come from Friday afternoon. Not picking flowers from landscaped yards would definitely be one of the lessons Madison would soon learn but not today. Later, when the timing was right. That would be true for all the things she wanted to teach the young woman if they proceeded. Shasti wanted to mold her into a strong, self-assured, independent woman who could stand her ground against more dominant personalities.

"Including me," Shasti mused out loud and put the car in park. She followed Madison's precise directions, which included using the far elevator because it was faster and soon found herself knocking on Mrs. Park's front door.

"I'll get it," Madison called from inside. The door opened, and Madison's face lit up. "You came."

"Of course," Shasti said. "May I come in?"

"Yes, yes." Madison stepped back and gestured for her to come inside.

Shasti entered the apartment and took off her shoes, having been counseled that it was respectful to do that in Mrs. Park's house. Shasti didn't tell her that shoe removal was also customary in many Indian homes—including her parents'. The apartment was tastefully decorated and looked clean. And the view out the floor-to-ceiling windows was incredible.

Madison reached for Shasti's hand, shooting Shasti's blood pressure a bit higher than it already was. Madison pulled her into the living room, where an elderly Asian woman sat dozing in a reclining wheelchair.

"She wanted to be in the wheelchair and not in the bed when she met you," Madison whispered.

Ahh, yes, this was a woman whose body was failing her—her frail, emaciated look, the obvious Raynaud's disease in her fingers. The oxygen concentrator working in the background was another clear indicator. No, this woman didn't have much longer. Did Madison know that?

Mrs. Park roused from her nap and blinked her eyes a few times. "Girl!" she bellowed. It wasn't exactly a bellow since the woman was so obviously weak.

"I'm right here, Mrs. Park," Madison said and stood in front of her.

"Introduce your friend."

Madison made introductions and then sat down on the couch.

"How are you feeling today, Mrs. Park?" Shasti asked and moved a living room chair so Mrs. Park could see her directly.

Mrs. Park laughed. "Been better."

Shasti smiled and asked if she was in any pain. She couldn't help it. She was a mama bear and couldn't help protecting those that needed help. Her father, the lauded cardiac surgeon at Washington General Hospital, was disappointed that she "only" wanted to become a general practitioner and didn't want to follow in his footsteps. He eventually came around the day she received her ceremonial white coat after medical school. Helping people and problem solving were so innate in her that there was no way she could deny them.

Assessing that Mrs. Park wasn't in pain, she relaxed a bit.

"Girl!" Mrs. Park said, this time much more softly. "Get water for your girlfriend."

Shasti blanched at the word. What had Madison told her?

Once Madison was out of the room, Mrs. Park beckoned Shasti closer and whispered, "I need to speak with you in private. Send Madison out for a few minutes. To the office or something."

"Okay," Shasti was curious but decided not to speculate on what Mrs. Park wanted to speak with her about. Early in her medical career, she learned to let conversations flow naturally. Besides, she probably just wanted medical advice or something.

Madison came back in with a glass of water with ice for Shasti and a sippy cup with a straw for Mrs. Park. Shasti took both from her. "That was very thoughtful, peanut. Thank you."

Madison bounced on her feet. Her big grin made Shasti's heart warm. Shasti reached for her purse and dug out her keys. "Madison, would you please go to my car and get my black medical bag? It's in the back seat, probably on the floor." She handed over her keys with the car key out and prominent.

"Car alarm?"

"None," Shasti said, surprised that Madison would even think of it.

"Mail," Mrs. Park said.

"Okay," Madison said and bounced out of the apartment.

Mrs. Park didn't waste any time. "She doesn't know I'm on hospice. Her mommy didn't want her to know when she sent her down here. I'm going to a nursing home. Chrysalis Center."

Shasti swallowed hard, trying to shake the emotion from her voice. "I know it well. I've sent a few patients there myself. The hospice wing is well-staffed and is excellent."

"I've made peace with dying," Mrs. Park said. She paused for a moment to catch her breath. "But I disagree with her mommy's wishes. Phaneesa and Eugenia also think Madison needs to know everything. I want you to help her understand."

Shasti heart clenched. She was afraid this was where the conversation was headed. "I can do that."

"She trusts you." Mrs. Park reached toward Shasti. Shasti closed the distance and held the older woman's hand. "You will have to explain things. She is not dull and dim-witted like my daughter claims. Madi is smart. She just—"

She took a moment to catch her breath as Shasti assured her that she would take care of Madison. Mrs. Park nodded and then finished her thought. "She just hasn't gotten the love she needs. The care she deserves. My granddaughter-in-law tries, but she has her own issues."

Shasti was confused. She made soothing noises as she tried to put all the clues together. Then it suddenly dawned on her. "Mrs. Park, are you Madison's great-grandmother?"

Mrs. Park's relieved smile made Shasti's inner alarms quiet somewhat. "Yes. Please don't tell her until after I'm, you know, gone. Her mommy doesn't want her to know just in case…"

Shasti waited for Mrs. Park to continue. When the silence stretched out too long, she said, "In case of what?"

"Her grandmother is mean. That's my daughter. She is a narcissist, I think. The world revolves around her, and when I couldn't give her the world she thought she deserved, she turned her back on me. She got the whole family and neighbors and community to ostracize me." Another breathing break ensued. "After her step-father died, the only father she ever knew, I had a string of lovers in and out of the house. She thought I was disrespecting her father. I was lonely. I caught myself a nice Korean man, though, Mr. Park. I was happy with him. I thought she would settle after that. She didn't. My daughter is just plain mean and relentlessly cruel to her daughter-in-law."

"Madison's mother is your daughter's daughter-in-law?"

"Hard to keep track, I know. My granddaughter-in-law, I guess you'd say."

Shasti's ears perked up at the ding of the elevator. "I think Madison's on her way back."

Mrs. Park nodded. "She adores you," Mrs. Park said. "I had lovers much younger than me, too. I don't judge, but please help her. Please take care of that sweet girl."

"I will," Shasti said as the front door opened. "If she'll let me."

Chapter 9

Madison

"She's sleeping soundly," Miss Shasti said after they got Mrs. Park back in her hospital bed.

They headed to Madison's room to grab the baby monitor. Madison checked it, and it seemed to be working fine.

"Thanks for staying with me for a while," Madison said. "I think Mrs. Park likes you."

"I'm glad. I like her, too," Miss Shasti said.

They headed back to the living room, and Madison zoomed to the couch, landing with a bounce on one end.

Miss Shasti sat down on the other end. "Now, about the state of your room."

"I'll clean it. I promise."

"Text me pictures when it's finished?"

"Okay." Madison felt a wave of shyness overcome her as she asked, "Would it be okay if…"

Miss Shasti opened her arms in invitation, and Madison exhaled in relief. She scooted over into strong arms that wrapped around her snugly. She fit perfectly against Miss Shasti, her head landing on her soft breasts. Madison wasn't aroused sexually by it, even though she already had intimate knowledge of those soft breasts beneath her head. No, this was different. Way different. Miss Shasti was so nice. Madison couldn't believe she was in the snuggly arms of such an amazing woman who smelled so good and came to visit Mrs. Park and gave her an examination using her stethoscope and blood pressure thingy from her black bag, which looked like the black bags doctors used in those old-timey movies. It was a gift from her doctor father, she'd said. That was cool. Madison's own father hadn't given her gifts like that, but he let her help him whenever he did house and home repairs. Kwan was above that, according to her grandmother. Okay, fine. Whatever.

A squeeze and a kiss on the forehead roused her from her musings. "What are you thinking about, little one?" Miss Shasti asked softly.

Uh, oh. Her tone was cautious, sympathetic even. How did she know when Madison was troubled by something? Weird. "Miss Shasti, you're a doctor, right?"

"Mm hmm."

"What does 'hospice' mean? Phaneesa said it the other day, and the folder of papers they think I didn't read has the word written all over it. I could have Googled it, but I kind of didn't want to know."

"But you're ready to know now?"

"Yes, Ma'am. I think so."

"Okay," Miss Shasti said. There was a strange resignation to her voice, like the way Katia sounded right before she told Madison she was done with her.

"It's okay, Miss Shasti," Madison said. "I can handle it. They all think I can't handle stuff, but I can. And I think I even know."

"What do you think it is?"

Madison exhaled in a sigh and whispered, "Mrs. Park is going to die."

Miss Shasti made a small, sad noise. "That's right, peanut. Hospice is an amazing organization with doctors, nurses, and all kinds of folks who help sick people transition."

"Transition to, like, heaven?"

"Sure. When a person is ill, and it's determined that they won't ever get better, the focus changes to making sure they're comfortable and have a good quality of life with whatever time they have left."

"Is that why my mother sent me here to be with Mrs. Park? So, I could help her have a good quality of life?" Madison heard the uncertainty in her own voice and knew Miss Shasti must have heard it, too. "I should have been staying home," Madison said with sudden realization. "I went to the zoo all those times and the party. Mrs. Park can't go to the zoo or parties or even Rikki's coffee shop." Her chest tightened so much that she had to inhale and let her tears loose, or she'd be in hospice, too.

Miss Shasti's arms wrapped even tighter as she rocked Madison back and forth. A soothing hand brushed the hair off her forehead. "Shh, shh, shh," Miss Shasti comforted. "You didn't do anything wrong. You needed those short breaks so you could stay strong for your, uh, for Mrs. Park. And the nurses were here every day, right?"

Madison sniffed, and somehow a tissue was produced for her to blow her nose. That was kind of magic. Were Mommy Dommes part wizard or something?

"How do you know Mrs. Park?" Miss Shasti asked. There was something weird in the way she asked it, but Madison wasn't good at reading Miss Shasti. Not yet anyway.

"I didn't know her. She knows my family, I guess. She even knows my mommy. My leading theory is that she used to be a neighbor or something when she lived in Columbus." Madison shrugged and then blew her nose again. A hand went out for the used tissue, and Madison deposited it there. A fresh tissue was then presented. Yep. Miss Shasti was a tissue-producing wizard.

"I see," the wizard said. "And you're here all by yourself to take care of her?"

"Except when the nurses come. I can handle it."

"Oh, honey, I didn't mean to imply that you couldn't."

"They're coming tomorrow. The doctor, I mean, I think they're going to take her away. I overheard Eugenia on the phone today. She said something about packing up Mrs. Park's things. They haven't told me much."

"Yes, that's what's happening. I didn't realize it was tomorrow, but Mrs. Park wanted me to tell you that she'll be moving to a skilled nursing facility where she will get 24/7 care. It's right here in Denton Heights, near my clinic, and you'll be able to visit her every day."

"Will she ever come home?"

Miss Shasti shook her head.

"End game," Madison said, proud of herself that she didn't start crying again, even though she really really wanted to. After Miss Shasti left, that's when she could let loose.

Miss Shasti nodded. "I'm sure you'll be able to stay in the apartment for the duration."

"Okay." Madison hadn't thought about that. "And then do I have to go back home? To them?"

"To whom?"

"Columbus. My family."

"That's entirely up to you," Miss Shasti said, holding Madison at arms' length. It was kind of funny when she did that, but Madison liked it.

"I miss Mommy, but I don't want to go back there. I want to stay here with you."

"You're old enough to make your own decisions."

"Pfft. Oh, sure," Madison said. "Tell that to, oh, everyone in my life."

~~~

Madison got out of the car and watched as they wheeled Mrs. Park from the transport ambulance toward the new place. Seeing Mrs. Park in a bed outside in the air was kind of weird. What if it had been raining? Well, it wasn't, so yay. The place was kind of nice on the outside, she decided. There were pretty flowers and stuff all around, but they looked dry. Maybe they needed water or something. Or maybe they were going to die at this place like Mrs. Park would someday.

"Hang on," a voice called to her from the parking lot.

Madison turned, and she immediately started crying. Miss Shasti was running toward her. And in her nice lady shoes. Madison flung her arms around the slightly taller woman and buried her face in her chest. She felt like a baby crying, but she couldn't help it.

Miss Shasti made clicking noises with her tongue, which calmed Madison immensely. See? Wizard.

"Are you going to be okay, peanut?" Miss Shasti asked, holding Madison at arms' length.

Madison stepped away and swiped at her eyes. Wow. Another miracle tissue was handed to her. "I guess."

"I'm here now. Let's go in and help get Mrs. Park settled."

Mrs. Park's new digs in the hospice wing were sparse but nice, too, with the flowery fabric curtains and colorful sheets. After visiting for a while, the nurses told them it was time to leave because visiting hours were over, and they were strict about that. Madison followed behind Miss Shasti's car to her house. It was already after dinner time, and neither of them had eaten.

"Grilled chicken sandwich, okay?" Miss Shasti asked once they were in the house.

"I love chicken. No pickles, please." Madison bounced on her toes in the kitchen. "And I like mayo, please."

"You're a very polite young lady, aren't you?"

Madison shrugged and then did as Miss Shasti directed her. She wiped the table with a clean dishcloth and then set it with the plates and stuff Miss Shasti handed her. Madison liked having someone tell her what to do. She *really* liked having someone direct her and make clear what was expected. No guessing. No fuss. No muss. And no yelling when she did something wrong. That part was nice, too.

After they ate and Madison helped clear the table and do the dishes, Miss Shasti asked if Madison wanted to do something special with her. Madison nodded and then gazed toward the upstairs bedroom expectantly.

"No, dear. Not that." Miss Shasti led the way into the living room. The fun one. Not the stuffy one. "We're still getting to know each other, okay?"

"Okay." Madison did her best to keep the disappointment out of her voice.

"You seemed intrigued by my rope session with Lydia at Miss Tilda's party. Would you like to try that?"

"Being a prisoner?" Madison's eyes grew wide.

"Not that part. Although maybe one day you'd like to try bondage, who knows? I tied a harness on Lydia. Would you like me to tie one on you? It might help us both take our minds off the heavy things right now."

"I'm going to visit Mrs. Park every day at the nursing home or whatever it's called."

"That's very thoughtful of you," Miss Shasti said. "My clinic is only about a mile south on Kirkland, so you'll be nice and close."

"Miss Shasti?"

"Yes, dear?"

"I don't want to be tied to some structure."

Miss Shasti laughed, and Madison's head dropped. She looked down at her lap.

"Oh, honey. I'm not laughing at you, I promise. Come here."

Madison didn't move for a moment, but then she remembered how good being in Miss Shasti's arms felt.

"I wasn't going to tie you down to anything, little one. Just the harness around your body. You'll be free to move your arms and legs, and you can even walk right out the front door anytime you want to."

"I don't want to leave, and you smell really good."

Miss Shasti chuckled. "That's nice to hear." She released Madison from her squeezing hug. "So, do you want to be my rope bottom for the evening?"

"Okay."

"Don't sound so enthusiastic." The teasing lilt to Miss Shasti's words made Madison relax a little. "We can stop anytime. In our community, we use safewords."

"Red, yellow, green," Madison said, proud of herself.

Miss Shasti narrowed her eyes in question.

"I did some more reading on that website."

"Did you now?" Miss Shasti said. "Why don't we tie while you tell me what else you learned."

"Okay," Madison said. "I'll say 'red' if things get too weird or uncomfortable for me. According to everybody on that website, it means you have to stop doing whatever you're doing."

"That's absolutely right. Yellow means pause the action and rest. Green means go, go, go. Now, if you'll excuse me for a minute, I need to run upstairs for the rope." She returned minutes later with the same bag full of ropes she'd had at Miss Tilda's party. "Pick your color." Miss Shasti held out five different coils of colorful rope.

"Red," Madison said and then giggled.

"Why are you giggling, you silly one?" Miss Shasti pulled out two bundles of red rope and then put back the bigger of the two.

"Because I said, 'red.'"

Miss Shasti had a perplexed expression on her face until she didn't. "Oh! Like the safewords. I get it. Did you know I can say, 'red,' too?"

"You can?"

"Mm hmm." Miss Shasti directed Madison to sit on a comfy footstool. "Dommes sometimes need to stop things, too." She held the red rope out toward Madison. "Ready?"

"I think so." Madison stretched and wiggled until she got her nerves out. Well, not all of them, but some. "Go."

"You mean 'green?'" Miss Shasti teased and then joined in when Madison laughed.

"You're funny, Miss Shasti," Madison said, feeling shy again.

Miss Shasti moved close, wrapped the doubled-over rope around Madison's waist, and then slid it under her tiny barely-there boobs. They couldn't even in good conscience be called boobs. Bumps, maybe? Madison would have laughed out loud at the thought, but Miss Shasti's body was really close to hers. She could feel her body warmth. And she smelled so good, like clean soap or something. And her cleavage was right there in Madison's face. She swallowed. Hard. Her breathing deepened as Miss Shasti worked. Madison was aroused, but she wouldn't let Miss Shasti know because nothing was going to happen anyway.

The red rope continued its path up and over Madison's right shoulder, got tucked underneath her new boob belt in the front, and then went up and over her left shoulder. Miss Shasti moved behind her, did something that Madison couldn't see, and then the rope went under her left armpit. It kind of tickled and Madison giggled.

All motion stopped for an overlong moment causing Madison to look behind her.

"I asked you a question," Miss Shasti said. "Did you not hear me?"

"Did I 'knot?'" Madison giggled. "Get it? K-N-O-T?"

Miss Shasti smiled, but the smile didn't reach her eyes.

Madison cleared her throat and said, "Sorry. What did you say?"

"I asked if you were comfortable."

"Oh, yes. It just tickled for a minute." Madison looked down at the red ropes circling her body. "It's like decoration. Sexy decoration. I like it."

Miss Shasti moved in front of her and snaked the rope underneath the front part, effectively pulling up Madison's bumps. Madison was amazed that she had anything for the ropes to hold up. At Miss Shasti's urging, Madison told her what she'd read about submissives and Dominants on the *Kinks* website and how she understood better what Miss Shasti had been saying about consent. It was everything. If you don't agree to something, then it shouldn't be done. And more importantly, Madison realized that she was allowed to have an opinion in the first place. That's why Miss Shasti asked Madison if she wanted to be roped in red and didn't just make her do it. Miss Shasti needed permission, and Madison gave it. Miss Shasti answered questions too, but she postponed a discussion about why some people liked getting hit with paddles and crops and stuff. "Another time, peanut," Miss Shasti had said. "That's kind of a big topic."

They worked silently for a while, and Madison relaxed into the smooth and efficient movements. Miss Shasti had said she was new at this rope stuff, but it didn't feel like it. Madison felt like she was under the care of an expert. Like someone who was an artist and Madison, the prized subject of that art.

A soft kiss on her cheek startled her into the present. Madison sighed. She felt so…blissful. A hand stroked her cheek. She sighed again. It was more like a sigh-moan combo. She was feeling really, really peaceful. Almost floaty. She opened her eyes after realizing they were shut. Miss Shasti loosened the rope around Madison's neck and then locked eyes with her. Madison looked up at Shasti's lips. So close.

"Please kiss me," Madison pleaded.

Miss Shasti moved closer, placed both hands on either side of Madison's head, and tilted it down. The kiss to Madison's forehead was not what she wanted, and she groaned at the betrayal. She wanted to say, "Red," but knew that wasn't what safewords were for.

Miss Shasti chuckled. "In good time, peanut. Right now, I believe you're experiencing sub-space. A floaty kind of happy space. Yes?"

"Yes, Ma'am." Madison closed her eyes again. She couldn't ever remember feeling so peaceful. "Can I keep the rope on for a while?"

"Of course," Miss Shasti said. "Would you like to cuddle on the couch? Just cuddle."

"Yes," Madison said and stood up. Normally she would have leaped to her feet, but she was moving in a cloud or something.

Miss Shasti guided her to the couch, and they both assumed their increasingly familiar cuddle position. A strong arm went around her. Another kiss was given to her forehead. Loose strands of hair were brushed off her face. Madison snuggled into the warm body protecting her. Yep, she decided, cuddles were the best thing ever.

They snuggled together for quite some time. Sometimes Miss Shasti rocked them both, and sometimes they were still.

"Is there a Domme-space?" Madison said without preamble.

"Yes, sometimes, Domme's can get into that wonderful space, too."

"Did you get there?"

"I think I'm in Domme-space now with you safe in my arms."

"Mmm," Madison murmured. "I like that."

A kiss to her temple followed. Madison wondered how much lipstick she had on her head at this point. It would take a scrub brush to get it off, but she didn't mind. At all.

"It's too late for you to drive home now," Miss Shasti said. "And I don't want you to be alone in the condo tonight anyway. I have a spare room you can sleep in, but we'll have to blow up the air mattress first."

"I can't sleep with you?"

"No, dear. We're still—"

"Getting to know each other," Madison finished.

"Right. Now I want to point out something to you about protocols. You've done a lot of reading on the website, but there's always more to learn." Shasti stroked Madison's cheek. "Interrupting me like that is not acceptable. I won't interrupt you either unless it's for your safety. That would be one of my many rules should we go further."

"Go further?" Madison sat up so she could look at Miss Shasti straight on. It sounded like something important was about to be said, and she didn't want to miss a word.

"What do you think about a trial period? Maybe a month or so."

"A trial period?" Madison rubbed her eyes. Despite wanting to stay focused, she was getting sleepy.

"Yes. Where we see if an MD/lg dynamic is what we both want."

"Mommy Domme, little girl?"

"Mm hmm."

"Do I have to wear diapers and suck a pacifier?"

Miss Shasti chuckled. "No, of course not. What made you say that? Do you *want* to wear diapers and use a pacifier?"

"No! But I read on Kinks that a lot of littles like diaper stuff. Not me. I'm not *that* little."

"No diapers then," Miss Shasti said with mirth in her eyes. Madison liked it when Miss Shasti was happy. And she seemed really happy right now talking about MD/lg stuff. "But there will be rules," Miss Shasti continued. "Like bedtimes and healthy eating and other things. But we will discuss all the rules together. To be fair, we would have to agree at the start that as your Dominant, I make the rules for both of us. The rules I make will be for our mutual benefit. I want you to thrive and be the best Madison Kim you can be."

"And you would be the best Dr. Shasti Balakrishnan, M.D. *you* can be?"

"Yes, good girl. You understand that. I'm pleased."

Madison narrowed her eyes. "And when you're not pleased?"

"Punishment. Naturally."

"Oh," Madison said. This was the not fun part. "Punishments like what?"

"Toys taken away for a short time. Early bedtime. No dessert. Extra chores."

"But there will be desserts sometimes?"

"Mm hmm," Miss Shasti said and chucked her on the chin.

"Since I have to get up early tomorrow, I suggest a bedtime for us both at 10:00 pm."

"Can I sleep with you in your bed?"

Miss Shasti's eyebrow went all the way up to the sky.

"I guess that's a no," Madison said. "Oh, yeah, we have to get the air mattress filled up. I forgot."

"So, what do you say to a one-month trial period? We'll make it official if we're both happy with the arrangement on this same date in July. And at any time, if either of us wants to back out and end things, we can."

"Okay."

"Okay, what?"

"Okay, I'd like to go for the trial period."

Miss Shasti smiled. "I forget that you're brand spanking new."

"Spanking?" Madison asked wide-eyed.

"Just an expression, although we can try that one day if you're up for it."

"Why in the world would I voluntarily volunteer to get a spanking?" Madison shook her head. It was the most ridiculous thing she'd ever heard of. Well, after grown-ups wearing diapers who didn't need diapers, unlike Mrs. Park, who *did* need diapers.

"You'll change your mind on spankings, I'm sure. But getting back to my point. Our community has protocols, one of which is addressing Dominants by their honorifics. Miss Shasti or Ma'am or even Mistress. So when you address me, I'd like you to use one of those."

"Okay," Madison said. Oh, no. The eyebrow went up again. "Okay, Miss Shasti."

"There you go. That's a good girl." Miss Shasti patted Madison on the thigh and said, "C'mon, let's lock up and go upstairs to get that air mattress filled and make your bed."

Once Madison was standing, Miss Shasti grabbed her by the rope harness and pulled her along behind her. Tingles raced through Madison's body, some of them reaching her hot spot. Maybe this trial period wouldn't be so bad after all.

Chapter 10

Shasti

The morning had been hectic at the clinic. Before Shasti's first appointment at 8:30 am, a walk-in patient came in with head trauma. Apparently, his attempt at cleaning the garage ended with a head laceration needing two staples. He'd jumped on the second staple, but it went in smoothly, and she didn't have to redo it.

A traditional summer cold came in next, and then a sports camp physical for a young man hoping to become a professional basketball player one day. He was tall enough, that was for sure.

And now, she finally had a couple of minutes to hit the restroom. Back in her office chair, she sent a text to Madison asking how things were going at the nursing home. She'd forgotten to set up texting protocols with Madison, but there was time for those rules. The little dear had already pushed some boundaries two nights ago when Shasti found her sleeping on the floor of Shasti's room and not in the guest room on the air mattress. She said she wanted to be close to Shasti but didn't want to break any rules by getting in bed with her. That was sweet, but she had broken a rule. If Shasti let that one go, Madison would push further. Shasti had learned that from experience.

Amber had been the queen of pushing against Shasti's good nature, and it only ended in heartache for both of them. Shasti wasn't fulfilled, and Amber wasn't getting the kind of Dominance she craved. Amber was a full-on brat, not a *little* like they'd both thought. Put simply, Shasti wasn't a brat tamer. Not like Rikki, who'd had a string of brats, tamed them, and they all left her for one reason or another. Eileen was the biggest of them all. Shasti didn't know how Rikki was going to tame that one. She didn't seem tamable. Shasti suspected that Rikki needed to get out of the brat business. She was never going to be happy with that kind of submissive. But she didn't know how to tell her friend that.

There was a soft knock on her office door.

"Come on in," she called.

Her business partner, the one that had taken a chance on a young doctor from the east coast a little over a year ago, walked in. "Reggie said you dropped by my office?" Dr. Allie Littrell, an attractive blonde in her early fifties, let herself in. She was a tiny woman, but most people never noticed that once they experienced her might.

Shasti gestured to one of the empty chairs in her office, inviting her colleague to sit. "You didn't have to come by. I was going to check in again later."

"I'm here now," she said. "You have the Henderson girl next?"

"Mm hmm," Shasti said with a sigh. She'd voiced her frustrations to Allie in the past when she was coming up empty. "I've not exhausted my ideas. It may be a 'simple' case of vertigo or even 'simpler' case of puberty." She made air quotes around any word with simple in it.

"But you don't truly think that's what's going on," Allie said knowingly.

"No, but I have a few more tests to do. Insurance should cover them, but that's not what I wanted to ask you." Shasti took a quick breath. She wasn't sure how to phrase it. "I have a friend that I'd like a checkup done on. Hearing test in particular."

"School checkup?"

"Yes, like that, but she's no longer in school. I'd do it myself, but I don't trust that I can be objective. She'd be a new patient."

"I'd be happy to help, Shasti," Allie said and looked at her watch. She stood. "Set it up with scheduling, and I'll take care of it."

"You're a life saver. I just…" She was mortified when tears filled her eyes. "I just don't think anyone has ever taken care of her."

"She's more than a friend, isn't she?"

"Possibly," Shasti admitted but didn't go into details.

A pat on her arm and a sympathetic smile told Shasti everything would be okay.

Once Allie left, Shasti checked her phone. No return text from Madison. It was time to re-read the Henderson file again anyway.

She'd only gotten ten minutes of reading done when there was a knock on the door. "The Hendersons are in room eight," one of the medical assistants assigned to her said.

Shasti grabbed the file, stood up, and headed to room eight. After greeting the young patient first, she greeted Mrs. Henderson. She settled on the wheeled stool and read over the vitals the MA took. "Everything looks good here. Well, the blood pressure does look a bit on the low side," she said to Jessie. "But nothing out of the ordinary. You might be the first person I've ever met with the opposite of white-coat syndrome."

Jessie smiled, but Shasti could tell she didn't know what white-coat syndrome meant. The young girl looked healthy on the outside. She was well-groomed. Her long dark blonde hair was shiny, and she had clear, smooth skin.

"Any episodes this week?"

Mrs. Henderson answered for her daughter. "Yesterday morning, she had to come home from school. I had to cancel a few appointments with clients to get her. Her father is useless right now."

"What does he do?" Shasti asked. It probably didn't matter to the case, but the mother seemed to want to vent.

"Besides sending the alimony checks late and canceling his time with his daughter so he can spend time with the twinkie he left me for?"

Shasti pressed her lips together.

"He works in banking. In Cincy."

Shasti nodded. There was a lot of stress at home then. That might be important. "The labs came back pristine again. This is very good. We're in the elimination game now. I have a few questions for Jessie. You are menstruating, yes?"

"Yes," Jessie said, sounding like she'd rather be anywhere other than sitting on an examination table answering invasive questions.

"Cramps and discomfort? Are they manageable?"

Jessie nodded.

Shasti reviewed the timing of the fourteen-year-old girl's periods and didn't find any pattern syncing them with the dizziness episodes. She seemed healthy in that regard. Unless…

"As I said, we're in elimination mode. I'd like to do a pregnancy test."

"Absolutely not," Mrs. Henderson said, looking appalled at the mere suggestion.

"Just to eliminate. If I ask my colleague to consult on Jessie's case, that will be one of the first things she'll ask about."

"Mom," Jessie said. "It's okay. I can pee on a stick."

"How do you know—"

"I took Health this year. Remember?"

Mrs. Henderson let loose the biggest sigh Shasti had ever heard and said, "Fine."

Shasti had her staff do another blood draw in addition to a urine sample to send to the lab for analysis. The pregnancy test was done in house, though, and it didn't take long for the results to pop up on

Shasti's laptop screen. "Negative," she said to the room. Mrs. Henderson grunted as if that whole thing had been a waste of time.

After checking Jessie's ears for wax buildup or anything out of the ordinary, she sent her down the hall for the hearing test. When that came back fine, she was still at a loss.

The eye movement test showed that Jessie tracked her pen almost perfectly. Various head positions produced no dizziness. Balance tests showed nothing.

Shasti had booked two back-to-back slots for the Henderson family, and they were reaching the end of both slots.

"We've ruled out diabetes, and today we've ruled out a few more things like vertigo. I don't think that's what's causing the issues."

Mrs. Henderson sighed and nodded. "You've done so many more tests than Dr. Murray ever did. That's why we came here. Thank you."

"Of course. Of course. We've got ourselves a real challenge."

"Mom," Jessie said, "we're going out for ice cream, right?"

Mrs. Henderson smiled at her daughter. "Of course. There's a chocolate fudge brownie cone in your future." She turned to Shasti and said, "It's a Henderson Family tradition. Go to the doctor, stop for ice cream."

"I like that. I'll have to pass that on to my patients with kids. I have a couple more questions for Jessie, if you don't mind."

"Please," Mrs. Henderson said and gestured toward her daughter.

Shasti stood tall and put her best Domme face on. "Are you eating?" Girls her age often got caught up in body image issues and played around with starvation or purging diets.

"Yes, Mom made oatmeal yesterday morning for me. She even sprinkled her famous cinnamon sugar mix on top."

"Lunch? Dinner?"

"She eats," Mrs. Henderson interjected.

Shasti nodded and then raised her eyebrows at Jessie, expecting an answer from the young girl herself.

Jessie looked confused momentarily but then said, "Yes, I eat. Mom makes good lunches. She even scoops out chocolate pudding into these to-go containers." Jessie smiled at her mother, and Shasti relaxed momentarily. It seemed like mother and daughter had a good nurturing relationship.

"Have you been drinking alcohol at school?"

"No," came the quick and honest reply unless this kid was amazing at lying.

"Drugs?"

There was a slight hesitation, and then she said, "No."

Shasti pursued. "Marijuana?"

"No." Jessie looked insulted.

"Cocaine?"

Jessie laughed, and when she said, "No," Shasti believed her.

"Heroin, crystal meth?"

"No and no." Jessie seemed agitated. "I don't do any of those kinds of things."

So, what do you do? Shasti wondered, her eyes flitting back and forth, analyzing the young woman's truthfulness.

"A friend's ADHD medication?" Shasti continued. "Ritalin? Adderall?"

"No, Dr. B, I don't do stuff like that. I promise." Jessie looked at her mom as if for help with the onslaught from the crazy doctor.

"Thank you for your honest answers," Shasti said, making some notes on the chart. She updated the blood test order form requesting an extensive tox screen for common popular drugs. There had been that slight hesitation on Jessie's part. It might be nothing, but it might be something. They were in elimination mode anyway. "Jessie, go ahead and get dressed while I chat with your mom in my office." She pushed the intercom button and asked the MA to get Jessie in about five minutes or so.

Once back in Shasti's office, she said, "We'll continue to search. But young people are into experimentation."

"Are you accusing my daughter of something?" Mrs. Henderson asked, obviously taking offense.

"No," Shasti said succinctly. "But we need to be aware that peer pressure is real. And not everyone has caring adults around them like she does. I'd pay great attention when she comes home from school. Ask her teachers privately if they've noticed any mood changes in the long run or on a day-by-day basis. Your divorce is recent, yes?"

"Yes," Mrs. Henderson said, letting loose an angry sigh. "Finalized about six months ago. No one seems to care, though. None of my friends have been around to help me through this. It's like I've been shunned. It's embarrassing for them to be with me or something. Divorce isn't catching. Just wait until they're in the middle of their divorces, see if I come running to console them. Doubt it. And on top of that, my mother moved in a few months ago. She's still with Dr. Murray, but she's got a host of health issues I must stay on top of. She needs more exercise if you ask me, but no one listens to me."

Shasti handed Mrs. Henderson a tissue and then stood up.

"I'm sorry you're going through all of this. And Jessie's issues aren't helping."

"No, but at least I get the occasional call from my supposed friends whenever Jessie has one of her episodes. They care more about her than me."

"There have been a lot of changes in your lives recently. Maybe Jessie is experimenting with substances in order to find something. Peace and balance, perhaps? I don't know." She walked Mrs. Henderson to the door. "Watch her behavior. Ask her teachers. Try not to accuse her of anything. That would be counter-productive until we're sure of something."

"Thank you, Dr. B," Mrs. Henderson said and shook Shasti's hand. "I appreciate your caring approach."

Shasti said a few more consoling words and ended with, "Take care," when the MA brought Jessie to her office.

Mrs. Henderson nodded, and she and her daughter walked toward the reception area.

Shasti made copious notes in the file and then leaned back to rub her eyes.

"Mr. Baldwin is ready in room seven, Dr. B," the MA said after knocking on her office door.

Shasti sighed. No rest for the weary. "Be right there." She pulled up his file. She usually liked more than a twenty-second lead-in before seeing a patient, but she'd needed the extra time on the Henderson case. Mr. Baldwin would get her best, she thought firmly as she headed for exam room seven.

~~~

Shasti and Madison sat at the kitchen table, finishing dinner. Madison ate the last of her spaghetti and wiped her mouth on her napkin.

Shasti took a sip of water and said, "Miss Phaneesa told me she didn't think you'd eaten while you were at the nursing home."

Madison shrugged. Shasti raised an eyebrow.

"Words," Madison said. "I know."

Shasti nodded.

"I had a bag of potato chips and some of Mrs. Park's lunch that she didn't eat. Like her jello and, um, what else?" She looked up at the ceiling as if trying to find the answers there. "Oh, yeah, her red fruit punch. It was okay. Kind of watered down."

"Let's pack a lunch for you to bring tomorrow. Does that sound okay?" Shasti picked up their dinner plates. Madison grabbed their salad bowls and cups and met her at the kitchen sink.

"Okay. Thank you."

Shasti put down the plate she was rinsing and looked at Madison.

"Okay. Thank you, *Miss Shasti*," Madison said quickly. "Sorry, this is new. Do you want me to finish the dishes, or should I go up and do my punishment?"

"Upstairs with you. The vacuum is—"

"In the hall closet," Madison finished. "Oh, shoot. I'm sorry. I interrupted you."

"On your knees, please," Shasti said and pointed at her feet with two fingers.

"What?" Madison looked around as if someone would help interpret what she was supposed to do.

"Get down on the floor on your knees. You can sit back on your heels if you wish."

Madison did as she was instructed and hung her head. "I'm sorry if I did something wrong. I don't remember all the rules, Miss Shasti."

"Ahh, but you remembered my honorific just now, didn't you?"

"Yes, Ma'am," Madison said, but there was no joy in it.

"You're on your knees in front of me because you are to remember that I am your Dominant. You do not ever interrupt a Dominant. Not me or Miss Rikki or Miss Tilda."

Madison put a hand up, obviously desiring to speak. Shasti had all she could do not to burst out laughing. "Yes, Madison."

"And Daddy Vic, Mr. Seamus, Mr. Tom, Mr. Josef, and Miss Lydia."

"Actually, the first three are correct, but Josef and Lydia are submissives. You can use honorifics with them if you wish, but only if they don't mind. Many subs don't want that."

"Oh," Madison said with a tired sigh. Yes, it was time to get her to bed.

"Up, up, up with you," Shasti said. "Rug inspection will be in ten minutes. Both rooms. My bedroom and the guest bedroom, where you will sleep the entire night on your air mattress. Understood?"

"Yes, Miss Shasti," Madison said, leaping to her feet and then bounding up the stairs.

Shasti shook her head. Madison was going to be a handful, wasn't she? Was she up to the task? Only time would tell.

After a moment or two, Shasti heard the upstairs vacuum cleaner whirring with slow and steady strokes. Ahh, good. Madison wasn't rushing through it. Shasti busied herself in the kitchen, cleaning up and packing a lunch for Madison. She honestly didn't know what the young woman liked to eat. That knowledge would come in time, so she packed a sandwich where the layers could easily be removed. Turkey, cheese, tomato, lettuce. A no-sugar-added applesauce container would also go in the bag.

Shasti threw in a plastic baggie filled with pretzels. It was the only kind of snack food she had in the house. A bottled water completed the homemade lunch. Shasti didn't have any brown paper lunch bags, so she pulled out a plastic grocery bag from the pantry and wrote Madison's name on it. She drew a smiley face next to Madison's name, filled the bag, and then tossed it in the fridge right in front so Madison would see it the following day before heading to the nursing home. She made a mental note to take Madison shopping. A lunch box or bag would definitely be on the list.

The vacuum cleaner headed to the guest room overhead. Good, she was following directions well. And the punishment surely did fit the "crime." If Madison was going to sleep on the floor again, Shasti wanted to make sure the carpets were halfway decent. Should she just let Madison sleep in the bed with her? Madison wanted to. And Shasti, well, she did, too, but she had to take this one slowly. She'd moved way too fast with Amber, and she wasn't going to make that same mistake twice. If she and Madison were going to get into a deeper long-term relationship, she wanted to make sure it was based on a solid foundation and not the short-term excitement of easy and ready sex. Like with Amber. A one-month trial period wasn't that long to wait. Was it?

"Finished, Ma'am," came the call from the second story.

"Be right up," came the answer from the Domme in the kitchen, hoping with fingers crossed that she was doing the right thing.

Shasti washed her hands and then bounded up the stairs. She hoped Madison would be amenable to what she was about to suggest.

"Miss Shasti?" Madison said, closing the closet door where the vacuum was stowed.

"Mm hmm?"

"I think I need to go back to the condo tomorrow."

"If that's what you want," Shasti said.

"I'm probably going to get thrown out by Ms. Elena, the condo manager. She's really pretty, but she has to do her job and all."

"We'll talk to Ms. Elena about what happens next, okay? I can stop by tomorrow after my workday is finished. Bring us some takeout?"

"You would do that?"

The look on Madison's face was as priceless as it was needy. Shasti opened her arms, and Madison dove into them. Shasti held her tight and rocked her for a moment.

"Peanut?"

"Mm hmm?" Madison's voice was muffled because her face was buried in Shasti's blouse.

"How about a bath? And before you get any ideas, I mean just for you."

Madison pulled back and shrugged. Obviously, she wasn't convinced this was a good idea.

"Before you turn it down, let me show you what I have for bath time." Shasti reached for Madison's hand, led her toward the guest bathroom, and opened the linen closet door. A big plastic barrel filled with shiny new bath toys sat on the floor. She hadn't gotten them for Madison specifically, just for someone someday.

Madison's eyes lit up. "Okay."

Shasti beamed. She'd let the lack of honorific go. There had to be a balance for that kind of thing, and a reprimand would be counterproductive at this moment as she tried to earn trust.

"Pick out a few toys. No, not all," Shasti said as Madison made to dump the entire contents in the tub. "Just a few. And when you're finished, you'll rinse them off and put them back in this plastic barrel."

"Yes, Ma'am," Madison said, not looking at Shasti. She pulled out toy boats and sea creatures along with Shasti's favorite – the miniature penguin that squirted water. Wait 'til Madison figured out it could do that.

Shasti turned on the tub water and waited until it got warm before plugging the drain. "Bubbles?"

All motion stopped as Madison stared at her wide-eyed. Tears filled her eyes as she looked from the bottle of bubble mixture to Shasti's face. "Really?"

"Why not?"

"Okay. I've never had bubbles before. Too expensive."

"Never?" It was Shasti's turn to tear up. She blinked them back as best she could and said in as calm a voice as she could muster, "Well, now's as good a time as any to try them. Sound good?" She waited for a nod from Madison before dumping in a few capfuls.

"Are you going to stay in here with me?" Madison asked.

Shasti couldn't read whether Madison wanted her there or not. "That's up to you," she said cautiously.

"You'll see me naked," Madison said with a teasing lilt to her big eyes.

"You've seen *me* naked," Shasti countered.

"Oh, yeah. Turn-about is fair play, I guess." Madison started shedding her clothes. At that moment, Shasti realized that Madison wasn't shy about showing her body. No, she had only been concerned that Shasti might be uncomfortable.

Not a single ounce of body fat on her, Shasti thought as Madison got in the tub. "Not too hot?"

"It's perfect," she said with an almost orgasmic moan. Shasti tried not to stare as she took in the lean body in the tub. If all went well, she'd have plenty of time to explore that body. They'd have plenty of time to explore each other.

Shasti let Madison play 'sea creatures destroy the Imperial fleet' for a while and then suggested that the actual washing process begin. Washing Madison's back was soothing for Shasti, for both of them, judging by Madison's soft exhales. No signs of scoliosis or anything abnormal. No signs of tenderness, either. Good. Shasti handed Madison a washcloth and some body wash so she could wash the rest of her body. Amazingly, Shasti had to give her some instructions when it came to washing. It was as if Madison had never been shown how to wash her ears or feet or anything properly. Hopefully, she was learning.

Bath time for her *little* was one bucket-list item, and being allowed to wash her *little's* hair was another. Amber never wanted bath time or pampering in the shower unless it led to sex. Madison practically purred as Shasti worked out the tangles using a cream rinse, especially for that purpose.

"Hands over your eyes," Shasti said before dumping fresh water over Madison's head and hair. "One more time. You are such a good girl. You take instruction so well."

"Am I forgiven then?"

"For what?"

"Sleeping on the floor of your room?"

Shasti kicked herself mentally. She had forgotten to give closure to the punishment.

"Umm, yes," Shasti said. "You accepted your punishment, and as far as I'm concerned, your transgression is forgiven and forgotten. We don't need to revisit it, and I, certainly, won't bring it up again."

"Really? That's not how things work at my house," Madison said, sinking the cargo ship with the world-dominating squirting penguin.

"Oh?"

"My grandma would bring up stuff my mother did, like years ago when she and my dad first got married. You know? Hold it over her head. Me, too. Even my dad. You just got used to it."

"It won't be that way with me, Madison. Unless it's for your safety."

"You're very concerned with my safety," Madison said with a giggle. "Like maybe you'd say, 'Remember that time you stuck a fork in the outlet, Madison? Best not try that again.'"

Shasti chuckled. "Is that what I sound like? But, yes. Things like that." She stood up from her seat on the edge of the tub. "Okay, water monkey, time to rinse off and put your toys away." She pointed to the detachable shower head. "You can use that to rinse off. Just take care not to spray the whole bathroom." And that was why bath time was happening in the guest bath and not the master, Shasti thought with the wiseness of Saraswati. "I'll leave you to it and get you a big towel to wrap up in when you're finished."

133

Madison didn't make a move to get out of the tub as if she hadn't heard Shasti and continued to sink her boats with the sea creatures.

"Madison?" The tone was stern but not sharp.

"Okay, fine." Madison unplugged the drain and then stood up. She clearly wasn't happy about bath time being over. She watched as all her toys got pulled toward the drain and into the tiny whirlpool. Keeping her gaze on the toys, she turned on the shower and got a full blast of water in her face. "Boomph," she sputtered until she got a handle on the shower head.

Shasti turned and left with the biggest smile on her face. "Bath time. Check," she whispered under her breath and made a checkmark in the air.

Shasti returned and wrapped Madison in a large white bath sheet as Madison shivered on the cold tile. "Come on," she said, let's get you dry and in your bed."

"Not with you?"

"No, peanut." Shasti sighed. "We haven't known each other very long. I want us to experience each other a while longer before we get that intimate."

"Okay. I'm okay with that, but not really. I'm disappointed I can't snuggle with you all night."

Shasti kissed Madison's forehead and then wiped at it even though her lipstick was long gone. Madison snuggled into Shasti even though she was wrapped up tight like a little Madison burrito.

"I put my toys away," came the muffled voice.

"I saw that. I'm very proud of you for being so responsible. Very grown-up."

Madison bounced in Shasti's arms. "When I feel more grown-up, can we have sex?"

Shasti almost choked on the question. "It's okay to have needs, peanut." Her fingers caressed Madison's youthful cheek. "I have needs, too."

"I know."

"And, yes, one day, I think that will be possible. And I'm glad you already understand that you must be feeling big."

"I know. I know."

"Okay, little one, we need to get you some pajamas," Shasti said. "I guess you'll have to swim in a pair of my old lady shorts and a t-shirt." A million ideas were running through her brain. Internet ordering would probably be the best idea. Buying a onesie for a twenty-something-year-old woman might be embarrassing for all involved. Best to keep this one under wraps. Not everyone gave consent to be part of other people's kinks.

Chapter 11

Madison

Thursday evening, there was a knock on the condo's front door. "I'll get it," Miss Shasti said. "That's got to be the delivery girls."

"How do you know it's girls?" Madison asked from the couch where they had been cuddling after visiting Ms. Elena in the condo office. Apparently, Mrs. Park's fees were paid up for the next few months, so Madison was free to stay for a while. She didn't know where she would go if she got kicked out, but Ms. Elena reassured her she had at least two more months there—through the rest of the summer at least. Yay.

Miss Shasti didn't answer Madison's question but opened the door wide. On the other side stood Miss Rikki and Daddy Vic. Madison leaped to her feet and ran to them. "Hi, you guys." She gave Miss Rikki a full wrap-her-arms-around-her hug. She gave Daddy Vic a side hug because she wasn't a full-on hugger like Miss Rikki.

"Good to see you, Madison," Miss Rikki said. Miss Shasti guided Miss Rikki to the kitchen with all the bags of food. This was so awesome. It was going to be a party.

"Squirt," Daddy Vic said, "you've got some amazing digs here." She tousled Madison's hair, causing her to giggle. "I need a tour."

"Okay," Madison said. She wanted to reach for Daddy Vic's hand, but she didn't. Miss Rikki would have taken it, but not so much Daddy Vic.

Madison showed Daddy Vic the condo, including Mrs. Park's bedroom with the stupid hospital bed and oxygen machine she'd never use again. She tried not to tear up but couldn't help it. Daddy Vic frowned and pulled Madison into a quick hug. "Sorry this is happening, squirt. But we need you to be tough and strong. Miss Shasti needs you to be strong, too."

"She does?" Madison asked, wiping her tears away.

"She cares a lot about you. We all do, and it hurts us when you're hurting."

"It does?"

Daddy Vic nodded. "This room is huge."

"Mine is the same size, except I don't have a private bathroom. I have to use the communal one near the living room."

"Come on. Show me this cavernous room of yours."

As soon as Madison opened the door to her bedroom, she knew it was a mistake.

"Madison Kim," came the stern voice from behind her. "You told me you were going to clean your room."

"Uh, oh," Miss Rikki said from somewhere.

"I, uh, I'm sorry." Madison hung her head. Why was she always doing the wrong thing? "I think I've been at the nursing place and then at your house and haven't had time."

"That is true," Miss Shasti said, her tone softer. "But a promise is a promise. How about tomorrow, after I'm done with my patients at 4:00, I come over and supervise clean-up? And if it's not done by the time I have to leave, there will be consequences."

"Not more consequences," Madison muttered.

"Excuse me?" Miss Shasti said. Her tone was not fun, and having other people hear it wasn't fun either. But! Madison kind of liked the fact that someone was paying attention to her in a good way. "I meant to say, 'Yes, Ma'am,'" Madison amended.

"Better," Miss Shasti said and then addressed the group. "Let's eat." She guided them to the kitchen table where Madison and Mrs. Park never sat, not even once.

As they filled their plates with the world-famous, according to Miss Rikki, Chen's Chinese food, the grownups talked and kind of gossiped a little. Madison wasn't going to point out what they were doing, but she was all ears anyway. Sometimes they turned away from her and talked behind their hands, so she couldn't hear what they were saying, but that was okay. These were friends who cared about her.

"So, where is the famous Eileen this evening?" Miss Shasti asked Miss Rikki.

"I left her in the office doing payroll," Miss Rikki said. "I'll pick her up on the way home from here." She turned to Madison and said, "This view is amazing. I wish you could keep this place. I think you can see the coffee shop from here."

"You can. It's kind of panoramic." Madison kicked her feet wildly back and forth. A firm grip on her thigh told her to stop. So, she did.

"This would make a great bachelor pad," Daddy Vic said as if scheming. "I'll have to find out what the rents are in this complex. Do you know how much units go for here, squirt?"

"Like rent?" Madison shook her head. "Mrs. Park told me that she owns it. Like, she doesn't pay rent."

"I'm sure there are homeowner's or maintenance fees," Miss Rikki added.

"Probably." Daddy Vic flicked her head to get the stray lock of hair out of her eyes. She was butch like Katia, but she was cool and suave, unlike Katia. Daddy Vic was handsome, too, with her white button-down shirt and black jeans. Her boots were cool, like she was a cowboy or a Texas ranger or something. "I can't afford to buy a place like this, but I have to do something because Mac and all his boy toys are driving me insane. It's a new guy every friggin' week. And who are these guys? I have to lock up my stuff in my room because I don't want anything to walk."

"Can't you talk to him?" Miss Rikki asked. Whoa, she sure loved lo mein noodles judging by the fresh mound on her plate. Madison asked Miss Shasti if she could have some more, too. Yay. Request granted.

"I *have* talked to him," Daddy Vic said. "To no avail. It's time, you know? I mean, he's been my best guy friend since forever, but sometimes living with somebody just doesn't work."

Madison hung her head. Maybe that's why Miss Shasti didn't want her to sleep in the same bed as her. It wasn't working out.

"Nope. Nope," Miss Shasti said and lifted Madison's chin. "No moping this evening."

"Okay," Madison said. She was surprised that anyone had even bothered to notice her mood. "Okay," she said again and sat up taller. Three swings of her legs were once again thwarted by the stiff grip on her thigh. "Sorry," she said in apology.

The grownups talked some more while Madison zoned out. Mrs. Park had looked pretty bad today. Her skin was gray, if you could believe that, and she didn't even wake up to smile at Madison. Not once. The other day Miss Shasti told her they were keeping Mrs. Park "comfortable" until it was time. Time for her to cross over, transition, walk across the rainbow bridge. People had thrown all those phrases at her as if she needed reminding about Mrs. Park's limited future, her numbered days, her ending walk on this earthly plane. Whatever time Mrs. Park had left, Madison vowed to be by her side every minute she could.

"So, peanut?" Miss Shasti said as everyone pushed their plates aside, apparently finished. "I asked Miss Rikki and Daddy Vic here this evening so I can give you some news."

"Did Mrs. Park die?"

Miss Shasti glanced at Miss Rikki and then nodded. "Yes, honey. I'm sorry. I asked the nursing home to call me whenever it happened."

"When?"

"This afternoon. Right after you left, sweetie."

"Right after I left?"

"Mm hmm," Miss Shasti said. "Maybe she was waiting until after you said goodbye."

Tears welled up in Madison's eyes. "I held her hand a lot today. And I kissed her on the hand before I left."

"She knew you were there, squirt," Daddy Vic said softly.

"I kept having to sign stuff while I was there," Madison said. "I don't know why."

Miss Shasti gestured for them to move into the living room and sat on the couch. She patted the seat next to her for Madison to sit on and pulled her into a side hug. Daddy Vic sat in the high-backed chair that nurse Eugenia always sat in when she was there.

"You okay, kiddo?" Miss Rikki asked as she slid into Mrs. Park's fancy recliner. That was okay. Mrs. Park wasn't going to need it anymore.

Tears welled up in Madison's eyes again.

"Aww, c'mere." Miss Shasti pulled her close.

Madison buried her face in Miss Shasti's shoulder and tried hard not to cry in front of her friends.

"It's okay," Miss Shasti soothed. "Let it out, little one. We need to cry sometimes. It helps the body manage the stress of bad news like this."

Madison answered by way of a sob. "I hardly even knew her," Madison said, swallowing hard between bouts of tears.

"How long have you been here?" Daddy Vic asked gently.

"Since January first."

"About six months," Daddy Vic said after doing the math. "That's a pretty long time. I think you really helped her while you were here, didn't you? Miss Shasti tells us that you've also been a big help at her house."

"She did?"

"She did," Miss Rikki said. Miss Rikki was so pretty. She was a redhead, although her hair wasn't really red, it was kind of coppery orangey brownish. She always stood straight upright and tall. She was not freakishly tall, but everyone at the coffee shop knew she was in charge.

"So, peanut," Miss Shasti said, "for whatever reason, and I don't know why, but Mrs. Park wanted me to wait until after she passed to tell you something."

Madison sat upright and took one of the wizard's magic tissues, and wiped at her eyes. She took another and blew her nose. She wasn't sure why Daddy Vic and Miss Rikki smiled when she did that, but whatever.

"What is it?"

Miss Shasti, usually so strong and stoic, took a shaky breath and wiped at her own tears. "Little one, Mrs. Park was your great-grandmother."

Madison sobered instantly. "What do you mean?"

Shasti took a deep breath and let it out. "She didn't want you to know any earlier in case her daughter found out where she was and that she was still alive."

"She's not alive anymore," Madison said and looked down. A gentle finger lifted her chin.

"I know, sweetie. I'm so sorry," Miss Shasti said. "Mrs. Park's daughter is the grandmother you live with. Mrs. Park was your father's grandmother."

"Really?" Madison's eyes got big. "Mrs. Park didn't like my grandmother. Wow. That means Mrs. Park didn't like her own daughter."

"Apparently, there was a big falling out when Mrs. Park's husband passed away all those years ago."

"Mrs. Park liked my mommy, though."

"Mm hmm. And you. She liked you very much." Miss Shasti shrugged as if she didn't hold the key to Madison's family. Neither did Madison. Did anyone?

The three grownups and Madison talked for over an hour after that, and then Miss Rikki and Daddy Vic said they had to leave. They gave their condolences as they left. Madison wasn't sure what that meant exactly, but it must have had something to do with Mrs. Park's passing away.

Once the front door was shut behind her departing company, Madison took Miss Shasti's hand. "Thank you for helping me."

"Of course. This is what Mommy Domme's do. I would do it even if—"

"Even if we weren't on a trial period?" Uh oh. The raised eyebrow again. What did she do? What did she do? Her mind frantically searched for the infraction. Oh, shoot. "I'm sorry for interrupting you, Miss Shasti." She fell to her knees and hung her head. "I wasn't thinking."

Miss Shasti pulled her up and into a hug. "Given the circumstances, I think I can forgive it this time." She let Madison go and said, "And, yes, I would be here helping you even if we weren't in a trial dynamic."

"How much longer?" Madison heard the whine in her own voice.

"Another three-and-a-half weeks."

"That's sooooo long."

"Let's pack a bag for you with fresh underpants, pajamas, and clothes for tomorrow. Bring any toys you want. Bring your tablet or laptop."

"I don't own a tablet or laptop," Madison said. "Not here or at home. I always had a loaner from the school library because our family could only afford one laptop, and you-know-who always got first dibs. He is in college after all."

Miss Shasti seemed, like, angry or something but said simply, "You streamed Mulan the other day." She led the way to Madison's messy room. It wasn't dirty, except for the almost finished glass of chocolate milk on the dresser, the old pizza crusts in the box on the floor, and the empty ramen noodle cups everywhere.

"I watched on my phone." Madison pulled out her grandmother's cast-off android phone and wiggled it around.

"Ahh, I see," Miss Shasti said. There was an odd lilt to her voice that Madison wasn't sure she truly heard. "There's been a change in plans. Tomorrow morning, I'll drop you off here, and you will have this bedroom cleaned and vacuumed to my satisfaction by the time I get here. Understood?"

"Yes, Ma'am."

"Suitcase?"

Madison shook her head but ran to the closet and pulled out her Brookside High Softball duffel bag. Coach Meers always let seniors keep the bags at the end of the season. Her mother had packed her stuff in it the morning she got put on the bus for Cincinnati.

"Get to packing, kid," Miss Shasti said as she picked up the pizza box and glass of milk. "You have ten minutes to pack everything you want at my house. I don't want you to be alone tonight."

"Okay." Madison called after her, "Can I bring my sword?"

"Yes," came the faint answer from the kitchen.

~~~

Madison smacked Billy on the arm once they were on the path to Africa. "Tag, you're it!" She raced down the path toward the giraffes and lions.

"Oh, no, you don't," Billy said, chasing after her.

Madison glanced over her shoulder. He was so cute, thinking he could catch her. She actually slowed down a little so he could.

"Okay, okay," he said, completely out of breath. "You win." Billy looked cute in his khaki cargo shorts and blue batman t-shirt. His boyish, dirty blond hair made him look like the boy next door. She wished he lived next door. But then again, Madison wasn't really sure where she lived anymore. It had been two weeks since Mrs. Park passed away, and Madison hadn't spent one single night at the condo. She stayed with Miss Shasti, who was afraid Madison would be scared and have bad dreams. Miss Shasti had even let Madison sleep in her bed sometimes. But no touching. At first. More than once, though, Madison had woken up as the little spoon, and it was so perfect that she never wanted to move.

"Say it," Madison said, looking over her shoulder as she stopped jogging. She was a little more out of breath than she should be. Hmm, maybe she needed to start working out again. The yoga she did with Miss Shasti was cool and all, but she missed working out with the team. Well, until she became known as the "rug muncher" to her teammates. And then somehow, the whole rest of the school found out and started calling her that, too. Even the stupid boys pressed themselves against her any chance they got. No one ever stopped them. Well, Latisha did that one time in the hallway when there was no teacher around. But that one time didn't make a difference because the boys kept getting bolder and bolder. Who knows what would have happened if Coach Meers and the chorus teacher hadn't...No, she didn't want to think about that day which turned out to be the last day she physically went to school. Some grownups had finally figured out that Madison was getting super harassed by, oh, everybody, and they looked out for her. Coach Meers was probably the main one. She could be fierce when you crossed her.

"Say it," Madison repeated.

Billy held his side as they moved out of the way of zoo visitors walking the path. "Fine. Madison rules. Billy drools." He rolled his eyes. "Whatever."

Madison bounced on her toes and watched Miss Shasti and Mr. Seamus make their way up the wide pathway toward them.

Madison jumped when Billy started talking out of nowhere. "Are you under consideration with Miss Shasti?"

"What does that mean? Like a trial period?"

"Yes, exactly." Billy took one last deep breath and let it out. "Did she list you as her sub on her *Kinks* page?"

Madison shrugged. "I don't have a *Kinks* page, but she showed me hers a while ago."

"Wait, you don't have a *Kinks* page?" Billy frowned as if Madison had just dissed the Queen of England. "You have to get one. Ask Miss Shasti, and please heed my advice here. Do not try to make one on your own." He rolled his eyes. "Believe me. It will go badly, and your Domme will be angry and take you over her knee."

Madison gasped. She surprised herself at how cartoonish it sounded to her own ears. "Like for a spanking?"

Billy nodded big. The grownups were almost upon them, so Billy leaned in close and said, "Not all spankings are bad. Fun-ishment spankings are fun. I mean, they hurt, but they hurt good. Know what I mean?" He elbowed her in the side, and she pushed him away playfully.

No, she didn't know what he meant and had no chance to ask since the grownups were suddenly right there.

"Hey, speedy Gonzales," Mr. Seamus said to Madison. "Miss Shasti tells me you've been a good girl. She said you cleaned out your room at the condo and have kept your things neat and tidy at her house."

Madison stood up taller and twisted from side to side. "Yes, sir. I even rolled up the cords and hoses on the oxygen machine and put it near the front door. I washed the sheets on the hospital bed and unplugged everything, too. They came and got that stuff last week."

"This zoo trip is your reward, apparently," Mr. Seamus said and got them all walking again. "I'm happy Billy and I were invited." He looked pointedly at Billy, who seemed to finally come out of his fog, and said, "Thank you for inviting us, Miss Shasti."

"Anytime, Billy."

"Thanks for coming with us," Madison said. "Hurry, hurry, hurry. The park closes at five o'clock."

"It's only ten in the morning, peanut," Miss Shasti said.

"Oh, I usually rush because, you know, I have to…had to" Her chest tightened up as she remembered having to rush home to take care of Mrs. Park. She blinked back the stupid tears that kept building. Miss Shasti pulled her into a side hug as they walked.

"We know, sweetie." Miss Shasti sighed. "You really helped your great-grandmother when she needed it." She gave one of Madison's braids a light tug which made Madison smile. Miss Shasti sure liked playing with Madison's hair. Some days it was a ponytail, and other days, it was one braid or two like today. The bun on top of the head that one time was super weird, but Miss Shasti said Madison would come to like that style. She also said it made Madison look sexy and grown-up. Those were definitely words to store in the memory banks for future use. Especially the word 'sexy.'

Madison swiped at her nose with the side of her index finger. "Can we have Dippin' Dots?" It was an odd thing to say when Miss Shasti was trying to comfort her, but maybe Dippin' Dots were just the comforting she needed.

"Think long and hard about what sweet thing you want," Miss Shasti said. "Because there will be only one. Isn't there an ice cream stand in here somewhere? With gummy bear toppings?"

Madison's eyes grew big. "Yes, there is," she said slowly. Holy cow, she had almost blown her chance for ice cream. What had she been thinking? Her grandmother would have said, "You weren't, obviously."

A smack on her arm stopped all irritating thoughts about her grandmother. "Tag, you're it." Billy took off toward the giraffes that were now in sight.

"Pfft," Madison said, waiting a moment to give him a bigger lead. Like the cheetahs in the Cheetah Encounter, Madison took off and overtook Billy in a matter of seconds. She patted him on the back and said, "Tag, you're it."

After giraffes, lions, cheetahs, and all manner of African animals, they made their way around the zoo. Madison kept looking back at Miss Shasti, wondering if maybe she liked Mr. Seamus. *Like* liked him. But maybe not. Miss Shasti said she didn't like boys that way. Well, Mr. Seamus was a man, of course, but maybe she was bi or something. Or polyamorous. She'd read about those kinds of people that had relationships and sex with different people simultaneously. Was Miss Shasti like that?

"Hey, Billy," Madison said, using a tone that meant this was for his ears only. She was still a little mad at him for dissing the bird encounter, but the look Miss Shasti shot her told her to let it go. They could see the bird encounter another time. Fine. Whatever. The reptile house Billy dragged them to was pretty cool, actually.

"What?" Billy was transfixed on a massive python in a glass-walled cage. Miss Shasti and Mr. Seamus sat on a low wall talking quietly to each other. Good, she had Billy all to herself.

"Mr. Seamus doesn't just have you, right? Like he has a few more guys at home?"

"Mm hmm," Billy said, clearly distracted by the sleeping python. "This thing eats its prey whole. It can swallow a human."

"That's kind of scary," Madison said, looking at the snake for the first time. She tapped the placard on the fence. "And this says people have them as pets. No way."

"Not me," Billy said as they moved on to the tarantula tanks. "Why do you want to know about Papa?" Billy tapped the glass. The large black furry creature didn't move. It was probably aggravated that everybody kept tapping its house.

"I'm curious. That's all."

"Papa has four subs. I'm his only *little*, though. There's Mark—he's nice. He works at Miss Rikki's coffee shop. She's nice, too."

"I like both of them."

"Umm, DeShawn is quiet. He's really really submissive. I think he's kind of shy, too, so naturally, Mark and Sanjey pick on him. I feel bad. DeShawn's the new guy, so you know. Lowest one on the totem pole. I don't know what that means, but that's how Papa describes it."

"DeShawn's the cute Black guy with the cool facial hair? He was at the party, right?"

"Yeah. Sometimes Papa makes him watch me when he goes to be with Mark or Sanjey, you know, for their private times. Sometimes I hear Mark yelling as Papa whips him in the basement."

"Mark consents to that?"

"Yes, he does. He loves it. He told me. Did you know that Papa is teaching Miss Rikki how to wield the whip?"

"Really?" Madison's eyes were wide again. "I don't think I'd want that, like ever." Did Miss Rikki whip her sub, Eileen? If so, good. Eileen wasn't nice.

They moved past the vipers and rattlesnakes and poison dart frogs. All of which were very interesting, but Madison was much more interested in Billy's home life. "Have you ever had private time with DeShawn or the other guys?"

"No, no. Papa won't allow that. They don't know how to be gentle with me," Billy said. "But he lets them be with each other sometimes, but not all the time. He cages them up."

"What does that mean?"

Bill leaned in close and said, "You know. He locks up their pee-pees, so they can't, you know, get excited or have sex."

"Whoa," Madison said wide-eyed. "That's a thing?"

Billy gave her his full attention as he nodded. "Just wait until October. Papa calls it 'Lock-tober,' and we all get caged. Maybe Miss Shasti will lock up your private parts, too." His brow furrowed, and he added, "But I have no clue how that would work on a girl." He smacked her on the arm and said, "Come on, let's go see the alligators. Maybe it's feeding time."

Madison looked behind her to make sure Miss Shasti and Mr. Seamus were following. Miss Shasti smiled at her, and Madison smiled back. She felt her cheeks get warm and something nice settle in her chest. She liked Miss Shasti. Really liked her. *Like* liked her.

Did Miss Shasti invite Mr. Seamus along so she could pick his brain about having a house full of submissives? Miss Shasti's house was kind of big. Lots of bedrooms. Was it four or five? And that big yard could hold parties like Miss Tilda's. Madison looked back again, and Miss Shasti made an "Are you all-right" question with her face. Madison smiled and then waved like a silly person. Miss Shasti smiled back, telling her she understood, and Madison's whole body bloomed with feels. Uber gooey sugary feels.

Madison liked going to the zoo with Billy and Mr. Seamus, but she wished she could be alone with Miss Shasti right now. It was so not fair that she had to wait one and a half more weeks before Miss Shasti decided if she was going to keep Madison or give her away to someone else. And they hadn't even had sex yet. Not real sex. Yep, kind of wasn't fair.

Chapter 12

Shasti

Shasti knocked on the door to exam room sixteen, her business partner Allie's favorite exam room. It was ridiculous that it had taken over two weeks to get an appointment for Madison in Shasti's own health clinic. One that she half-owned. But that meant their practice was thriving, which was a good thing.

"Hey," Shasti said to Madison, who sat on the exam table in only a hospital gown.

"Hi, Miss Shasti," Madison said, almost relieved.

Shasti smiled at Madison and then turned to Allie. "Thanks for staying late. How did it go?"

Allie nodded as if getting her thoughts together. Uh, oh, this might not be good.

"First of all, Madison gave HIPAA authorization to you, her mother, Soo-jin Kim, and someone named Rikki Carmichael, so I am legally free to discuss the results of her physical with you. Isn't that right, Madison?"

"Yes, Ma'am," Madison said, swinging her legs. One raised eyebrow at Madison halted the swinging.

"Pretty healthy young lady here," Allie said. "Lungs sound good, and she's strong. Her hair and nails are looking okay, but I'd say there were some long-term nutritional deficiencies at some point, so a healthy diet will be important. Under your care, Shasti, she'll be in top shape in no time." She looked down at the notes on her laptop and added, "Just a couple of things I'd like you to follow up on, but I'd like you two to talk it over and decide what you want to do. For example, her eyes look healthy, but I think she needs corrective lenses."

Shasti nodded. "A referral to Dr. Nix then?"

"Sounds good." Allie made a note in Madison's file on the laptop. "Reggie will print the referral for you when you leave." Allie looked from Shasti to Madison and back again. "And a dentist trip is sorely in order. I didn't see anything major, and she says she's not in pain, but I'd get her set up with annual checkups right away."

It was all Shasti could do not to let her blood pressure skyrocket. How could Madison's family…No, she would seethe later. Right now, she needed to be present and nurturing to this dear sweet *little* who might be overwhelmed. Clearly, visits to doctors and dentists were non-existent in Madison's childhood. And besides, she had to keep calm because Madison might think Shasti was mad at her. Far from it.

"And finally, the ears," Allie said. "There is extensive hearing loss, but I believe it is due to the excessive wax build-up on both sides. I'd like to go ahead and get some of it out today, all of it if I can. And if she needs a specialist, we can find her one, but we'll see if I can get it all."

"You always like to care for your patients in-house, don't you, Dr. Littrell?" Shasti asked for Madison's benefit.

"Always." Allie looked at Madison and said, "I take care of my patients as if they were part of my extended family."

"See, peanut?" Shasti said. "You're in excellent hands."

Madison nodded, swung her legs twice, and stopped on her own as if remembering she shouldn't be doing that.

Allie closed her laptop and stood. "You two talk things over. I'll be in my office. Buzz me if you want to proceed today."

"Thank you, Dr. Littrell," Shasti said and looked pointedly at Madison.

Madison took the hint immediately. "Thank you for helping me, Dr. Littrell."

The smile Allie shot Madison was a genuine one. Once Allie was out of the room, Shasti said to Madison, "How do you feel?"

"Okay, I guess," Madison said. "When can I get dressed?"

Shasti chuckled. "Soon. Let's talk about the ear wax situation. I think we should let Dr. Littrell try to remove it. It will—"

"Okay," Madison interrupted.

Shasti wanted to raise her eyebrows and reprimand Madison for interrupting but didn't. Before she could say anything else, Madison said, "She gave me a woman's wellness exam." Her voice turned to a whisper. "And she's checking me for STDs and stuff, too."

"Mm hmm," Shasti said. "Best to check everything, right? I regularly get checked and am always STD free. That's a good thing to know, right? Especially since you didn't ask about that before you, uh, you know."

Madison frowned and then looked down. "I'm sorry. I should have, I guess." She looked back up and said, "That part of the exam was quick, and she said it was really important, and I figured you would think it was important, and I didn't want you to be disappointed with me, so I told her it was okay." Before Shasti could respond, Madison blurted, "I've been really helping you, Miss Shasti. Like fixing your broken gate to the backyard, reattaching that loose wire in the lamp, and bracing that shelf in the pantry. You need better tools, though, but are you sending me away, Miss Shasti? I know I'm in bad shape, but I can be helpful. Could you not send me back to Columbus? Give me to somebody here. Okay. Will you? Please?"

Shasti pulled her into a hug and rocked her. "I'm not sending you away, sweet thing. Whatever gave you that idea?" She stepped back and ran her knuckles down the sweet, scared face. "As a matter of fact, I was thinking, maybe in a few days from now, oh, Saturday perhaps, about asking you to be in an official full-time dynamic with me. And if I did ask you that sometime on Saturday, what do you think you would say?"

"On Saturday? Like two days from now?"

"Mm hmm."

Madison searched Shasti's face for a moment as if trying to decide if she was serious, and then a small smile crept up her face. "I would say yes, Miss Shasti. I would say yes."

"And, on Saturday, if I were to ask you to live with me in my house and make Denton Heights your permanent residence, would you also say yes?"

Madison leaped off the table, her gown opening up in the front, and slammed a hug into Shasti. "Would you really ask me that? Really?"

Shasti nodded and kissed Madison on the forehead.

"Then I will say yes, on Saturday, I mean, because I can't think of anything better than that."

"You'll be mine then?" Shasti asked, her heart so full that she was sure Allie could hear the loud thumps in her office.

"Yes, of course, I'll be yours. Would that make you mine, too?" Madison seemed shy when asked, but Shasti put her fears at ease.

"Of course. We'll be partners. Through thick and thin."

Madison squeezed Shasti again, almost knocking the wind out of her.

"Can I call you something other than Miss Shasti?"

"I guess, but why?"

Madison laid her head on Shasti's shoulder. "Because Billy and all the other subs call you that. I want you to be special. I want them to know that you're mine and only mine. That's part of it, right? No other partners or whatever like Mr. Seamus?"

"No other partners for either of us. Agreed."

"Yay," Madison said into Shasti's shirt collar and wiggled around.

"Okay, wiggle butt," Shasti said. "Get back up there. I'll tell Dr. Littrell that you're ready for the procedure."

"Will you stay?"

"If you want me to," Shasti said.

Madison nodded as she hopped up on the table. She swung her legs to and fro, and Shasti did nothing to stop it. Let her have her joy. Shasti used the intercom to let Allie know the procedure was on.

Allie and her MA took quite some time to clear all the wax, but Allie declared both ears a success and gave Shasti aftercare instructions. Since Madison was so woozy, Shasti helped her get dressed, sat her in a wheelchair the MA ran out to fetch, and wheeled her to her own office. She helped Madison lay down on the couch while her equilibrium rebalanced.

Shasti plopped down in her executive chair and caught up on charts and emails. She wasn't very productive because she kept stealing glances at her new, not-yet-official submissive. Okay, on Saturday, it would be official. She tossed her work stuff aside and texted Rikki and Victoria to give them the good news and get the ball rolling. Rikki texted back with her congratulations and said she would get the word out and would take care of everything, including the special things they'd discussed earlier. After verifying times for the collaring ceremony and subsequent party afterward, Shasti sat back in her chair and watched her future doze on the couch.

After half an hour or so, Madison sat up. "Hi," she said and used that endearing wave that melted Shasti into a puddle.

"I have thoughts," Shasti said.

"Whoa," Madison covered her ears with her hands. "Holy shit. That was really loud."

"Language, young lady," Shasti said, being sure to reprimand quietly. "Your ears are sensitive right now."

"Sorry," she whispered. Madison blinked her eyes a few times and then swiveled her head toward the door. "What's that?"

"Sounds like one of the MA's getting room eight ready for tomorrow."

"I heard that. This is weird." Madison swiveled her head toward the window. "I hear a bird. Look, look—a cardinal. I heard him. That's the name of your street, Miss Shasti. Cardinal Lane. Named after the Ohio state bird." She looked back at Shasti and hung her head. "Sorry for cursing. I'll do extra chores or pushups or something, but this is so cool. I can hear stuff."

"Thank you for your apology." Shasti held in her own emotions and couldn't help the smile on her face. "How about this? We drop by the condo, get more of your things, and then get some take-out to bring home?"

"Okay, Miss Shasti," Madison said and stood up unsteady. "Whoa." She held her hands out on both sides for balance. "They really dug and dug in my ears, didn't they?"

"They did, but Dr. Littrell did everything safely. She said you probably won't need an ear specialist after all, and with some proper ear care, you won't ever have to go through this again."

"Thank goodness." Madison looked at the cardinal again and then asked, "Did I dream it, or are you really making us official? On Saturday?"

Shasti was on her feet with her arms wrapped around Madison in an instant. "It's real, baby. It's real."

They headed out of the clinic via the side door, and Shasti drove them to the condo. The ding of an incoming text forced her to stay in the car, letting Madison get a head start. Ahh, it was her parents. She'd been a bit awol lately, so she sent them a quick text saying she was doing well and would give them a call on Sunday – their usual call day. Would she tell them she was in a new relationship? Maybe. She'd play that one by ear. She smiled at her mother's return text. The one that said she loved her. Shasti sent a return text saying she loved them, too, and waited. Yep, true to form, her mother sent one more text. This one told her to enjoy her evening. Shasti didn't dare text back because her mother had a serious case of last-text syndrome, so she left it at that.

Before she could get her texting app closed, she heard Madison calling for her. She looked up to see Madison beckoning for her to come into the condo office. When Shasti entered the office, Elena, the pretty Latina property manager, sat behind an official-looking deep cherry desk. Her long deep black hair was pulled back into a tight high ponytail, giving her a more extreme look than Shasti thought the job of condo manager warranted, but whatever. And the well-fitting suit seemed kind of stifling. Shasti forced herself to stop with the negativity when she realized that what she was feeling was classic jealousy. Elena was not about to scoop up her darling new submissive and whisk her away. *Get a hold of yourself, Shasti.*

Madison had a pen in her hand and looked like she was about to sign something official.

"Stop," Shasti said. "What's happening here?"

"Mrs. Park's lawyer called," Elena said. "He had a copy of the will."

"And this?" Shasti gestured to the official-looking paper.

"Well, apparently, Mrs. Park left the condo to her great-granddaughter." She gestured toward Madison with an open hand.

Shasti was floored. "Do you have a copy of the will?"

"Just the part that pertains to the condo." Elena rooted around her desk and handed the printout to Shasti.

Shasti's hand on Madison's shoulder effectively halted all signing and further movement. She wasn't that well-versed in legalese, but it seemed pretty straightforward. "Looks like you own a condo, little one."

"Really?" Madison said wide-eyed. She looked from Shasti to Elena and back again. She rubbed one of her ears as if the noise level was bothering her again.

Shasti nodded instead of speaking.

"Whoa," Madison said and looked down at the form she was about to sign. "I'm allowed to have a condo?"

"Yes, honey," Shasti said with a muted chuckle. She took a seat next to Madison. "Good things are allowed to come into your life."

"Like you?" Madison said. The look on her face was pure something. Love? Lust? Both? Yes, both.

Shasti cleared her throat. They weren't alone. "Um, yes," she said to Madison. She could see Elena's grin out of the corner of her eye. Good. She wasn't judging them. Shasti didn't care, but she was soon to be the official worrier of all things Madison. Madison had had enough abuse and neglect for a lifetime, and it was time to change that. Yes, this beautiful soul in the next chair over was about to be hers.

Shasti looked over the form. "I think we'll get in touch with this lawyer before signing anything, but it does look legit."

"I've seen these before," Elena said to Shasti. "They're real. But I appreciate you looking out for this one. She's got a pure, innocent soul. Not every day, something worth well into six-digits falls into your lap."

Elena then bombarded them with information about the condo, including the obligatory maintenance fees. She rooted around her desk for a thick booklet of condo rules which included procedures for filing grievances, renting the unit, and a dozen other fun things Shasti knew she and Madison would be reading at some point.

An incredible warmth seeped through Shasti's core. Someone, finally, in that family, had the nerve to think about Madison and had the guts to take care of her. *Good for you, Mrs. Park.*

"Okay, come on, kiddo," Shasti said. "Let's get your stuff, get food, and go home." And by home, she meant the house on Cardinal Lane.

~~~

Shasti had been looking forward to this moment ever since Madison asked if they could do another rope scene. Okay, she hadn't used the word "scene" per se, but that's what it was.

"Why do I have to be in my underwear for this one?" Madison said as she took off her shorts and t-shirt. "And why do I have to stand?"

"Those are the cutest little boi shorts," Shasti said, running her hand down the side completely not answering Madison's questions. Tomorrow was the big official collaring day, but this evening was designed to solidify their commitment to each other in both their minds. Shasti was all in. She had to make sure Madison was, too.

Shasti found the center of her rope and draped it over Madison's neck. She'd wanted to do the rope play in her bedroom, but that would tip her hand too soon. One overhand knot resting against Madison's spine later, and Shasti was ready to create the series of four knots that would travel down Madison's front. She kept her eyes on her work but felt Madison's quiet gaze on her. Somehow, she wasn't sure how, but she felt Madison relax and submit to the smooth rope wrapping around her body. A soft exhale told Shasti that Madison was content. Good.

Shasti measured the hanging rope for length and then created the happy knot. She'd tried it on herself a few times but never on an actual rope bottom. She looked Madison right in the eyes as she reached a hand between Madison's thighs and tapped first one inner thigh and then the other.

Madison's eyebrow raised in question, but she spread her legs slightly as bidden. Ahh, yes, her breathing was changing already. That was quick. Shasti snaked the rope through Madison's legs and was pleased when the happy knot hit the area where Madison's clit would be under the boi shorts. Shasti stepped behind Madison and pulled up, causing the knot to make serious contact. Madison's sharp intake of breath told her that she'd hit the mark.

Shasti looped the ends of the rope through the loop created by the original knot. She tugged up a couple of times as if adjusting things, but in reality, she was causing the happy knot to rub against ground zero. Madison made a slight strangled sound causing Shasti to smirk behind her victim.

She separated the rope, brought the individual ends around and then up and over Madison's small breasts, and then created another line underneath. Yet another went around Madison's waist nice and snug. As she created the friction knots in the back, it was all Shasti could do not to reach around and splay her hand over Madison's stomach and pull her closer. Her lips would be on Madison's neck, instantly devouring her. The tiniest of moans escaped during an exhale. The slight tilt of Madison's head let Shasti know that Madison had heard it. Oh, yes, Madison knew what was going to happen. Soon.

Shasti secured the final knot and tucked the remaining ends in the back. She made a pretense of checking her work by running her hands down every rope line in the back. Without lifting her hand, she ran it around Madison's torso to the front. She traced the lines over and then under Madison's breasts. Madison's nipples peaked behind the cotton sports bra, but Shasti didn't comment or even meet Madison's gaze. Shasti ran her hands slowly down the lines leading to the happy knot but stopped shy of it. She stepped closer. She looked up to see Madison's eyes glazing over with lust and arousal. Shasti's own breathing had gotten heavier. She looked from Madison's eyes to her lips.

"Please, Miss Shasti," Madison said with a half-moan. "Please kiss me."

Shasti closed the distance, her lips slamming into Madison's with a need so great that she almost scared herself. Madison's arms went around Shasti's neck; Shasti's went around Madison's waist and pulled her tighter. Madison's lips were soft but urgent. Shasti slipped her tongue into Madison's mouth, and Madison received it willingly. Tongues stroked tongues. Moans matched moans. Shasti insinuated one thigh between Madison's and pressed against the knot. Madison's head lolled back as she moaned at the touch. Her eyes fluttered closed. Hey, not bad for a first kiss.

"Miss…"

"Yes?" Shasti did her best to sound nonchalant but knew she wasn't pulling it off.

Madison was breathless when she said, "Mistress, please. Please take me. Here. Upstairs. Anywhere."

"You sure?"

"Yes, yes, yes. I consent," Madison murmured and captured Shasti's mouth again in a feverish kiss.

Shasti reluctantly pulled away but grabbed the center knot under Madison's breasts and pulled her toward the stairs to her bedroom. Shasti climbed the steps backward, amazed that she could do so, but she didn't want to lose contact with the young woman in her grasp.

Madison resisted Shasti's pulling when they reached the full-length mirror. "This is beautiful, Miss Shasti." She gestured to her reflection.

"Thank you," Shasti said, hearing the huskiness of her own voice.

"Too bad you have to take it off me now." Madison's tone was almost shy.

"Let me get some pictures first." Shasti took several pictures from all angles, including a few without Madison's face. Those would be good for Madison's inevitable *Kinks* page.

Satisfied with the pictures, Shasti moved behind Madison and made good on her previous fantasy. She reached around Madison's body, splayed her hand on Madison's stomach, and pulled her back until their bodies met. Her lips found Madison's neck, kissing and licking and sucking.

"Please, Mistress," Madison pleaded. "Please take this off me. All of it." Madison tugged on the knots.

Shasti stepped back and cursed her non-foresight in the removal of the rope harness. She grabbed the juncture of knots against Madison's back, maneuvered Madison to the bed, and practically threw her on it. She undid the knots as quickly as possible, peppering the young woman beneath her with kisses everywhere a knot had been. This was the young woman whose STD screening came back clean and clear that very morning, giving Shasti the early green light. The collaring ceremony was less than twenty-four hours away. Close enough.

The long red rope got tossed aside, and Shasti teased a finger under Madison's bra. "May I?"

"Consent given." Madison sat up and let Shasti remove the pesky article of clothing.

"So pretty," Shasti said, stroking Madison's breasts with her fingertips, teasing the already erect nipples. She pushed Madison on her back and asked permission to remove the boi shorts, which she got instantly. The light earthy scent from Madison's arousal catapulted a jab of lust through Shasti's core. "You keep trimmed," she said in surprise.

"Yes," Madison said succinctly.

"Beautiful." Shasti leaned down and placed a kiss on the trimmed hairs covering Madison's mons. She kissed her way back up Madison's now nude body, savoring the trip. Which new spot would become a favorite? She reached the small breasts and dipped her head to tease one nipple and then the other with her tongue. Madison arched up in an attempt to increase the pressure, but Shasti backed away. She gave up the game immediately, though, and used both hands to scoop one breast into her mouth. She sucked and licked and nipped and then focused on the other.

Madison lifted her pelvis, obviously trying to create contact. It was time. Shasti moved up and captured Madison in another searing kiss while her hand moved down Madison's body. She didn't hesitate or tease this time. Shasti's fingers slaked their way over Madison's mound, made brief and seemingly accidental contact with her clit, and slid through the slickness Shasti knew would be there. Shasti moaned her approval into Madison's mouth, and Madison moaned her own into hers.

Shasti swirled two fingers around Madison's labia, coating them well, then swirled them around Madison's erect clit. Oh, yes, this woman was ready to burst. Madison bucked her hips in perfect rhythm to Shasti's swirls, and then Madison's head lolled back into the pillow. Her hips stopped bucking. It was like all time and space ceased to exist. Madison's orgasm ripped through and broke the ephemeral stillness. Her back arched, her hips bucked, and her face contorted as if in pain. One hand flew to the back of Shasti's head as she crushed her lips against her lover's.

As the kiss slowed and the bucking hips ceased, Shasti pulled back and kissed Madison on the forehead, one cheek, and then the other. "Are you okay?"

Madison moaned her exhale. "Yes. I didn't know it could be like this."

"Like what, baby?"

"So good. I've never cum so fast or hard." Madison blinked her sleepy eyes open and captured Shasti's lips again to kiss her several times. She fell back on the pillow with a sigh. "Thank you, Mistress. Thank you. I love you so much." She swiped at the tears in her eyes.

Shasti blinked back her own tears as she said, "I love you, too, peanut."

They lay quietly in each other's arms for a few minutes until Madison maneuvered herself on top of Shasti. Shasti nodded her permission as Madison began undoing the buttons on Shasti's shirt. "I know you'll fall asleep as soon as you cum, Mistress, but I have to ask if I can stay here and sleep next to you after you do."

"Yes, yes, yes," Shasti said, grabbing Madison's chin tenderly. "This night and every night after that."

The smile taking up Madison's entire face told Shasti she'd made the right decision. Many right decisions.

Chapter 13

Madison

Madison was trapped against the countertop, her back to the sink. Miss Shasti's hands gripped the edges on either side, effectively keeping her imprisoned. That was okay, though. Madison's own arms were wrapped around her mistress's neck as they kissed passionately.

"You slay me, peanut," Miss Shasti said breathlessly.

"We didn't get much sleep last night," Madison said mischievously. Sex with Miss Shasti had been outstanding. It was way more than she ever thought possible with anyone. And morning sex? Waking up to someone kissing you all over? Yes, please.

"Sleep is for sissies," Miss Shasti said with a smirk.

Madison could tell by the deepness of Miss Shasti's voice that she was aroused. Again. But they couldn't go back upstairs for more because Miss Shasti said company was coming over. That was nice, but wasn't Miss Shasti supposed to ask her to be her forever person today? Or official partner or whatever it was called? Maybe after the company left. Another incoming kiss. No time for troubling thoughts.

"You called me Mistress last night," Miss Shasti said after devouring Madison's lips with her own.

"Was that okay? I read on *Kinks* that some people call their person Mistress."

"I like it. Will that be what you call me from now on?"

Madison nodded, then remembered that Miss Shasti—no, Mistress liked actual words in response. "Yes, Mistress." She couldn't help the grin spreading up her face.

"Good."

The doorbell rang, and Mistress moved out of the way. "Tag, you're the door person today."

"Okay." Madison skipped to the front door and opened it wide. She had a too-late thought that maybe she should have peered through the peephole to see who it was, but oh, well.

"Billy," Madison screeched, "what are you doing here?"

"I don't know," he oh-so-obviously lied. He took off for the kitchen before she could call him on it. He had a big box under his arm.

Madison didn't know what to do, so she ushered in her next company. "Hi, Mr. Seamus. Come on in. Mistress is in the kitchen. Can Billy and I go out back and play?"

"Not just yet," Mr. Seamus said. "He's kind of dressed up at the moment. So are you. You look nice."

"Oh, thanks." She shut the door behind him. Madison looked down at some of the new clothes Mistress had ordered online for her. There was a short-sleeved button-down shirt with panda bears on it because Madison liked the zoo so much and new shorts that fit Madison so much better, according to Mistress. Mistress had run her hands all over Madison in those shorts that morning, saying she liked how Madison's "firm ass" looked in them. It was fun to think of Miss Shasti as Mistress. It reminded Madison about all the sex they'd had since the rope session. Hopefully, Billy and Mr. Seamus wouldn't stay too long because maybe she and Mistress could try afternoon sex.

She was headed back toward the kitchen when the doorbell rang again.

"Miss Rikki," Madison gushed as she opened the door. "Hi, hi, hi."

"Hi there, kiddo." Miss Rikki walked right past her into the kitchen without another word. She carried a couple of bags in her hands.

"Hi, Eileen," Madison said but got no acknowledgment from the short-haired older woman. She was older than Miss Rikki. That seemed weird that a submissive was older than her Dominant. She'd ask Mistress about that later. Eileen was carrying a big box. Shoot, was everyone moving in or something?

Madison barely had the door closed when she saw movement out front. "Daddy Vic!"

"Hey, squirt," Daddy Vic said as she came in. "This is Heather."

"Hi," Madison said and watched the woman named Heather take off her overcoat. Madison's eyebrows almost reached the ceiling. How in the world could this woman with the long blonde hair and high heels not get arrested for wearing practically nothing in public? You could see her actual areolas and nipples under the short mesh shirt. And you could see the underside of her boobs. And her shorts? You could see the V heading toward her hot spot. Whoa.

Daddy Vic and Heather didn't linger by the front door. Nope, they took their bags and boxes toward the kitchen. Madison liked the way Daddy Vic put her hand on the small of Heather's back, possessively guiding her toward the kitchen. The conversations in the kitchen were getting louder, but they were just talking about food and who knows what else? And where had Billy gone? Maybe they could play 'Battle for the Kingdom' again.

She groaned out loud, frustrated as heck when the doorbell rang again.

"I'll get it," she called back toward the kitchen, getting no answer. "Okay. Whatever."

She opened the door, and to her surprise, Mr. Seamus's other three sub-boys were there. "Hi, Mark. Hi, Sanjey. Hi, DeShawn." Each one held a bag, and each one smiled at her in turn but said nothing in response.

"O-kay," Madison said, wondering where everyone's manners were today. Did she have a booger on her face or something? A quick swipe around her face said no.

Lydia arrived next, making Madison wonder who was running the coffee shop. Mr. Tom was with her, of course. And then there was a whole bunch of other people she recognized from Miss Tilda's party. She let them all in because apparently, everyone in Denton Heights was coming over today. There went any chance of afternoon interactions with Mistress. *Sigh.*

Madison sat in one of the very uncomfortable chairs in the formal sitting room and pulled the curtain over with her foot so she could watch out front for the arrival of more company. Yep, a car pulled into the driveway, and two people got out—two very important people.

"Miss Tilda and Mr. Josef are here," Madison shouted toward the kitchen. She wanted to run in and tell Mistress, but the guests were already walking toward the door.

Madison opened the door before they had a chance to ring the bell.

"Hi, hi, hi." Madison opened the door and made a please-enter gesture.

Josef nodded, but Miss Tilda wrapped Madison up in a tight hug. When she finally let Madison go, she said, "This is a big day for you, my dear. Now come on." She held out her elbow for Madison to hold on to. Shouldn't it be the other way around? "Come with me, and let's see what all the fuss is about this afternoon."

Madison heard Mr. Josef shut the front door, so at least she wouldn't get in trouble for leaving it open. It was July, after all, and the air conditioning was on.

They rounded the corner to the kitchen, and Madison jumped when the mass of people stopped talking all at once. The quiet was weird. Miss Tilda stopped in front of Mistress and then unlinked their arms. She said to Mistress, "I believe this belongs to you?"

"We'll find out in a few minutes, won't we?" Mistress said, her cheeks getting darker. Was she blushing?

Madison looked from Mistress to Miss Tilda, who was being led to a comfy chair by Mr. Josef, and then looked back to her Mistress. She flew into Mistress's arms. The soft chuckling and "Awws" from all those people in Miss Shasti's house were kind of unnerving. "What's happening, Mistress?" she whispered.

Mistress put Madison at arm's length and said, "Madison, you've made me so happy. You came into my life when I thought I'd never find someone as wonderful as you. Someone who will let me take care of her and someone who seems to understand how to take care of me, too."

Madison's eyes grew wide as Mistress got down on both knees right there on the kitchen floor. "I want us to be together, peanut. To grow together and help each other through life. Madison, will you do me the honor of being mine? Being my submissive *little*?" She reached into her pocket, pulled out the most awesome pink leather collar, and held it in her hand.

Madison had no idea what to do. She looked at the crowd, and no one moved. Many were smiling, and then Miss Rikki smiled even more and nodded her head ever so slightly. What did all this mean? Oh! Oh! Oh! Mistress was making it official. Holy macaroons! She was asking in front of everyone.

"I think you've left her speechless," Miss Tilda said. More chuckles came from the people, including Billy. She was going to have to tackle him later for laughing.

Mistress continued to hold up the collar until Madison finally blurted. "Yes! Of course, I will. I didn't know what you were doing. This is making it official, right?"

Mistress nodded.

"Okay, then. Yes, I'll wear that if it means I can be yours and you can be mine, and you take care of me, and I take care of you."

A hand on her shoulder pressed down slightly. It was Miss Rikki. Madison took the hint and kneeled in front of her kneeling Mistress. Mistress showed her the engraving in the leather collar. It read, "Property of Miss Shasti." Madison grinned and nodded. Mistress fastened the collar around Madison's neck, grabbed Madison's cheeks with both hands, and said, "You've made me very happy." Madison didn't answer with her voice. Instead, she lunged forward and locked her lips with Mistress's.

When the kiss broke off, Madison registered the clapping for the first time. She put both hands over her ears and let Mistress pull her to her feet and into a protective hug.

"Do I wear this all the time now?" Madison said, running her fingers along the smooth collar.

"No," Mistress said succinctly. "Only at special events or playtime. I have something to give you later that you can wear daily."

"I didn't get you anything," Madison said, knowing she had messed up royally. Mistress had even told her that Saturday would be the day. Maybe Madison's grandmother was right—maybe Madison really was selfish and always put herself first.

Comforting arms wrapped around Madison. A kiss on the forehead told her everything was going to be okay. "That's not protocol, little one," Mistress said. "Dominants shower their subs with gifts. Your gift to me is your submission."

"Okay," Madison said, totally not understanding that at all. "Can we eat now?"

Miss Tilda's laugh was the loudest of them all. And this time, Madison understood that the people weren't laughing at her. They were happy, and it was kind of a good feeling. Being in Mistress's arms felt good, too. No, it felt great. Even better, it felt like home.

~~~

The official collaring day had been one part exhilarating and one part exhausting. Most of the guests were gone, except for Miss Rikki and Daddy Vic and their two subs. Now that Madison had a better understanding of power exchange stuff by observing the Dominant and submissive relationships in action at the party, she understood more of what her mistress wanted from her.

Madison sat at the kitchen table, exploring her new tablet. Miss Rikki said everyone pitched in because they'd heard she didn't have one. The only person who knew that she didn't have one was Mistress, so she must have gossiped about that. Oh! Maybe she asked or suggested or even hinted strongly to her friends to get Madison a tablet. Aha! Mystery solved. But Madison still wasn't quite sure why all those people had gotten her stuff. She kept waiting for Mistress to open some gifts. That never happened, but no one seemed weirded out by it. It must have been some kind of protocol or something. There was so much she still had to learn about this community she had just ceremoniously entered into. She hoped it wasn't a cult. Nah, it couldn't be. Miss Shasti said she could leave anytime she wanted to. But where would she go?

She went back to the tablet and tried to find the *Kinks* website online. Billy showed her how to do it, but she was used to her phone, not this big thing. She could always video chat with him later when the company was gone. Or she could ask Mistress. She was plenty smart.

"She needs guidance and someone to be in her corner," Mistress said to the last of the departing guests. She had gone with them to the front door to see them out.

"She has a lot of people in her corner now," Miss Rikki said.

"She's a pistol," Daddy Vic added. "What's not to like?"

"She's positively adorable," the scantily clad woman named Heather said.

"She is," Mistress agreed. "Thank you all for making today happen."

"It's what we do," Miss Rikki said. "Okay, I've got a sub to tie up once we get home, so I'd better get moving."

"Oh, yeah," Eileen said.

"Same," Daddy Vic said, making the whole group laugh. "Bye, squirt," Daddy Vic called to her.

Madison leaped to her feet and ran toward the front door. She gave hugs all around and said her thank yous again even without having to be told by Mistress.

Once they left, Mistress shut the door firmly and locked it.

"You're all mine, peanut." Mistress grabbed Madison's hand and led her back to the kitchen table.

"And you're all mine, too," Madison said and picked up the tablet.

"Mm hmm. Coffee?"

"Oh, yes, please," Madison said. "Do you want me to make it?"

Mistress cocked her head to one side and shook her head. "Thank you for offering, though."

"Welcome. I saw DeShawn and Heather and those other subs, like, doing everything for their Dominants, and I figured I'm supposed to do the same for you. Otherwise, you might change your mind about keeping me or something."

Mistress's expression softened, if that was a thing, and she said, "Again, thank you for offering, but I don't expect you to wait on me hand and foot. We'll divvy up the household chores equally and help each other. How does that sound?" Before Madison could answer, Mistress added, "That toolset that Daddy Vic got you was above and beyond, so I think maybe you'll end up being the handy-girl around here. That stuff's out of my jurisdiction."

Madison smiled. "'Handy-girl,'" she echoed. She liked it. "Did you see the Supergirl t-shirt Billy got me? It has a cape sewn in."

"I did see it. It's perfect. That tablet the group got you was more than enough for a collaring gift, but you got into their hearts, didn't you, sweet thing?" A kiss to the top of the head, right on the crown, followed. It made Madison woozy. Kisses on the forehead were excellent, but that kiss was amazing.

"Hmm?" Madison said. She was feeling spacey.

Mistress laughed and said, "I'll get the coffee going. You pull up the *Kinks* website. It's time for you to officially have your own page."

"Yay," Madison said and quickly went back to work. She was able to calm her mind enough to recall Billy's instructions. She remembered! You have to tap the plus sign to open a new page. "Got it open, Mistress. Should I log in as you?"

"Nope, nope. You're getting your own account."

"No way! Really?"

"Really."

They spent the next half hour or so setting up Madison's page. The only pictures they had to post were the rope bondage pics, but they were careful not to use any with her face or identifying marks. Madison also uploaded a picture of her Mulan figurine from her phone and another internet photo of Princess Merida. Mistress said those were good because they showed her personality. She did, however, remind Madison never to post anything that was too identifying or personal. There were a lot of creeps out there who didn't always have a person's well-being in mind. When Mistress said that, they both got quiet. Madison was thinking about Katia and the *pretties* and the *stupids* in Columbus. She wasn't sure what Mistress was thinking about.

"And now for the best part of all," Mistress said. "Remember the relationship status section we skipped?"

Madison nodded.

"We get to fill it in now." Mistress instructed Madison on what options to tap, and Madison's eyes widened when the giant list of relationship types popped up. They scrolled through and found *little*.

"That's me, right?"

"Mm hmm."

Madison checked the box, and then another section popped up. "What does this part mean?"

"It wants to know who you belong to."

Madison's heart skipped a beat. "I get to tell everyone on here that I'm yours?"

Mistress nodded. "And as soon as we're done here, you're going to help me reword my relationship status and my blurb because this Mommy Domme is no longer looking for a *little*. I found her."

Madison smacked a hand over her eyes, and she grinned so hard that her cheeks hurt. She suddenly felt dizzy. "Is all of this real?" She rubbed at her temples with the hand covering her eyes. "I'm afraid I'll wake up, and it will all be gone. I mean, why would anyone bring me gifts like these?" She removed the hand from her eyes and gestured toward the tablet and the other gifts piled high on the table. "All the tools and games, Star Wars action figures, and even you—" Madison turned to look at her mistress. "You got us annual passes to the zoo because you said I loved the zoo so much. No one's ever done stuff like that for me. Why would they—I don't understand."

Madison looked around the room, kind of trying to find an escape route. Fight or flight, her Mistress had called it once.

Mistress reached for Madison's hand and held it. The tone in her voice was soft and soothing. "Baby, this is why I wanted to make it official with you. I want you to see that you are worth being loved. Everyone here today loves you, including me, and wants to see you thrive."

"What do you mean by 'thrive?'"

"A lot of things go into that," Mistress said. "First and foremost, I want you to feel safe."

"I do."

"And I want you to feel loved and taken care of." Mistress ran the knuckle of her index finger down Madison's cheek. Madison leaned into it.

"I do."

"And I want you to be able to stand up for yourself, too. Like against those bullies in Columbus."

"Bullies?" Madison hadn't ever thought about them that way. Well, the *stupids,* maybe. Yeah, they were all stupid jerk bullies.

"But I also understand that you need someone, well, let me rephrase. You seem more comfortable looking to me to make big decisions and take the lead.

"Oh, yes. You're in charge, Mistress."

Mistress smiled. Madison liked it when those smiles went all the way up to her eyes and beyond. "That's one way to phrase it."

"You're in charge in lots of places, like at your job. Dr. Littrell is, too. You're both kind of no-nonsense. You always do the right thing, and you listen to what people say."

Mistress nodded.

"And, and, like at that fancy restaurant you took me to last week. You know, when I had to get really dressed up, and we realized that I didn't have any nice pants or shoes, and then you ordered me clothes online? The restaurant with the white tablecloths and the hot bread and butter to die for?"

"Mamma Mia's? Near the condo?"

"Yes, that one. You ordered for me after asking what I liked, and then you sent it back when they messed up my fettuccine order. I never would have done that. I would have suffered through it." Madison threw her head back as if in agony.

Mistress chuckled, and the sound made Madison realize how comforting it was to be alone with her.

"So 'thriving,'" Mistress said, returning to the original thread, "means that Madison gets to be happy and healthy and live her best life."

"I still don't understand why people care."

"Well, you help everyone feel good by showing them it's okay to laugh and to have fun. It helps them relax."

"Me? I help people relax?"

"You sure do, peanut." Tears brimmed Mistress's eyes. "With the exception of your mommy and your high school softball coach, I don't think many people in your life have told you or shown you what an amazing person you are. No one in Columbus has shown you that you're worthy of love, affection, and attention. But today's collaring ceremony was my public way of showing you and all the witnesses here that I am making a promise to keep you safe, healthy, and happy."

"A promise to help me 'thrive?'"

"Yes."

"And…" Madison narrowed her eyes. "And I can help you thrive, too?"

"I'm counting on it."

"I might not know how, but I'll do my best, Miss Shasti. I mean, Mistress."

"Both of those work, peanut. I love you, sweetheart."

"I love you, too, Mistress."

Mistress reached into her skirt pocket and pulled something out. "I don't want you to wear your pink leather collar outside—it'll create too many questions, but I hope you'll accept this bracelet instead." She showed Madison the circular wooden design.

"What is that?"

"It's a triskelion," Mistress said. "It's the symbol for BDSM. Look on the back."

"Oh!" Madison said excitedly. "It turns. It says, 'Property of Miss Shasti.'" Madison looked into her mistress's eyes. "Your property. I love it." She threw her arms around her Mistress's neck and hugged her. "Thank you." She sat back down and held out her wrist. "Can you put it on me?"

"Of course."

Mistress put the bracelet on her, and Madison admired it for a moment. She pushed the unfinished Kinks page aside and stood up. She looked at Mistress's lap and moved toward it. Mistress received Madison gracefully and pressed her cheek against Madison's. Madison let the warm feels wash over her and then moved away to look into Mistress's deep brown eyes, and then she leaned close enough until they were breathing each other's breaths. Mistress closed the distance and kissed her. Madison kissed back, soft, slow passionate kisses, a lifetime of kisses.

Chapter 14

Shasti

It was mid-morning on Sunday, the day after the collaring party, and they were still in bed. Shasti squeezed the young woman in her arms. "I love making love with you in the morning."

"I'm still pulsing," Madison said and rolled on top of Shasti. "I love you, Mistress."

"And I love you." Shasti tugged at the pink collar that Madison still wore. "Are you ever going to take this off?"

"Nope." Kisses to Shasti's face followed the word.

"Not even in the shower?"

"Oh, maybe." Madison began a trail of kisses down Shasti's neck and shoulder blades.

"No, no, no, you insatiable thing. You're going to kill me." When Madison made no move to stop her kissing excursion, Shasti said, "Out, out, out. Go turn on the shower and get it warm for us."

"Shower sex!" Madison exclaimed and bolted off Shasti's body. She ran past the master closet and into the master bathroom. "Your bathroom is for sex. Mine is for bath time and toys."

"Sounds right," Shasti called after her lover. Lover. Mm hmm. And what a lover Madison turned out to be. Shasti might be the Dominant in all other aspects of their relationship, but Madison had clearly taken the lead in the bedroom so far. That would change, but it was working out just fine for now. Pinning Shasti's arms above her head with one hand while the other worked magic down below had been unexpected but not unwelcomed.

"Mmm," Shasti moaned, squirming at the memory. Suggesting nipple clips and strap-ons, none of which they'd tried yet, but the mere suggestion coming from her submissive was enough to heighten her arousal.

She was about to doze off again when Madison broke the stillness by saying, "Hey." Shasti opened her eyes and looked up. Madison was peeking out of the big closet. She had on the biggest boo-boo face Shasti had ever seen. "I was going to jump out and scare you when you went by." She hung her head as if horribly disappointed.

Shasti burst out laughing. "Oh, you were, were you?" She sat up and then reluctantly got out of the bed. "I may just have to punish you for this planned impertinence."

Madison's eyes got wide. "Like a 'fun-ishment'?"

Shasti strode by Madison in all her naked glory and latched onto Madison's hand as she went by. She headed for the steamy shower beyond. "Sounds like a wonderful idea. I'm not sure you're ready, though."

"Yes, I am," Madison said.

"I'll think about it." Shasti took the collar off Madison's neck and pulled her into the shower.

The washing of skin that occurred was interrupted by another type of skin contact. Shasti wasn't sure if she started it or if Madison had. Didn't matter. They were both very satisfied at the end and had to rewash themselves in cold water. Not fun, but the closeness they shared outweighed any temporary chill.

Once dressed, they shared coffee on the back patio, watching the finches flit to and from the new feeder Madison had thoughtfully purchased and put up. Famished, they headed back inside for breakfast. Shasti wouldn't let Madison help this time and suggested she check out their *Kinks* pages to ensure they were accurate and conveyed what they wanted.

"Does my alias still sound okay?" Madison asked.

"*Little_peanut*?" Shasti said. "I love it."

"Yay," Madison gushed. "Does this part still sound okay for my page?" Madison started reading. "'I discovered there was a word for how I always felt my whole life. And that word is *little*. I may not be into diapers or pacifiers, but I like Mulan and playing Battle for the Kingdom with my other *little* friend Billy.'"

"Sounds good so far," Shasti said and put the final touches on the cheese omelets and side dishes of fruit she'd made for the two of them. The fruit was a way to get some healthy nutrition into the young woman who had never learned to eat correctly. She'd bet money there would be more of a fight regarding vegetables. If she was a betting woman, that is. "Read that next part. It's my favorite."

"Okay. It says, 'An amazing woman found me. She gives me structure, offers guidance, teaches, challenges, and loves me. She is *Cincy_MommyDomme*. I am trying my best to make her happy and give her what she needs also. I am (and we are) a work in progress. Thank you for reading my page.'"

"I love it," Shasti said and placed Madison's breakfast plate in front of her.

"What's this?" Madison picked out the speared piece of cantaloupe. She popped it in her mouth and pulled out the tiny plastic cocktail sword. "Whoa! This is so cool." She speared a honeydew chunk and repeated the process several times, declaring each piece of fruit to be another enemy of Mulan's new dynasty defeated by Madison/Mulan herself.

"I love you," Shasti said, unable to hold it in any longer.

"Thank you, Mistress. I love you, too. And this food is so good. I appreciate you taking care of me so much. What can I do for you today besides afternoon sex later?"

"You have a one-track mind, Madison."

"Can't help it. You're so sexy, and you make me shiver."

"I do, huh?"

"Mm hmm. From the minute I really looked at you in Miss Tilda's kitchen. I kept thinking about you even after I ran away."

"I'm glad you're not running anymore," Shasti said. "But there is something we need to discuss."

"What's that?"

"After breakfast."

"Okay, Mistress," Madison said and dug into her omelet.

Shasti also ate her meal and wondered how this next part would go. She debated putting it off for a while, even bargaining with herself that after Labor Day in another month and a half was better. But she knew that for what it was—avoidance. Best to rip that band-aid off ASAP.

"Finished," Madison said and pushed her plate away as if being timed. "Now, what did you want to discuss? A trip to the sex toy store?" Madison waggled her eyebrows.

"I've created a monster, haven't I?"

"Only if that monster gets to taste you again." Madison stood up, grabbed the now-empty breakfast dishes, and brought them to the sink to soak. When she returned, she moved behind Shasti's chair and asked, "May I touch you, Mistress?"

"Yes. Thank you for asking this time." Shasti laughed, remembering a month ago when Madison had tried to give her a shoulder massage without consent.

Madison's strong fingers made deep circles along Shasti's tight shoulder muscles. The fingers and hands worked their way down her arms and back up. When the fingers moved down Shasti's chest and began a slow massage of her breasts, Shasti tilted her head to one side in invitation. Soft lips contacted her neck, causing a sharp intake of breath. Gentle teeth replaced the lips, and Shasti exhaled in clear arousal. No words were needed. Madison moved the entire chair back with Shasti in it and then kneeled in front of her. Shasti should have but didn't stop the casual lifting of her skirt, the tucking of it into the waistband. Strong arms pulled her by the hips to the edge of the chair.

"Is this what you had in mind that other time?" Shasti heard the huskiness in her voice, knowing Madison heard it, too.

"Mm hmm." Madison parted the thighs she knelt between. With help, she eased Shasti's panties down and pulled them off one leg but let them dangle off the other.

Teeth found Shasti's mons first and bit lightly as if the owner of the teeth was sending the message that Shasti was about to be devoured. Soft kisses replaced the light bite mark. The young woman giving the kisses looked up into Shasti's eyes as her tongue darted out and made elongated sweeps of Shasti's slick center. Shasti's core clenched as she took a mental snapshot of the highly erotic scene. Another sweep had Shasti squirming in the kitchen chair.

"Mmm," Shasti moaned. "Such a good girl." She reached down and ran her fingers through Madison's loose hair. A braid later. Yes. So she could pull Madison back up the stairs and have her way with her. Or no. A fun-ishment. Maybe. Downstairs. On that couch.

One more extended sweep of that talented tongue brought her back to the present. "Fuck me, Madison." Shasti was so turned on. She undulated her hips. Her burning need pleaded for satisfaction.

Madison eased two fingers inside Shasti's center and turned them upright to caress the eager g-spot. Madison slid those wonderful fingers in and out slowly. Shasti was already in the clouds as pure arousal enveloped her entire body. She shivered as waves of ecstasy pulsed from her toes to her core to her head and back again. She'd never had a lover so tuned to her body and needs. Her head rolled on its own as she fought to keep her eyes open.

What torture. What exquisite torture. She fisted the hair within her grasp and pulled the head to the epicenter. "Make me cum, baby. Make Mistress cum."

With her head pressed against her Mistress, Madison had no choice but to put her lips and tongue to the task. A soft kiss to Shasti's clit was followed by that skillful tongue swirling and stabbing and swirling again. Lips sucked lightly and then harder.

Shasti felt the stirring of orgasm. Yes, yes, yes. With her eerie sixth sense, Madison knew it too and increased the pace of her pumping fingers. She added a third finger without missing a beat. Oh, yes. Shasti was filled.

Shasti's phone shattered their bubble as it rang an incoming call. "No, no," she said as Madison reached for the phone with her one clean hand. Her other hand continued pistoning. "Let it go to—" There was no holding back the orgasm that had built its own sandcastle around them both.

"Hello?" Madison said into the phone.

Shasti slammed her hand over her mouth as the orgasm hit her full force. She slammed her other hand on top of the first as she faintly registered Madison greeting her parents on the phone. Pulse after pulse wracked her body as the orgasm ripped through her. It was all she could do not to pass out. She struggled to catch her breath as the aftershocks claimed her sanity.

"Oh, yes, she's here," Madison said politely. "Hang on one moment, Mrs. Balakrishnan. I'll see if she's coming."

Shasti grabbed the phone and hit the mute button. Double checking that it was toggled, she grabbed the back of Madison's head and jammed it back into her center. A quick second orgasm followed, and when she successfully stopped her eyes from rolling into the back of her head, she leaned down and kissed Madison on the mouth with such passion that she almost forgot her parents were waiting.

Shasti kissed Madison one more time and picked up her phone.

"Hi, Mom," she said after unmuting. "Sorry for the delay. I was deep in the middle of something."

"Is everything okay?" Shasti's mother asked. "You sound out of breath."

"Fine. Fine." Shasti shot Madison a scandalous look. Madison buried her face behind her hands.

"Who was that polite creature that answered your phone?"

"That was Madison." Should she, or shouldn't she? Honesty was one pillar in the foundation of her relationship with Madison, so yes. Yes, she would. "She's my girlfriend."

"Girlfriend? Oh?" Shasti's mother had an excited lilt to her voice. Good. Maybe things were changing on that front. "What does she do? Does she have a job?"

"Why don't you ask her yourself?"

"Me?" Madison mouthed as she got up from her kneeling position, now suddenly shy about talking on the phone. She wiped her mouth and then licked her fingers mischievously.

Turnabout is fair play, Shasti thought as she nodded. "I've put you on speaker phone, Mom." Shasti pulled up her panties and fixed her skirt. "Is Dad there, too?"

"Right here," Shasti's father said, his voice faint.

"Hi, Mr. Balakrishnan," Madison said into the phone.

"Doctor," Shasti whispered.

"I mean, hi, Dr. Balakrishnan. Hey, you're a doctor like Mistr— just like Miss Shasti. That's neat."

"Hello, Madison," Shasti's father said. "What are your intentions with my daughter?"

Shasti rolled her eyes. He was teasing, but Madison didn't know that. "Dad, stop. She intends to make me happy. Isn't that right, peanut?"

"Yes, that's right. And she intends to make *me* happy, too," Madison said in her oh-so-adorable way of speaking that made the whole world brighter.

"Well, that's perfect then," Shasti's father said.

"And when were you going to tell us you were in a relationship, daughter?" her mother asked without a hint of mirth.

"It's new, Mom," Shasti said. "And I'm telling you now. That's why I asked Madison to answer the phone." She sent a playful scowl at Madison as if to say they would talk about it later.

Before Shasti's mother could point out any more of Shasti's transgressions, Madison jumped back in and said, "I own a condo, Mrs. Balakrishnan. And I will be renting it out for income. There are maintenance fees and stuff, but it should get a healthy profit."

"Oh, you're in real estate," Shasti's mother said, sounding impressed.

"Yes, Ma'am," Madison said. "And I'm also going to inquire at PETology and see about a job there."

"Oh?"

"Yes," Shasti interjected while shrugging at Madison as if to ask why she hadn't heard about this new idea. "Madison is going to use the condo as a foundation for her income while she pursues her dream of working with animals."

"I am?" Madison mouthed.

Shasti shrugged and made a face that said, 'Hey, why not?'

"That sounds exciting, Madison," Shasti's mother said. "It's wonderful when young people go after what they want. She sounds young, Shasti."

"I'll be twenty-three in September," Madison said and swung her legs back and forth on the chair.

"A libra?" Shasti's mother asked.

"Yes, Ma'am."

"Good. Good. That's a good match for you, Shasti. Aries and Libra are on the opposite sides of the zodiac wheel, so it's a good match if you respect each other's boundaries and develop trust."

"Getting back into astrology, Mom?" Shasti asked with a slight shake of her head. She wasn't judging. Her mother simply flitted back and forth from interest to interest and hobby to hobby.

"She's also into crocheting now," Shasti's father added. "Be ready for scarves this winter." His voice sounded a little closer this time.

"That's great," Shasti said and meant it. "How's my baby sister?"

"Juggling home, husband, and career. You know how it is."

"I do now," Shasti said. "And I love it."

The words sent Madison's legs swinging to and fro again. She mouthed the words, 'I'm not your husband' and bugged out her eyes.

Shasti waved her silliness away and then hit the mute button. "Baby, go put on one of your new outfits. And get your backpack. We're going out."

"Where?"

"Coffee shop."

"Excellent." Madison leaped to her feet and tore up the stairs to her room. The room they still had to paint and fix up as a safe space for her beloved *little*.

Shasti unmuted before she was done laughing.

"It's so good to hear you happy, daughter," Shasti's mother said. Shasti thought so, too.

They chatted for a while longer, and Shasti got the news about her family's comings and goings and her sister's challenges trying to get pregnant. Satisfied that all seemed well with her family, with the pregnancy exception, Shasti told her parents that she had to get going. They wrapped things up, and her parents even remembered to include Madison in their goodbyes. That warmed Shasti's heart as she tapped the end-call button.

"They loved you," Shasti said.

"Yay." Madison twirled around like a ballet dancer.

Shasti stood up. "I need some cleaning up, so give me a few minutes to, err, freshen up."

Madison winked at her with the most lascivious grin Shasti had ever seen.

~~~

Coffees in hand, Shasti and Madison sat in their usual seats in the far corner of Rikki's shop.

"Did you mean it, little one? About getting a job at PETology?" Shasti took a sip of her wonderful Mark-made coffee.

"Yes," Madison said. And that's all she said. She was busy coloring in her bird book with the new set of colored pencils that Rikki and Eileen had gotten her.

"Because?"

"Because I've mooched off you enough." Madison didn't look up. "You're nice and all, but I'm grown up enough to pull my weight."

"All eighty pounds of you," Rikki said, coming to sit with them.

"I weigh more than that, Miss Rikki," Madison said, finally putting down the coloring project. She took a sip of her coffee. It wasn't a sugar-filled, whipped-cream laden thing either. Shasti was putting a stop to that nonsense as of today.

"I know, kiddo. I know," Rikki said. "Hey, I love your Katniss Everdeen t-shirt. Now that was one strong woman. Who got that for you?"

Madison looked down at Katniss, pulling back her bow. The arrow was pointed up and off to the side. "I forgot their names, but it was the big lady with the Asian sub with no clothes on. She sat on the rug at the lady's feet. And why did all the female Dommes touch her?"

"Minjung is Miss Rowena's submissive, Madison," Shasti said.

"Oh, she's Korean, too. Well, except that I'm American. American of Korean descent."

"Mm hmm," Rikki said.

"Did that bother you that she was naked?" Shasti asked.

Madison shook her head, and Shasti tilted her head in warning.

"No, Ma'am," Madison said. "You touching her did, though. You said it was only you and me."

"Ahh, okay," Shasti said. "I promise it's just you and me, but Rowena asked the Dommes to touch Minjung without asking for consent because it helps keep her in submission."

"Feeling like an object?"

"Mm hmm. That's very insightful of you."

"Katia did that to me."

"Oh? I'd like to talk more about that later. Would that be okay?" Shasti exchanged a worried glance with Rikki.

"Yes, it's okay," Madison said.

"Would you prefer I don't touch her next time?"

Madison shrugged, but before Shasti could reprimand her for not using actual words, Madison said, "I guess it's okay as long as..." Madison looked down at the hands in her lap.

"As long as what, baby?"

Madison looked up. "As long as you could still be mine."

"Always." Shasti reached over the coffee table, grabbed onto Madison's knee, and shook it a few times. She tapped her wrist, and Madison looked down at the bracelet Shasti had given her. "That, right there, tells you that you belong to me. If you ever forget, turn the disc over and read what it says."

Madison did just that and showed Rikki, who seemed impressed.

"I'm glad because I want to stay yours," Madison said. "I thought maybe Minjung would want to talk to me because we're both East Asian, but she didn't even look at me. She just kneeled at Miss Rowena's feet." Madison had kind of forgotten that one bad part of the party.

"Minjung is more than a submissive, Madison," Rikki said gently. "She's Rowena's slave and doesn't speak unless Mistress Rowena gives her permission. But rest assured. Their relationship is consensual."

"How do you know?"

Rikki exchanged a glance with Shasti, and then Shasti said, "We watch out for each other. We informally make sure all subs and Dominants in our community are safe."

"So, someone will make sure I'm always safe?" Madison asked.

"Always," Rikki said. "And they make sure I'm safe, and Miss Shasti, too. Everybody."

"That's cool," Madison said.

Rikki patted Madison on the knee and then blew out a sigh so big that it got both Shasti and Madison's attention.

"What's up?" Shasti said. There was no sense asking Rikki if everything was okay because clearly, it was not.

"Ahh," Rikki said. "I got a credit card bill for over a thousand dollars. It's not my credit card. I didn't buy anything on it. Massages and high-end restaurants. Stuff like that."

"You reported it, right?"

"I did, but apparently, it's my word against the credit card company's. I somehow have to prove my innocence. I got the bill the other day, but the longer this lingers, the lower my credit score. And then it's only a matter of time—"

"Stop," Shasti said.

Rikki took a deep breath and let it out. "I know. I know. I can't spiral into the unknown. Aunt Tilda already had this talk with me."

"Get a good lawyer if it can't be resolved."

"You and Aunt Tilda are on the same wavelength."

"Sorry this is happening, Rikki," Shasti said. "Keep us posted, okay?"

"Will do. And Eileen is bugging me to buy her a Mercedes, a convertible Mercedes."

"Does everyone think you're made out of money?" Shasti asked. She knew Rikki was barely scraping by with the coffee shop. It was why she had to live with her Aunt Tilda, to help keep expenses down.

"Right? I think I've spoiled her too much." Rikki stood up and asked, "Hey, has she come by to say hello yet?"

Shasti shook her head. As far as she was concerned, it was a blessing.

"She will," Rikki said. Her expression changed to one of Dominance, and Shasti understood what was happening. Greeting them was part of Eileen's punishment for something.

"I'll let you know after she does."

Rikki nodded and sighed again. "Thank you. I knew you'd understand. And now, I have to get back to work."

Shasti watched her friend walk away. She realized that Madison was watching her watch Rikki.

Madison whispered, "Is Miss Rikki okay?"

"Hopefully. She just got thrown a curve ball recently, but she's dealing with it." Speaking of curve balls. "Uh, peanut, come sit next to me."

"Okay." Madison bounded up and crashed onto the couch next to Shasti, who wrapped her arm around her shoulders and held her close.

"Remember back home—"

"I like when you call it 'home,'" Madison said and snuggled in.

Shasti had to halt her train of thought because Eileen was headed right for them with two brownies on a plate.

"Hey, Madison," Eileen said and handed her the plate.

"Thanks, Eileen," Madison said. Normally she would have been over the moon about being handed brownies, but even Madison knew there was something about Eileen that sucked the happiness out of any room.

Eileen glanced over and said, "Hello, *Miss* Shasti," in greeting. The word 'Miss' was practically hissed. Shasti never knew what she'd done to Eileen to earn such disdain, and she'd probably never know.

"Hello, Eileen," Shasti said in a normal tone. As long as Eileen didn't mess with her relationship with Madison, it would be okay.

"I have to go," Eileen announced and returned to the counter.

Shasti and Madison silently watched Eileen walk away, and then Madison set the brownies down on the coffee table untouched. Shasti said nothing and pulled her little one closer.

"Let's get back to our discussion, shall we?"

"She disrespected you," Madison said.

"I know."

"She's supposed to greet you first."

"I know."

"What's her problem?" Madison pounded a soft fist on her own thigh.

Shasti sighed. "I'm not sure, peanut. I'll speak with Miss Rikki about it later, okay?"

"Yes, Ma'am."

"Okay," Shasti said. "Do you remember back home when I said I had something I wanted to discuss with you?"

"Oh, yeah. I forgot. We kind of got distracted. Hee hee hee." Madison giggled behind her hand.

"That we did." Shasti took a deep, cleansing breath and let it out. "I think it's time to go to Columbus."

Madison's face fell. "You're kicking me out already?"

"Oh, no, no, no, silly. I want you to visit your mommy and the rest of your family, and while we're there, we can fetch a few of your things. If that's okay with you."

"Fetch a few of my things?" Madison looked around the coffee shop as if searching for meaning in the words. "What do you mean?"

"You must have clothes and treasures and things in your room that you want to have here. Like old yearbooks or your softball glove?" Ahh, that last one got her attention.

"I guess."

"The primary goal is to visit your family. It's been quite a while."

"Almost seven whole months," Madison clarified. "And, yes, I would like to see Mommy."

"And I'm sure she'd love to see you."

"You can meet her, Miss Shasti. She'll like you."

"I hope so. And I'd like to meet the rest of your family, including your grandmother."

"Why?" Madison's smile faded.

"To get a sense of your childhood and your life BS."

"My 'life bullshit?'"

Shasti laughed. "BS means 'Before Shasti.' Your life before me."

Madison burst out laughing, causing more than a few customers and staff to look their way. "My life BS. I love it. When would we go?"

"We'll have to wait until after the lawyer and dentist appointments next week, and then there's your eye appointment the week after that." Shasti thought for a moment and added, "I also have to consider my work schedule. We can make a long weekend out of it, maybe. I have some vacation time I can take. You can show me the sights in Columbus. I'll have my very own tour guide."

"August sometime, maybe?"

"Mm hmm. I suppose. Sooner rather than later is best."

"You'll have to call Mommy, I guess. You know, to set that up."

"I'll take care of all of that," Shasti said. "And maybe your Mommy and father can come to visit us here sometime. Your brother, too?"

Madison shook her head. "No."

"Why not?"

"They'd just ruin it here for me."

Shasti's heart broke for Madison. But maybe it was a good sign that she understood the toxic environment she'd grown up in was the cause of her anxiety.

"Mistress?" Madison said, leaning into Shasti's hug. "Is it okay that I miss Mommy? Will you get mad?"

"Never. I am not replacing your mommy."

"Even though you're my Mommy Domme?"

"You can think of me as your caregiver if that helps you. Some people use CG/lg as their acronym. Caregiver/little girl."

"Okay, thank you," Madison said, looking down and pulling at her shirt. Shasti had gotten used to this look. It meant that Madison was thinking seriously about something. "Mistress?"

"Yes, peanut?"

"Can we buy some thank you cards? I should send thank you cards to everyone that bought me a present."

"That's a lot of people."

"I know, but I want them to understand that I appreciate them. And they should know I'm grateful they're looking out for me. And looking out for you, too."

Shasti's heart melted as she held her now-official *little* snuggling in her arms. "That's a perfect idea, peanut. Perfect. Like you."

Chapter 15

Madison

There was no way Madison was getting out of the car until Mistress got there. Dentist offices were on everyone's register of known scary places. She hadn't been to one since she was little. Maybe seven or eight years old. Her grandmother thought it was a scam. *It was a waste of money*, she'd always say. Apparently, both Dr. Littrell and Mistress thought it was a good idea, so that's why Madison was sitting in Mrs. Park's gold Cadillac that Madison now officially owned in the parking lot of *All Smiles in Denton Heights*.

And how about that? She owned a car now. The lawyer they'd met with yesterday morning gave it to her. Well, it was in Mrs. Park's will, of course. But then there was that other part. The part about the bank account. She still didn't understand how she and Mrs. Park ended up having a joint bank account, and all of Mrs. Park's money was now officially hers. Well, it would be once all of Mrs. Park's debts were figured out and paid off. Mr. Hill, the lawyer, was the—what was the word? Madison couldn't remember, but he was the one who would determine what Mrs. Park's assets were and what the debts were and all that stuff, but eventually, all of Mrs. Park's stuff was going to be hers, including the condo like Ms. Elena said. That still really confused Madison, but Mistress was helping her make sense of it.

But the even bigger question was why Mrs. Park left it all to Madison in the first place. Made no sense. They only knew each other for, like, a minute. Maybe she was supposed to give it all to Mommy?

She'd have to ask Mistress about that. At the moment, though, it was much too much to think about. She had other big fish to worry about.

Relief washed over Madison as Mistress's BMW pulled into the lot. She pulled up right next to Madison's gold monstrosity.

"Why are you laughing?" Mistress asked when they both got out of their respective cars.

"Because I own a pimp mobile."

Mistress's eyebrows raised to the sky. "I hadn't thought about it like that. Hey, let's ask the dentist to put in a gold tooth. Right in front."

The thought of that both intrigued and frightened Madison. "No, thank you, Ma'am." She pressed her lips together as if to ward off gold-tooth implanting dentists from getting near her.

Mistress held out her hand, which Madison gratefully took, and then said, "Ready?"

"No, but I know we have to do this."

"I'm glad you know that." Mistress pulled open the door and let Madison enter first.

After letting the receptionist know who they were, they sat down to fill in the paperwork. "You'll need to change your address officially to Cardinal Lane, peanut. Won't you?"

"Yep," Madison said and kicked her feet wildly. She was glad Miss Shasti didn't stop her from swinging her legs because she had a lot of pent-up energy that needed to go somewhere, and Miss Shasti had already counseled her that she would have to stay really really still while in the dentist's chair, otherwise, you could get hurt. Miss Shasti didn't think it was funny when Madison said it might be safer *not* to go after all and that they should just stay home. That didn't go over well because here they were.

"Madison Kim," a Black woman wearing light green scrubs with flying toothbrushes and toothpastes all over them, called for her. She was older than Miss Shasti and seemed nice. Madison smiled at her flying toothbrushes, and the lady put her arm around her shoulder.

"My name is Vicky Bowen, and I'm a registered dental hygienist. I'll be cleaning your teeth today if that's okay with you."

"Yes, Ma'am," Madison said. She glanced over her shoulder, making sure Miss Shasti was still following. "Is it okay if my girlfriend comes in?" Madison whispered, "I'm a little scared. I haven't been to a dentist in a while."

A slight squeeze from the arm around her shoulders was soothing, but the words were even soothier. "Of course. I understand you're a bit of a newbie to all this."

Madison nodded and then remembered to use words. "Yes, Ma'am." She jumped when a shrill grinding noise broke the stillness.

"It's okay," Miss Vicky said. "That's the noise of a drill."

"A drill?" No way.

"Yes. It's a small drill just for teeth. Dr. Hernandez has to first drill out all the decay in the tooth before filling in the cavity. Don't worry. She caters to cowards and newbies. The patient can't feel it at all. The sound, seriously, is the worst of it."

"Okay, Miss Vicky," Madison said. "Thank you for telling me."

Miss Vicky got Madison settled in the big reclining chair that looked one part comfortable and one part not so much. Miss Vicky showed her everything that would be used during her cleaning that afternoon.

Afraid to move, Madison said, "Mm hmm," as quietly as she could.

"You can still talk, Madison," Miss Shasti said. "Once Miss Vicky starts, though, that's when you have to be still."

"Okay." Madison blew out the biggest sigh making the two other women in the small room chuckle. "Miss Shasti, I submitted that job application at PETology this morning. I forgot to tell you."

"Oh, that's wonderful, peanut," Miss Shasti said. "We'll talk about it this afternoon at my office, okay?"

"Okay," Madison said. She liked hanging out in Miss Shasti's office at the health clinic. It was private, and Madison liked being close to her. Not that they had sex there. That would never happen, but she had her backpack and could color or watch a movie on her new tablet now that she had a good case for it.

Miss Vicky got to work and told Madison everything she was going to do before she did it. Having the x-rays taken was okay. They didn't hurt at all, but the suctiony thing now in her mouth was really weird. Both Miss Vicky and Miss Shasti praised her when she figured out how to get the sea of spit into the sucking tube. She was about to wiggle at their praise, but Miss Vicky said, "Be still, please." And Madison froze again.

Madison definitely did *not* like the metal tools coming at her face and into her mouth. And the scraping sounds sucked. Seriously? Could this possibly be good for you? Sometimes Miss Vicky hit a spot, and Madison would tense up and whimper.

"I'm sorry, little pup," Miss Vicky would say. "We'll make sure Dr. Hernandez checks those ouchy spots."

Finally, after a hundred years, Miss Vicky used this electric toothbrush thingy and "polished" her teeth. Would they be shiny like the gold Cadillac outside? Miss Shasti's Beemer needed a wash, didn't it? Maybe Madison could convince Billy to help her wash and wax it. But Madison wanted it to be a surprise. How could they do that? Maybe at the health clinic while Mistress was working, saving the lives of countless Denton Height's residents. Yeah, maybe that. Did they have a hose there?

"Madison?"

"Hmm?" Madison made the mistake of looking up into the bright light over her head. She blinked a few times until Miss Vicky came back into focus.

"We're all done."

Madison let out a sigh so big that her lips flapped as the air went by. "Thank goodness." All done! Maybe this dentist stuff wasn't so scary after all.

"Madison," came the quiet but stern reprimand from the corner chair.

"I mean, thank you, Miss Vicki."

"You're welcome, little pup." Miss Vicky turned, and Madison jumped when she saw the scary Dr. Hernandez looking down at her.

"Hello, Madison," Dr. Hernandez said.

"You know my name?"

"Of course," the dentist said. "I make it a point to know who my patients are." She was a tall Latina woman with a slight accent like Katia's mother. Dr. Hernandez's hair was pulled back in a bun, and she wore sturdy glasses with chains along the sides. It made her look really really smart. "Now, give Vicky and me a minute to review your x-rays, and then we'll start the examination."

"Examination?" Madison was positively deflated. They weren't done. She remembered now. Miss Vicky told her that x-rays were first, then the cleaning, and finally, the dentist lady would come and examine her teeth. Oh, no. Maybe she'd have to use that tooth drill on her teeth. Would she slip and puncture a hole into Madison's brain? She wanted to go home.

"Madison," Miss Shasti said quietly, "you're okay."

"I am?"

The dentist and Miss Vicky both chuckled.

"You are," Miss Shasti said. "In fact, I have something back at my office to give you if you continue to be as good for Dr. Hernandez as you've been for Miss Vicky."

"Like a present?"

"Yes," Miss Shasti said. "Now, don't let Dr. Hernandez hear this, but we usually go out for ice cream after medical appointments, but I think we'll postpone that for another day when your mouth and gums aren't so sore."

"I heard nothing," Dr. Hernandez said. "Open," she said to Madison and then stuck more metal things in Madison's mouth. The suctiony thing was gone, thank goodness, but right now, she was tired of keeping her mouth wide open for so long. The dentist lady was nice, but this whole dentist trip sucked. She'd give it a two out of ten and a "would not recommend" to anyone who asked. And the only reason it even got a two was because the people were nice.

Once the dentist finished her examination, without using a drill thank you very much, Miss Vicki taught her how to floss and brush her teeth properly. Madison had been brushing mostly okay, but she had a few stylistic things to adjust, like not mashing the toothbrush against the teeth. Oh, and brushing the inside of her cheeks and her tongue. Who knew that was a thing?

"You're fortunate, little pup," Miss Vicky said, helping Madison sit up. She removed the funky napkin clipped over her chest. "Only three cavities, and you haven't been to a dentist in fourteen or fifteen years." She looked at Miss Shasti and said, "That's incredible."

Miss Shasti nodded her agreement as to the incredulity, but Madison was too tired to care. She was a little woozy now that she was sitting upright.

At the checkout place, Madison opened her wallet and handed Miss Shasti her brand-new dental insurance card that had come in the mail the other day. She even got a health insurance card, too. And a vision card. She felt kind of grown-up having these things in her wallet, and Miss Shasti had assured her that even though insurance costs money each month, it would save her a lot of money in the long run. Saving money was cool. She trusted Miss Shasti.

They had to make two more appointments for the dentist over the next couple of weeks because her stupid cavities had to be taken care of with that little drill thing sooner rather than later. Once the appointments were set and entered into the family calendar on her phone, Madison got back in her pimp mobile with her sore but freshly polished teeth and followed Mistress to her health center. Noting the presence of a hose bib but no hose on the side of the building where Mistress parked, Madison rejoiced. Maybe she could pull this car washing thing off.

Once in the privacy of her office, Mistress wrapped Madison in a full-body hug. Madison lay her head on Mistress's soft chest. Her boobs were like pillows. Sigh. It was funny how she thought of Mistress as Miss Shasti when they were out in the wild with other people, but as Mistress when they were alone like this. Calling her Mistress was personal and private, and she wasn't sharing that with anyone.

"Thank you for being such a good girl with Miss Vicky and Dr. Hernandez today," Mistress said. "You were very polite, thanking everyone in the office."

"I knew you'd want me to do that," Madison said. "And I was very very good in the chair the whole time. Wasn't I?"

"You like to please me, don't you?" Mistress asked.

"Yes," Madison said shyly. She had been quick to trust Mistress, and that trust was only growing. Maybe Mistress really liked her for more than just the sexual stuff Katia had taught her to do.

"And that pleases me." Mistress rocked them both from side to side. "Greatly."

"I like when you're happy with me." Madison smiled against Mistress's chest. "And, you know what else?"

"What, peanut?"

"My mouth is kind of pulsing and hurting. I don't think I could enjoy ice cream right now."

"I knew that would happen," Mistress said, releasing Madison from the all-encompassing hug.

Madison ran her tongue over her newly cleaned teeth. "My teeth are so smooth. Look!" She opened her mouth, so Mistress could see how smooth her teeth were.

"Very nice," Mistress said and then kissed Madison on the top of the head. "Go to the bathroom, wash your hands, and I'll give you your present when you come back."

"You like ordering me around, don't you?"

"Is that how you see it? Me ordering you?"

Madison looked down and to the left. "Not really. But you always give me lots of instructions on what to do next and stuff."

"Do you want me to stop?"

Madison looked up, concerned. "No, no, no. I just—never mind."

"Go wash up, and we'll talk when you come back, okay?"

"Yes, Ma'am." Madison headed out of the office. She hoped she hadn't blown it. She didn't mean to be mean to Mistress. She just hadn't said it right.

One of the medical assistants greeted her by name as they passed in the hallway. Madison guessed they were all getting used to her being there a lot. She greeted her back and then did the tasks Mistress had asked her to do.

"I'm back," Madison said as she opened the door to the office.

"Good." Mistress stood up from her desk and sat on the couch. "Come sit. That's not an order, just a request."

"Ugh," Madison said. "Mistress, I didn't say it right. I like when you tell me to do stuff. I really do. I used the wrong word."

"I'm just trying to guide you, baby. To help you understand how to make good choices."

"I know," Madison said and finally sat down. "Am I in trouble?"

"No, honey. No. But, tell me, is there anything I've asked you to do that would have caused you harm or was unfair?"

Madison thought for a moment. "No. Except my teeth hurt now."

Mistress chuckled but said nothing.

"I know. I know. It's for the greater good because I would look weird driving around in my pimp mobile without teeth in my face."

Mistress chuckled even louder and pulled Madison toward her. It was funny how her butt slid so easily on the black leather.

"I like you helping me," Madison continued, trying to dig herself out of the hole she'd gotten into. "I like how sometimes you ask what I think before just telling me what to do. Like at the lawyer's office when he asked about the car."

Mistress nodded and said, "It's my nature to help like that. To want to take care of you. And I think that your innate nature wants someone who will do that. You want someone to be there to help. Making decisions can be extremely hard all by yourself. It's like flying blind."

"Yes, it is." Madison snuggled against the warm body she now shared a home with. Whoa. That was kind of cosmic. "Mistress?"

"Mm hmm?"

"I called you my girlfriend in front of Miss Vicky. Was that right?"

"That was perfectly right. I consider you my girlfriend, for sure. You're also my *little*. The one I take care of in all kinds of ways."

Madison rocked back and forth. Her energy was coming back to life. "And I'm not sure how, but do I take care of you, too?"

"Yes, baby," Mistress said with a kiss on Madison's head. "In so many ways."

"Can I have my present now?"

Mistress burst out laughing. "Yes, of course." She got up and sat at her desk. She pulled open the bottom righthand drawer and reached in for a bag. "Here you go. This is for being a big girl today. I'm very proud of you."

"Thank you, Mistress." Madison ripped through the brown paper bag and pulled out a box filled with Mini-Wheels cars, a truck, and a boat. Ooh, and a school bus. "For me?"

"Mm hmm," Mistress said. "I figured we can keep them here in the office, and then you can play with them whenever you're stuck here."

Madison threw her arms around her Mistress and thanked her over and over with kisses. "Can I play now?"

"Sure," Mistress said. "I have some charts to go through, but as long as you're relatively quiet, you can play."

"Yes, Ma'am."

Madison dropped to her knees next to her Mistress and hugged her legs. "I love you."

"And I love you, peanut."

Madison stayed on the floor next to her Mistress. To move to the couch or anywhere else would have been too far away. Way too far. She pulled each of the eight vehicles out of the box and began building an imaginary freeway system right there on Mistress's carpet. Funny how the road took itself right into the well under Mistress's desk. Obviously, Mistress had to scooch over, but she understood that providing infrastructure with a new highway was extremely important. And it couldn't be helped that the new road ran right up and over her feet. In fact, the road kept crisscrossing her feet several times. The bus even got stuck right on top of Mistress's toes. Funny how that happened.

As Madison ran the VW bug along the carpet, extreme tiredness overcame her. She closed her eyes. She couldn't help it. A quiet humming from above told her that all was well with the world, so Madison succumbed and let herself fall asleep at Mistress's feet.

~~~

"I was thinking," Mistress said as she put the dinner dishes in the dishwasher.

"About what?" Madison wiped the kitchen table one last time. Dinner had been scrump-dilly-ish-ous. It was all soft foods like mac-n-cheese, cottage cheese, and apple sauce. They even had pudding because Madison had eaten all her protein-laden cottage cheese. She'd never had cottage cheese before, and it was pretty okay. It looked weird with the curds and all, but it was creamy and necessary to be allowed to have dessert. And dessert was butterscotch pudding that Mistress made right from the box and everything. She was such a mom.

"We should go shopping." Mistress closed the dishwasher door, leaned against the sink, and then wiped her hands on the dish towel. "Once all this lawyer stuff and your doctor and dentist appointments are finished, we can go to Columbus for our mini-vacation, and you can wear some new outfits."

"Clothes shopping?" Madison knew her tone conveyed that she'd rather poke an eye out with an ice pick.

"It won't be so bad, Madison." Mistress checked her watch. "Looks like we have time for a movie or a board game if you want. You pick."

They moved to the fun living room and sat down on the couch. Madison wanted to sit in Mistress's lap, but that would have been weird and needy, so she sat on the far end of the couch.

"Mistress? What's fun-ishment? I mean, Billy was talking about it the other day. He said, like, it hurts, but it's awesome. That makes no sense whatsoever, right?"

Madison paled when Mistress's smile left her face. Holy cannoli, it was scary.

"Madison Kim," Mistress said, her voice stern, "do you think I am the walking dictionary of all things BDSM? Do you think you can just ask me any question, and I'll have the immediate answer, simply because you've asked?"

Madison looked around the room, trying to find a place to hide.

"Get over here, young lady."

Madison leaped off the couch and stood in front of her Mistress, her hands in front of her face. She peeked around one hand to see just how mad Mistress was.

"What should we do about your impertinence?" It was then that Madison saw the slight smile creep up Mistress's face. Oh! She was play-acting.

"Fun-ishment me?" Madison said, hopeful.

"Exactly." Mistress moved to the middle of the couch. "Take off those shorts."

"Yes, Ma'am." Madison undid the button and then pulled down the zipper. Mistress reached over, yanked the shorts down to the ground, and motioned for Madison to step out of them. She kicked them to the side.

"Go get your new play collar."

Madison was already zipping out of the living room before saying, "Yes, Ma'am." She was back down in record time, handing the pink collar over.

Mistress wrapped the collar around Madison's neck, had her spin around, and then buckled it in the back. She tugged on one of the D-rings gently for two reasons. One was to make sure the collar wasn't tight, and the other was to let Madison feel Shasti's Dominance. She tugged Madison closer by the collar, slid a thumb on each side of Madison's boi shorts, and yanked them down to her ankles. Without taking them all the way off, she commanded Madison to lay across her lap face down. Madison found herself ass up on top of her Mistress.

A warm hand caressed her exposed skin. "You are not going to like this at first," Mistress said. "But then it will begin to feel different after a while." A second hand joined the first, caressing warm skin, and it was kind of nice. "You'll tell me how it feels when I ask."

"Yes, Mistress."

"What are your safewords?"

"Yellow and red."

"Ready?" Mistress's hands stopped their stroking and waited.

"Yes."

A sharp smack hit her right butt cheek, and Madison cried out at the surprise of it. Of course, she knew fun-ishment involved a spanking, but *ouch!* Another smack on her left cheek. She had been ready that time and only groaned. Mistress laid down two more smacks, one on each cheek.

"Color?" The warm hands were back caressing and soothing.

Madison moaned before saying, "Green, Mistress."

"Why are you getting this spanking, young lady?" Four more smacks made contact before Madison could answer.

"I assumed you were a walking dictionary."

"And was that appropriate behavior?" Gotta love those warm, soothing, swirling hands.

Madison's legs parted in invitation. Maybe those hands would venture to the inside of her thighs and even higher because, for some reason, the pain from the smacks was turning into sultry heat at her hot spot.

Two more smacks hit her cheeks. "Answer your Mistress."

"Yes, Ma'am." Had there been a question in there somewhere? "Please don't stop, Mistress," Madison said. "Please keep going." She squirmed, trying to spur her lover on.

More smacks came from her lover's hands. They caused such blissful pain. It was…excellent.

The more Mistress hit the same spots over and over, the more Madison squirmed. Moaning became a necessary relief from the pain. She couldn't help it.

"Yellow," Madison said. "Please, Ma'am. Rub me. All of me." The warm hands were gentle. Until they weren't. One hand grabbed her right butt cheek and squeezed, causing Madison to screech in pre-orgasm. She opened her legs wide. Her breaths came out in gasps. "Please touch me." She winced as the other hand grabbed another handful of butt and squeezed.

"You want me to make you cum, little pup?"

Madison snorted a laugh back. That's what Miss Vicky had called her. "Yes, Mistress. Please, touch me. I'm going to cum on my own in a second."

Mistress released one butt cheek and sank two fingers into Madison's slick center. Madison bucked against her Mistress. The free hand let the handful of skin go and then pulled up on the collar, effectively tightening it around her neck. Mistress was in control. And that was more than okay.

Madison had no words. There was nothing in her world except Mistress's hands and fingers. The free hand let the collar go and then smacked her butt three times in quick succession. The hand then rubbed her hot skin while the other pistoned in and out. Madison matched her Mistress's rhythm as she bucked in ecstasy. A low growl started somewhere in her toes and then shot through the top of her head as the orgasm tore through her. The fingers in her body continued to move, even as Madison stopped undulating her hips. Breathing became a challenge as Mistress milked out powerful aftershocks.

When Madison's breathing finally became somewhat normal, she collapsed and felt rigor mortis setting in. "Holy sex goddess, Mistress."

"Are you okay?" Mistress removed what must have been very wet fingers from Madison's body.

Madison moaned as the fingers vacated the premises. "Thank you for loving me. And fun-ishmenting me."

Mistress chuckled and said, "So it was okay for you?"

Madison scoffed. "Phenomenal."

"Green light then for fun-ishments in the future," Mistress said as if taking notes. She nudged Madison off her lap gently and then pointed to her lips as she leaned forward. Madison gave her the silently requested kiss.

Standing in front of Mistress with her boi shorts around both ankles and her arousal running down her inner thighs was weird. Mistress must have noticed because she said, "You need a shower."

"Your bathroom or mine?" Madison crossed her fingers on both hands and prayed for the correct answer.

"Are you kidding?" Mistress stood up and yanked Madison's boi shorts back up into their proper place. "Fun-ishments aren't just for subs. Mistress needs taking care of, baby."

"Right answer!" Madison leaped in the air, grabbed Mistress's hand upon landing, and pulled her toward the stairs to the magic shower. Soon Mistress would be the one crying out as Madison's skillful fingers did their thing. Hopefully, neither of them would get much sleep that night. Madison kept her fingers crossed for that wish to come true.

Chapter 16

Shasti

Shasti tapped her pen on her paper desk calendar. She had electronic calendars, of course, but there was nothing like having the entire month laid out on paper so she could plan her life. Her father always had one on his desk at home and what was good for the elder Dr. Balakrishnan was good for the daughter. Yikes, she couldn't believe it was already August. She also couldn't believe it had been over six weeks since she and Madison had gotten together.

"So, peanut," Shasti said to Madison over the phone, "remember that your mommy and I settled on a weekend to visit."

"I know. I can't believe it," Madison said.

"So, make sure you tell them that you'll be out of town for our Columbus trip from August twenty-fourth through August twenty-seventh."

"But what if PETology doesn't hire me because I'm already asking for time off?" The worry was clear in Madison's voice.

"It's called a pre-existing condition, peanut. All employers understand that when interviewing candidates."

"Okay, I'll tell them, and if they don't hire me, then maybe I can get a job somewhere else." Madison still sounded a bit worried.

Shasti gushed with pride. "I'm proud of you, you know."

"How come?" Shasti could hear Madison beaming all the way across town.

"Your eye doctor visit last Tuesday."

"I can't believe I have to get glasses."

"Oh, but you'll have that sexy librarian thing going for you," Shasti said. "And I'm particularly proud of you at your dentist appointment last Wednesday. Two of the three cavities filled and not a peep from you."

"Well, just that one time," Madison said. "She hit a nerve. That sucked."

"And only one more filling to go next week."

"And then I'm perfect?" Madison said. Ahh, now she was shy again.

"You've always been perfect to me, sugar," Shasti said.

"Sugar causes cavities, Mistress," Madison warned. "But, um, you do owe me ice cream trips for my dentist visits. And then one more next week."

"I do, don't I?" Shasti looked over the calendar on her desk again. "How about one tomorrow? It's Saturday, and we can go to that DIY store and pick paint colors for your room."

"I can't believe I get to have my own room in your big house, Mistress. But…"

"Uh, oh. I hear dissension in the ranks. What's on your mind?"

"Do I still get to sleep in your big bed with you every night?" Madison said the words slowly as if she was afraid of the answer.

"Absolutely, my dear," Shasti said, hoping her voice conveyed the right amount of enthusiasm. "But every big girl needs her own room for her personal treasures."

"Yay," Madison said. "I get to have personal treasures."

"And don't let us forget to get rollers and brushes, too. I have to make a list. We'll go clothes shopping at the mall after that, and finally for ice cream in the food court. Sound good?"

"All except the trying on clothes part," Madison said glumly.

Most girls would clamor for a shopping trip, but Madison wasn't like most girls, now was she? And that's what had attracted Shasti to her in the first place. "But there's ice cream," Shasti said in her best persuasive tone.

"Bribes will get you everywhere, Mistress," Madison said with just the right amount of mirth in her voice.

As much as she didn't want to, Shasti had to return to work. Unlike the first health clinic she worked in back home, it wasn't expected that the doctors hand off their patients to one of the physician's assistants after a patient's first visit. Of course, they had PAs at the health clinic, but they were there to supplement, not replace. And, besides, she didn't want to be *that* doctor. "Hey, baby?" Shasti said. "I have to get going."

"I know," Madison said glumly. "But I kind of do, too. I'll let you know how my interview goes this morning. Can I stop by and bring you lunch or something later?"

Shasti almost choked at Madison's kind thoughtfulness. "Yes, that would be nice. Thank you. I'll text you once I've figured out a good time."

"I love you," Madison said softly.

"And I love you," Shasti said just as softly. They took an entire minute saying their goodbyes before Shasti reluctantly ended the call.

She did have charts to review, including Jessie Henderson's, who was coming in that morning for the follow-up regarding the labs drawn at her last visit, but Shasti's thoughts went back to Madison. As they often did.

During their fun-ishment session last week, Shasti had given Madison a small taste of impact play and the barest hint of bondage. Soon the collar would have a leash attached to it. When? Shasti wasn't sure. She was letting it unfold naturally. And rope play—that was going to escalate quickly into bound limbs, one leg at first and then maybe both. Once both arms were bound, Madison would feel the helplessness Shasti wanted her to experience. The helplessness that would float on the loving care and trust that Shasti would provide. That would take time, but then and only then would Madison truly be free.

And Madison's questions the day after her first erotic spanking were intense. Shasti had expected nothing less, though. It was good that Madison was questioning things.

"Why did I get so turned on, even when it hurt?" Madison had asked.

Shasti explained the scientific reasons that pain could cause pleasure. "When a mistress spanks or paddles your bottom," Shasti said, "your brain and body flood with endorphins and adrenaline."

"Adrenaline makes the fight or flight thing happen, right?"

"Mm, hmm," Shasti said. "And endorphins make you feel good. Runners call it a runner's high. Sex creates endorphins, too."

"Like when I made you cum in the shower last night?"

"Mmm," Shasti said, remembering the brilliant flood of chemicals coursing through her body. "Endorphins make you feel good."

"Soooo," Madison said, squinting her eyes. "Okay, so you're saying that spankings and running and sex all create these endorphins that make you feel good?"

"Yes."

"Will you ever hit me with a paddle or a crop or whatever?"

"We can explore that if you want."

"Mark at the coffee shop likes to get whipped," Madison said.

"He does."

"And Miss Rikki whips Eileen. Does Eileen get endorphins?"

"Of course, but Miss Rikki must be very careful. Whipping is an extreme form of play and can go wrong quickly. I won't ever do that with you."

"You said even Dommes use safe words. So, you're calling red when it comes to whips." Madison's amusement spread over her entire face.

"Exactly."

"Mistress?"

"Hmm?"

"I love the spanking you gave me, not just because of the endorphins and stuff. I loved it because you were the one doing it, and I felt safe with you because I knew that you only wanted to make me happy."

Shasti had tried her best not to tear up that day and tried her best not to tear up again now as she sat in her office. She reached down and opened the bottom right-hand drawer. She pulled out the yellow school bus and wheeled it across her desk calendar. "I love you, little peanut," she whispered to the universe, sure that Madison would feel it.

~~~

Shasti would not allow herself to look as confused as she felt walking into exam room seven. "Good morning," she said to Mrs. Henderson and her daughter, Jessie.

"Good morning," Mrs. Henderson said.

"Morning, Dr. B," Jessie said. Her tone was quite chipper, as if she was happy to be sitting in nothing but a paper exam gown on a Friday during summer vacation from school.

Shasti looked over the information the MA had taken. "Your vitals look good today, including the blood pressure." She looked up from the laptop and smiled. "Any incidents?

"None for a while," Mrs. Henderson said.

Shasti walked up to Jessie and began her examination. Her heart and breath sounds were good. Everything else she checked came back normal for a girl her age.

"You look good today, kiddo," Shasti said. "But there was this one anomaly on your last set of blood and urine tests."

"What's that?" The fear in Mrs. Henderson's voice was almost tangible.

"Jessie tested positive for…" Shasti hesitated. She was afraid to say it because it must be wrong. "Positive for LSD. The hallucinogenic drug lysergic acid diethylamide." She let that hang in the air for a moment. Sometimes the best thing to do around a patient was to stop talking. Body language could betray a patient's truthfulness or confirm it.

Jessie looked positively stunned and looked from her mother to Shasti. Mrs. Henderson, on the other hand, had no expression at all. Wouldn't a mother balk at the idea? Wouldn't a mother say something right about now? Shasti pictured Madison on the exam table and Dr. Littrell telling them that Madison had tested positive for LSD. What would her reaction be? She'd demand a recount or say something like, "Surely that can't be true."

But Mrs. Henderson sat there and said nothing.

"We will obviously test again to make sure," Shasti found herself saying. "But we simply can't rule it out just yet."

Mrs. Henderson nodded slowly but made no eye contact with Shasti or her daughter. What was going on in her head?

"Has anyone given you anything at school to take, Jessie?" Shasti asked.

"No," Jessie answered. "I mean, some of the kids smoke pot and do edibles—"

"That better not be you," Mrs. Henderson said, finally snapping out of her daze. "I can't take much more of this." There were tears in her eyes. The poor woman was stressed out.

"Mom," Jessie said, "I don't do that stuff." Jessie sounded truthful. Seriously, either this kid was a fantastic actress who could beat any lie detector test known to humankind, or there was something else going on.

"I can't help you if you're not honest with me," Shasti said, standing as tall as she could and lifting her chin. There was no smile on her face or comfort in her voice.

"I don't do that stuff you said, Dr. B." Jessie added, "Mom, I don't do LSD or pot or anything like she said."

Deflection, Shasti noted. She was pointing the blame elsewhere. Yes, something was going on. Shasti had to find out what. School being out was a variable. Maybe the physical school environment had been affecting Jessie. Or maybe Jessie and her classmates had been experimenting with drugs, but now that it was summer, she didn't see them as often. Shasti couldn't rule those things out.

Shasti stood up and paged one of the MAs. When Kelly came in, Shasti sent Jessie off to get yet another set of blood and urine samples taken.

Mrs. Henderson stayed behind. "It can't be LSD, Dr. B. It can't be. Her teachers told me she and her friends seem fine. Nothing weird except her dizziness and fatigue. I've got her on a short leash. When I'm at work, her grandmother is there with her. She's not allowed out for longer than two hours, and when she comes home, she always seems fine. I check her eyes and make her speak to me."

"I understand," Shasti said. "Give me a moment to go over these results again."

"Of course," Mrs. Henderson said. "I have to make a work call anyway. Excuse me." She got up and left the exam room.

Shasti turned on the swivel stool and scrolled through her notes. There was a connection between LSD and hypertension, she knew. And Jessie's blood pressure had been relatively low during her last visit. But if Jessie hadn't ingested anything to make her sick, then it might be time to send them to a cardiologist. If anything, that might eliminate more variables. But what a costly venture that would be. And Mrs. Henderson already had a deadbeat ex-husband who wasn't paying regular alimony. The poor woman was at the end of her rope. It must be difficult for Mrs. Henderson to be going through this alone. Her friends weren't very supportive of the divorce, if Shasti remembered correctly. That's got to sting. There was the grandmother, of course, but apparently, the grandmother also had health issues and seemed more of a burden than a help. When did Mrs. Henderson get relief?

Something niggled at Shasti's memory. Friends. Ahh, yes. It was something Mrs. Henderson said during a prior visit. She'd said that her friends offered sympathy and came by every time Jessie had one of her spells. Something was dawning on Shasti. Something sinister that she didn't want dawning. But it did.

Mrs. Henderson gets sympathy and attention whenever Jessie gets sick.

Shasti was stunned by this revelation. Her gaze darted toward the door. She hit the intercom to the front desk. When Reggie answered, she said in a passive run-of-the-mill tone, "Reggie, please ask Dr. Littrell to locate Form MSBP for exam room seven."

She'd never had to use this protocol in all her years of practicing medicine. She'd only read about it or seen it in bad movies.

Like puzzle pieces falling together, Shasti might very well have the solution. Was it the right one? She didn't know. But she had to explore it. Carefully, though. It could blow up if she were wrong. And she needed Allie's help right now.

Jessie was still getting labs taken on the other side of the clinic, and who knew where Mrs. Henderson was. Thankfully neither of them was there when Allie knocked and let herself into the exam room. There was no form, of course. It was code to isolate the parent from the patient.

"Tread very carefully, Shasti," she warned. "You must be one hundred percent sure."

"I'm not, but I need to talk to the patient alone."

"I'll keep Mrs. Henderson occupied in my office," Allie said. "I'll ding your cell phone with a text when I have her."

"Thank you," Shasti said, letting out a sigh. "I'll be careful."

Allie nodded and let out a similar sigh. It wasn't every day you suspected a mother of Munchausen Syndrome by proxy.

Jessie came back in and asked where her mother was. Shasti shrugged and said, "Work call, I think." The ding of a text from Allie came in. Good, she had Mrs. Henderson in her office.

"Whatever," Jessie said. Her disappointment with her mother's absence sounded like a regular occurrence.

"Let me ask you a few more questions while we wait for your mom to come back. Now that it's summer, what do you eat? Do you cook for your grandmother?"

"Pfft," Jessie spat. This must be a point of contention in their house as well. "Nope. Mom makes everything. Plastic bowls are filled with food and labeled with our names on them. One time I ate Grandma's lunch, and mom had a fit. I thought it was the same soup. How was I supposed to know? Grandma gets the low sodium blah blah blah." Jessie waved her hand like she was over it.

"So, your mother makes all your food during the school year and also at home during the summer."

"Yeah, she's *Super Mom*." The sarcasm in Jessie's voice was pretty clear. "But sometimes when I'm allowed to go out, I dump the lunch she made me and have Hungry Hamlet's with my friends," Jessie said. "Don't tell her, okay?"

"I won't." Shasti knew she didn't have much time left. "Do you take any medications? I know. I know. I've asked you this a thousand times."

"Nothing. Maybe some cough medicine when I have a cold, but the last time was in the winter. I had a headache one time, and she gave me a baby aspirin. I mean, come on, I'm fourteen. Am I not old enough for a real aspirin? My friend Kat takes Advil for her cramps every month."

"Have you tried Advil?"

"No, Mom would have a fit."

"Does she often have fits?"

"When it comes to Dad, yeah. But not, you know, all the time." Jessie looked down and picked at her nails. It seemed like she didn't want to betray her mother.

There was a quick knock on the door, and Mrs. Henderson reentered.

"Okay," Shasti said quickly, too quickly. *Chill, chill, chill,* she warned herself. Do not tip your hand. Frankly, she didn't have enough evidence, only a strong suspicion. And that wasn't enough to lay down an accusation. "I'll put a rush on the new tests. If they come back clean, I'll have to recommend a specialist."

"I was afraid of that," Mrs. Henderson said.

Shasti turned to Jessie and said, "I'm glad you've been feeling better this summer. Hopefully, whatever was affecting you has run its course, but we need to continue to watch it."

Shasti stayed in the exam room after the Hendersons left. "LSD? Seriously?" If the next round of tests came back positive, then Shasti was going to recommend counseling. Maybe she should recommend that anyway. It sounded like the family needed to work some things out. And if it genuinely was MSBP, then hopefully, the counselor could find out why Mrs. Henderson was giving some kind of drug or substance to her child just to get attention for herself.

"I don't know how to prove it, Jessie," Shasti said out loud. "And you clearly don't know your mother is doing this to you." *If she truly is,* Shasti reminded herself. She had absolutely no proof and couldn't act like she did. Her medical career would be finished if she didn't tread lightly as Allie warned her to.

~~~

Lunch with Madison was positively delightful. It helped the dark Henderson cloud following her around that morning. Not only did Madison bring soup and sandwiches from the Indigo Café, but she also brought Billy along. Billy had the day off from his job at the photocopy place and was hanging around with Madison. The three of them ate in her office, and Madison took great delight in showing Billy the bottom right drawer dedicated to her toys. He'd said she was a lucky duck, to which she said she wasn't a duck. And then he insisted she was a duck because she walked like one, and then it was on. Shasti put her elbows on her desk, her chin resting on her fists, and watched the fun banter between the two *littles*. Much too soon, Billy said he had to leave and that Madison would drive him home. Shasti hugged Madison for an overlong time, causing her to squirm and say that she couldn't breathe.

The two *littles* had been gone for about a half-hour, but Shasti was too shaken by the Henderson revelation to get much paperwork done. Her thoughts wandered back to her new relationship. That was a safe place. Maybe she'd make a special dinner for Madison. Or they could go out. They should celebrate. Madison said her job interview went well that morning, and she liked the manager. They would call her in a week to tell her whether or not she got the job. Maybe they should wait until she actually had the job before celebrating. "Cart before the horse, Shasti," she mumbled to herself.

There was a soft knock on her office door.

"Come in," Shasti called, thinking maybe Madison had come back.

Allie walked in and closed the door behind her. She sat down on the couch without invitation. She sighed and said, "How much proof do you have?" Obviously, she was referring to the Henderson family MSBP situation.

"Not enough," Shasti said. "But the signs are there. Something is going on. The positive LSD test is a huge curve ball, though. And the family changed doctors. That's another sign of Munchausen. It seems to be adding up, yet there could be many other explanations."

"Have you prescribed any treatments?"

"Nothing yet," Shasti said. "Just healthy eating, exercise, and water intake. Allie, I don't want to simply throw things at this. It could make things worse. If I treated the symptoms without genuinely knowing the cause, that might be construed as medical abuse."

Allie nodded, and they talked more about the details Shasti had on the case. As they spoke, nothing new came to light, so Allie said, "I'm on board with this possible diagnosis, but before you pull the trigger, please talk it over with me first because we'll have to enlist law enforcement, Child Protective Services, counselors."

"I will," Shasti said. "And I understand that if we delay too long, then that might be considered negligence. Also, not good. I've ordered a rush on the labs she gave today."

Allie stood up. Her expression was grim. "Let me know when the labs come back. Maybe together, we'll see something." She headed toward the door and then stopped and turned around. There was a big smile on her face. "I can't believe I almost forgot. You have to see this.

They came and asked permission first, so don't be upset. I think exam room eight will have the best view."

Shasti stood up, perplexed. Don't be upset? Best view of what? She understood as soon as she got to the window in exam room eight. Outside in all their sneaky *little* glory were Madison and Billy washing her car. Shasti laughed and said, "Those little devils. They said they were driving Billy home." Both were soaking wet, but it was the perfect activity for a hot August day.

"I had a feeling you didn't know," Allie said. "I'll leave you to it then."

"Thanks."

Shasti pulled out her cell phone and texted Madison.

> SHASTI: Lunch was wonderful. The company even better. What would you like to do for dinner later? Eat in or go out?

Hidden behind the cracked blinds, Shasti watched from the exam room window as Madison pulled her phone out of her back pocket.

> MADISON: (heart emoji) Hi, Mistress. Hmm. Maybe eat in and then "eat in." Ha ha ha.

Shasti was glad Allie had left. Madison was in a promiscuous mood.

> SHASTI: Sounds good to me, peanut. Where are you right now?

Madison beckoned Billy over and showed him the text message on her phone. They both started laughing and then talking animatedly to each other, probably about where they should say Madison was. Before Madison could perjure herself, Shasti opened the blinds and knocked on the window. Both Madison and Billy looked over, their startled faces instantly transformed into shock at getting caught. Shasti made a heart shape with both hands as she smiled at them.

Both Madison and Billy waved frantically. Shasti gestured for them to finish the job they'd been doing and then waved that she was leaving the window. Shasti texted Madison as she headed back to her office.

SHASTI: You and Billy are so sneaky! But thank you for taking care of me, peanut. Come in when you're all done. AFTER everything is put away, that is. Where did you find a hose and bucket?

MADISON: Bucket, sponges, hose, sprayer, and car soap were all bought today at that DIY store. I paid with my own money. And, okay, we'll come back in when we're done. We're kind of wet, though. Is that okay?

SHASTI: Of course. And thank you again for being you. You are special to me.

MADISON: (heart emoji) (heart emoji) (heart emoji)

Shasti sat at her desk, wondering two things. How in the world had she gotten so lucky finding Madison, and how in the world could a mother do to her child what it appeared Mrs. Henderson was doing to hers?

Chapter 17

Madison

Joy. Another clothes store. That's exactly what Madison wanted to do on a Saturday afternoon. She was already carrying seven thousand bags filled with clothes, shoes, and all kinds of stuff Mistress bought at those zillion other stores. She even had Madison try on "cute bras." Now that was embarrassing. They weren't even sports bras, so what was the use in having them?

Madison sighed dramatically, hoping Mistress would take the hint. All she got was a raised eyebrow and a scolding look. Fine. Whatever. Yay—clothes shopping. Fake it until you get ice cream, right?

"Ooh, this is cute." Mistress held up a shirt with a giraffe outlined in sparkly sequins. Actually, it was kind of cute. Madison threw her a thumbs up and looked for a place to park it. Why don't these stores have benches or something for the people who couldn't care less about clothes? Arghh.

Madison trailed behind her mistress around the boutique, whatever the heck a boutique was. It was a store. In the mall. Get over yourself. Anyway, Mistress finally had a big enough pile for Madison to try on. The tall saleswoman let them stash their already purchased bags and boxes behind her counter before heading into the try-on room.

Oh, thank goodness. This try-on room was a single-serving one. Private. The one in that other store was like a giant open locker room.

Madison had to take off her clothes in front of strangers. She usually didn't mind taking off her clothes, but now that she thought about it, that was only in front of lovers. Well, to be perfectly real, the *pretties* in Columbus weren't really lovers. They were receivers of sex. That's all. Katia made her take off all her clothes before she took care of Brooke that first time and every time after. Was that really necessary? Brooke didn't touch her. Not once. Madison thought it was so she couldn't run away after telling Katia she didn't want to lick Brooke's privates. But Katia just laughed and made her do it anyway while waiting downstairs.

Mistress organized the "outfits," as she called them, in the order they were to be tried on and paraded by a very-excited-to-be-trying-on-clothes Madison.

Madison tried not to sigh but simply said, "Yes, Ma'am," and got to work in the dressing room. She heard Mistress talking with the saleswoman outside, so she had a moment to breathe. She wanted to get to the ice cream part already. She was so tired. They had spent ages in the DIY store getting paint and supplies first thing that morning, and Madison had kind of wanted to go right back home to get started. They'd picked a light dusty rose color for the walls and a darker rose color for the trim work. She'd never been allowed to paint her room before or have color or posters on the walls. Back home, everything was white, white, white except for the people in it.

Madison giggled, prompting Mistress to ask, "Everything okay in there?"

"Yes, Ma'am," Madison said.

"So polite," the saleswoman said. Uh oh, their voices were really close now. They must be right outside. She'd better get moving.

Madison took off her Life is Good t-shirt and then turned to reach for the sparkly giraffe shirt. She caught movement out of the corner of her eye and whirled toward it. In an instant, her world came full circle.

It was a mirror. She stared at her reflection, horrified at the person she saw there. It was her. She started shaking. In all her pretending to be someone who could be loved, that mirror told her she was that same stupid, worthless girl from Columbus. The one who would never amount to anything. The one too stupid to go to college. And the one too helpless to stop the boys pushing her against the lockers face first, grabbing her by the hips, and dry humping her in front of all their friends.

She sat down hard on the bench. A sob escaped before she even knew it was there.

"Who do you think you are?" Madison spit at her reflection. "You're nobody. No one really cares about you, Madison Kim. You. Are. Nothing." A groaning sob came out next.

The door flew open, and Miss Shasti was on the bench in an instant. She threw her arms around Madison and pulled her close. Madison wouldn't let herself be held and yanked out of the embrace with a squeal. She slid to the far side of the bench and cried. All this attention Miss Shasti was giving her? Madison wasn't worth any of it. Miss Shasti was a doctor. What was Madison? Madison was nothing. She didn't even have a stupid job anymore. What an idiot. She slammed the side of her fist against her thigh. No one should have to look at her or even be in the same room as her.

Miss Shasti tried to touch her again, but Madison recoiled. She didn't want to taint the nice lady who tried to be nice to her. Being nice to Madison must be her community service charity or something.

Mistress said to the saleswoman, "I saw you had a restroom. Could you please grab a few paper towels and wet them? Not too drippy." The saleswoman must have nodded because Miss Shasti said, "Thank you."

She turned her focus to Madison. "I'm not going to touch you. Can you tell me what happened?"

Madison swiped at the angry, disgusted tears on her cheeks. "You shouldn't be seen with me. You're too nice and good and way way above me. I'm no good. Don't buy me things. It won't help. I'm not..." She couldn't think of the right words but said, "I'm not worth it. Seriously. You should leave. I'll get the bus and go home. To Columbus, I mean. They know who I am there. And what I'm not. You haven't figured that out yet. You're really nice and all, but it makes no sense." Madison swiped at the tears that just wouldn't stop.

The saleswoman brought the requested towels and then shut the door, giving them privacy. Madison let Miss Shasti rub a cool paper towel along her wrist and forearm.

"Can you breathe for me?" Miss Shasti asked. "Deep breath in. Yes, that's it. Hold for a second, and, yes, yes, slow exhale. Good girl." The cool towel made its way to Madison's other wrist and then to the back of her neck and forehead. A fresh towel started again on her wrists. So good.

Miss Shasti said nary a word but continued her towel therapy. She even started humming. It was a kid's song that Madison liked. Something about a bear and a bee and their fight over honey. In the end, the bear and the bee became best buddies. It was a funny story. Madison wasn't surprised when one of those amazing forehead kisses came next. That was good, too. The towel therapy stopped, and Madison let herself be pulled into a light hug. Miss Shasti rocked them both slightly, still humming. They sat like that for many long minutes.

"Mistress?"

"Mm hmm?"

"Can we go home now? I'm kind of tired."

"No ice cream?" Mistress held Madison at arm's length and looked comically distressed. She put a hand to her forehead. "Just checking for a fever."

Madison laughed. "I'm not sick. Just tired. Can you lay down with me when we get home?"

"Mm hmm. Can I be the big spoon?"

"Always," Madison said.

They stood up, and Madison put on her shirt. "I like that giraffe shirt. Sorry I didn't try on any of the clothes."

"That's okay. I'm buying them all, anyway." Mistress opened the door from where she sat on the bench and gestured to the saleswoman to ring everything up.

Once the saleswoman left with the clothes, including the giraffe shirt, Mistress said to Madison, "You can try everything on at home. Later. How about this? When we wake up after our nap, how about we pick up a pizza and go keep Miss Rikki company at the coffee shop?"

"Okay," Madison said. "Can we not tell her I had a mental breakdown in the store?"

"I won't if you won't," Mistress said. "But you and I are going to talk about this at some point. When you're ready. Would that be okay?"

"Yes, Ma'am."

Mistress put her hand out, and Madison took it. She was still trembling a little and knew that Mistress felt it. Together they stood up and headed for the cash register and then home.

~~~

A week later, Madison was sitting in yet another doctor's waiting room. This doctor wasn't a medical doctor, though. She was a head doctor. A shrink. And she was going to help Madison take care of her "Life BS." She and Mistress kept laughing about that. Her "life bullshit." Ha!

The waiting room had neat, framed photographs on the walls depicting soothing scenes. She guessed that was the goal of the pictures because they were kind of calming. One was a mountain with a soaring bird in the sky, another was a bunch of pine trees with a shaft of sunlight slicing through them, and the big one right in front of them was an ocean at sunrise, or maybe it was sunset. Who knew? Depended on your perspective, maybe. All she knew was that she promised Mistress she would listen to the doctor and answer whatever questions she asked. And she was to answer honestly. No worries. There was a promise of ice cream after this appointment, and there would be no mental breakdowns standing in the way this time.

Her nose itched, and she moved her hand to scratch it, but Mistress was holding that hand and wouldn't let go. Fine. Madison had another perfectly good nose-scratching hand anyway. A simple solution for a simple thing.

"This place is cool looking for a psychologist's office," Madison said. She patted the new-looking couch she and Mistress sat on together. "Is this the couch I'll lie down on and tell the doctor all my troubles?" Madison swooned just to make Mistress laugh, which she did. That was always the best—making Mistress smile.

"I'm so pleased how your room turned out," Mistress said. "That paint color looks so good. Doesn't it?"

"I love it. I know it's a pinkish color, but I like how it sometimes looks lavender in the morning."

Mistress chuckled. "I think we got more paint on ourselves than on the walls."

"You started it," Madison accused. Mistress had dapped her nose with a dusty rose-colored finger. Oh, yes, and then soon Mistress had a dap on her chin. Somehow, and Madison wasn't sure how, but in and amongst all the laughing and wrestling, paint got all over their faces, arms, and legs.

"That's not how I remember it," Mistress said and looked innocently toward the ceiling. Aha! Clearly, she was fibbing.

Madison scoffed and said, "I can't wait for my bed to get here." Madison kicked her legs back and forth, hitting the couch on every backswing. A hand gripped her thigh. Okay. Time to stop kicking.

Just then, a well-put-together Black woman walked up the long open hallway toward them.

"Ouch," Mistress said.

"Oh, sorry." Madison had been squeezing her hand hard.

"It's okay to be nervous, peanut."

"Okay."

"Hello," the pretty doctor said. She looked like she was a tiny bit older than Mistress. And, yeah, she was really nice looking with her tight-fitting professional suit. Her hair was in a million thin braids, all pulled back into one thick ponytail. It was so cool looking. And her red glasses matched her red lipstick, and both contrasted nicely with her deep brown skin.

"Madison," Mistress said and patted her on the back. "Dr. Sumner asked if you were ready."

"Oh, sorry." Madison felt her cheeks get warm. "I'm ready, I guess. I don't know what to do."

"First, we'll go back to my office," Dr. Sumner said. "Your mistress will stay in the waiting room until we're done. Does that sound okay?"

Madison nodded and then whispered to Mistress, "She knows you're my mistress?"

Mistress chuckled. "Yes, baby. Remember, I told you that Dr. Sumner is a BDSM-friendly therapist."

"Ohhhh yeahhhh," Madison said dramatically as she put a single finger up in the air.

"You can talk to her about anything and everything," Mistress said. "Hold nothing back. I'll be out here and won't hear a thing."

"Okay." Madison looked down at her feet, feeling shy in front of the psychologist or therapist or whatever she was called.

A friendly hand reached out in front of her. "Shall we head to my office?"

"Okay." Madison took the therapist's hand and let herself be led down the sunny hallway to the therapy room. There would probably be a couch and tissues. Lots and lots of tissues. Dr. Sumner would ask, "How does that make you feel?" and then jot down all the things that were oh-so-very wrong with Madison on her handy notepad. Madison was sure there would be a lot of things to write down. Maybe Dr. Sumner would need seventeen notepads for all of it.

Dr. Sumner told her where to sit—yep, right on the couch. The doctor sat in a well-worn swiveling chair across from the couch. There was a solid-looking wooden coffee table in between them. Too bad there wasn't coffee. Madison took a moment to look around. On one side of the room, the side they were in, the doctor's desk stood in the corner in all its regal glory. It was dark wood with fancy designs cut into the legs and looked like the desk of a powerful CEO or something. The fancy books on the floor-to-ceiling bookshelves behind the desk were also impressive. Maybe Mistress would let her have a bookshelf in the room that was going to be hers. She had so many books in her room back home. Home in Columbus, she meant. Maybe Mistress would let her bring some back when they visited in two weeks. Hopefully. Fingers crossed.

Madison then took in the other side of the therapist's room. Holy hippopotamus! It was decked out with toys galore. There were bins with all kinds of colorful things in them that she was dying to look at. And the floor was a rug with a meandering road printed on it. Gah, her Mini-Wheels cars were in Mistress's desk in her office. Maybe Dr. Sumner had toy cars here?

"Did you want to check out the toys, Madison?"

"Can I? Yes, please." At Dr. Sumner's nod, she bolted off the couch and looked in every bin until she found something suitable for running along the roads. It was a hillbilly pickup truck. All she needed was a bale of hay in the back, and she'd be set. She'd have a little gun rack in the front cab. But wait, no. She'd never shoot a gun. Hmm. Maybe a light saber or her sword. Yes, that's it.

"Can we talk while you play, Madison?"

"Okay." Madison got on the floor and ran the toy truck along the marked road, carefully staying in the correct lane. "Most of your toys are for babies." A simple statement that she said without looking up.

"And you're not a baby." Another simple statement.

Madison scoffed. "No. No. No. Just a *little*. You know what that means, right?" Madison sat back on her heels and eyed the doctor suspiciously. Was she a quack? Or did she know her stuff?

"I've worked with *littles* before, so yes, I do know. But why don't you tell me what you think it means."

Ahh, here we go. Where's the notepad? How does that make you feel? Madison giggled out loud but then cleared her throat. Mistress said she had to answer the doctor's questions. She'd better pay attention.

"It means that sometimes I want to play with toys, not baby toys, but like cars and swords and Chutes and Ladders and stuff. And I like when Mistress gives me a bath and washes my back and my hair and puts it in braids and stuff." Her chest was kind of tight, and she wasn't playing with the truck anymore.

"You love your Mistress, don't you?"

"Mm hmm." Madison's throat was tight with emotion. Someone better find those tissues. She stood up, making sure to grab the tiny pickup truck, and sat down in her original spot on the couch.

They chit-chatted for a little while about Madison's favorite foods and superheroes and stuff like that. Madison knew they were just in the get to know each other phase, but that was okay. It was helping her relax, and that was probably the whole purpose.

She was relaxed until Dr. Sumner said, "So can you tell me what happened in the dressing room at the Queen City Boutique?"

Madison was all over the place after that, but Dr. Sumner seemed used to rambling patients and got Madison back on track or an equally important track. Madison talked about the things Katia made her do and what the stupid boys did at school. She told the doctor the things her grandmother would say to her. She also told her about Mrs. Park and how all that time, Madison didn't even know that Mrs. Park was her great grandmother and she felt cheated not knowing the woman before then. That kind of wasn't fair of her family to do that.

"I told Mistress all of this, too, Dr. Sumner," Madison said and guided the truck down her right thigh toward her knee. "We had a 'heart-to-heart.' That's what she called it. She said it's better not to have secrets between us. 'Builds trust,' she'd said. Anyway, I told her everything I just told you. Some of it she already knew." The truck flew in the air, landed on her left thigh, and traveled back toward her hip.

"You haven't mentioned your mother," Dr. Sumner said. "You're going to visit her soon, aren't you?"

"Mm hmm." The knot was back in Madison's throat. *They always think it's the mother's fault,* Madison thought sarcastically. "I miss Mommy. And my dad." Another simple statement. Okay, two simple statements. *There you go, Doc. Do something with that.*

"How do you feel about seeing your mommy?"

"I can't wait. But I hope she'll be out of bed. She sometimes stays there for days and days. Mrs. Park said that Mommy has depression. Mommy lives with Grandma, though, so that makes sense."

"Would it be better for your mommy not to live with your grandmother?"

Madison shrugged. She hadn't really thought about what grownups should or shouldn't do for themselves. Before Dr. Sumner asked her to talk more about her mother or grandmother, Madison blurted, "Can I ask you a question?"

"Of course." Dr. Sumner's smile was so kind. So gentle. Madison knew Mistress was paying for this session, but she fully intended to pay her back for every single one of the doctors, dentists, eye doctors, and therapists once Mrs. Park's money got out of jail. There was a term for it, but Madison couldn't remember at that moment. Anyway, Madison felt at ease with the doctor, which was good.

"Do you think of yourself as African-American because everyone wants to call me Korean-American or sometimes Chinese-American as if all East Asian people are Chinese or something? I've never been to Korea, and I probably couldn't even find it on a map. I tell people, 'I'm American,' but it weirds them out or something. They say stupid things like, 'But where are you *really* from?' Stupids."

Dr. Sumner took the bait, probably knowing full well that Madison was avoiding the mother and grandmother topics, and spoke with Madison about being Black in a country that, for some odd reason, thought itself a white, Christian, English-speaking country.

At some point, Dr. Sumner realized they had gotten way off track, but the time had come to a close, so, hooray, they couldn't get back to topics that made Madison's heart hurt. She readily agreed to come back for another session the following week, and if that went well, they could make it a permanent weekly session.

When Dr. Sumner opened the door to walk Madison back to Mistress, Madison had other ideas. She ran down the long hallway, even though it probably wasn't allowed, and slammed into her Mistress, who was just getting up from the couch.

Wordlessly, Mistress's arms wrapped around Madison and held her tight. One forehead kiss later made Madison bounce so much that Mistress had to release her.

"I take it the session went okay?"

"Mm hmm," Madison said. And even though the doctor was standing right there, she added, "She's really nice, and she listens, and we talked about a lot of stuff, and she isn't a fan of the term African-American, but she's okay if other people want to use it for themselves and she has toys in there and, and, and—"

"Madison," Mistress said pointedly.

"Okay, okay." Madison stopped bouncing. "I'll slow down." She looked at Dr. Sumner and said, "Mistress tells me to slow down a lot."

Dr. Sumner smiled and said, "And that's okay. She looks out for you, doesn't she?"

Ahh, the therapy session was still going on, was it?

"Mm hmm." Madison looked up at her Mistress, knowing she had love spouting from her eyes.

Dr. Sumner said she'd see Madison next week and, before heading back down that long hallway, added, "Don't forget your homework."

"I almost forgot." Madison squeezed Mistress's hand. "We have homework."

"We do?"

"Yep, I'll tell you once we're in the car. It's easy peasy homework."

They made Madison's next appointment at the reception desk and headed outside to the sunny parking lot. Holding hands with Mistress on the way to the car, Madison said, "Mistress?"

"Mm hmm?"

"You know how you said you wanted to keep me?"

"Yes. I still do."

"Well, maybe I believe you."

Mistress made a weird kind of strangled noise and then swallowed a few times. "Thank you, peanut." Oh, Madison understood. Mistress was choked up with emotion. "Yes, I want to keep you, baby."

Madison raised the hand she was holding and kissed the back of it. "I love you."

"And I love you."

Once back in the Beemer, Madison started a quiet but steady chant of "Ice cream, ice cream, ice cream."

Madison giggled when Mistress joined in, and they headed to *Ice Dreams* down on Kirkland past Mistress's office.

Chapter 18

Shasti

Shasti was now one hundred percent sure that therapy for Madison would help. She had hesitated before suggesting it to her *little* because she didn't want to set her off again. But all seemed well, and having Shasti as a sounding board would supplement Dr. Sumner's work. It was only five hours or so after the session, and Madison had yet to tell her what the homework assignment was. And apparently, they both had to do it.

"Baby," Shasti said to Madison, who was washing up the dinner dishes, "I've got all the leftovers in the fridge."

"Can we have tacos again tomorrow?" Madison asked. It wasn't exactly an interruption because Shasti had technically finished her sentence. She just hadn't finished her thought, so she let the lapse in protocol slide.

"Did you forget? We're going to Miss Tilda's for Sunday dinner tomorrow afternoon."

"Dinner in the afternoon? And, yes, I did forget."

"We can have tacos again on Monday. You're starting at PETology on Monday, aren't you?"

Madison turned toward Shasti and smiled big. "Yep. I will soon be a contributing member to your household."

"*Our* household."

"Whatever you say," Madison said as if she wasn't convinced this was her home as well. That would take time, Shasti figured. "Should I wear my collar tonight?"

"That would be nice," Shasti said. "I like my girl to know her place."

Madison beamed at Shasti. "At your feet, Mistress."

"And in my bed."

Madison's face beamed even brighter. "Can we have sex now?"

Shasti burst out laughing. Oh, yes, Madison was a keeper. "Uh, maybe. I have some work to do upstairs in my office. You're welcome to join me after you finish cleaning up, but you must stay very quiet. Or you can stay down here if you want. I won't be too long."

"I'll come up to be with you," Madison said.

"All right, but you have to dress appropriately." Shasti bit her bottom lip. "Boi shorts and that cute turquoise tank top. The tight one. No bra."

Madison made an odd noise, but it was a good noise. Funny how Shasti was beginning to be able to read Madison's moods. She wasn't one hundred percent there but getting closer all the time.

"I have this e-reader app on my new tablet," Madison said. "I'm going to find a book about BDSM and *littles* and Mommy Dommes. If that even exists."

"Ooh, let me know what you find." Shasti stood on her tippy toes to kiss Madison on the crown of her head. She laughed when Madison purred. Shasti patted her *little's* butt and headed up the stairs, and Madison went back to scrubbing the pan in the sink.

Once settled at her desk, she turned on the computer and logged into her case files. She knew Jessie Henderson's case number by heart, and it uploaded quickly. Like any good detective, she went over the clues from the beginning. She tried to keep an open mind as she sifted through the details but to no avail. No new information or ideas were coming through. And the MSBP diagnosis? Well, that looked kind of thin, too. There was no real hard evidence to prove the mother was hurting her child.

Shasti hated losing. She hated being unable to figure out a diagnosis, which meant she couldn't help a patient.

"Ahh, the new lab results are in." Shasti clicked on the download tab. She waited for it to open up and then scanned them intently. "Are you kidding me?" She blinked her eyes and looked at the date of the test. Yes, these were the latest results. "Why do you keep testing positive for LSD, kiddo?" she muttered to her screen. She printed out the results and highlighted the LSD note. "There are no other signs that you've taken that drug." She sat back and blew out a long sigh. Her cheeks puffed up as she did so.

Madison knocked shyly on the open door.

"Come on in, sweetie." Shasti let her gaze roam over Madison's outfit. Those tight little boi shorts contoured wonderfully to Madison's curves. And the tank? Mm hmm. Nice and tight across her chest. Shasti's ogling must have aroused Madison because two peaks grew from her breasts.

"I'll be quiet," Madison whispered. "I'll be on the floor right here."

"Perfectly good couch right there," Shasti suggested.

"You and Dr. Sumner are always trying to get me on a couch for one reason or another." Madison rolled her eyes dramatically, making Shasti laugh.

Just then, Shasti's phone dinged an incoming text. It was Rikki. Why was she texting now? Shasti flicked it open. Rikki wanted her to call when she got a moment. "Madison, I have to call Miss Rikki. You stay right here, okay? I'll be in the bedroom."

"Yours or mine?"

"Ours," Shasti said and waggled her eyebrows.

"Can I use your printer, Mistress?"

"Of course." Shasti pointed to the wireless printer next to her desk. "Password is on that post-it note."

"Nice security," Madison called after her.

Shasti closed her bedroom door just as Rikki picked up. "What's going on, Rikki?"

"Another one," Rikki said. "I got another fucking notice. Somebody has my information and maxed out another credit card. The credit card companies, two of them at this point, are threatening to sue me."

"Keep your lawyer posted and send him copies of everything."

"I did," Rikki said. "I just need to vent, and I can't tell Aunt Tilda about this. She'll worry too much. Hopefully, it's nothing, right?"

"Here's hoping," Shasti said. "Have you told Eileen?"

"I have. She can be cold sometimes, but she's been very sympathetic and attentive. That part's been nice."

"I'm glad," Shasti said and meant it. Rikki and Eileen had been together about seven months at that point. They were still getting to know each other, and maybe Eileen wasn't such a joy suck after all. Shasti wanted the best for her bestie. Rikki was the first real friend she'd made since her big move to Denton Heights a little over a year ago.

They talked for a little longer, and Shasti asked Rikki for a favor. Something for after the dinner tomorrow afternoon, and Rikki said she would be happy to oblige after she cleared it with her aunt.

"And Eileen, of course," Shasti said.

"Yes, of course. Consent is always number one."

They said their goodbyes and were about to disconnect when Rikki said, "Oh, and I'd prefer my, uh, situation stay between us."

"Of course," Shasti said. "That's why I took the call in another room."

"Love you, friend," Rikki said.

They said their final goodbyes, and Shasti headed back to her office. She stood in the doorway admiring her girlfriend lying on her stomach on the floor with her legs bent at the knees. Oh, yes. Shasti had gotten lucky, all right. Madison was an incredible young woman whose potential had yet to be tapped. And Shasti was determined to help her live her best life.

It looked like her girlfriend was reading a novel, so she must have been successful finding something to download. And, yes, it was okay to think of Madison as her girlfriend. She was that, indeed, and so much more. Hmm, how big was her girlfriend feeling this evening? She mentally cleared her throat and sat back in her chair.

"Everything okay?" Madison asked, looking up from her tablet. "Were you talking to Miss Rikki about me?"

Shasti sat in her office chair facing Madison. "No, sweetie. Rikki sometimes needs to talk to me about grown-up stuff. About things going on in her life."

"Like the way I talk to you?"

"Mm hmm," Shasti said.

"Is Miss Tilda okay?"

"She's fine. We'll see her tomorrow."

"Yay," Madison said and looked back at her tablet. "Mistress? I printed a list of BDSM movies. Maybe we can watch some."

"Excellent idea." Shasti swiveled back around to face Madison.

"And, um," Madison sat up, her back against the loveseat, "I had this chorus teacher in tenth grade. His name was Mr. Valente. I mean, that probably still is his name, but anyway, this one day, they thought he was drunk at school, and they fired him, but really, he had diabetes, and no one knew it. He knew it but never told anybody, and he had a diabetes event or whatever it's called."

"A hypoglycemic reaction?"

"I guess. They hired him back once they got it all straightened out and stuff, but I thought maybe your LSD thing isn't really LSD. Maybe it's something else. Maybe those lab people came to the wrong conclusion or didn't have the real thing in their database or something. I don't know."

Shasti didn't answer right away. She had too many thoughts swirling in her mind because Madison was absolutely right. Something else could be masking as LSD. Why hadn't she thought of that? Shasti sighed, disgusted with herself.

"I wasn't snooping, Mistress," Madison said. "You were muttering when I got up here. I overheard you. And then I guess my brain must have marinated on that, and then I remembered about Mr. Valente."

"I believe you weren't snooping, peanut. But you understand I can't talk to you about my patients, right?"

"I know. I know. I'm sorry."

"Don't be sorry, little one." Shasti turned back to her computer. "I'm going to explore your idea for a while, and then we'll do your homework."

"Ohhhh yeahhhh!" Madison wiggled on the carpet. "We're supposed to come up with three good things in our lives. Things that make us happy. And then we have to say three things that make us, um, not happy. No, no. She said, 'three things we're working on because everybody should be trying to better themselves in one way or another.' Something like that. But I'll read on the floor until then, okay? I found a book about lesbians in a Domme/sub relationship, so imma just read that, okay?"

"Go for it."

Madison rocked back and forth and then plopped down on her stomach again.

Shasti minimized her case file and lab results and opened a new browser window. She typed in "False positive for LSD."

The results were many and varied, but she finally found a refereed journal article to peruse. She scanned the introduction and found nothing useful. Once she was in the heart of the article, there it was. Plain as day. The puzzle pieces in her head slowly came together, forming a complete picture. "That's it!" she said out loud. "That's got to be it."

She held a finger up when Madison asked her what was wrong. Shasti tapped open her text app and texted Allie. She knew it was late, but this just might be the answer.

> SHASTI: Sorry to text so late. I think I have it figured out. What's causing the Henderson girl's symptoms, I mean. I can't talk on the phone right now, so I hope you're okay with texting.

It took an entire minute before Allie got back to her, but it was well worth the wait.

> ALLIE: Tell me.

Shasti relayed the information in the article, and they texted back and forth as Allie asked for more details. She asked for a copy of the article, which Shasti gladly forwarded and then printed a copy for herself.

> ALLIE: First thing Monday morning, call that family and get them all in your office ASAP. The child, the mother, AND the grandmother who is now a possibility.

SHASTI: Yes, exactly. I hadn't considered her before.

ALLIE: Let me know when. I will be hovering nearby.

SHASTI: I will. And we'll need law enforcement and child protective services if it goes one way, not the other. Because I think I know what, but not who or why.

ALLIE: I'll take care of the professionals.

SHASTI: Excellent. Thank you. I'll see you Monday. Thank you for responding so late on a Saturday evening.

ALLIE: Just watching a movie with my hubby. Your text is more exciting than this predictable shoot-em-up movie. It was his pick tonight.

Shasti chuckled, and then they texted their goodnights. Shasti swiveled around to face Madison. "You!"

"Me?"

"Yes, you. You may have just saved this young girl's life."

"How?"

"You might have provided the missing link, baby."

"Yay." Madison wiggled on the carpet.

Shasti couldn't help herself. Her gaze shifted to that enticing part of Madison she loved to stroke. Okay, fine. There were a lot of

Madison parts she liked to stroke, but this particular part had captured her attention.

"Uhh, Mistress?" Madison looked up coyly at Shasti. "Are you, like, checking out my butt?"

"Mm hmm," Shasti said. "Bring it here."

Madison practically leaped to her feet and fell into Shasti's open arms. Shasti remained seated while Madison insinuated herself between Shasti's opened legs. Shasti's hands reached around and grabbed two handfuls of Madison over her tight boi shorts. She squeezed and kneaded the soft flesh making Madison giggle. Shasti let go and then ran her hands over the smooth cheeks. Madison's small breasts were right there for the taking, but something was in the way. Clothes.

"You don't need this," Shasti tugged on Madison's tank top, and Madison whipped it off.

Madison leaned down to whisper in Shasti's ear. "My three good things are these. One – Miss Shasti. Two – kisses from Miss Shasti. And three – cuddles with Miss Shasti. Four—"

"You only had to name three."

"But there's so many."

"Mmm. That's good." Shasti was distracted by Madison's mouth being so close to her ear. She wanted to kiss those soft lips, but she needed to be latched on to one of those breasts in front of her five minutes ago. Shasti first placed a kiss on the pink collar around Madison's neck and then gave tender kisses on the small but budding flesh. Madison's breathing deepened as Shasti licked a nipple and then sucked it into her mouth. Shasti not only heard Madison's moan but felt the reverberations through her lips. Madison boldly placed both hands on the back of Shasti's head and pulled her tighter. She wanted more pressure. Shasti obliged and then wrestled herself away to service the other breast.

"Mistress," Madison said, her voice thick with lust, "please take me to your room."

"*Our* room. And, yes, ma'am," Shasti said, making Madison giggle at the role reversal.

Shasti stood up, and Madison grabbed her hand, letting herself be led out of the office. Once in the dark bedroom, Shasti pressed Madison against the wall and smashed her thigh between Madison's parted legs. Using her fingers, Shasti tilted Madison's chin up and looked her in the eyes for several long moments.

"One," Miss Shasti said, "Madison. Two – your soft lips. Three – Madison loves me, and I love her. Four—"

"Kiss me, Mistress," Madison interrupted. "Please."

And Shasti did. She kissed Madison until she was writhing. Shasti pulled back out of breath.

"Why are you still wearing those shorts?" Shasti asked in all seriousness. "Take them off." She left Madison breathing heavily against the wall and turned on the bedside light. She twisted the dimmer, creating an intimate glow, and then pulled down the comforter and top sheet.

"I like it when you're bossy." Madison said this while taking off the aforementioned boi shorts and tossing them aside.

"Mmm," Shasti said, licking her lips. "You are a delicious dessert, and I am ultimately going to devour you, but first—" She maneuvered Madison to sit on the side of the bed and then rummaged through the bottom drawer of her dresser. "Here they are." She pulled out two pink wrist cuffs that matched the pink collar Madison had received at her collaring ceremony. Unbeknownst to Madison, two pink ankle cuffs would make their appearance at some point. But not tonight. She put the wrist cuffs on Madison's wrists.

Shasti went to close the drawer but spotted a new purchase. Yes, this would do tonight. She pulled it out and said, "Be right back." She hustled into the master bath to clean and sanitize the purple strap-on dildo. It had never been used, but she liked to clean her toys before and after.

She brought it back and held it up for Madison to see.

"Yellow," Madison said and folded her arms over her chest.

"It's for *you* to wear," Shasti said. "Not me." She wanted to make sure Madison understood the game that was afoot.

"Really? Green, green, green!" Madison stood up so fast it made Shasti laugh.

"Excellent, but we'll talk later, maybe tomorrow, about the yellow call. Okay?"

"Yes, Mistress," Madison said the words, but her eyes were on the harness. "I've never worn one of those before."

Shasti showed her how to put it on and adjusted the straps snugly. "Look at yourself in the mirror." As she said the words, she instantly regretted the suggestion, but luckily Madison only looked at the phallus dangling in front of her body and didn't have a repeat freak out like she'd had at the mall the weekend before.

Madison jiggled her body, making the phallus bounce all around. The grin on her face was so worth it as she grabbed the base and stroked it a few times. "This is weird. I can't imagine dealing with this thing permanently attached to your body."

Shasti did her best not to laugh.

"Umm, things I don't like," Madison said. "One, Mistress still has all her clothes on." Madison stood with her hands on her hips. It was quite the comical look with the phallus sticking out in front of her.

"Undress me then," Shasti said. She turned away mostly because she needed to wipe the smile off her face. It was hard because Madison was so freakin' adorable at that moment.

With tentative hands, Madison removed all of Shasti's clothes, although Shasti had to help unclasp the bra. Mm hmm, that was something her peanut would have to get better at. Madison placed the clothes gently on the chair instead of tossing them on the floor like she did with her boi shorts. Shasti pushed Madison backward until her legs hit the bed, and she fell back onto it. Shasti told Madison to scooch over a bit until she was flat on her back in the middle of the king-sized bed.

With more finesse than she ever remembered having, Shasti climbed over Madison and settled herself on top. She kept her weight on her hands and feet in a plank position, so their bodies barely touched. Well, except for the phallus sticking straight up touching Shasti's pelvis.

Slowly, inch by inch, Shasti lowered her lips to Madison's. They kissed without touching anywhere else. For now, Madison got to remain unsecured to the headboard. And that wouldn't happen tonight, either. Shasti merely planned to Velcro the cuffs together. This way, Madison could break free anytime she wanted. Slow and steady wins the race. That was something her father always told her, and he would never ever know how she was applying that wisdom tonight.

Their kiss deepened, and Shasti's arms started to shake. She lowered her knees to the bed on either side of Madison's hips, letting the phallus stand tall in front of her, resting against her stomach. She lowered her upper body until their breasts met. Madison moaned at the same time Shasti let out a lusty breath.

Shasti kissed her way across Madison's face and then sucked in an earlobe causing Madison to shiver. Madison's arms went around Shasti's neck loosely but firmly. Kisses along Madison's neck above and below the collar elicited more shivers. Madison's hands moved to rub up and down Shasti's arms as if she needed to be in constant contact with her Mistress.

Shasti sat up. "Guide it inside me, baby." Shasti's voice was thick with need. She lifted up slightly.

Madison held the phallus upright and maneuvered the tip until she found the soft flesh it was meant for. Shasti lowered herself slowly, keeping her gaze locked onto Madison's.

A spike of lust ran through Shasti when Madison's hands latched onto Shasti's hips as if to help her move. Shasti got into a good rhythm riding up and down on the dildo inside her. She felt her flesh swell and opened her legs wider. The angle was tiring, so she let herself fall forward on top of Madison but held herself up by her arms. Madison let one hip go and guided Shasti's closest nipple into her mouth.

"Yes, baby, that's it. Suck. Suck harder." Shasti moaned and shifted her weight so the other breast would get equal attention. Madison obliged. "Fu-uck," Shasti said, making the word into two syllables. "Move your hips, honey. Fuck Mistress. Make me cum."

Madison inexpertly thrust her hips, trying to get the right angle on the penetration. She finally figured it out and sped up, much to Shasti's literal pleasure.

"Yes, yes, yes," Shasti cried out. Those were her last words until that distant spark she'd been nursing ignited and shot blinding hot through her body. She threw her head back as light took over the darkness behind her closed eyes.

She rocked her hips in time with Madison's as she eked out the pulses throbbing around the phallus. "Good girl. Good fucking baby girl." Shasti opened her eyes and slowed down her gyrations. Madison knew instinctively to slow down as well.

Shasti's energy was spent. Her arms collapsed, and she twisted to one side to avoid falling onto Madison.

She awoke moments later to soft kisses on her forehead and face. "Mistress," the soft voice said, "that was epic."

"Mmm," was all Shasti could manage. She'd had good sex with lovers before, but there was something about the trust, love, and adoration she had for Madison—that they had for each other—that made it otherworldly. And, truly, they had just begun exploring each other, exploring what they could be for each other.

"Mistress, let's never have sex on a high wire because you'll pass out, fall off, and die."

With the little strength she had, Shasti laughed. "Go get me some water, baby. Please?"

Madison hopped off the bed, her purple phallus bouncing in the breeze as she ran out of the room and down the stairs to the refrigerator. Shasti's chest bloomed with endorphins. Yes, she loved that young woman rushing to get her water. Was their relationship progressing too quickly? Maybe, but she didn't care. Nurturing and loving Madison and being loved back was like a calling. It was natural and necessary, like life itself.

"Here you go, Mistress." Madison handed her an unopened bottle of water.

Shasti sat up and drank several gulps before handing the plastic bottle to Madison. Madison barely took a sip when Shasti snatched it back, an evil grin on her face. "Take that off," Shasti pointed to the strap-on that Madison still sported.

Shasti put the water on her nightstand, watching intently as Madison undid the straps and slid the contraption off. She held it out as if unsure where to put the purple phallus. Shasti pointed to a towel she'd laid out for that purpose. When Madison returned to her side, Shasti pulled her into the bed and covered her face, neck, and bare chest with kisses. These were not tender, slow kisses. No, they were hungry, passionate kisses designed to make the recipient understand that she was about to lose all control. A soft whimper told Shasti that the recipient understood this.

Shasti leaned over her lover and removed a lock of hair off her face. She then pulled one unresisting arm and then the other over Madison's head and smashed the light pink Velcro patches together.

"Pull them apart," Shasti commanded. Once Madison did so, Shasti asked, "Color?"

"Green."

"Good. Keep those wrists velcroed together and above your head."

"Yes, Ma'am." Madison's voice was breathy. Good. She liked this game. There was so much more of this game to come down the road.

Shasti speed kissed her way down Madison's body and then lay a soft kiss on Madison's trimmed mons. She looked up to see Madison watching her every move. Shasti slid a thumb around the wet labia within easy reach. She slid the tip of her thumb inside. "Color?"

"Green. I like you inside me," Madison said eagerly.

Shasti eased her thumb further inside and gently pistoned in and out. She made sure to caress the upper walls hoping the G-spot was there and ready to play. Madison arched her hips. Oh, yes. The spot named G was wonderfully willing to play in this evening's events. Shasti rubbed it lovingly, enjoying Madison's soft moans. There was no hurry in her movements. The G-spot was part of the overall clitoral network with thousands of fabulous nerves with only one purpose: pleasure. And Madison clearly felt that as she rode a heightened flood of hormones. Her eyes were closed, and her head lolled lazily from side to side as if riding a sea of clouds. Her mouth opened slightly as she basked in the pleasure that Shasti was giving her.

Shasti's thumb kept up its work as she leaned down and kissed the spot where the still-hidden clit was. She dug her tongue in, revealing the shy little pearl, and then blew gently, making it grow in size. Madison's moans intensified as she undulated her hips, clearly digging what Shasti was doing. Shasti licked the swollen nub and then sucked gently in rhythm to her pistoning thumb. She swirled her tongue, causing Madison's hips to rise off the bed, taking Shasti with her.

Shasti's own flood of hormones hit her as she witnessed Madison's heightened arousal. She intensified her thrusts, licks, and sucks until Madison's body went rigid. For a split second. And then she roared as her orgasm hit. Her entire body shook as her climax gushed all over Shasti's still working mouth and thumb.

Madison bucked her hips for a while and then finally came to a stop. Shasti stopped all movement and pulled out. Madison's breathing was ragged, and she closed her legs, obviously sensitive.

"Miss—" Madison's eyes rolled back as an aftershock hit her.

Shasti slid up and showered her girl with kisses. "So good, baby."

"Mmm," was all Madison could get out. Another aftershock shook her body.

"Oh, my," Shasti said, stroking Madison's forehead. She kissed the forehead until two cuffed arms, Velcro freed, went around her neck and pulled her into a passionate kiss.

After a moment, Madison pulled back and said, "Mistress." She got the whole word out this time, but that was it.

Shasti chuckled and said, "Are you okay, sweetie?"

"Mmm," was all Madison could say. She rolled away from Shasti but reached back for Shasti's arm so they could cuddle.

After pulling a sheet over them, Shasti obliged, happy to be the big spoon to Madison's little.

Chapter 19

Madison

The dishes and forks and stuff were really classy and high-end. Madison didn't know if Miss Tilda should trust her to set the fancy dining room table, but Miss Shasti said it would be okay. Only one time did she ding a knife on a plate. She didn't break the plate or anything, and no one seemed to notice, but her nerves were still jangling.

Miss Rikki and Eileen were back in Miss Tilda's kitchen fussing with the food, which smelled so good and got Madison's tummy rumbling so much that she was ready to gnaw off her own arm. Would they have warm rolls? With butter? That would be so excellent. Josef had been instructing her how to set a proper table, but he had to go answer the door. Two people she didn't know were also coming to the dinner. That was okay, but her stranger-danger spidey senses always perked up around people she didn't know.

"It's been too long, Tilda," a female voice in the living room said. "Shasti," the voice then said, sounding surprised. The sound of a hug happening in the other room made Madison want to run in there and tell whoever this stranger was not to touch her Mistress. She belonged to Madison. Madison had the collar to prove it. At Miss Shasti's house, but still, she had one.

"So good to see you, Olga," Miss Shasti said to the stranger. "Ahh, hello, Doug. Looking fine this afternoon."

The stranger named Doug didn't say anything back. Rude much? Maybe Madison would give him a piece of her mind, too. And what kind of name was Olga, anyway? It sounded like a mean old Russian nurse's name. Yeah, and she was probably like Grandma. Pull you into a hug only to pinch you somewhere. You never knew where, either, because she kept changing it up as if she was ultimately trying to pinch every square inch of you. She hoped Miss Shasti hadn't gotten pinched when the stranger hugged her.

"You okay, kiddo?" Miss Rikki asked as she placed a steaming bowl of broccoli on the table. "You look upset."

"I'm okay, Miss," Madison said, hoping she had used good protocols or whatever it was called.

"Oh, good," Miss Rikki said. She turned to Eileen, who had brought in a couple more side dishes of unknown substances, and said, "I think I heard Olga and Doug arrive, so if you could please get the last of the side dishes, I would appreciate that."

"Okay," Eileen said.

"Let Josef bring in the pot roast."

"Okay."

Madison raised both eyebrows. There should have been a "Ma'am" or something at the end of one or both of those responses. Even Madison knew that. Was Eileen really a sub?

"And, Madison," Miss Rikki said, "would you please go inside and tell everyone they can come in and sit at the table?"

"Me?" Madison knew her face looked as stricken as she felt. "Ma'am?"

"If you're too shy, go tell your Mistress, and she can relay the message. But..."

Oh, no. A life lesson or something was coming. Miss Rikki liked strong subs, Mistress had told her. She wanted them to be independent and not hide behind their Dominants.

"But I should do it because you asked me to. Right, Ma'am?" Madison's stomach flipped a little bit and not from starvation. Miss Rikki was nice, and Madison didn't want to piss her off as much as she didn't want to interrupt all the grownups in the other room.

"You got it, kiddo." Miss Rikki winked and then headed back into the kitchen.

Madison took a deep breath. She didn't know why she was so shy in Miss Tilda's house today. The last time she was there, she and Billy tore it up with their running and games. That was the day she met Miss Shasti, pretty Miss Shasti. Oh, wait! Mistress was there, in the other room. Everything would be okay.

Madison walked through the open doorway to the living room and made a beeline for Miss Shasti, sitting in a cool-looking rocking chair. Madison stood in front of her but off to the side because she didn't want to interrupt. When her Mistress finally turned to look her way after a hundred years, Madison smiled and waved her goofy wave. Her Mistress's smile reached her eyes, and she pointed with two fingers to the floor at her feet. That was their signal for Madison to plop down and lay her head on Mistress's thigh. A casual hand petted her head. If Madison could purr, she would have. She closed her eyes and listened to the grownups' conversation, but not really.

"Madison?" a voice called from far away. It sounded perplexed. It was Miss Rikki.

Oh, shit. Madison sat bolt upright. "Dinner's ready," she said to Miss Shasti. "That's why I came in here. To tell everyone."

The grownups in the room chuckled and stood up.

"I'm sorry, Mistress," Madison said, her eyes filling with tears. "I forgot. I messed up. I embarrassed you."

Miss Shasti stood and motioned for Madison to stand as well. She pulled Madison into a soothing hug and whispered, "You're okay. You just forgot. No harm, no foul."

"We used to say that at softball," Madison said, her head buried in Miss Shasti's blouse.

"I know. I've heard you use it with Billy."

"I wish he were here," Madison said, her truth finally coming out. She hadn't been nervous until they pulled up in the car. And then her nerves spiked when she realized Billy wasn't coming nor any other *littles*. She was the only one. Sighhhhhhhh!

"Come on, peanut." Miss Shasti reached for Madison's hand and led her into the dining room.

"There's our shy girl," Miss Tilda said. "You're next to me, honey." She pointed to the empty chair next to her. Miss Tilda was old. Really old. Like in her eighties or something old. Her completely white hair was done up in a bun like the last time Madison had been at her house. She was wrinkled, too, but that's what happened when you got old. Her alpha sub, Josef, was also there. He lived in the house with Miss Tilda. Miss Rikki and Eileen lived there too, but upstairs. Mistress had told her that Miss Tilda had a lot of subs under contract—whatever that meant—but only Josef would be there at the dinner. He was Miss Tilda's main man. Okay, Mistress hadn't used that term, but that's what he was, and he got to live in the house just like Madison got to live in Miss Shasti's house.

"Shasti, please sit there," Miss Tilda said. Oh, good. Mistress would be next to Madison, telling her what fork to use and stuff.

They sat down, and then Miss Tilda introduced her to Miss Olga. She was an older woman but nowhere near as old as Miss Tilda. She was, maybe, in her fifties? Madison wasn't sure, but her graying hair was striking, and she sat up so straight and tall. She had these eloquent high cheekbones and a kind smile.

"Are you Russian?" Madison asked, causing the table to twitter in laughter.

"No, dear," Miss Olga said. "I was born in Norway, and my parents emigrated from there to Minnesota, and then, somehow, I ended up here in Denton Heights, Ohio."

"You're very pretty," Madison said and then regretted it. Maybe that would make Miss Shasti upset, you know? Upset that Madison thought another woman was also pretty. Ugh. She couldn't do anything right.

"Well, thank you, Madison," Miss Olga said and then turned to Miss Tilda. "She's adorable. Just like you said." Miss Tilda nodded.

Eileen brought the beverages around, and Madison was floored that she was allowed to have pop with dinner. Wait. What kind of trickery was this? The can said zero calories. Diet pop? "What is this, Mistress?"

"It's sparkling water," Miss Shasti said. "I picked a lemon flavor for you, and if you like it, maybe we can stock up at home. They have all kinds of flavors like watermelon and grapefruit, my favorite."

Grapefruit? Ugh. Madison made a face. Who in their right mind would want grapefruit-flavored anything? Double ugh.

"Go ahead and try it," Miss Shasti urged.

Madison took the smallest of sips. Hmm. It was bubbly all right. And, yeah, it tasted pretty good. Lemony. It didn't have the amazing goodness of pop, though. She took a bigger sip and decided it would do. Yes, very much. She took another big swig.

"Do you like it?" Miss Shasti asked.

Uh, oh, the most giant burp was heading back out. She might get in trouble, but she couldn't *not* do it. "Yes, Ma'am," she burped the words and then trailed the burp until its final bitter note.

The table erupted in laughter.

"That was impressive, kid," Eileen said, shooting Madison a genuine smile and a thumbs up. "Inspiring even."

"Somebody, get me a spoon," Miss Tilda gushed. "I just want to eat her up."

"Madison Kim," Miss Shasti said, trying to be stern but failing miserably because amusement had taken over her entire face.

"Sorry," Madison said, but was she? She couldn't remove the smile from her face.

Just then, something bumped her leg. She knew Miss Tilda had dogs, but she'd been told they were in another room until later. She turned to see what had touched her and screeched. A grown man was on his hands and knees on the floor. "Mistress!" Madison screeched again, clutching her arm.

"Doug!" Miss Olga called. "Get back over here. Don't bother Madison."

He defiantly put his chin on Madison's leg and whimpered, kind of like a dog but kind of not.

"You're not a dog," Madison said as her high blood pressure lowered slightly. "Oh, Mistress! He's a fox. See his ears and nose? And, holy Canidae Vulpes, he has such an awesome tail." Without waiting for her Mistress to respond, she asked Miss Olga, "Can I pet him? On his head?"

"Be gentle," Miss Olga said.

With a somewhat shaking hand, Madison patted the grown-man fox on the head between his ears. He made a happy sound, so Madison patted him again and giggled.

Just then, Josef entered the dining room with the giant platter of Sunday pot roast and placed it on the table.

"Doug," Miss Olga commanded, "come." Doug, the fox, did go to her side, but not before bumping his forehead against Madison's legs a couple of times playfully.

"He's a fox," Madison whispered to her Mistress.

Miss Shasti nodded and then put a finger up to her lips for quiet.

Miss Tilda reached her hand out for Madison's, and Madison dutifully gave it before she understood that they were all going to hold hands around the table. Oh, no, Miss Shasti had to hold hands with Eileen. Madison definitely didn't like that. At all. Miss Rikki had her hand on Doug the fox's head on one side, and Miss Olga did the same on the other. That was funny. Josef held hands with Miss Tilda, his Mistress, which was so nice to see. He was a quiet man, but really really nice.

Miss Tilda bowed her head, so Madison did, too. "Bless this family, some by blood and some not, as we gather together as kindred spirits. May we continue to support each other and help each other grow. Bless the hands that prepared this meal and those that helped get this shindig together."

Madison giggled when Miss Tilda, such a proper lady, said, "shindig." A tightening hold on her hand from Miss Shasti's side told her that had not been a cool thing to do.

"Amen," Miss Tilda finished her speech.

"Amen," Madison said, noting that not everyone at the table said it, but that was okay. 'You do you,' Coach Meers always said when Madison confided that she felt different because she didn't look like any of the other girls at school. And that's what people were doing at this table—being themselves. Doug was a fox right now. Cool. Eileen was scowling. Nothing new there.

As the food got passed around, Madison didn't have to do anything except pass bowls because Miss Shasti filled her plate for her. Miss Olga fed Doug with her fingers, and he ate heartily from her hand. It was so cool to watch. Madison wondered if Miss Shasti would let her feed Doug, too.

She scoffed when two pieces of broccoli hit her plate.

"Broccoli is good for you," Miss Shasti said. Good, she didn't sound mad.

Madison mumbled the next, not even caring if anyone heard her. "The only good broccoli is dead broccoli."

Bemused, Miss Tilda patted her arm, but then she held on as if to get Madison's full attention.

"Uh oh," Eileen said.

And Madison knew immediately why Eileen said those words when Miss Tilda's full Domme persona came out. "Your Mistress put that on your plate for a reason, young Madison." There was no mirth to her voice this time. She looked over at Miss Shasti and said, "I suggest a book report, or whatever you kids call it nowadays, about the benefits of broccoli in particular and vegetables in general."

"Excellent idea," Miss Shasti said. "She'll be reminded once we get home."

"I'm sorry, Mistress," Madison said, hanging her head. "I'm sorry for being rude, Miss Tilda. I'm…I'm sorry." Tears kept trying to bubble up from her chest, which is not where tears came from, but Madison fought against them anyway. She thought about the foxes she'd seen at the zoo instead.

"Good girl," Miss Shasti said. "Thank you for the apologies. That was very grown-up of you."

Madison nodded and pushed her food around on her plate. Obviously, she needed to choke down both broccoli things at some point, but first, she'd devour some mashed potatoes and then some pot roast. She hated when she messed up like this. Sometimes she had entire days of doing everything wrong. Maybe her grandmother was right. Madison wasn't worth the money spent to feed and house and clothe her. Miss Shasti had spent so much money on her already. But, no, Madison would be gainfully employed starting tomorrow, and Miss Shasti would get every dime of her money. Every dime. PETology might not pay as much as being a doctor, but it might help defray the costs of putting up with such a worthless person like herself. A charity case that everyone had to be nice to.

A hand belonging to someone by the name of Mistress stroked her thigh soothingly. Lips belonging to the same person kissed her cheek. "It's okay, baby," Miss Shasti said. "I've got you. Okay?"

Madison looked up into the most loving eyes she'd ever seen, and that was all it took. Those tears she'd stuffed down came shooting up to the surface like they'd been waiting for the starter's gun at an Olympic race. Madison buried her face into Miss Shasti's side and wept quietly. A gentle nudging on her other thigh told her the fox had returned. He rested his chin on her leg and made a quiet whining sound in sympathy. No one at the table said anything, which almost made it worse.

"You're my sensitive girl today, aren't you?" Mistress said, and then one of those magic tissues appeared so that Madison could dry her eyes. Mistress's question wasn't really a question, more like a non-judgmental observation, and that was fine. It was nice to have your feelings acknowledged for a change. It was nice to be seen and not for a bad thing, wasn't it? Yes, it was.

Madison dabbed at her nose because to out and out blow it would probably be wrong at the dinner table. She petted the fox next and thanked him for making her feel better. He made a happy noise and returned to his Mistress when she called for him.

She didn't look up at anybody and then ate her meal in the order she'd devised to get the two broccolis in her system.

Once dinner was finished, Madison helped Eileen and Josef clear the table and put the food away, although Josef did most of it. Then Miss Rikki suggested they head down to the dungeon for a demonstration. Madison was concerned. She looked from Miss Rikki to her own Mistress and back again. Was Miss Rikki going to whip

Eileen? Right there in front of them? Was Eileen going to holler and scream in pain?

Everyone stood up, and Madison cupped her hands around her mouth and whispered into Mistress's ear, "Yellow."

"You'll be okay, Madison," Miss Shasti said. "It's not a whipping. Is that what you thought?"

Madison nodded.

"Just an old-fashioned flogging, but if you want to leave the room at any time, tell me. Please don't just run off. Is that understood?"

"Yes, Ma'am," Madison said. Somehow her chin had ended up between Mistress's thumb and forefinger. "Where's Daddy Vic? I thought she was part of this inner circle."

"Inner circle?" Mistress chuckled and said, "Victoria has a date with a new girl." She guided Madison toward the basement stairs.

"Another new one?" Madison let her jaw fall open. "What happened to Heather? I liked her."

Mistress shrugged and rolled her eyes as if to say she knew not what happened in Daddy Vic's world.

Once in the basement, Mistress sat in one of the comfy chairs Josef had pulled over. Miss Tilda and Miss Olga sat in the other two. Mistress gave Madison the hand signal, and Madison happily sat at her feet and wrapped her arm around Mistress's calf. Too bad Mistress was wearing pants because it would be nice to feel skin on skin right now. Doug, the fox, lay down at Miss Olga's feet, and Josef sat on a low stool at Miss Tilda's. Madison reasoned that since he was kind of old, he got a stool to sit on. He was, like, completely gray and balding after all.

Miss Rikki talked quietly to Eileen near the big X on the wall. Was she going to be attached to it? Oh, yes. Yes, she was. She wore both wrist and ankle cuffs. Unabashedly, Eileen took off her shirt and then unhooked her bra. Madison's eyes got big. Eileen's boobies were showing. Right there in front of everyone, boys included.

Miss Rikki turned Eileen toward the X and attached her wrists and ankles to it with sturdy-looking clips. She then placed safety goggles on Eileen, who frowned.

Miss Rikki looked at her audience a safe distance away and said, "Normally, we don't use the goggles, but it's a good safety move for today because we have an audience, and one or both of us might get distracted. Her safety is of my utmost concern." Eileen scowled, and Miss Rikki added, "And she's not happy about it."

"Safety is really important," Miss Shasti said low to Madison.

"That's why we have safe words, right?" Madison looked up at her Mistress and felt her heart gush with love for the woman who seemed to want to take care of her for a while.

"Mm hmm." Mistress pointed back to the action.

"This is a flogger," Miss Rikki said. "These tails are leather, but they can be made from anything really, like suede or nylon." She motioned for Madison to come up and feel the leather.

"Soft," Madison said, trying not to look at Eileen's exposed boobies. She hurried back to Mistress when Miss Rikki told her to.

"Mm hmm," Miss Rikki said. "Soft, wide strips mean she'll get more of a thuddy experience. That, she tells me, can feel almost like a massage. How hard I hit also determines the level of pain." She leaned in and asked Eileen something, obviously something no one else was supposed to hear, and Eileen nodded. And then Rikki planted a kiss on Eileen's mouth. Madison figured Miss Rikki had to, seeing Eileen's boobies hanging free and all. She had to relieve the sexual tension somehow, right?

"My goal is to make sure I don't wrap the tails around her shoulders or neck, but if I do, she has the glasses on for protection. And I'll make sure I don't hit this area." She gestured toward Eileen's lower back. Oh, the kidney area. That's really good. Safety first. Miss Rikki stood back and then gently twirled the wrist holding the flogger back and forth. The tails made a soft sound against Eileen's back, and the motion became mesmerizing after a while. Miss Rikki pointed out how Eileen's back was turning a bit pink, which was Miss Rikki's signal to up the pace. Whoa, she moved that flogger so fast, and Eileen wasn't making a sound or trying to jump out of the way or anything.

Miss Rikki reached for a second flogger and started doing this cool double back-and-forth pattern. But now, Eileen was starting to squirm a little bit. She moaned, too, as if to relieve the pressure or something. Her body slumped but being attached by her wrists meant she didn't fall. The cuffs were bearing most of her weight, it looked like. Madison couldn't imagine how Eileen felt at that moment, but her breathing had become heavy and ragged like she'd just played an entire basketball game.

Maybe that was Miss Rikki's cue to slow down because she did and then ultimately stopped. Eileen moaned, and it sounded like she was aroused or something. Maybe she was. Who knew? Miss Rikki then did something really cool. She pulled out this piece of soft-looking material and caressed Eileen's angry red back.

Eileen lifted her head and moaned in gratitude that her Domme was taking such excellent care of her.

"She's hit sub-space," Miss Rikki said quietly. "I need to let her ride it out." Miss Rikki unclipped Eileen's ankles first and then held Eileen up as she undid the wrist cuffs. Eileen turned in Miss Rikki's arms and began peppering her with kisses and soft murmurs Madison was sure no one else was supposed to hear, but she did. Eileen wanted Rikki to have sex with her. Right then. Right there.

"Dessert upstairs, everyone," Miss Tilda announced, and Madison leaped to her feet. She held her arm out to help Miss Shasti up. She did that because she watched Josef do it for Miss Tilda. Subs were supposed to be helpful. Madison had to remember that.

Once the group was upstairs, the unmistakable sound of Eileen screeching in orgasm hit them. No one reacted, but Madison's eyes were wide open. Is that how loud she was when she came the night before? When she'd squirted for the first time in her life? She hadn't known that's what happened, but Mistress told her the following day and seemed really proud of herself for causing it to happen.

"Mistress?"

"Mm hmm?" Mistress said. They were back in their assigned seats at the dining room table. Mistress was stirring the coffee Josef had just poured her. Madison wanted coffee, too, but maybe littles weren't allowed to have coffee in Miss Tilda's house. Bummer.

"When you made me cum last night, and I squirted and then kind of passed out, did I go into sub-space?"

Miss Shasti put a hand over her eyes and shook her head. "She has absolutely no filter sometimes."

Miss Tilda and Miss Olga were doing this weird breathy kind of laugh through their noses like they didn't want to laugh but couldn't help it. "We speak and act freely here, Shasti," Miss Tilda said. "You know that."

Mistress uncovered her eyes and kissed Madison on the forehead. "Yes, dear. You were kind of floaty and blissful, right?"

"It was so nice."

"G-spot orgasms can do that."

"Hmm," Madison said. "Can I give you a G-spot orgasm later?"

"Okay, okay," Mistress said. "Enough." She sounded like she had reached her limit on something. She seemed embarrassed, too, even though Miss Tilda said they could talk about anything. "We'll talk more about this later. Okay?"

"Okay," Madison said, and then her eyes lit up. Josef was pouring her a cup of coffee, too. Oh, right! Dommes got served coffee first. That made sense. Look! Josef had given her a white mug with a rainbow unicorn on it. He smiled at her when he finished. "Thank you, Josef. I love my mug." His smile made her heart warm.

Mistress added some creamer to Madison's coffee and her own. She waved away the sugar, much to Madison's disappointment. Mistress was serious about this sugar thing, wasn't she?

While the grownups talked, Madison looked around at the room full of people and a fox. She also thought about the two people still in the dungeon. Each one of them, in their own way, had made her feel special. Each one had taken care of her and tried to make her feel seen and heard and, yeah, loved.

Those stupid tears were back. Idiots. Why couldn't they take a day off?

"Baby?" Mistress produced a magical wizard tissue.

"I'm okay," Madison said and wiped her tears. Again. "I'm not used to people being so nice to me."

Mistress pulled Madison into a hug so tight that she almost couldn't breathe. Kisses covered her head and face. "You are so loved, peanut. By everyone." She released Madison enough for her to look around. Kind faces smiled back at her. Even the fox was smiling.

Chapter 20

Shasti

Shasti hadn't been this nervous since the day she met Madison. "You have your lunch? And your wallet?"

"Yes, Mistress," Madison said. "I'm only going to work, not into battle."

"I know. I know." Shasti pulled her into one last hug, released her, and then patted her on the butt. "Go on, now. Before I change my mind and shackle you to my side today."

"You'd do that?" Madison's eyebrows shot to the sky. She seemed to like the idea.

"Go on," Shasti said, hoping Madison didn't see the tears welling up in her eyes.

Madison leaned in for one last kiss and headed for the front door. "I love you, Mistress."

"And I love you, baby. Go on." Shasti remained frozen in the kitchen, listening to Madison's car start up and then drive away. She exhaled a big sigh. "Why was that so hard?" That little peanut of hers had gotten under her skin in only two months. And Madison had totally pulled everyone into her orbit at Tilda's Sunday dinner, too.

Thinking of Tilda made her frown. She knew Tilda was only trying to help, but Shasti hadn't planned on scolding Madison about the broccoli comment. She wasn't even going to punish her, just have a conversation about vegetables in general at their next meal together.

Madison was smart. She assimilated information quickly. But now, they had a research paper to write.

Shasti had felt so bad watching Madison choke down the broccoli. She had been a real trooper. Shasti didn't want to force bad-tasting food on Madison since the pressure might cause her to become anxious around new foods. Maybe Shasti should look for a kid-friendly broccoli recipe. With cheese? Something like that.

She tucked that thought aside, and her brain went to an unpleasant thought without her permission—Columbus, Ohio.

"That family of yours has done a number on you, kiddo," Shasti said out loud and poured her second cup of coffee. "And those friends? They weren't friends." She'd like to give all of them a piece of her mind and then some.

Shasti picked up her phone and reread the last text exchange with Madison's mother.

> SIN-JOO KIM: We are all looking forward to seeing Madison on the weekend of the 25th. I miss my baby. I hope she is being a good girl for you. She can be a handful.

> SHASTI: She is a delight. We'll text again when the date gets closer to reconfirm.

There was no return text. Shasti made sure in her opening text to Madison's mother to introduce herself as Madison's girlfriend. Mrs. Kim didn't seem to bat an eye and said it was nice to meet Shasti and that she was happy Madison had found someone so nice. Ahh, but would that hold up when they met in person?

Shasti figured she'd text again after Madison's next therapy session on Saturday. No, not after—during. That would give her something to focus on while Madison was with Dr. Sumner. But then again, Shasti was rethinking it. Seriously, was it too soon to visit the family? Maybe Madison wasn't ready. Should they wait until Dr. Sumner had a chance to really dig in with the therapy and make some inroads with Madison? Or maybe they should rip that band-aid off now? It was so hard to know the right thing to do.

Shasti sipped her coffee and checked her watch. Madison's bedroom furniture was due to arrive between eight and ten that morning. Why did some days feel like you were already behind before they even started? Hopefully, the delivery people would get there earlier, so Shasti could get to the clinic and make her phone call—that important call to the Henderson family. It was bad enough she'd had to ask one of the PAs to take her morning patients. They were all fairly routine appointments, but still, she hated doing it. She'd return the favor at some point.

Shasti leaned back against the counter, unsure what to do with herself. And she was leaning, not physically but mentally, toward postponing that Columbus visit. Shasti was the one who had pushed it on Madison, after all. She wanted Madison to be free of all that BS in Columbus with her family, and this time, BS did stand for bullshit. Would she ever be free of it? Was Madison ready to go back? Move some things out? Maybe not. Maybe they could just visit. Have lunch out with the family. No big move, just pick up a few things.

Or was Shasti afraid that Madison would decide to stay once they got there? That was a possibility, and that stupid pendulum clock ticking impossibly loud in the front room was fraying her nerves.

Shasti groaned. She didn't know what to do. "Let it unfold naturally," Shasti said out loud. But what part of all that was "natural?"

Her phone dinged an incoming text. "Now what?" She put her coffee down and tapped open the text. Ahh, the furniture people were in the driveway, and it wasn't even eight o'clock yet. Excellent.

She tucked her phone into her pocket and opened the front door. She guided them to Madison's room and made sure they put the bed together since she'd paid for that service. The white metal open-framed platform bed was just as lovely as it looked on the website—plenty of places on both the headboard and footboard to attach wrist and ankle cuffs. And the white looked so good against the dusty rose walls. The matching whitewashed dresser, nightstand, student desk, and bookshelf were moved in, making the room look lived in. It was all coming together as Madison's official room. She'd have her own private space. Maybe seeing the room full of furniture would help Madison understand that this home was hers too.

Shasti was not sorry to see the two high wing-backed chairs, the heavy dining room table, and six dining chairs go back out the front door. Since those items were still within the return time, she decided they didn't fit the life she and Madison were building together. Madison would be so surprised. Shasti wasn't sure why she'd purchased them to begin with. Maybe to have something heavy to anchor the house down with, ensuring that she'd made the right decision buying it? Who knew? What she did know was that she and Madison would decide what to do with those front rooms together.

Shasti tipped the workers and was heading out the door when her phone dinged again. She whipped the phone out of her pocket, adrenaline rushing through her. Was it Madison? Was she okay?

She breathed a sigh of relief. Madison's glasses were in. It looked like they were taking a trip to Eyeglasses O-Rama that evening. Maybe dinner out? Wait, no. They had leftover tacos to finish. And Madison might be too tired after a full day of work and then an eyeglass errand. The black-framed rectangular glasses had looked so cute on Madison.

It was as if she had put her own glasses down on the counter that day and then put them back on. Shasti knew enough to order a backup pair, and she hoped Madison would be able to manage both without losing or scratching either.

Shasti sent Madison a text telling her they'd pick up her glasses after work and that she loved her. When she didn't get an immediate reply, she tucked her phone into her purse and headed to the clinic.

Once in her office, Shasti powered up her computer and noticed that the PA was still working with Shasti's nine-thirty appointment. She glanced at the notes already taken, and all seemed well with the patient. It was just a routine semi-annual checkup, and the labs looked normal. Since nothing was pressing or urgent, she let the PA finish it. Shasti had always hated it back in D.C. when a more senior physician barged in and took over. She'd get the debrief from the PA later and sent her a note requesting an update on the three appointments she'd missed that morning.

She glanced at the clock. She had just enough time to get that Henderson phone call in. She clicked open the file and then punched in the numbers for Mrs. Henderson's cell phone. It went immediately to voice mail. Shasti didn't want to leave a voicemail of this magnitude, so she decided to try a few more times throughout the morning before switching to the home phone number. She also didn't want to hand the task over to Reggie to schedule. Mrs. Henderson would want to know why, and Shasti needed to be the one to explain things.

It was a jam-packed day, but by the end, she'd finally gotten through to Mrs. Henderson, who cautiously made an appointment for late Thursday afternoon. One would think the mother would have been overjoyed when Shasti said she had a strong theory about what was causing the issues. Or maybe Mrs. Henderson's hesitation was due to the fact that Shasti wouldn't tip her hand and reveal the potential cause over the phone. Shasti sent Allie an inter-office message, so she could set up the proper authorities to be on hand that day. Shasti had no idea whether they would need them or not, but by law, they had to report it. And it was a definite possibility that the Hendersons would be a no-show that day.

~~~

It was finally Thursday afternoon as Shasti waited in her office, trying to keep her cool. The Hendersons were there, in whatever exam room Allie had assigned them. She was just waiting for the MA's signal to come in. The days preceding had flown by. Madison had been so enamored by her glasses and the fact that blurry objects in the distance were now clear that she wanted to wear them during her bath and to bed. The poor dear started her period in the bathtub that Monday night and had to switch to a shower, but it explained why Madison had been tearful the day before at Tilda's Sunday dinner. Heightened hormones had made her baby emotional. Shasti made a note in her phone's calendar to keep track of Madison's cycle. Maybe they needed to avoid a Columbus visit or any other stressful event during her pre-menstrual time.

Madison had also been shocked Monday evening to find the "old geezer" furniture in the front rooms gone but happily fell in love with the new furniture in her room. For three nights running, they moved everything except the bed around to see what combination worked best. Shasti didn't care where any of it ended up. She was happy and relieved that Madison accepted the room and the furniture as her own.

And what also relieved Shasti's mind was that Madison seemed to be gliding in smoothly at her new job at PETology. Madison came in knowing what was required and seemed to be making friends with the woman in charge of the animals. Madison was allowed to put the birdfeed and water into their cages only once her stock work was done.

In fact, after three days of work, Madison was so happy that she begged to make love to Shasti. Madison wanted to try that "g-spot orgasm thing" on her, and even though Madison was "out of commission" because of her period, that didn't mean she couldn't "make Mistress happy." And make Mistress happy she did. Madison vowed to keep trying until Mistress "squirted across the room." Yeah, that wasn't going to happen, and Shasti had tried to explain that she had never ejaculated like that, but hey, if Madison wanted to keep trying, Shasti would not be the one to discourage her.

Yes, things were looking good and solid for the inhabitants living on Cardinal Lane, but things were about to get rocky for those on County Road 126.

A knock on her office door pulled Shasti back into the present. "Your four o'clock is here." Allie opened the door. "Room four." Ahh, right by the lobby where the law enforcement would be. "We're all set out here."

The signal from Bree, the MA in the exam room, came, and Shasti stood up. "Got it." She smoothed down her white lab coat as she stood up and then grabbed her laptop.

Allie walked her to the room, put a hand on her upper arm, and squeezed. She said no words, but Shasti nodded her understanding of the silent communication. Yes, she would be firm but gentle. No, she wouldn't out and out accuse. They'd gone over that multiple times during the last few days.

Shasti took a deep breath and let it out slowly. She'd learned that trick from a med school classmate. It was amazing how quickly her pulse rate decreased. She opened the door and greeted Jessie and her mother warmly. The grandmother was also there, looking utterly miffed at being dragged out of the house, but Shasti greeted her warmly, as well.

"You've met Bree, of course." Shasti gestured to the MA, who they had arranged to stay in the room as a witness. "Let me just pull up your vitals," Shasti said. She didn't need to because she had watched them show up in real time when Bree put them in a few minutes ago. "Looking good, kiddo."

Jessie beamed from her seat on the examination table.

"Why are we here?" Mrs. Henderson asked, clearly another miffed woman in the Henderson household. "She's had no incidents, and you were vague on the phone."

Shasti nodded. She wanted Mrs. Henderson to know that she'd heard her and understood. Always let patients and their caregivers know you've listened to them. This advice had come from her father, not from anyone in med school.

It was a bit crowded in the small exam room with five women inside, but it couldn't be helped. Shasti purposely remained standing but out of the way of the door. If one of the three were going to flee, she wouldn't stop them. Law enforcement outside would do it. In fact, she could hear the walkie-talkie in the distance. Did they hear it, too? Did one of them understand what was up?

Shasti cleared her throat as a spike of nerves cropped up. "As you know, Jessie has been testing positive for LSD."

"What?" the grandmother asked, clearly having been kept out of the loop. "No granddaughter of mine would ever do drugs." She tilted her head sideways as she glared at Jessie. Jessie said nothing to her grandmother's unspoken question.

'Don't state things as facts,' Allie had advised. Use softer words like 'believe' and 'it seems.' Shasti said, "I don't believe LSD was in her system."

"No?" Mrs. Henderson said.

"It seems we may have been getting a false positive. This means the tests they ran showed up incorrectly as LSD. But it may be something else. After researching substances that sometimes give false positives for LSD, I came up with this list." Bree handed her the three printouts from her clipboard, and Shasti gave them to the patient and her family members. Shasti knew they probably wouldn't be able to understand the medication names, but that was okay. She was about to explain the first one.

"Diltiazem, also known as Cardizem." Shasti paused as the grandmother's head lifted. Shasti continued, "This medication is used to slow heart rate and relax blood vessels. The extended-release version treats both chest pain and high blood pressure."

"Isn't that your blood pressure medication, Mom?" Mrs. Henderson asked her mother.

"Yes."

A one-word response. That didn't show guilt. The grandmother looked so perplexed that Shasti was ready to rule her out as a suspect. The medication? That was still on the table.

"The side effects of this medication, among other things, can be dizziness, tiredness, slower heart rate, nervousness," Shasti said, slowly naming Jessie's symptoms. She remained standing and decided to stop speaking. She needed the information to sink in and for either Jessie or Mrs. Henderson to have an epiphany. Which one would put it together? Which one already knew? Which one would blink first?

The grandmother looked completely confused but seemed to know enough to stay silent. Mrs. Henderson looked up at Shasti as if waiting for more information. When none came, Mrs. Henderson turned and looked at her daughter. Jessie's expression was unreadable as she looked from Shasti to her mother. The two Hendersons locked gazes. The weight of silence was heavy in the exam room. Mrs. Henderson's expression changed from one of confusion to concern as her brow furrowed. Jessie's turned to anger, and then, Shasti wasn't sure, but it looked like guilt.

It was all Shasti could do not to say something, even though the silence was so thick it was terrifying.

"Jessie," Mrs. Henderson said softly, "what have you done?"

Jessie blinked back tears and looked up and then away from her mother. Her legs were crossed at the ankles, and the back of one heel banged rhythmically against the exam table.

"Oh, Jessie. Honey." Mrs. Henderson scooted forward in her chair. It was obvious that she didn't know whether or not to hug her child or scold her. "Tell me what happened."

Jessie's head whipped back around, and her eyes were like lasers boring into her mother's soul. "I just…"

Shasti stayed silent. Mrs. Henderson did as well.

Jessie took a deep breath, and her words came out in a torrent. "Grandma takes four of those a day. She says it makes her feel better. I wanted to feel better, too, so I snuck a few from one of her bottles. When I took that first one, it didn't make me feel better at all, and then you had to come to school. It was—" Jessie started crying, and Shasti offered her the tissue box. Jessie took the whole box, ripped out a tissue, and wiped at her eyes. "When you came to get me, you looked at me, like, for the first time since Daddy left. You paid attention to me. You were worried about me. Me! And we went for ice cream after Dr. Murray's, like we always did with Daddy. And, and—" Jessie's sobs choked off any further words, and Mrs. Henderson's arms were around her daughter within seconds.

"Oh, honey," Mrs. Henderson soothed. "I didn't know you were hurting like this." She looked over at Shasti and nodded. What the nod meant; Shasti wasn't sure. "I've been subsumed with this divorce and work and Grandma coming to live with us that I forgot the most important things. None of that matters unless we're all happy and feel loved." She gestured for her mother to stand up and join the hug.

"Love you, chickadee," Jessie's grandmother said and got her own personal hug from Jessie.

"Why did you keep taking the medication, honey?" Mrs. Henderson asked.

Jessie looked away. Shasti knew the answer. So did Mrs. Henderson, but like Mrs. Henderson, she wanted to hear it from Jessie's own mouth. "I liked your attention, Mom. And then you took me here, and Dr. B was so sympathetic, and everyone here is so nice." She turned to smile at Bree, who smiled back.

"I see," Mrs. Henderson said, and Shasti could already see the wheels in her head turning. Hopefully, the wheels were turning in a way that would benefit Jessie and the entire Henderson family. One could hope, and Shasti did hope.

Shasti let the family hug and regroup before interjecting. She sat down on her stool, not feeling like she needed to assert her authority as much. When she felt it was time, she said, "I have two things. One is a recommendation, and the other is an unfortunate side effect of all this."

The grandmother sat down, but Mrs. Henderson held on to her daughter. "Go on."

Shasti waited until Mrs. Henderson choked back a fresh batch of tears.

"I recommend family counseling. I have a couple of reputable family therapists Dr. Littrell has recommended to her patients for years. She is quite confident they can help." She took the two business cards from Bree and handed them to Mrs. Henderson.

"And the 'side effect?'" Mrs. Henderson asked, pocketing the business cards.

"I was required under law to report this suspected situation to Child Protective Services. They're waiting outside to interview you. And me."

"I understand," Mrs. Henderson said.

"I'll send them in." Shasti asked Bree to send in the CPS officer and fill in Dr. Littrell.

The CPS officer asked for a recap from Shasti and the family and then dismissed Shasti, who returned to her office. Allie was waiting for her there.

"I didn't know how that was going to go," Shasti said and plopped down in her desk chair. She blew out a long sigh. "It felt like a detective novel in there," Shasti said. "But the girl ultimately fessed up to taking her grandmother's blood pressure meds."

"Just to get her mother's attention. Munchausen Syndrome," Allie said from her seat on the couch. "You recommended the therapists?"

"Mm hmm. This is out of our hands now, isn't it?"

Allie nodded and then stood up. "Keep me appraised of any new developments, okay?"

Shasti nodded.

"Oh, and you have a new admirer."

"I do?"

"Bree. She gushed over how calm and cool you were in there and how amazing it was that you got the girl to confess."

Shasti laughed. "Don't tell her that my nerves are still clattering."

"I won't." Allie turned and headed out the door, closing it behind her.

Shasti took a moment and then sent good thoughts out to the universe for Jessie and the rest of the Henderson family to find peace and happiness. That done, she opened her laptop to prep for her five o'clock patient. Seven o'clock couldn't come fast enough. The Henderson appointment had taken a lot of emotional energy from her.

She pulled out her phone and texted her sweetie.

SHASTI: I hope you're having a good day, love. Remember that I won't be home until after seven.

MADISON: Hi, Mistress!!! (heart emoji) (kiss emoji) (happy emoji)

MADISON: I had a good day. I am stopping by the condo to check on it. I wish the lawyer would call with Mrs. Park's paperwork stuff. Sighhhhhh!

SHASTI: How about I give him a call tomorrow?

MADISON: Or…I could.

Shasti raised her eyebrows. Wow. That was so…mature.

SHASTI: Yes, of course, you can. During your lunch break, maybe?

MADISON: Okay. Oh, and I'm making you dinner, btw. It'll be ready when you get home.

Shasti's eyebrows had just recovered, but they were shooting right back to the sky.

SHASTI: Can't wait! What are we having?

She should be prepping for her five o'clock, but texting with Madison was much more fun.

MADISON: It's a surprise. Because it might not come out right. But! You're the detective over there. Think about the ingredients I put in your shopping cart at Kroger the other night.

SHASTI: Hmm. I'll just wait to be surprised, baby. I have to go now. I love you.

MADISON: And I love you, Mistress. (kiss emoji) (kiss emoji) (kiss emoji)

Shasti had pretty much figured out Madison's meal would be some kind of chicken casserole with noodles. The bag of frozen peas and carrots that Madison had put in the cart was encouraging. Maybe her baby was actually absorbing the wisdom Shasti was trying to impart. Pulling all of Madison's love and sugar inside her soul, Shasti stood up, ready to tackle another two hours of playing doctor.

Chapter 21

Madison

As Madison set the shopping bag down on the coffee table, it clunked more loudly than she'd intended, but thankfully Dr. Sumner didn't flinch or even scold her.

"I bought you some stuff," Madison said. "Well, they're for your non-baby patients to use, but I guess they're yours technically." Madison had purchased an identical set of Mini-Wheels cars that Mistress had gotten for her, so now Madison would have some at Dr. Sumner's and one at Dr. Shasti Balakrishnan's office. She giggled.

"Thank you for the toys, Madison. That was very thoughtful of you. And would you like to share your amusement with the rest of the class?" Dr. Sumner asked, a bemused smile on her face.

"I have toys everywhere I hang out." She pulled all eight vehicles out and meticulously parked each one side-by-side in the imaginary parking lot that used to be known as the coffee table. Without a word, she stood up and rooted around the toy bins until she found the other truck she'd played with last time.

"And why do you have toys everywhere?" Dr. Sumner asked, leaning forward.

"So I have stuff that makes me feel nice for a while because sometimes things go south fast, and then I'm sad."

"Oh? For instance?"

Madison shrugged and pulled the VW bug out of its parking spot. The family that owned the bug had to go to the store to buy food.

"Like when Mommy said we were going to Aldi's. Kwan and I would be so happy. We might convince her to get ice pops or something." She was quiet for a moment and then said, "I had to write a report about the benefits of vegetables and stuff because Miss Shasti wants me to be healthy. Did you know that vegetables have nutrients like fiber which helps you poop, and vitamins and minerals like potassium which lowers your blood pressure? Apparently, Dr. Sumner, and this I didn't know, but broccoli, in particular, is awesome. It's packed to the gills with vitamins, including Vitamin K, which I had never heard of, but Vitamin K is supposed to help your blood clot properly and build strong bones." Madison banged the side of her fist against her forearm. "See? Strong bones. It also has antioxidants, which supposedly help you not get cancer and stuff."

"I love broccoli," Dr. Sumner said. "So why do your nice feelings 'go south?'"

The VW bug was back on the coffee table road, picking up speed as it went. One final push and it soared off the table and crashed to the carpet below. "Sometimes Grandma would get in the car. She sucks the air out of everything she does, Dr. Sumner. Kwan and I knew we weren't getting anything if she came along. And even Mommy knew that she wouldn't be able to get half the stuff on her list when Grandma came."

"Why was that?"

"Grandma is…" She couldn't put it into words. It was almost like talking about her would manifest her right there in front of them. "She wears these house dresses. It's always the same style, and her hair is pulled back severely. She never smiles. Okay, maybe once in a while, but she never likes anything Kwan or I do. We're too loud or watch too much TV with Grandpa or just…breathing." The school bus pulled out of the parking spot and accelerated so quickly that Madison hoped the school children inside were buckled up because the bus rocketed over the cliff and into the raging river below that used to be Dr. Sumner's carpet.

Dr. Sumner didn't say anything, so Madison continued, "You never know what kind of mood Grandma's in or what she's going to fuss about. Our family has no friends. I have no friends. Back in Columbus, I mean. Grandma says the family is best because other people take advantage of you. She always told us that we'd all be nowhere without her. That makes no sense, Dr. Sumner. Grandpa and Daddy are the ones who have jobs to pay the bills and buy the food. Mommy's the one that raised us kids and cleans the house and stuff. Grandma won't let Daddy help Mommy because it's 'women's work,' she always says. She says that *she* was the one, not Grandpa, who had raised my Dad, after all. Yeah, whatever." Madison picked up the sports car and flung it. It bounced once on the coffee table, careened way past the raging river, and hit the big mountain on the other side, which Dr. Sumner probably called a chair. "But what does Grandma do? Nothing. Mommy and I are the ones that clean. Daddy and Grandpa are in charge of maintenance stuff like fixing the cars, taking care of the yard, and putting up shelves or whatever. Daddy would let me help sometimes, so that's why I know how to fix things at Miss Shasti's house now."

Madison took a breath and said softly. "But seriously? What does Grandma do except fuss and fuss and fuss at us and tell us we're no good and pinch me?" Madison's voice was rising. "I can take it, but when she does the same stuff to Mommy, and then Daddy does nothing to help her? I hate Grandma, Dr. Sumner. I. Hate. Her."

Madison pressed her lips together and refused to let the tears of frustration fall down her face. She'd never once said words like that out loud. She sat back on the couch and looked at nothing.

"Do you still hate her?" Dr. Sumner asked. "Now that you live with Miss Shasti far away from her?"

"When I think about her, yes," Madison said. She braved looking up. Dr. Sumner's expression was kind. "And I think about Mommy still there, and it tears my heart out. She can't, like, live her own life. I wish Mommy could come live with Miss Shasti and me. Mistress could maybe take care of her, too?" Madison shrugged.

"What about your dad?"

Madison shrugged again. She had no idea what to do about that. Grandma picked on him, sure, but she didn't attack him as much as she attacked Mommy, who wasn't even a blood relation.

"Tell me about your friends in Columbus."

Dr. Sumner sure was asking a lot of questions today. Last week must have been the introductory session where nothing major got dredged up. But Madison kind of understood why Miss Shasti wanted her to be there. It all stemmed from her stupid breakdown at the mall. Fine. Madison would unload all the crappy crap from her life. Why anyone would even care was beyond her, but fine. Ready? Here goes.

"Kwan and I rarely had friends over. Well, I wasn't allowed. That's why I went when Katia invited me to her house near the end of senior year. Yay, I finally had a friend. And then we started having sex, like that first day. It escalated so fast, but you know. It was Katia. She was pretty and the captain of the team and all."

Madison remembered how special she'd felt when Katia invited her over that first time and touched her intimately, saying she wanted to try some things out with Madison. Madison had stars in her eyes, that was for sure.

"And even when Katia made me be with those other girls in her room, I kept going because I thought she still liked me. I thought she was my friend. When I told her I didn't want to keep doing those things with those other girls, she laughed and told me that I had to, or she'd tell everyone at school what I was doing to Brooke, Alaina, and Latisha." Madison looked up right at Dr. Sumner. "But that didn't matter, did it? Because everyone found out anyway. Including my brother's stupid friend Dalton, who was allowed to come over for some reason." Madison set her chin firmly and refused to cry over Dalton, the jerk.

"Did something happen with Dalton?"

Anger pressed against Madison's eyes, and a lone tear escaped making a solitary track down her face. Thank goodness Dr. Sumner didn't push the tissue box closer because Madison would have thrown it at the chair/mountain and not been sorry.

Madison nodded.

"Do you want to tell me?"

Madison shrugged.

"You're safe here, Madison," Dr. Sumner said. "And Miss Shasti is right outside. See this button?" She pointed to an intercom on the side table near her command chair.

Madison nodded.

"I can push that and talk immediately to the receptionist who can have Miss Shasti in here in seconds."

"Seconds?"

Dr. Sumner nodded. "Do you want to try it?"

Madison shook her head and began the sordid tale. "I was in my room laying on my bed reading. He and Kwan had been smoking pot in the backyard, and they came in to go to Kwan's room or something. But Dalton came into my room instead. I told him to get out. He didn't get out, Dr. Sumner. I sat up, but he pushed me back down and got on top of me. I felt his hard thing through his sweatpants. I tried to push him off me, but he was a big fat kid. He was heavy. I couldn't do it. I kept trying."

Madison pushed on the bridge of her nose. Despite her new glasses, her vision was blurry. Blurry from those stupid tears that wanted out. Fuck you, tears. Stay in there. Madison blinked, and a few of those renegade tears spilled over.

Dr. Sumner stayed mightily quiet. Madison figured she should keep going.

"He pressed his big fat smelly hand over my mouth when I called out for Kwan. I tried to bite his hand, but he hit my face with the other and started pressing himself against me. He was humping me, Dr. Sumner. Through our clothes. He got faster and faster, pressed harder and harder, then made this weird strangled face and held his breath. He pressed against me a few more times and fell on me."

Madison stared into space as she told the story. It was as if she was there standing in her room watching it happen to her younger self.

"He got off me then, his hand still on my mouth, and said if I told anyone, he would come back and hurt my Mommy and then me." I scrambled to the side of the bed once he got off me, and do you know what he said to me after that?

Dr. Sumner lifted her head as if to tell her to go on.

"He said he was going to fuck me for real next time. No clothes."

"Oh, Madison," Dr. Sumner said. "I'm so sorry you had to deal with that. You were so young."

"But if I'd only locked my door, fought him harder, or yelled for Kwan when Dalton first came in my room uninvited. Un. In. Vited."

"His actions were not your fault, Madison. You are not to blame. He assaulted you."

"Mommy told me that."

"So you told your mother?"

Madison nodded. "Dalton wasn't allowed in our house anymore, but we didn't press charges on him or anything. You know, I keep going over that day in my head. What if I had done this, or he had done that? Sometimes it goes on this endless loop in my head."

"And does thinking about that day help?"

Madison snorted out a sigh. "No. Not at all. And then all the boys at school heard about it. They kept cornering me at my locker every day, taunting me. Some tried to grab my non-existent boobs. I don't know why they thought they could do that. And then there was that day—" the words got lost in her throat. She had intended to say them, but it was like she was out of air or something. A mega-sob came out from somewhere in her past. She tried not to relive the events of the gang of boys pushing her into the empty chorus room and holding her arms behind her.

A hand touched her arm. She shoved it away. She barely recognized that it was Dr. Sumner. It was too real and in sync with the nightmare playing in her head. The boys taunted her with names. They held her arms tighter behind her when she fought back. One boy wrapped both hands around her mouth to quiet her screams.

She couldn't remember what boy had done what, especially because she didn't know them all, and she knew she was in big trouble when another boy undid the button on her jeans and started to pull her zipper down. This wasn't right. She didn't want this. She didn't want this.

"Madison Kim, look at me," a stern voice said. Mistress's voice. Madison looked up. "I'm here, baby." The voice was softer.

"Mistress?" Madison looked around. She wasn't in the chorus room. She wasn't in Columbus. There were no boys here.

She leaped into Mistress's arms and buried her face into loving softness. "I'm sorry," Madison cried into the soft folds of her Mistress's bosom. "I'm so sorry."

"You have nothing to be sorry about, sweetie." One of those amazing kisses hit her crown and decreased her stress level.

Mistress even did that humming thing again. The same bear and bee song. It was so nice when they decided to share the honey at the end. That's what friends did. Not what Katia, those girls, Dalton, or any of those boys did.

Madison let her Mistress sit them down on the couch together, side by side. Madison pulled her glasses off, placed them in Mistress's waiting hand, and wiped at her eyes with the back of both hands. She felt all kinds of puffy and snotty and everything. Ahh, a magic tissue appeared. "I'm sorry that I'm crying again, Dr. Sumner."

"Best therapy," Dr. Sumner said. "Gotta let out all that pent-up stuff."

Madison reached for Mistress's hand and held it tight. She needed an anchor because she had to finish the tale. She looked up at Mistress and felt the love caress her like she hoped it would. They smiled at each other, and then Mistress kissed her forehead. When she started to rub off her lipstick, Madison protested. She wanted the power of Mistress on her like a tangible weapon as she finished the story.

"So, the most amazing thing happened then, Dr. Sumner."

"Oh?"

"Coach Meers and Mr. Valente, the chorus teacher, busted through the door and saved me. I'm not kidding. They pulled the boys off me and the rest scattered so fast." Madison saw Mistress exchange a confused glance with the therapist, but that was okay. Madison would fill her in later. "Coach called out their names as they were fleeing the room. She then came to me and pulled me in her arms, not in a creepy way, I promise. She told me I was going to be okay. She took me back down the hall to the girls' PE office, and then the school psychologist came, and I told them everything that happened. All. Of. It."

"All of it? Katia? The girls? Dalton? All of it?" Dr. Sumner asked.

"Mm hmm," Madison said. "Because it wasn't right, Dr. Sumner. Katia wasn't my friend. I realized that in Coach's office. And I know what could have happened with Dalton if he'd come back and what could have happened that day with those boys. I know. I know. I know." Her chest got tight again but loosened up when Mistress's magic love sprinkled over her.

"I'm sorry if we're going over my time, but I want to say one, no, two more things," Madison said.

Dr. Sumner nodded and gestured for her to go on.

"Coach Meers helped me so much. I didn't have to go to school after that day. I missed the rest of the softball season, but I didn't care. And I got to take finals and AP exams at a different place, but it all counted. I didn't go to graduation, and my family was okay with that. You see, and this is the second thing I wanted to tell you, my grandmother called me a slut and told me that I'd brought shame on the family. She said I must have done something to make the boys act like that."

Miss Shasti groaned beside her.

"No, no," Madison said, holding up a finger. "I think I understand now. I think my grandmother has something wrong with her. Like she has a faulty empathy switch or something. I just figured that out." Madison looked up at Dr. Sumner. "I know I did nothing wrong, Dr. Sumner. Well, with those boys, I mean. I didn't 'entice them' like my grandmother said. And I was really confused about Katia until, like, right now. She was an abuser, wasn't she? Like, she used me. In a mean way."

"Yes, she did," Dr. Sumner said. "She absolutely took advantage of your good and innocent nature." She looked up at Mistress and said, "I recommend a quiet evening at home tonight for Madison."

Mistress nodded. "We're planning on ordering in and watching a movie."

"We are?" Madison sat back, stunned. Awesome.

"I was going to surprise you. We can watch *Brave* or whatever you want." Mistress leaned in and rubbed noses with Madison. "Eskimo kisses," she murmured.

"Mistress!" Madison leaned closer and said out of the side of her mouth, "You can't use that word 'Eskimo' anymore."

Mistress sat back and said, "Oh?"

"It's considered bad. Outsiders gave the Inuit people that name. Europeans, I think, and the native people are rejecting that label now."

"I didn't know that. Thank you for enlightening me," Mistress said. Her face had this interesting expression. Like she was completely impressed with Madison or something.

Dr. Sumner chuckled from her command chair and then said to Miss Shasti, "And she's been told she's not 'smart enough' for college."

Mistress closed her eyes and shook her head as if she couldn't believe the audacity of some people. "She's very concerned with labels."

"People should be allowed to label themselves," Madison said to the grown-ups. They knew that, right? Part of her was wondering if maybe she *was* smart enough to go to college. Nope, there was no way she'd survive.

"Madison," Dr. Sumner said, "if it's okay with you, I'd like to see you a couple of times a week for a little while. Would that be okay?"

Madison's head swiveled to look for the answer on her Mistress's face.

"What do you think, peanut? Twice a week for a little while?"

Madison nodded. "Maybe so because we've barely scratched the surface of all of Madison's issues and childhood traumas." Before Dr. Sumner made a note that Madison was disassociating by referring to herself in the third person, she amended, "*My* issues and childhood stuff."

"There you have it," Miss Shasti said to Dr. Sumner.

Dr. Sumner extended the session a little bit longer and asked Madison about her homework assignment. Madison diplomatically gave her three big things she was grateful for, none relating to sex or how amazing Mistress's sexy kisses were. And the things she needed to work on? "I'm trying to figure that out, Dr. Sumner. Except there is this one thing I'm currently working on." The tone of her voice became very conspiratorial as she turned her gaze to Mistress and waggled her eyebrows.

Dr. Sumner laughed and said, "Okay then. I don't think I want to know, but how about we hone that list together in the next session?"

"You'll have me all figured out by then?" Madison quipped.

"We're figuring you out together, aren't we?" Dr. Sumner's smile reached her eyes, and Madison felt her cheeks get warm. She'd told Dr. Sumner a lot of private stuff, stuff she hadn't even told Mistress yet. But Dr. Sumner seemed trustworthy. Mistress wouldn't have brought her there if she wasn't.

Madison nodded and then apologized for the earthquake that wrecked the cars falling off the coffee table cliff. "I'll tell you later," she said to Mistress, who raised a curious eyebrow. Madison picked up all the fallen vehicles, even those still in their parking spots, and tossed them into one of the high bins. Maybe the babies wouldn't be able to reach this high, and Madison's toys would be relatively unscarred, except by her.

They said their goodbyes to Dr. Sumner, made the new appointment for Wednesday evenings with the receptionist, and headed out into the parking lot. It was on an overcast afternoon, which should fit her mood, but oddly, didn't.

"Mistress?" Madison said after pulling the driver's door open for her.

"Oh," Mistress said, surprised at Madison's chivalrous move. "Thank you, peanut." Once Madison got into the passenger seat and buckled up, Mistress asked, "What did you want to say?"

"Umm, what does narcissistic personality disorder mean? I saw that on Dr. Sumner's notes next to the word grandmother and then, like, three question marks."

"You probably shouldn't have looked at her notes, Madison."

"I know, but she dipped her notepad down, and the words were so interesting looking that I read them upside down."

"I suppose Dr. Sumner may suspect that's what your grandmother has. And before you ask me more, I really don't know. You should bring that up on Wednesday when you see her again."

"Okay, I will." Madison said the interesting words silently to herself again so her brain would commit them to memory. "And, Mistress?"

"Yes, honey?"

"As much as I want to see Mommy, do you think we can go to Columbus another time? Like maybe after Dr. Sumner fixes me a little more? I don't think I can deal with all of that right now." She pushed her hands in the direction of Columbus to ward it away.

"I was leaning the same way, baby," Mistress said and pulled the car onto Kirkland.

"Oh, good. I didn't want you to be mad."

"Never."

"You were mad about the broccoli thing."

"Actually," Mistress said, "I wasn't. Miss Tilda was the one who suggested the punishment. Not me."

Madison furrowed her brow as she replayed last Sunday's broccoli incident in her brain. "Wow. You're right. But it's okay if you get mad at me sometimes."

"Let's go home, baby."

"Okay. This therapy session is O-V-E-R." Madison lay her head back on the headrest and closed her eyes. Was Mistress a knight in shining armor saving Madison from her old stupid life? She opened them and turned to gaze at the beautiful woman driving her home. Home.

"Mistress?"

"Mm hmm?"

"I love you." Madison reached for one of Miss Shasti's hands even though she kind of needed it to drive. She borrowed it long enough to kiss once and then returned it.

Mistress looked over at her and smiled one of those amazing smiles that made Madison go all oogly inside. "And I love you, baby."

Chapter 22

Shasti

Four months after the breakthrough session with Dr. Sumner, Madison and Shasti sat in what had become their designated seats at Rikki's Coffee Shop two days before Christmas, admiring the decorations. Rikki had taken a break to join them, and Victoria was taking a rare moment to socialize with them.

"It looks so festive in here," Shasti said to Rikki and gestured to the twinkling lights around the front window.

"Miss Rikki," Madison said from her favorite couch.

"Yes, kiddo?"

"You should put arcade games or something in here. You could get rid of that bookshelf with books no one ever reads and put them there."

"Madison!" Shasti reprimanded.

"Oh, sorry," Madison said, but it was obvious that she didn't understand that she had potentially insulted Rikki.

Rikki waved it away and pushed a stray lock of hair behind her ear. She looked a bit tired. "Actually, that's not a bad idea," she said to Madison.

Madison bounced on the couch and then drank her coffee. Somehow, and Shasti wasn't sure how, but Madison had convinced her it was okay to have a sugary whipped-cream latte with sprinkles. It must be the Christmas season, Shasti reasoned. It had made her overly generous.

"Ooh, ooh," Madison said excitedly. "Remember when Mistress and I went to the Festival of Lights at the zoo for our six-month anniversary two weeks ago?"

Both Rikki and Victoria nodded.

"You should go, Daddy Vic," Madison said. "The lights are so nice once it gets dark. And you can bring your newest sub there and be all romantic and stuff."

Victoria chuckled but didn't take offense. She was as smitten with Madison as the rest of them. "Sounds like just the thing," Victoria said. Her entire black ensemble, including black leather boots, made her look like she was headed to a funeral or something. At least she was out and about on the eve of Christmas eve and not hiding away at home until the festive season was wrapped up and gone.

"It was so good," Madison continued. "Mistress got me a Christmas present there, but I can't have it until we unwrap presents on Christmas day."

"Two more days to go," Rikki said. She looked striking with only a few strands of her long auburn hair pulled back and the rest cascading down over her shoulders. And that vintage Adolfo jacket looked stunning over her red turtleneck. Shasti glanced down at what she was wearing. A long forest green skirt, sensible winter boots, and a bulky sweater. Hmm. Mom clothes. Maybe she'd work on her style in the new year.

Shasti's thoughts were pulled back to the present when she heard Madison say, "It's this sloth whose arms velcro around your neck and hangs down, but the best part is that if you turn it sideways, it becomes one of those airplane pillows you put behind your neck." She made a half-circle behind her neck to demonstrate. "Mistress is taking me on a plane next summer to D.C. to visit her parents and go to a beach. A beach! At the Atlantic Ocean. I've never seen the ocean. I've never been on a plane."

"She's never been out of Ohio," Shasti added. Madison looked up at her Mistress and shrugged. It was so endearing that both Rikki and Victoria awwed.

"What was your favorite part of the festival?" Victoria asked.

"The luminaries were cool," Madison said with a ready answer. "Especially the lion and the watering hole scene. They made the water out of twinkling blue lights like those white ones you have, Miss Rikki."

"That sounds cool," Rikki said. She glanced over her shoulder toward the front counter. Everything must have been okay because her attention quickly returned to the group.

"They said the zoo has over four million lights, Miss Rikki," Madison said.

"Wow," Rikki said. "Just think about that electric bill." She smiled, but Shasti noticed that the smile didn't reach her eyes. Rikki had a heavy load on her and had confided in Victoria and Shasti that more fraud had been discovered. The idiots that had stolen her identity had taken out a big loan in her name and used the coffee shop as collateral. Shasti vowed to help her friend in whatever way she could, knowing full well that Rikki would be too prideful to ask. But still, she would try. And she would try to make sure Madison didn't find out. That was a request from Rikki, who didn't want Madison to worry. Shasti was in full agreement.

Victoria must have sensed Rikki's change in mood and asked, "What part was the most fun, squirt?"

"The train ride was cool, but going there with Mistress was the best because she's…" Madison cleared her throat. "She's…"

Rikki and Victoria awwed again, and Shasti held her arms out to receive a flying hug from her girl.

Once returned to her original seat on the couch, Madison said, "Christmas is actually fun this year. The Masquerade ball was fun, too."

Victoria laughed and said, "All those dances you did. You've got some rhythm, kid."

"Billy didn't even know how to Floss." Madison shook her head. "I had to show him."

"My favorite was when you guys did the running man," Miss Rikki added. "No, wait. Gangnam style. No, no! The one where you swept your legs from side to side."

"New Kids on the Block?"

"That's the one."

"I'm not a *little* aficionado, as you all know," Victoria said, "but all you *littles* in your matching toy soldier costumes was freakin' adorable."

"I agree," Shasti said. "We got some good pictures." Seamus had the idea initially and enlisted his tailor, Robert, to put all the outfits together. It was well worth the cost because it may have been the first time that Madison felt like she belonged somewhere in a group of her peers.

"All right, landlord," Daddy Vic said to Madison, changing the subject. "You called me here for a reason. What is it?"

"Oh, uh," Madison looked over at Shasti and then away. "It's a private matter." She stood up and beckoned Victoria to follow her. Victoria stood but looked over at Shasti with a quizzical expression. Shasti simply shrugged and shook her head to say that she had no idea what her *little* was up to. The two of them headed to the far corner of the shop near the "never-used" bookshelf.

"Victoria loves living in the condo," Rikki said to Shasti. "What a windfall for Madison."

"That whole Mrs. Park situation was unreal," Shasti said. "And lucky for us, the condo was rentable, and the condo management takes care of everything."

"You know Madison's old room there?"

"Mm hmm."

Rikki leaned in, so Shasti did as well. "Vic wants to make that into her playroom."

Shasti burst out laughing. "Oh, no. Really?"

Rikki nodded. "Victoria, everyone." She pointed both hands as if highlighting Victoria to an audience.

Shasti laughed again but then frowned as she watched Madison and Victoria putting their coats on by the front door. She nodded toward them.

"Oh, my," Rikki said. "I think your *little* is getting kidnapped."

Shasti scoffed. "I think it's the other way around."

A text dinged on her phone.

VICTORIA: Is there a price limit on this?

SHASTI: I'm seriously in the dark and don't know what's happening.

Madison waved as she and Victoria headed out the door.

VICTORIA: Oops. Never mind. Forget I said anything. Over and out.

Shasti showed Rikki the text exchange. "Well, Christmas is only two days away, Shasti."

Shasti nodded and then sighed.

"Handful?"

"No," Shasti said, "and yes. She's perfect for me." Shasti couldn't help taking a tiny moment to thank the universe for bringing Madison to her.

"Things are still tense in my house," Rikki said and moved closer.

"The uh, Eileen incident at the ball?"

"Mm hmm. Aunt Tilda just won't let me have this. She says Eileen is nothing but trouble."

"Eileen can be hard," Shasti said, trying to find the right words, "but she does what you ask her and seems to satisfy your Domme needs." There. Had she said enough?

"True enough, but I don't know why Aunt Tilda tried to pick a fight with Eileen during the ball. All Eileen did was volunteer for Mistress Dominique's impact demonstration. Dominique was just trying to drum up business for her dungeon downtown. Aunt Tilda accused Eileen of, how did she phrase it, 'looking for the next best thing.'"

"Your aunt saw something that wasn't there," Shasti said. They'd already gone over it several times, but Rikki was having difficulty letting it go. She loved her aunt. Owed her life to her aunt, she'd said on more than one occasion. But having her aunt speak ill of her lover and submissive? That was too much for Rikki.

"And then when I defended Eileen to my aunt? She was having none of it. Why can't Aunt Tilda just let me be happy?" Rikki sighed. Neither of them knew the answer. "Eileen thanked me later for defending her. Did you know that?"

"No, but I'm glad she recognized what you did for her and how hard that might have been for you."

"I'm beginning to hate these Christmas masquerade balls. They never work out for me." Rikki turned her head toward the front counter again. The line had gotten long. "Ahh, I better get back there and help. You okay here by yourself?"

"Of course," Shasti said. "Go on. I'll just wait here until Victoria brings my baby back."

Rikki patted her arm and glided to the counter. "Next in line," she said, her voice strong and sure.

Rikki was strong. Although she was going through a rough time with the fraud and her aunt's dislike of her girlfriend, she'd get through it. She'd started this coffee shop business against all odds, and she'd find a way back to happiness. Hopefully, sooner rather than later.

~~~

Madison scampered, yes, that was the only word to use, back into the living room. She held two fresh cups of coffee in festive Christmas mugs, one in each hand. "Merry Christmas, Mistress," Madison said and carefully handed Shasti one of the mugs.

"Merry Christmas to you, too, peanut." Shasti took a sip and watched as Madison did the same. The act of doing a grownup thing like drinking coffee juxtaposed against her pink onesie with teddy bears all over it was a bit surreal, but it captured the essence of Madison perfectly.

Shasti took another sip. "Almost time for the call with your Mommy."

"Ooh, yes, it is." Madison leaped up and grabbed her tablet off the charger. No sooner had she situated herself on the couch than the video call from her mother chimed.

Shasti beamed, more in relief than anything. This video call was the one thing she had truly wished for Madison for Christmas. That Madison's family would show her their love.

"Mommy! Hi!" Madison yelled at the tablet screen. "Look at my onesie." She scanned her outfit using the tablet. "And see my sloth?" She velcroed it behind her neck and let it hang down.

"Oh, how cute, Madi," Madison's mother said. "You look adorable."

"Thanks, Mommy. Merry Christmas. I'm glad you can be on the phone with me and not…"

Aww, her baby was getting choked up. Shasti wasn't sure if she should sit next to Madison on the couch and hug her or let her work it out with her mother. The latter. Yes. Let mother and daughter have their moment. A little privacy might also be in order.

Shasti stood up, took her coffee, and headed to the kitchen. She'd pre-made a cheese quiche for Christmas morning, a hint she'd seen on one of those cooking shows she'd been obsessed with before Madison came into her life and had made a mental note to make one if she ever had a *little* to share Christmas morning with. It also helped that Madison liked quiche. Check went the mental bucket list item. She turned on the oven, put the quiche in, and set the timer.

She also made a small fruit cup for each of them and brought them back into the living room. If Madison wanted to partake, she could. If not, no worries. Shasti almost laughed at how big Madison's eyes got at the food heading her way.

"Oh, how nice," Madison's mommy said, referring to the fruit cup. "Miss Shasti takes care of you, doesn't she?"

"Yes, Ma'am," Madison said and put a spoonful of fruit in her mouth.

"I'm glad. Miss Shasti, can you hear me?"

"Yes, yes, I'm here." Shasti sat down next to Madison and waved at Madison's mother through the camera. Madison's mother was looking so much better. There was a healthy glow to her skin, and the dark circles under her eyes had lessened substantially.

"I know it's not Thanksgiving, but I have so many thanks to give you," Madison's mother said. "First of all, thank you for finding and taking care of my little girl. She needed someone like you to be her mentor, guide, friend, lover."

"Mommy!" Madison said at the mention of the word lover.

"Aww, it's okay, Madi," Madison's mother said. "We're all adults here, aren't we? Except one of us is in a onesie."

Madison cracked up, causing both older women to chuckle with her. "I'm twenty-three and one-quarter now, Mommy."

"How can that be, Madi, when I'm only twenty-nine?" Madison's mother chuckled at her own joke and then added, "And, Miss Shasti, I need to thank you and Madison for urging me to get out of the house. Yoga has been a godsend. I made some friends right away. And, Miss Shasti, your recommendation of Dr. Perfero as a therapist has been another godsend. Your grandmother fussed at the cost, Madi, but thanks to the money you shared with me from your inheritance from Mrs. Park, I can do it."

"I wish I'd known who she was, Mommy," Madison said. "Mrs. Park, I mean."

"I wanted to tell you so many times, but for her safety and sanity, she begged me not to. I'm glad that you at least got to meet her. Right, Madi?"

"Yes, Ma'am."

"How formal. Are you a good girl for your Miss Shasti?"

"Yes, Ma'am," Madison said and glanced up at Shasti, who was still sitting next to her. "She's my girlfriend, Mommy, and we've been together for six months, one week, and one day. She and Dr. Sumner convinced me that not all people are stupid and take advantage of you. They showed me that I'm worthy of love and affection and that what those kids in high school did to me was on them, not me." Madison turned her voice into a whisper and said, "And I even understand that Grandma has her own issues. But Mommy?"

"Yes, honey?"

"Miss Shasti loves me. Like, a lot. And I love her a lot, too, so I'm going to live here with her from now on. Is that okay?"

"Oh, Madi, of course," Madison's mother said without hesitation. "I'll miss you. I already miss you—you know that. But we're not that far apart. You can come here to visit, and we can go there. I knew you'd have to launch at some point, and I only want the best for you."

"Mommy, Miss Shasti thinks that sometime in the spring might be a good time to visit and clean out my room while we're there. Then you can use my room for yoga or something."

"Looking forward to it, pint-sized," a male voice said.

"Daddy," Madison squealed. "Hi!"

"You look good, Madi. We can't wait to see you." Madison's father leaned closer and smiled a toothy grin into the camera.

"Me, too." Madison reached over and squeezed Shasti's hand as her father said he had to fix a loose cabinet in the kitchen. Shasti covered a smile. It seemed like the Kim family was always on the lookout for cabinets needing repair.

"Madi," Madison's mother came back into view, "we're looking forward to your visit, but I am so glad you were able to get out of here." The last part she whispered, but then picked up in a regular-volumed voice, "Dr. Perfero is helping me find my power. I've been sticking up for myself more, 'taking my power back,' he calls it. Even Daddy is doing it. He sticks up for me. I have a couple of friends now, too. I met them at yoga, but now we're in a women's bowling league together."

"Bowling, Mommy?"

"Yes. I might have inherited my athleticism from you, I think, Madi. I'm quite good."

Madison laughed but didn't say anything.

"It's a good outlet for me, and your daddy encourages it, too. He says I'm becoming the woman he married. I guess I lost myself somewhere in there."

"Good for you, Mommy," Madison said, her shoulders visibly relaxing. "I don't know what I'm becoming, but it's good." She glanced up at Shasti and said, "Really good."

Shasti couldn't help it. She kissed Madison on the top of the head right there in front of Madison's mother. Oh, well. Honesty was the best policy, she'd always said. She excused herself when she started to smell the quiche. From the kitchen, she heard Madison tell her mother about all the presents she had gotten. After a while, she heard them wrap things up and say their final goodbyes. And then there was silence.

"Everything okay in there?" Shasti called from the kitchen as she put two steaming slices of quiche on two separate plates.

Madison cleared her throat several times and said, "Yes." Aww, the poor baby was choked up.

Shasti presented Madison with the quiche and sat beside her girl, their thighs touching. "Happy tears, peanut?"

"Mm hmm," Madison said. "Mommy looks so good. I'm so glad I met you, Mistress. You're helping Mommy and me. And Daddy, too. You're like our savior."

Shasti wanted to scoff but knew Madison was in a vulnerable state. She simply said, "I love you, baby."

"And I love you, Mistress." Madison held up the plate of food in her hands as if noticing it for the first time. "Oh, wow. Thanks. This smells so good. We can eat on the couch?"

Shasti nodded and, before taking her first bite, said, "I have a couple more presents for you, and then I thought maybe we'd use that rope you got me for Christmas."

"Ooh, yes, please. Another hip and waist tie?"

"Mm, sounds lovely," Shasti said. "Maybe a Frog tie, and if that goes well, I may extend it to a Futomomo." Before Madison could ask, Shasti added, "Both bind your thigh to your ankle, and you're flexible enough for me to do it."

"Sounds like fun," Madison said.

Mm, yes, it did, Shasti thought.

Once they finished their quiche, Madison brought the dirty dishes and forks into the kitchen, and when she came back, Shasti had two red envelopes ready to hand to Madison.

"These aren't very romantic gifts, sweetie," Shasti said as Madison returned to the couch, "but I wanted you to know that I'm all in. That you're going to be taken care of."

"Which one should I open first?"

"It doesn't matter."

Madison carefully opened the first envelope and saw an application partly filled out. "A bank account? With you?"

Shasti nodded. "A joint account we put money into for household expenses, vacations, and car maintenance—things like that. I will insist, however, that you also have your own personal account as well. This way, you can still have your independence. We can go to the bank next week and set that up if you're okay with this."

"That's such a good idea. You're taking care of me, aren't you, Mistress? Taking care of us?"

"That's the idea." Shasti smiled at her *little*, pleased that she obviously liked the idea. "Go ahead and open the other one."

Madison was just as gentle with the second envelope as she was with the first. "No way! A credit card? Holy grownup responsibilities, Mistress. Can I handle this?"

Shasti chuckled. Her peanut was so silly, sometimes. "Of course, you can. You need to establish credit, so having a joint credit card with me is one way to jumpstart that. Now, before you try to buy the Cincinnati Zoo, there is a low credit limit on this because you're just starting out."

"The credit card company wants to make sure I won't mess things up?"

"Something like that. Now, my rule is that we only use the card for essentials and only for convenience. Make sure you already have enough money in the bank to cover whatever you buy."

"You're so wise," Madison said, making googly eyes at Shasti. And Shasti was falling for it. Oh, yes, their rope session later was definitely going to end up in the bedroom. That was for sure. Maybe all four cuffs and a certain pink collar would come into play—

"Mistress?" Madison said.

"Hmm?"

"You were daydreaming," Madison said with a laugh.

"Mm hmm. I went somewhere really good." Shasti waggled her eyebrows.

"Mistress, I have two more gifts for you, too. I didn't forget to give them to you. I just wanted to give them to you last." Madison leaped to her feet and pulled out two packages from under the couch. "Open this one first," she said, handing the small box to her.

Shasti carefully unwrapped the snowman wrapping paper and discovered a white jewelry box. She opened it and pulled out a silver necklace.

"It's real silver," Madison said. "The two pieces, when put together, make an infinity sign, which symbolizes us. Together forever." She put both hands up in the air as if to say, "Tada."

Shasti's chest squeezed with emotion. "I love it," she said, her voice high and tight. She pulled Madison in for a hug and ended up kissing every square inch of her face. Madison squirmed, but in a good way.

Madison whispered, "Daddy Vic helped me pick it out the other day. You know, the day you thought she kidnapped me?"

Shasti nodded knowingly and then asked Madison to put the necklace around her neck. Once placed, Shasti reached up and lovingly touched the metal. "This is so special. Thank you."

"You're welcome, Mistress." Madison picked up the last gift and said, "This next one isn't expensive, but it represents how you make me feel. Special. Cared for. Like I matter to you. I feel, you know, loved."

Shasti's tears were back. She opened the gift and found the back of a picture frame. She turned it over, and her vision became completely blurred with emotional tears. Under the glass in the frame was Madison's coloring book picture of two birds. One bird held its wing over the other as snow fell around them.

Softly Madison said, "This is you." She pointed first to the mama bird and then to the baby bird. "And this is me. I know it's not professional or anything, but it's kind of us, and the other day I saw it in my book and thought, that's Mistress and me because she put me under her wing."

Shasti pulled Madison close and cried softly. Madison seemed to know enough not to ask if anything was wrong. She must have known they were happy emotional tears.

When Shasti finally got a hold of herself, she blew out a sigh and wiped at her tears. She said, "I've had a lot of successes and good things in my life, but Madison, you are by far the best thing that's ever happened to me." Shasti's lips covered Madison's, stealing away any possible response.

When the steamy kiss ended, Madison said, "Best Christmas ever," and reclaimed Shasti's lips for another steamy encounter.

"Upstairs," Shasti said, her voice thick with emotion. "Grab the rope. You're about to be devoured."

"In a good way, I hope." Madison leaped to her feet, reached for the rope, and tapped her Mistress on the arm. "Last one upstairs has to do the tying."

Shasti's heart threatened to burst as she watched the pink onesie containing her life's joy run toward the stairs.

~~~ THE END ~~~

National Sexual Assault Hotline

Hours: Available 24 hours

USA: 1-800-656-4673 www.rainn.org

Newsletter Signup

Sign up for Danielle Grainger's newsletter to keep up with new releases. She also likes to recommend books to read (other than her own, of course).

Find the sign-up on Danielle's website: www.daniellegrainger.com

Reviews

Reviews help get books like this one into the hands of readers who enjoy books like them. It's often difficult for readers of certain, err, tastes to find books they enjoy. Would you consider writing a review? Get the word out. Thank you for the help.

About the Author

Danielle Grainger

Dani is an instructor who currently resides in the southeastern USA with several pampered fur babies. She has always been an avid reader and ventured into writing after reading several novels she felt didn't accurately represent the BDSM lifestyle. With so many rampant misconceptions, she took a chance and crafted admittedly idealized versions of possible experiences. Dani hopes not only to entertain her readers but to enlighten and educate them as well.

Dani's Website:
www.daniellegrainger.com

Dani's Facebook:
facebook.com/danielle.grainger.7777

Dani's Instagram:
DaniGrainger84

Dani's Pinterest:
danigrainger84

Dani's Goodreads Page:
www.goodreads.com/author/show/19699760.Danielle_Grainger

Books by Danielle Grainger

THE DENTON HEIGHTS SERIES

The Denton Heights Series comes BEFORE the Bernadette Series. This group of books tells the stories of the beloved characters who populate the Bernadette Series world and live the BDSM lifestyle. We find out more of the origin stories of Madison and Shasti; Jaleesa, Tina, Harriet, Dana, Deshawn, and Kari; Marta and Shanice; Rowena and Minjung; Lisa and Rachel. The Denton Heights series is basically the "Prequel" to the Bernadette Series.

Under Her Wing (Denton Heights Book 1)
(The Shasti and Madison Story)
A lesbian age-gap erotic romance with light BDSM aspects.

2023 GOLDIE FINALIST

Madison Kim finds herself on a bus headed to Denton Heights, Ohio, a suburb of Cincinnati. Her mother sent her there without notice to care for an elderly Korean woman Madison had never met. Madison is twenty-two-and-three-quarters years old, has a high school diploma, but isn't smart enough to go to college...so they tell her. Now she spends her time caring for Mrs. Park, going to the beloved Cincinnati Zoo, and watching movies on her outdated phone. She's not really sure why she's there, but she's taking it day by day. And then she meets strong nurturing Miss Shasti at a tea dance.

Shasti Balakrishnan has been looking for someone to call hers for more years than she cares to count. She wants a woman to love and care for in a nurturing Mommy Domme/little girl scenario. She's thirty-two and already a partner in a thriving medical clinic in Denton Heights, but truth be told – she's lonely. She thought she'd found a companion in Amber back in D.C., but that fizzled out once they realized they weren't what each other wanted—or needed. And then she meets adorably precocious Madison at a tea dance.

ISBN: 978-1-953734-10-5 (e-Book)
ISBN: 978-1-953734-13-6 (Paperback)

In Her Cage (Denton Heights Book 2)
(The Jaleesa and Tina Story)

A lesbian/asexual interracial polyamorous erotic romance with BDSM aspects including Dominance and submission.

Jaleesa Whitmore is a lesbian Domme in and out of fast relationships fueled by sex. She didn't understand addiction. Not yet, anyway. Although she had almost one full year sober, she was done with it. She was moments from heading down the familiar road of drinking that always made her feel good and filled that void. She was about to get her life back on its old track when a fateful encounter with a stranger, who would become a trusted friend, halted her downslide. She didn't know it then, but this encounter would not only lead her to a series of events and people that would change how she looked at life but how she approached it.

Tina Jenkins likes women but is asexual and afraid to try for another relationship. She does understand addiction. Just shy of eleven years clean of her opioid addiction following a dental procedure right out of high school, her parents carefully constructed and monitored everything in her world. It didn't matter that she was thirty-one years old and still living in the pink bedroom in her childhood home. It didn't matter that her mother now had to work from home, and her parents had to track her location and do routine searches of her bag, car, computer, phone, and room. None of it mattered because she was clean.

And then asexual Tina meets promiscuous Jaleesa. And everything changed. For both of them.

ISBN: 978-1-953734-28-0 (e-Book)
ISBN: 978-1-953734-29-7 (Paperback)

Within Her Grasp (Denton Heights Book 3)
(The Marta and Shanice Story)

A lesbian age gap interracial erotic romance with light BDSM aspects.

"Within Her Grasp" is an age-gap interracial lesbian romance that tells the tale of two women who had settled for unhappy lives. And then they meet.

White, thirty-something Marta Ingersoll was done with people. She just wanted to be left alone at work and at home, thank you. Her inside cat and the outside stray were all she needed. And her sister, Nora, too, of course. But that was it. And then, one fateful afternoon, her instincts to save a woman in obvious distress kicked in, and her life was shoved onto a strange new course.

Black, twenty-something Shanice Ward never got a break. Life had thrown challenge after challenge at the young woman, and this latest thing was too much, but it wouldn't stop. Woken up from a sound sleep by someone trying to remove her clothing, she shrieked for him to leave her alone. He didn't, but then, the most amazing thing happened. She discovered that superheroes were real, and one had just flown into her room to save her, and her life was shoved onto a strange new course.

ISBN: 978-1-953734-30-3 (e-Book)
ISBN: 978-1-953734-31-0 (Paperback)

THE BERNADETTE SERIES

Dr. Bernadette Garneau holds a Ph.D. in Mathematics and has just gotten out of a four-year relationship. Shortly after the breakup, she began an exploration of her repressed sexual desires. One message from a beautiful and powerful online Mistress and Bernadette leaps into the world of BDSM. The Mistress takes charge, and Bernadette reels in the heady power this stranger has over her. She has gotten a taste of the life, and she wants more. She needs more. Several online and in-person experiences with BDSM and Power Exchange have led to cravings she doesn't quite understand. A brief sexual exchange with an online Goddess unleashes an incredible pain-to-pleasure connection that she hadn't understood before. As she sifts through the posers and one-night stands, she homes in on what her submissive nature needs from a Domme.

The Bernadette Series follows Bernadette's journey into the world of BDSM and her search for love and sexual satisfaction. As she said, "I want a monogamous partner who wants to not only love and nurture me but who also wants to drape me over her lovely couch and have her way with me."

Wrecking Bernadette
(Book One in the Bernadette Series)
A lesbian erotic novel with heavy BDSM aspects featuring Dominance and submission.

Dr. Bernadette Garneau holds a Ph.D. in Mathematics and is four months out of a four-year relationship. One good thing about breaking up is that Bernadette is free to explore her repressed sexual desires. One message from a beautiful and powerful online Mistress, and Bernadette leaps into the world of BDSM. Mistress Ciara takes charge, and Bernadette reels in the heady power this stranger has over her. She has gotten a taste of the *life*, and she wants more. She *needs* more.

ISBN: 978-1-953734-00-6 (e-Book)
ISBN: 978-1-953734-14-3 (Paperback)

(S)mothering Bernadette
(Book Two in the Bernadette Series)

A lesbian erotic novel with heavy BDSM aspects featuring Mommy Domme, little girl.

Dr. Bernadette Garneau's universe is pushing her toward change. Her initial experiences with BDSM and Power Exchange have led to cravings she doesn't quite understand. A brief sexual exchange with an online Goddess unleashes an incredible pain-to-pleasure connection she hadn't understood until that encounter. But after sleeping on it, she clearly understands that this Goddess would never be the long-term relationship she seems to be seeking.

Disappointed, she wonders if she should just give up and move back to California to be closer to her family. That is until she meets Mama_Luvs, an online Mommy Domme. The woman is nurturing yet stern from the start and is just … perfect. And then Mama_Luvs wants to meet. Starry-eyed Bernadette packs for a New Year's Eve weekend, hoping that this time she's found *the one* – the one who wants to love and nurture her but who also wants to drape her over a couch and have her way with her.

ISBN: 978-1-953734-01-3 (e-Book)
ISBN: 978-1-953734-15-0 (Paperback)

Becoming Bernadette
(Book Three in the Bernadette Series)

A lesbian erotic novel with heavy BDSM aspects featuring Dominance and submission.

University professor Dr. Bernadette Garneau has fallen in love with the world of BDSM. She has a nascent interest in the pain-to-pleasure connection, but she has yet to find partners interested in nurturing the soul within her body that they play with. Admittedly, she's had incredible sexual encounters with experienced Dommes, but all of them left her feeling cold for whatever reason. Most of them simply wanted a sadistic roll in the hay. Bernadette wants a strong Domme who will love and nurture her *before* flogging her on a St. Andrew's cross and *afterward* when her body is spent.

One afternoon, she finally musters up the courage to venture out and meet some new friends in the local BDSM community. In walks a tall, handsome butch woman with fantastic hair and a confident stride. When this woman asks Bernadette, "Are you collared," Bernadette truthfully answers, "No," and accepts a dinner invitation for that very evening. She is walking on stars when she gets home at 2 a.m. after an ethereal sexual liaison. On the one hand, she wonders who she is becoming – she's never been this promiscuous. And on the other hand, she wonders if this strong butch woman could finally be the Domme of her dreams.

ISBN: 978-1-953734-02-0 (e-Book)
ISBN: 978-1-953734-12-9 (Paperback)

Desiring Bernadette
(Book Four in the Bernadette Series)

A lesbian erotic romance novel with heavy BDSM aspects featuring Dominance and submission.

Rikki Carmichael finally feels that deep Dominant/submissive relationship she has been craving ever since her Aunt Tilda introduced her to *the life*. She embraced her dominant side early on, but finding a suitable submissive woman who wanted more than a quick roll in the dungeon proved elusive. That is until Professor Bernadette Garneau arrived on the scene. Now collared and committed to Rikki, will Bernadette prove to be different, or will she turn out like all the others — fickle and full of lies and deception?

And will this perfect sub stay with her when she realizes Rikki's ship is sinking? She'd almost lost the coffee shop she owns when creditors came knocking down her door en masse seeking payment for debts that weren't hers. Rikki managed to keep most of her staff and friends in the dark about it, but she has not been able to get out from under it. With high stakes all around, Rikki looks for the peace she is seeking within her relationship with Bernadette. If this one fails, it may be time to leave the life entirely and go live in a cabin somewhere isolated in the woods. But buying a cabin takes money – money she just doesn't have.

ISBN: 978-1-953734-03-7 (e-Book)
ISBN: 978-1-953734-09-9 (Paperback)

Danielle Grainger

Loving Bernadette
(Book Five in the Bernadette Series)

A lesbian erotic romance novel with heavy BDSM aspects featuring Dominance and submission.

Bernadette Garneau, a beloved professor of mathematics, is a natural submissive. She likes structure and rules and finally found a way of life and a woman who would provide those things for her. The BDSM community she stumbled upon in Denton Heights, Ohio is where she found Rikki Carmichael, now her dominant partner and fiancée. Rikki is everything she's dreamed of. Yes, Bernadette found the captain of her ship. With Rikki's support and guidance, maybe other parts of her life can finally come together, too – like the respect she deserves but hasn't gotten at the university. Why won't anyone see that she deserves to teach those upper-level courses? And to move out of that closet of an office? What do they know that she does not?

Rikki Carmichael, the respected owner of Rikki's Coffee Shop in town, has finally found the woman of her dreams in super-smart and super-real Bernadette Garneau. Bernadette is a submissive who instinctively knows how to take care of Rikki and accepts Rikki's need to be in charge. Bernadette is the first submissive Rikki's ever had that wasn't solely out for her own gain. Once Rikki can climb out of the deep financial debt she's found herself in, she will finally make their engagement to be married public.

Miscommunication, faulty assumptions, and unmet expectations threaten this union seemingly made in heaven. When life comes at them hard and fast, they must rely on their bond and their loving self-made family of friends.

ISBN: 978-1-953734-08-2 (e-Book)
ISBN: 978-1-953734-11-2 (Paperback)